SLAVE
OF MY
THIRST

Also by Tom Holland

Lord of the Dead

SLAVE

OF MY

THIRST

TOM HOLLAND

POCKET BOOKS

New York   London   Toronto   Sydney   Tokyo   Singapore

POCKET BOOKS, a division of Simon & Schuster Inc.
1230 Avenue of the Americas, New York, NY 10020

Copyright © 1996 by Tom Holland

First published in Great Britain by Little, Brown and Company (UK) Ltd.

ISBN: 0-671-54052-1

First Pocket Books hardcover printing October 1997

10 9 8 7 6 5 4 3 2 1

For my parents.
Blood will out.

'Rubbish, Watson, rubbish! What have we to do with walking corpses who can only be held in their grave by stakes driven through their hearts? It's pure lunacy.'

Sir Arthur Conan Doyle, *The Adventure of the Sussex Vampire*.

———————

'The blood is the life.'

Bram Stoker, *Dracula*.

PREFACE

London,
15 December, 1897.

To those whom it concerns—

If you are reading this letter, then you will no doubt suspect the danger you are in. The lawyers you have approached are under instructions to deliver to you a body of papers. The story they reveal is a terrible one. Indeed, only recently did I understand its full extent when a copy of Moorfield's book was sent to me from Calcutta, together with a bundle of letters and journals. Start with Moorfield's book, at the chapter titled 'A Perilous Mission' – I have left three letters where I found them within the pages of the book. Otherwise the papers are arranged by myself. Read them in the order in which they have been placed.

My poor friend. Whoever you may be, whenever you may read this – do not doubt, please, that what is recorded did occur.

May God's hand protect you.

Yours in grief and hope,

ABRAHAM STOKER.

3

PART ONE

PART ONE

*Extract from the memoirs of Colonel Sir William Moorfield, C.B.,
C.M.G., D.S.O.*, With Rifles in the Raj *(London, 1897).*

❦

A PERILOUS MISSION

*A secret mission – 'Shmashana Kali' – a mountain journey – the bloody
idol – an ominous discovery.*

I come now to perhaps the most extraordinary episode of my whole
long career in India. In the late summer of 1887, when the boredom
of garrison duty had become almost unbearable, I received an
unexpected summons to Simla. There were no details of what the
mission might be, but since the heat on the plains was by now pretty
sweltering I was not averse to a jaunt up to the hills. I have always
had a love of mountains and Simla, perched high on a promontory
above cedars and mists, was certainly a place of striking beauty.
However, I had but little time to admire the views, for no sooner had
I arrived at my allotted quarters when a message came to me from
one Colonel Rawlinson, ordering me to report to him at once. A
quick shave and a change of uniform, and then I was on my way
again pronto. Had I known where the meeting was to lead, I might
not have walked with such an eager step – and yet the thrill of
soldiering was in my blood again, and I would not have exchanged
it for all the world!

Colonel Rawlinson's office was set apart from the regular H.Q.,
down a side street so dark that it seemed more suitable to a native
bazaar than the quarters of a British officer. Any uneasiness I may
have suffered on this account, however, was soon banished by my
first sight of Colonel Rawlinson himself, for he was a tall, spruce
man with a hint of steel in his eye, and I found myself liking him
instinctively. He led me straight away into a teak-lined study, filled

7

with maps and decorated along the walls with the most extraordinary collection of Hindoo gods. There were two men waiting for us there, seated at a circular table. One I recognised at once – it was old 'Pumper' Paxton, my commanding officer from Afghanistan! I had not seen him for five years now – yet he looked as hale and hearty as he ever did. Colonel Rawlinson waited as we exchanged our greetings; then, once we had finished, he introduced the second man, who had been sitting until this moment obscured by shadow.

'Captain Moorfield,' said the Colonel, 'please meet Huree Jyoti Navalkar.'

The man leaned forward; he bobbed his head in the native manner and I saw – with a sense of shock, I don't mind admitting – that the fellow was not even a soldier, but your typical Babu, a fat, sweating office-wallah. Colonel Rawlinson must have observed my surprise, yet he offered no explanation for the Babu's presence; instead he began to flick through some papers, then stared up at me again, that look of steel still glinting in his eye.

'Outstanding career record you have here, Moorfield,' he said.

I felt myself getting red. 'Oh, that's all rot, sir,' I muttered.

'I see you gave a good account of yourself in the Baluchistan show. Get into the mountains at all, did you?'

'I saw a bit of action there, sir, yes.'

'Fancy seeing a bit more of the hills?'

'I'll go wherever I'm sent, sir.'

'Even if it's not in your regular line of soldiering?'

I frowned at this and caught old Pumper's eye, but he just looked away and said nothing. I turned back to Colonel Rawlinson. 'I'm willing to have a crack at anything, sir.'

'Good man!' he smiled, patting me on the shoulder, then reaching for his swagger stick. He crossed to a large map hanging on the wall, and as he did so his face froze once again into an expression of deadly seriousness. 'This, Moorfield,' he said, tapping with his stick at a long purple line, 'is the frontier of our Indian Empire. It is long and, as you yourself will know only too well, it is thinly protected. And here' – he tapped with his stick again – 'is the territory of His

Imperial Majesty, the Russian Tsar. Observe further, this zone here
– the mountains and the steppes – these belong neither to Russia
nor to ourselves. Buffer states, Moorfield – the playground of spies
and adventurers. And right now, unless I am very much mistaken,
there is a storm brewing there, a mighty tempest, and it seems to be
blowing towards our Indian frontier.' He tapped at an area left blank
on the map – 'Towards here, to be precise.' He paused. 'A place
named Kalikshutra.'

I frowned. 'I don't think I've ever heard of it, sir.'

'Not surprised, Moorfield, few have. Just look' – he tapped at the
map again – 'see how remote it is. High up as hell, and with only a
single road that leads to it – here. No other traversable way in – or
out. We've always been content to leave it well alone – no strategic
value, you see.' He paused, then frowned. 'Or so,' he murmured, 'we
had always thought.' His frown deepened. He stared at the map for
a moment more; then he returned to his seat and leaned across to
me. 'We're getting strange rumours, Moorfield. There's something
brooding there. A month ago, one of our agents came staggering in.
He was pale as death and carved with scars, but he also brought us
our first hard news. "I have seen them," he whispered, as a look of
the utmost horror crossed his face. "Kali." Then he shut his eyes, as
though too weak to utter what he wanted to say. "Kali," he repeated.
We left him alone, to get a good night's sleep. The next morning...'
Colonel Rawlinson paused. His lean, bronzed face seemed suddenly
pale. 'The next morning' – he cleared his throat – 'we found him
dead.' He paused again. 'Poor fellow had shot himself.'

'Shot himself?' I repeated in disbelief.

'Straight through the heart. Damnedest mess you ever saw.'

'Good God.' I breathed in deeply. 'What made him do it?'

'That, Captain, is what we need you to find out.'

Suddenly, the room seemed very still. I felt those damned Hindoo
gods gloating down at me. That we had a true mystery on our hands,
I didn't doubt. I knew full well how dangerous intelligence work
could be, and how brave the fellows were who took it on. Such men
were not in the habit of shooting themselves in a blind state of funk.

9

Something must have got to the man. *Something*. But what? I looked up again at Rawlinson.

'The Russians are involved in this business, then, you think, sir?'

Colonel Rawlinson nodded. 'We know they are.' He paused, then lowered his voice. 'Two weeks ago, a second agent came in.'

'Reliable?'

'Oh, the best.' Colonel Rawlinson nodded. 'We call him Sri Sinh – the Lion. Quite the best.'

'He'd seen Ivans,' said Pumper, leaning over to me. 'Scores of the beggars, done up as natives, marching up the road to Kalikshutra.'

I frowned. Something had just occurred to me. 'Kalikshutra,' I repeated, turning back to Rawlinson. 'Your first agent, sir – the one who died – if I remember correctly, he only referred to a "Kali". Might it not be possible that he was talking of a quite different place?'

'No,' said the Babu, whose presence in the room had gone clean from my mind.

'I beg your pardon?' I said coldly, for I was not used to being spoken to thus by anyone, let alone a Bengali office-man. But the Babu seemed quite unperturbed by my glance of disdain; he stared back at me rudely, then scratched at his rump. 'Kali is a Hindoo goddess,' he said, for all the world like a schoolmaster addressing some boy who has been slow with his prep. 'It is not a place.'

I must have looked hot at this, for Rawlinson cut me off pretty sharpish. 'Huree is Professor of Sanskrit at Calcutta University,' he said hurriedly, as though that served to justify anything. I stared at the man and he met my look, watching me with his insolent, fish-cold eyes.

'I am only a simple Englishman,' I said – and I flatter myself I made this sarcasm bite. 'I make no pretence of learning, for the Army camp has been my teaching-ground. Clearly then, I must let you explain to me this link between Kali, the goddess, and Kalikshutra, the place, for I readily admit I don't see it myself.'

The Babu bobbed his head. 'It will be a pleasure, Captain.'

He shifted in his seat and, bending down, picked up a statue, a great black thing which he then placed on the table in front of me. 'This, Captain,' he said, 'is the goddess Kali.'

Well, thank Heaven I'm a Christian, was all I could think, for the goddess Kali was the most frightful-looking thing, and no mistake. Pitch-black body, as I've mentioned, with swords in her six hands and a tongue dyed like blood. She seemed to be dancing on the body of a man. And that was by no means the worst of it, for only when I looked closer did I see her belt and the garland round her neck. 'Good Lord,' I murmured involuntarily. Human hands hung bleeding from her waist, and the garland was made of freshly severed heads!

'She has many names, Captain,' said the Babu in my ear, 'but always, she is Kali the Terrible.'

'Well, I'm not surprised!' I answered. 'Just look at her!'

'You misunderstand what such a title may mean.' The Babu smiled slyly. 'You must try to comprehend, please, Captain, that terror in our Hindoo philosophy is but an opening on to the absolute. What appals, inspires – what destroys, can create. When we experience terror, Captain, we are made aware of what the sages call *shakti* – eternal power – the feminine energy which underlies the universe.'

'Are we, by George? You don't say.' Well, I'd never heard such rot in all my born days, of course, and I'm afraid I let it show, but the Babu did not seem offended in the slightest. He only gave me another oily smile. 'You must try to see things as we poor heathens do, Captain,' he murmured.

'Why the devil should I?'

The Babu sighed. 'Fear of the goddess, terror of her power – to you it is just bloody bunk, I know, but to others it is not. Therefore, Captain – know your enemy – get into his mind. That – after all – is where Kali waits as well.'

Slowly, he bowed his head. He muttered some prayer under his breath. And then, as I watched, the Babu seemed to change before my eyes. It was the deucedest thing, but he seemed suddenly a soldier, possessed and cool, and when he spoke again he might have been lecturing the Chiefs of Staff. 'I have asked you, Captain Moorfield, to appreciate the nature of the devotion that Kali can inspire, for it is likely to be your most potent foe. Do not scorn it, just because you find it abhorrent and strange. Piety can be as dangerous as your soldiers' guns. Remember– only fifty years ago, Kali's priests in Assam were offering up the goddess human sacrifice. Had you British not annexed their kingdom, they would doubtless be offering it up still. And the British, of course, have never conquered Kalikshutra. We cannot know what customs are still practised there.'

'Good Lord,' I exclaimed, scarcely able to believe my ears. 'You surely don't mean to say ... not human sacrifice?'

The Babu shook his head. 'I say nothing,' he replied. 'No agent of the Government has ever penetrated far enough. However ...' His voice trailed away. He paused to glance at the statue, at its necklace of skulls and the red on its tongue. 'You asked about the link between the goddess and Kalikshutra,' he murmured.

I nodded. I liked the fellow more now, and I could sense he was ready with something pretty hot. 'Go on,' I said.

'Kalikshutra, Captain Moorfield, means – literally translated – "the land of Kali".* And yet' – he paused – 'it is an insult to my religion to say that Kalikshutra is Hindoo – for elsewhere in India the goddess is worshipped as a beneficent deity, the friend of man, the Mother of all the Universe ...'

'Whereas in Kalikshutra?' I asked.

'Whereas in Kalikshutra ...' Again the Babu paused, and stared at the statue's grinning face. 'In Kalikshutra, she is worshipped as Queen of the Demons. *Shmashana Kali!*' He spoke these words in a low whisper, and as he uttered them so the room seemed to darken and grow suddenly cold. 'Kali of the Cremation Grounds, from whose mouth blood flows in a never-ending stream, and who dwells amongst the fiery places of the dead.' And here the Babu swallowed,

---

*Calcutta, I have been informed, was built on such a site. The name of this second city of the British Empire was originally *Kali-kata*.

and spoke in a language I did not understand. '*Vetala-pancha-Vinshati*,' I heard, repeated twice, and then the Babu swallowed again and his voice trailed away.

'Sorry?' said old Pumper after a decent pause.

'Demons,' replied the Babu shortly. 'It is the phrase the villagers from the foothills use. An ancient Sanskrit term.' He turned again to look at me. 'And such is their fear of these demons, Captain, that the villagers who live below the heights of Kalikshutra refuse to take the road that would lead them there. And this is how we can be sure that the men our agent saw climbing up the road were not natives of the region, but foreigners.' He paused, then wagged his finger in emphasis. 'You understand me, Captain? *No natives would ever have taken that road.*'

There was a silence and Rawlinson turned to study me. 'You see the danger?' he asked, a frown on his face. 'We can't have the Russians in Kalikshutra. Once they establish themselves in a place like that, they are near as damnation impregnable. And if they do set up a base – well, it will be on the very border of British India. Perilous, Moorfield – deadly perilous. I don't think I need to emphasise that.'

'No indeed, sir.'

'We want you to recce those Ivans out.'

'Yes, sir.'

'You'll leave tomorrow. Colonel Paxton will follow you the day after that with his regiment.'

'Yes, sir. And how many men will I have with me?'

'Ten.' I must have looked surprised, for Rawlinson smiled. 'They'll be good, Moorfield, you needn't worry about that. Remember – you are only going to spy out the lie of the land. If you can take on the Russians yourself, then well and good. If not' – Rawlinson nodded at Pumper – 'send for Colonel Paxton. He will be waiting at the base of the road; he'll have men enough with him to sort the Russians out.'

'With respect, sir . . .'

'Yes?'

13

'Why don't we march in with the regiment at once?'

Rawlinson stroked the curve of his moustache. 'Politics, Moor-field.'

'I don't understand.'

Rawlinson sighed. 'This is a diplomat's game as well, I'm afraid. London doesn't want trouble on the border. In fact – and I shouldn't be telling you this – we've already turned a blind eye to a number of infringements in the region. About three years ago – don't know if you remember it – Lady Westcote was abducted, together with her daughter and twenty men.'

'Lady Westcote.'

'Wife of Lord Westcote, who had commanded in Kabul.'

'Good Lord,' I exclaimed, 'who took her?'

'We don't know,' replied Pumper, sitting up suddenly and looking angry. 'Our attempts to investigate were cut short. Sat on by the politicos.'

Rawlinson glanced at him, then back at me. 'The point is this,' he said, 'that the Raj can't be seen marching in to places willy-nilly.'

'Bit bloody late for that,' said the Babu. The rest of us ignored him.

Colonel Rawlinson handed me a neatly bound file. 'These are the best maps we've been able to run up. Not much good, I'm afraid. Also Professor Jyoti's notes on the Kali cult, and the reports from Sri Sinh – our agent in the foothills – I mentioned him before, I think?'

'Yes, sir, you did – the Lion. Will he be there now?'

Colonel Rawlinson frowned. 'If he is, Captain, then don't expect to run into him. Intelligence men play to different rules. One chap you may care to look out for, however, is a doctor – an Englishman – goes by the name of John Eliot. He's been working amongst the tribesmen up there for a couple of years now – setting up a hospital, that sort of thing. Won't usually have anything to do with the colonial authorities – bit of a maverick, don't you know? – but in this case he's aware of your mission, Captain, and he's game to help you if he can. Might be worth your while picking his brains. Got a lot of local knowledge. Speaks the lingo like a native, I'm told.'

I nodded, and made a jotting on the cover of the file. Then I rose, for I could see that my briefing was at an end. Before I left, though, Colonel Rawlinson shook my hand. 'Good God, Moorfield,' he said, 'but duty is a stern thing.'

I looked him straight in the eye. 'I shall try to do my best, sir,' I replied. But even as I said this I was remembering the agent who had shot himself, the unknown terror which had led him to crack, and I wondered if my best would prove to be enough.

Such forebodings only made me the keener to set out, of course, for no one cares to sit around and frowst when there's a bad business up ahead. Pumper Paxton, as an old hand himself, must have known how I was feeling, for he did me the great kindness of inviting me over to his bungalow that night, where we downed the old *chota peg* and yarned about old times. His wife was with him too, and his boy, young Timothy, a splendid chap who soon had me marching for him up and down the house. He was as promising a drill master as I had ever come across! We had a rare old time of it, for I had always been a favourite of young master Timothy's, and I was not a little bucked that he still remembered me. When the time came for him to retire to bed, I sat reading him yarns from some adventure book and I thought, watching him, how one day Timothy would do his father proud.

'That's a fine boy you have,' I told Pumper afterwards. 'He reminds me of why I wear this uniform.'

Pumper pressed my arm. 'Nonsense, old man,' he said, 'you have never needed reminding of that.'

I retired to bed in good spirits that night. When I woke up next morning at the crack of dawn, it was as though my dark imaginings had never been. I was ready for the fray.

We journeyed from Simla along the great mountain road. My soldiers, as Colonel Rawlinson had promised they would be, were good men, and we made rapid speed. For almost a month, as we travelled, I could well believe what has often been claimed – that there is nowhere more lovely in all the world, for the air was fresh, the vegetation glorious, and the Himalayas above us seemed to reach up to the sky. I remembered that these mountains were worshipped by the Hindoos as the home of the gods – passing below the stupendous peaks, I could well see why, for they seemed charged with a sense of great mystery and power.

At length, though, the scenery began to change. As we drew nearer to Kalikshutra it grew harsher and steadily more desolate, yet at the same time it was none the less sublime, so that the bleakness of the landscape served only to fill my thoughts. One evening, quite late, we reached the junction with the Kalikshutra road. A village straggled away from it, mean and poor, but still with the promise of human life, something we had not met with now for almost a week. When we entered the village, however, we found it deserted, and not even a dog was there to welcome us. My men were reluctant to bivouac there – said it gave them a bad feeling – and your soldier's second-sense is often pretty good. I too was keen to press on to our goal and so that same evening, though the sun had almost set, we began our march up the Kalikshutra road. Around the first steep corner, we passed a statue painted black. The stone had been worn away and had scarcely any features at all, but I could recognise the trace of skulls around the neck and knew whose image the statue represented. Flowers had been laid at the goddess's feet.

The next day, and the next after that, we toiled up the mountain-side. The path grew ever more precipitous and narrow, zig-zagging up an almost sheer wall of rock, while above the abyss burned a pitiless sun. I began to understand why the inhabitants of a place such as Kalikshutra, if indeed they existed at all, should be called demons, for I found it hard to believe that any human dwellings could lie ahead of us. Certainly, my own enthusiasm for mountains began to pall somewhat! But at last, as the second day began to dim into dusk, the path we were taking started to level out and we saw traces of green amongst the rocks ahead. As the sun's dying rays disappeared behind the cliff, we rounded an outcrop of rock and saw ahead of us a vast expanse of trees stretching upwards into purple

16

cloud, while still higher, just visible, gleamed the ghostly white of the mountain peaks. I stood for a moment to admire this splendid view; and then I heard a cry from one of my men who had continued down the path. I began to run myself, of course, and as I did so I heard the buzzing of flies.

I joined my man past a further crag of rock. He was pointing at a statue. Beyond it the jungle began, so that the statue seemed to stand like a sentinel guarding the approach into the undergrowth and trees. My soldier turned back to me, an expression of disgust on his honest face. I hurried up to join him, and as I inspected the idol I saw something slung around its neck – something alive. The stench was frightful. It reminded me of rotting meat and then I realised, as I watched the thing slung around the idol's neck, that I was staring at the swarming of maggots and flies, countless thousands of them, so that they seemed to form a living skin feeding on whatever it was that lay there underneath. I prodded the thing with my pistol butt; the flies rose in a buzzing cloud of black and there, maggot-ridden, hung a pile of guts. I cut them down and they fell with a soft thud on to the ground. As they did so, I saw to my surprise the gleam of gold. I smeared away the blood, and saw around the idol's neck an expensive-looking ornament. Even I, who have no eye for woman's things, could see at once that it was of a fair old workmanship. I inspected the necklace more closely; it was formed of a thousand tiny drops of gold, all strung together in a kind of a mesh, and must have been worth a pretty packet in anyone's book. I reached up to try to remove it. At that very same moment, a shot rang out.

The bullet whistled over my shoulder and pinged into a rock. I looked up and picked out our assailant immediately; he was standing alone on the crest of the ravine. He aimed his rifle a second time, but before he could fire I had the great good fortune to bag him in the leg. The man tumbled down the slope and I thought he might be done for, but not a bit of it, for he picked himself up and, using his rifle as a crutch, began to drag himself across to the road where we stood. All this time he was jabbering away, waving at the statue; I couldn't make out a word he was saying, of course, but I could guess his meaning well enough. I stood back from the statue, my hands raised to show I had no interest in his idol's gold. The man stared back at me, and for the first time I got a good look at him. He was old, with tattered pink robes and streaks of the most foul-smelling substance daubed across his face and arms, so that he stank to the very height of heaven. In short, he had *brahmin* written all over him. He looked pale, and his eyes were filling with tears. I glanced down at his leg. It was bleeding pretty bad, and I bent down to try and tend the wound, but as I did so the *brahmin* flinched away from me and started to let rip with his tongue again. This time, I fancied I caught the word 'Kali'. 'Kali,' I repeated and the man bobbed his head. '*Han, han, Kali!*' he screamed, then burst out into tears.

Well, the conversation was shaping up nicely and I was not a little perplexed as to what I should do next. Suddenly, however, I heard footsteps at my back.

'Perhaps I can be of assistance?' a voice said in my ear.

I turned round to see a man standing there, not in uniform but a European all the same. He had a thin, gaunt face, with an aquiline nose and rather the air of a bird of prey. He would not have been more than thirty, I estimated, yet his eyes seemed those of a much older man. I wondered who the devil he could be; and then suddenly – in a flash – it came to me.

'Doctor Eliot?' I asked.

The young man nodded. I introduced myself. 'Yes,' he said shortly, 'I was told you might be coming.' He stared down at the priest, who by now was laid out on the ground, clutching his leg and still muttering to himself.

'What's he saying?' I asked.

Eliot didn't answer me at first. Instead, he knelt down and began to tend to the *brahmin*'s leg.

I repeated my question.

'He is accusing you of sacrilege,' said Eliot without looking up.

'But I didn't take his gold.'

'You cut down the guts, though, didn't you?'

I snorted. 'Ask him why they do it,' I ordered brusquely. 'Ask him why they smear the idol with blood.'

Eliot spoke something to the priest. The old man's eyes dilated with fear; I saw him point at the statue and then sweep with his arm at the darkness of the jungle; I heard him mutter words I recognised, '*Vetala-pancha-Vinshati*' – words I had heard from the Babu back in Simla. Then the old man began to scream violently; I bent down beside him, but Eliot already had him in his arms and he brushed me away. 'Leave the poor man alone,' he ordered. 'He's in great pain. You've already shot him, Captain Moorfield – isn't that enough good work for now?'

Well, I was nettled by this comment, I freely admit, but I took the doctor's point – that there was nothing I could do – and so I rose to my feet. I had been intrigued, however, by the mention of the Babu's demons; Eliot must have read my thoughts, for he looked up at me and told me he would find me later on. I nodded again, then turned on my heels. His manner may have been a little short, but Eliot struck me as a sound man in the essentials, the sort of chap I was willing to trust. I went off to supervise the pitching of our tents.

Some time later, with the sentries posted and our camp ship-shape, I was sitting alone enjoying a pipe when Eliot joined me. 'How's your patient?' I asked.

Eliot nodded. 'He'll pull through,' he said as, with a sigh, he slumped down beside me where I sat. For a long while he said nothing at all, just stared into the fire. I offered him a pipe; he took it and filled it up himself. After several minutes' further silence, he stretched out like a cat and turned to me.

'You should not have tampered with the statue,' he said at length.

'Fakir still upset then, is he?'

'Naturally,' my companion replied. 'He holds himself responsible for appeasing the gods. Hence the golden jewellery, you see, Captain, and the goat guts round the neck . . .'

'Goat guts?' I interrupted.

'Why?' Eliot's bright eyes gleamed. 'What did you think they were?'

'Oh, nothing,' I grunted, tapping out my pipe. 'Just seems odd, I suppose – kicking up that fuss about some animal's insides.'

'Not really, Captain,' Eliot murmured, hooding his eyes again. 'Because you see, by insulting the goddess you have also insulted her worshippers, the dwellers of Kalikshutra – the very people whose country you are about to invade. The *brahmin* is afraid for his own folk, who live scattered around here amongst the foothills. He says that now there will be nothing to stop them from being attacked.'

'What, by the fellows higher up the mountainside?'

'Yes.'

'But I don't understand. I've left them the gold – surely that's what really matters? Why should anyone care for goat guts and blood? Why would that ever stop anyone's attacks?'

Eliot shrugged languidly. 'The superstitions here can sometimes seem rather strange.'

'Yes, so I've been told. Demon worship, and all that. What lies behind it, do you think? Anything much?'

'I don't know,' said Eliot. He poked at the fire and watched the sparks fly up into the night. Then he glanced back at me, and as he did so his air of relaxation seemed suddenly gone. I was struck again by the depths that seemed to wait behind his eyes, remarkable in a man so much younger than myself. 'Two years I have worked here,' he murmured at length, 'and there's one thing, Captain, that I am sure about. The mountain folk are terrified of something – and it isn't just superstition. In fact, it's what drew me to come here in the first place.'

'What do you mean?' I asked.

'Oh, odd things reported in out-of-the-way journals.'

'Such as?'

Eliot glanced up at me, and his eyes narrowed. 'Really, Captain, you wouldn't be interested. It's a rather obscure branch of medical research.'

'Try me.'

Eliot smiled mockingly. 'It's to do with the regulation and structure of the blood.' My face must have betrayed me, for his smile broadened and he shook his head. 'To put it simply, Captain, the white blood cells take a long time to die.'

Well, this had me sitting up, and no mistake. I stared at the man in astonishment. 'What,' I asked, 'you don't mean to say they can prolong a chap's life?'

'Not exactly.' Eliot paused. 'They may give the illusion of it, perhaps, but only for a while. You see' – he paused again – 'they also mutate.'

'Mutate?'

'Yes. Like a cancer spreading through the blood. It ends up destroying the nerves and the brain.'

'Sounds pretty grim. What exactly is the disease, do you think?'

Eliot stared at me; then he shook his head and looked away. 'I don't know,' he admitted reluctantly. 'I have only had a couple of chances to examine it.'

'But wasn't it to study the sickness that you came here?'

'Yes, originally. But I soon found out that the natives discouraged interest in anything to do with the disease and, since I am their guest here, I have respected their wishes and not pursued my research. I have had more than enough to do here as it is, establishing my hospital and fighting diseases which are all too well-known.'

'But even so – you did say you had seen a couple of people with your mystery disease?'

'Yes. It was shortly after Lady Westcote was abducted – you heard about that, no doubt?'

'Very briefly. A terrible case.'

'It appears,' continued Eliot dispassionately, 'that intrusions of such a kind, from the outside world, will always disturb the sufferers from the illness, draw them out from their hiding-places to stalk the foothills and jungles round about.'

'Goodness!' I exclaimed. 'You make them sound like wild beasts!'

'Yes,' agreed Eliot, 'but that is very much how the natives here regard them – as the deadliest of foes. And from my own observation of the two cases that I mentioned I think they are right to be so afraid, for the disease is indeed deadly – highly infectious, and destructive of the mind. That is why I am willing to help you now, for the presence of the

Russians here is dangerous in the extreme. If they remain here long, God knows how rapidly the disease may start to spread.'

'And is there no cure?' I asked, appalled.

Eliot shrugged. 'None that I know of. But the two cases I treated were not with me for very long. I had them a week or so, but it was a race against the process of atrophication. In the end I lost out – the brain-sickness got to them. Both the victims disappeared.'

'Disappeared?'

'Back to where they had come from.' Eliot turned and gestured at the forest and the distant mountain peaks. 'You know the legend,' he said. 'That's where all the demons live.'

'Are you serious?'

Once again, Eliot hooded his eyes. 'I don't know,' he said at last, 'but it seems clear that the higher up the mountain you go, the greater the incidence of these cases becomes. It is my theory that the local people have observed this phenomenon and explained it by constructing a whole mythology.'

'Meaning all this talk of demons, and such rot?'

'Exactly so.' Eliot paused, and slowly opened his eyes again. He glanced over his shoulder and despite myself I did the same. The moon, as ghostly and pale as the mountain peaks, was almost full, and the jungle behind us seemed a patchwork of blues. Eliot stared at it, as though trying to penetrate its very depths; then after a while he turned back to me. '*Vetala-pancha-Vinshati*,' he said suddenly. 'When the *brahmin* spoke that phrase, you recognised it, didn't you?'

I nodded.

'How?'

'I was told,' I replied, 'by a Professor of Sanskrit, no less.'

'Ah.' Eliot nodded slowly. 'So you've met Huree?'

I tried to remember if that had been the Babu's name. 'He was fat,' I said, 'and damnably rude.'

Eliot smiled. 'Yes, that was Huree,' he agreed.

'So how do you know him, then?' I asked.

Eliot's eyes narrowed. 'He visits here occasionally,' he replied.

'Up here?' I chuckled to myself. 'But he's so confoundedly fat!

How the devil does he manage it?'

Eliot smiled again faintly. 'Oh, in the cause of his research he could manage anything.' He reached inside his pocket. 'Here,' he said, taking out a folded sheaf of papers. 'Those articles I mentioned, the ones that persuaded me to come up here – it was the Professor who wrote them.' He handed the papers across. 'He sent me this one just a month ago.'

I glanced down at it. '*The Demons of Kalikshutra*,' I read. '*A Study in Modern Ethnography*.' And then there was a sub-title, in smaller print: 'Sanskrit Epics, Himalayan Cults, and the Global Tradition of the Meal of Blood.' I frowned. 'Sorry,' I said. 'Should I be interested in this?'

There seemed to be mockery in Eliot's glance. 'So Huree didn't tell you what "*Vetala-pancha-Vinshati*" meant, then?' he asked.

'Yes, of course he did, it's the word for demon.'

Eliot pursed his thin lips. 'Actually,' he said, 'around here it means something much more specific than that.'

'Oh, really?'

Eliot nodded. 'Yes. Something which, with my interests, I've always found particularly intriguing – the association of myth, with medical fact, you see, being particularly suggestive in the regions of the East . . .'

'Yes, yes,' I said, 'but tell me – what does the damn phrase *mean*?'

Eliot turned again, to stare at the jungle and the pale, ghostly moon. 'It means "drinker of blood", Captain,' he said at last. 'Now do you see? That is why the hill-people smear their statues with goat-blood. They are afraid that otherwise the demons will come and drink from them.' He laughed softly, and a strange sound it was. '*Vetala-pancha-Vinshati*,' he whispered to himself. He turned back to face me. 'There is an obvious English word for it,' he said, 'much more precise than "demon".' He paused. '"*Vampire*", Captain. That is what it means.'

I paused, staring at his face bathed silver by the moon, then opened my mouth to ask him if he really thought the tribesmen drank blood. At that very moment, however, I heard my sentries call out; I looked round and jumped to my feet. There was the sudden crack of a rifle shot. So much for our chat, I thought; as is ever the soldier's fate, I was being summonsed away by action's call. I hurried through the camp to find the sentries standing by the edge of the path. 'Russians, sir,' said one of them, still holding his gun. He gestured with the weapon. 'Out there, three or four of them. I think I got one of the bastards in the back.'

I drew out my revolver, then led the way carefully along the track towards the line of trees where the jungle began. 'They were over here, sir,' said one of the sentries, pointing towards a pool of thick shadow. I made my way through the undergrowth; there was no sign of anyone. I pulled away the creepers and stared around. The jungle was as silent and still as before. I took a step forward ... and then suddenly I felt fingers gripping my leg.

As though in slow motion, I looked down and fired. I remember seeing a pale face, its mouth wide open but its eyes cold and dead. Then the bullet smashed into its skull – I saw it disintegrate, and a shower of blood and bone was blasted into my face. Unpleasant – but the strange thing was, I stayed deadly calm. I wiped the stuff away from my eyes, then stared down at the corpse by my feet. There was the beastliest mess everywhere. As I bent down by the body, I could see a round bullet-hole in the back; my soldier had caught him bang in the spine. 'He should have been dead long before you got him, sir,' the sentry said, staring down at the bullet-hole. I ignored him and I rolled the corpse over. He was dressed in native garb, but when I felt in his pockets I found a tattered rouble note.

I rose to my feet and peered into the darkness of the creepers and trees. 'Damn it, but they are up there,' I thought. Rawlinson's intelligence had been correct – the Russians were indeed in Kalikshutra. My blood fairly boiled at the very thought. God knew what devilry they might be brewing against us! God knew what devilry against the whole British Raj! I glanced down at the corpse by my feet. 'Bury it,' I said, tapping at its side with my boot. 'Then, when you're replaced, get a good few hours' sleep. We have a long day ahead of us – we depart tomorrow at the first light of dawn.'

SLAVE OF MY THIRST

Letter, Dr John Eliot to Professor Huree Jyoti Navalkar.

6 June 1887.

Dear Huree,

I am leaving tomorrow with Moorfield and his men. One of the sentries shot a Russian soldier tonight, and Moorfield wishes to ascertain the full extent of the enemy presence here. I will accompany him as far as the Kalibari Pass.

I leave you this note because it is possible that I shall accompany him even further than that. If I do so, then it is equally possible I shall never return. For two years now I have lived amongst the people of the foothills, almost as one of their own. In all that time, I have kept my promise and never attempted to penetrate beyond the Pass to Kalikshutra itself. If I feel I can, I will keep to that promise now, for I would not willingly betray those who have been so welcoming and generous to me. But what the tribesmen most dreaded has already begun to happen: Chaos is indeed descending from beyond the Pass. Huree – the Russian who was killed tonight – I conducted the autopsy. There can be no doubt at all – *his white cells were diseased.*

I am very much afraid, then, that the sickness is starting to spread. It is too early yet to talk of an epidemic; but certainly the presence of Russian soldiers in Kalikshutra makes the prohibition on travelling beyond the Kalibari Pass seem futile. If we find further evidence of the disease below the Pass, then I shall feel that it is my duty as a doctor to investigate its nature more closely. The tribesmen will forgive me, I hope, if I can only find a cure. Goat's blood and gold, I think, may soon prove an inadequate defence.

I cannot deny that I feel a certain excitement at the thought of penetrating Kalikshutra at last. The disease that is surely raging there seems an extraordinary one. If I can identify it, then the whole programme of my research may well be resolved. Your own theory too, Huree – that the sickness explains the vampire myth – may also be proved.

Let us hope we shall have the chance to discuss all these matters. Until then, though, my best wishes,

JACK.

Extract, With Rifles in the Raj, *(continued).*

❦

INTO KALIKSHUTRA

A jungle expedition – first blood to us – an unsettling dream – 'Durga' – a soldier's wretched death – Kalikshutra – a grisly ritual.

My men, I knew, would relish the scrap ahead of us, and it was in high spirits that we set off the following morning. Even as we moved forward, however, I was careful to cover my back. The swiftest of my soldiers was dispatched down the path we had just climbed with a message for Pumper and his regiment, telling them to advance with all God's speed; two other of my men were left to guard the summit of the road. The seven remaining soldiers accompanied me, and alongside them came Dr Eliot. We would need a guide, he had told us, for the way was rough; he would take us as far as the Kalibari Pass, which he described as the gateway to Kalikshutra itself. I gave him a service revolver; he refused it at first, saying that he would never use it, but when I insisted he eventually gave in. I was glad of his company, for he was a stout fellow and the path did indeed prove very treacherous. As I have mentioned elsewhere, I was a pretty keen game-hunter out in India and I'd seen some thick jungle in my time, but nothing that ever compared with what we had to pass through now. A more effective barrier Nature couldn't have designed, and I began to get the queerest sense that man wasn't meant to penetrate it. Call it soldier's superstition – call it what you will – but all of a sudden I had a bad feeling about what lay ahead. Naturally I didn't let this show, but it worried me all the same, for I had noticed this instinct for danger in myself before while out hunting tiger and other big game, and I had learned to trust it. And now we were hunting the most dangerous game of all – man! – for at any time our quarry might turn and we, the hunters, become the prey!

We had a hard day's travelling. Not until nightfall did the jungle start to thin. At length I hauled myself up a rock face and Eliot, who was just behind me, pointed ahead. 'You see that crag?' he whispered. 'That's the cliff that looks over the Kalibari Pass.'

I stared at it. Beyond the Pass, I could see a road winding steeply up the mountainside. It was fearfully exposed, yet was clearly the route we would have to take, for on the other side of the Pass the mountain rose skywards in a sheer wall of rock, up and up for hundreds of feet. It seemed to form a plateau at the very top.

Eliot too was staring at it. 'Kalikshutra is beyond the summit,' he said.

'Is it, by George?' I muttered. 'Then it seems we're in for a fearful ascent. A more perfect spot for an ambush I have never seen.' And indeed, at that very moment the silence of the jungle was split by a shot. I turned and plunged back into the undergrowth; I could see pale forms ahead of me, like ghosts amongst the trees. My men formed a line about me; we began to fire and I saw the figures start to drop. Our shooting was deadly and fast. Soon the Russians had melted quite from view, either downed or fled. The jungle seemed as hushed in its stillness as before.

We continued our advance towards the Kalikshutra road, but had not advanced more than half a mile before they were at us again. Once more though, we repelled them, and again we were able to resume our advance. At length we reached flat and open ground, where the mountain road met the foot of the jungle, and I knew that if we went any further we would be entering the jaws of a fatal trap. I looked around me. There was a line of rocks along the edge of the road; I ordered my men to take position behind them, and no sooner had they done so than the air was chilled by a most unearthly cry.

'My God,' muttered Eliot.

Rising up from the shadows, almost it seemed from the very soil, was a line of men – their faces pale, their eyes like pricks of burning light. I steadied my troops. 'Fire!' I bellowed. There was a deadly crackle, and seven of the enemy fell back into the dust. 'Fire!' I repeated, and again we ripped out a hole in their line. Still they came at us, though, and I could see more figures rising from the dark: things were starting to seem pretty tight. I scanned the enemy line and observed, standing just back from the rest of his men, a Russian in a turban, sniffing the air. He said nothing, but the others seemed driven forward by his look and I knew him at once to be the man in command. I leaned across and spoke to Private Haggard, the best shot amongst us. Haggard aimed, a crack rang out across the rocks, and the turbaned Russian staggered and fell. At once the line of our attackers began to waver. 'Shoot him again,' I ordered Haggard, as I rose to my feet. 'At 'em, boys!' With a cheer, we advanced. The enemy began to fade before us – almost, it seemed, into nothingness. Soon only the bodies of their fallen were left. Silence reigned across the whole ghastly scene. The road, at least for now, was back in our hands.

I knew though that our respite would be temporary, and so my first priority was to post the guards. Meanwhile Eliot had been moving amongst the slain, making sure there was no one beyond the reach of his help, when suddenly he froze and called out to me. 'This one's alive,' he said, 'though I don't know how.'

I joined him. He was kneeling by the slim man in the turban, the commanding officer; the Russian had two bad wounds to his stomach, and blood was seeping out in a thickish flow. The officer's body seemed extraordinarily frail in Eliot's arms, and I too failed to see how he might still be alive. I bent down beside him and looked into his face. Then I whistled. 'Good Lord,' I exclaimed.

For it was not a man before me at all, but a woman, and a lovely one at that. Her face was pale, but not in the way of a European: instead it seemed almost translucent, and I realised that I had never seen a woman half so beautiful before. Even Eliot, who I had down as a pretty cold fish, seemed rather taken with the woman – and yet there was also something repulsive about her, something indescribable, and the beauty and horror were mingled together so that her loveliness seemed that of hell. You will read that and think I must have been pretty overheated – well, so I was and yet my instincts, I think, in the long term were to prove correct enough. I brushed back the woman's turban, and long black hair spilled out across my hand. I caught the glint of various gew-gaws and, I breathed in sharply, for I recognised them at once; they were almost identical to the jewellery I had seen round the idol's neck, back beyond the jungle. I bent down closer to have a better look; and as I did so our lady captive opened her eyes. They were deep and wide, in the manner that Orientals find most admirable in a woman, but they also burned as though lit by fire and I felt a shiver run through me as I looked into them, for they seemed full of hatred and a devilish power.

I rose to my feet. 'Ask her who she is,' I said.

Eliot whispered something, but her eyes fluttered shut again and she made no reply.

I glanced down at the gaping wounds in her side. 'Can you keep her alive?' I asked.

Eliot shook his head. 'There's nothing I can do, I repeat – this woman should be dead.'

'So why isn't she, do you think? Anything to do with your white blood cells, perhaps?'

He shrugged. 'Possibly. You'll notice, however, that her expression betrays no sign of the imbecility I would expect to find if she did have the disease – and which, incidentally, the other soldiers' faces *did* seem to betray.' He shrugged again. 'But I'm operating pretty much in the dark here. I'll give her some opium, I can't think what else to prescribe. I feel pretty helpless, I have to admit.'

I left him to his doctoring and wandered moodily amongst the bodies of the slain, troubled by what Eliot had said. I stared down into the faces of the dead; unlike their commander they had clearly been Russian, but their pallor was almost *too* waxy, *too* white. I remembered the man who had seized my leg the night before; his face had been similarly pale before I had blown it half-away, and I recalled how dead his eyes had looked. Eliot was right; the Russians *had* worn the faces of imbeciles – all save one, of course, that damnable woman with her burning eyes. I began to wonder about the disease, to fear how infectious it might truly be.

But I could not allow myself to brood for long. I sat amongst my men, swapping jokes and mugs of tea. They deserved their relaxation, for it had been a stiffish day and tomorrow, God knew, might turn out breezy as well. I glanced up at the road ahead of us. The more I studied it, the less I liked its look. It would be an act of bravery akin to folly, I knew, to follow it any further up the mountainside. I wondered if we should not wait for Pumper and his men, but I was mustard-keen to spy the land out further and have another crack at the Ivans up ahead. I remembered our prisoner. Whoever or whatever she was, she might prove a useful hostage to us. I rose and wished my men good-night; then I crossed back to Eliot, where his patient still lay.

'So, then,' I asked him, 'she's still alive?'

A shadow appeared to pass across his face. 'Look,' he replied and he drew back a blanket. The prisoner's eyes were still closed, but there was a faint smile on her lips and her cheeks seemed plumper and touched with red. Eliot replaced the blanket and rose to his feet. He crossed to the other side of the fire, and I noticed a second body stretched out there; it lay perfectly still.

'Who is it?' I asked.

Eliot bent down. Again he drew back a blanket and I recognised Private Compton, a good lad and usually the very picture of ruddy health. But now his skin was remarkably pale, just as the Russians' had been, and his eyes, which were open, seemed glassy and dead. 'Look,' said Eliot, and began to unbutton his patient's tunic. He pointed; there were scratches all over Compton's chest, and the wounds were vivid and raised like welts. I looked up into Eliot's eyes. 'Who did this?' I asked. 'What did this?' He slowly shook his head. 'I don't know,' he replied.

'And the pallor? – the look in his eyes? – dammit, Eliot, is this your disease?'

He glanced up at me; then slowly, he nodded his head.

'So where has it come from?'

'I told you before – I just don't know.' The admission of this ignorance seemed to cause him displeasure. He glanced through the flames at the body of the prisoner. 'It is possible, I suppose,' he said, with a wave of his hand, 'that she is infected. Her skin seems very cold and it has a certain pallid gleam, but otherwise she lacks the primary symptoms of the disease. It may be that she's a vector, transmitting it but remaining unaffected herself. The problem is, though, that I am not even certain how the disease is being spread.'

He sighed and glanced down at the wounds across poor Compton's chest; he seemed on the verge of saying something, but then he froze and stared through the flames at the prisoner again. 'I will keep a watch on her,' he said slowly, 'on her and on Compton.' He looked up at me. 'Don't worry, Captain. Leave me with the patients, and if anything happens I will let you know at once.'

I nodded. 'But please, for God's sake,' I muttered, 'don't let her die on us.' I glanced up at the road to Kalikshutra again. 'If we can only get her to talk, she might know of another way up that devilish cliff.' Eliot glanced at me and nodded; again he appeared ready to say something, but for a second time the words seemed to freeze on his tongue. I wished him good-night and left him staring into Compton's face, wiping the poor fellow's brow. Clearly we both had much to think about. I needed a good pipe, I realised. I sat down, and lit one. But I must have been more tired than I had thought, for even with the briar still between my teeth I began to feel my eyelids droop. Before I knew it, I was out like a light . . .

I had the queerest dream. This was unusual for me – I'm not a dreaming type – but the one I had that night seemed uncommonly real. I imagined that the woman, our prisoner, was by my side. I stood quite transfixed; I had a gun in my hand, but as I stared into her face I found I was slowly loosening my grip. The gun dropped to the ground, and its clattering woke me from my trance. I looked around and realised that I was in a palisade, and that the enemy were breaking in waves against our fire. But my men were falling – surely soon they would be utterly submerged. I had to help them – I had to man the walls – otherwise we would be broken and the regiment destroyed! But I couldn't move, that was the damnedest thing; for when I tried I found that I was frozen by the woman's eyes, trapped like a fly in a spider's web. She laughed. I looked around again, and I saw that everyone was dead – my own men, the enemy, all dead apart from me. Even the woman beside me was dead, I saw now, and yet she still moved, walking away from me as though she were some hungry pantheress. I felt drawn to her most terribly and I tried to follow her, but then I felt cold hands pulling on my legs. I looked down. The dead were everywhere reaching for me. Their eyes had the idiot stare of Eliot's disease, and their flesh was white, and chill as the grave. Helplessly, I felt myself being pulled down, submerged beneath soft, cold limbs. I saw Compton. His face was pressed against my own. He opened his mouth and a look of the most damnable greed suddenly burned in his eyes. His lips seemed to suck like a pair of hungry leeches as he brought them closer and closer towards my face. I knew he was going to feed on me. They touched my cheek . . . and I woke up to find Eliot was shaking me.

'Moorfield,' he was saying in a low, desperate voice, 'get up, they've gone!'

'Who?' I asked, rising at once to my feet. 'Not the woman?'

'Yes,' said Eliot, giving me a queer look. 'Have you been dreaming of her?'

I stared at him, astonished. 'How the devil did you know?'

'Because I did too. And that's not the worst,' he added. 'Compton is gone as well.'

'Compton?' I repeated. I stared at Eliot in disbelief and then, I'm afraid, such was my shock at the tidings he had brought that I rather bawled the good Doctor out. But he merely studied me, his eyes keen and his head angled so that he had even more the look of a hawk.

'Are you still determined to press further on?' he asked, when my anger had at length blown its course.

I didn't answer immediately, but looked up at the mountain peaks and the road that led towards them through the Himalayan night. 'There is a British soldier missing,' I said slowly. I clenched my fists. 'One of *my* soldiers, Eliot.' I shook my head. 'Damn it, but it would be a pretty poor show if we were to draw stumps now.'

Eliot stared at me, and for a long time he made no reply. 'You realise,' he said at last, 'that if you continue to take the road you are on, they will wipe you out?'

'Do we have any other choice?'

Again Eliot stared at me wordlessly; then he turned and began to walk towards the cliff. I followed him; he had the air of a man who was wrestling with his conscience, and I wasn't altogether too upset to see it. At length he turned to face me again. 'I shouldn't tell you this, Captain,' he said.

'But you are going to?' I asked

'Yes. Because otherwise you will certainly die.'

'I am not afraid of death.'

Eliot smiled faintly. 'Don't worry – I am only reducing the certainty of it to the level of high probability.' Then his smile faded, and he looked at the mountain wall which lay beyond the pass. Now that we were more directly below it, I could scarcely see to its summit, so high it rose. Eliot pointed. 'There is a way up,' he said, 'to the top.' The route, it seemed, was a pilgrims' path. 'It is called *Durga*,' Eliot told me, 'which is another name for the goddess Kali, and means in English "difficult of approach". And so it is – which is why the brahmins give it such supreme value, for they say that the man who can scale it is worthy of glimpsing Kali herself. Only the greatest of ascetics have ever attempted it – only those who have purged themselves through decades of penance and meditation. When they have attained the state of readiness, they ascend the cliff. Many do not succeed; they return, and it is from them that I have heard of the difficulty of the way. But a few – just a few – manage it. And when they reach the summit' – he paused – 'when they have succeeded, then they are shown the Truth.'

'The Truth? And what the devil would that be?'

'We don't know.'

'Well, if these *brahmins* attain it, why ever not?'

Eliot smiled faintly. 'Because, Captain, they never come back.'

'What, *never*?'

'Never.' Eliot's smile faded as he stared up at the mountain front again. 'So then,' he murmured softly, 'do you still want to go?'

A wasted question indeed! Naturally I prepared to set off at once. I chose my fittest man, Private Haggard, and my strongest, Sergeant-Major Cuff; the rest I left behind to make sure of the Pass and await old Pumper, whom I hoped would be approaching with his troops fairly soon. But in the meantime, with dawn still several hours off, I and my small band were already on our way. We clambered towards the far side of the Pass, over rocks at first and then, when the cliff started to rise sheer and featureless, up steps which had been carved out from the naked rock. 'According to the brahmin,' Eliot said, 'these will lead to a plateau perhaps a quarter of the way up. We must cross that and then continue our ascent up the remainder of the mountain face.'

Painfully, we began our ascent. The steps had been crudely carved and were often little more than toe-holds in the rock, sometimes vanishing altogether, so that it was pretty hard going and toughish on the legs. It was cold as well, and my legs began to cramp; after a couple of hours I started to think what fine soldiers the brahmins would have made, for they must all have been fitter men than we! I paused to draw my breath and Eliot, who was behind me, pointed to an outcrop of rock. The steps, I could see, twisted up across its face. 'Once we're over that,' he shouted, 'we're past the worst. The plateau will be only a gentle climb away.'

But goodness, did we have to earn that gentle climb first! It was virtually dawn by now, but in that bleak, exposed place the wind seemed more vicious than it had ever done, and it buffeted our bodies in screaming gusts as though trying to sweep us out into the sky which waited, blank and dark, below our swinging feet. It was a pretty grim experience; and then, just when I thought it could hardly grow more grim, I heard a scream. It was very faint, and then was lost on the shriek of the wind. I tensed, and Eliot too seemed to freeze against the rock. The wind fell and we heard a second scream, borne to us on a gust blowing up from the ravine. But beyond the ravine we couldn't see; the outcrop we were crossing had intervened. My blood felt like ice now; to continue on my way, thinking only of where to place my fingers and my toes, to worry about myself and not my men, was the worst kind of ordeal, yet it had to be done; indeed, I did it faster perhaps than if I had never heard the screams. Once I had reached safety, I followed the path as it wound back across the rock-face; I looked down and saw the ravine yawning distantly below, yet not so far that I couldn't see our tents. Remember too that it was almost dawn, growing lighter by the minute, and you will understand my consternation when I found that I couldn't see any of my men. Not a hint of movement. *Not a sign of them.*

I continued to gaze as well as my eyesight would allow, but it was as though every last one had just vanished into air. I remembered the screams I had heard, and I freely admit that I dreaded the worst. So too, it was clear, did Private Haggard. My three companions had all joined me by now and, despite my best efforts to chivvy them along, they observed the camp and its emptiness. 'Probably gone for an early-morning stroll, sir,' said the Sergeant-Major imperturbably; then he gestured at Haggard. 'Best keep an eye on him, sir,' he whispered. And he told me what I had not before realised, that Haggard had been a part of the expedition which had lost Lady Westcote – he had been in the area before and seen some pretty queer things. He was a brave enough chap, but rattled, for your average soldier will cheerfully take on a Zulu impi by himself, but give him a whiff of voodoo and he'll show you a stomach dyed a deepish shade of yellow. By this time we were crossing level ground; I began to wish we were still mountaineering, for Haggard, I thought, needed his mind kept busy.

The plateau we were crossing was about a mile deep. We made our way carefully, and soon joined a path that wound up through the rocks and had traces of recent footprints in the dust. We took to the heights, shadowing the path, and it wasn't long before we were approaching the base of another mountain front, rising sheer and seemingly even more insurmountable than the cliff we had just climbed. Eliot paused to scan the rocks ahead. 'There,' he said suddenly, pointing. 'That's where the path continues up the cliff.' I looked and saw a gaudily painted shrine carved out from the rock. I inched forward, searching for a way that wouldn't take us along the path, for I was on my guard despite the seeming calm, but as I lifted my head I felt Eliot's hand restraining me. 'Just wait,' he whispered. 'The sufferers from the disease are sensitive to light.' He pointed again, this time to the east. I looked. The mountain peaks were touched with pink. Eliot was right; the sunrise couldn't be far away.

'Sir,' whispered Haggard, 'what are we waiting for?'

I motioned him to be quiet, but Haggard shook his head. 'It was like this when they took the Westcotes,' he muttered, 'that poor lady and her lovely daughter – snatched away, them and their guard, just like now, gone into the night, just gone into the air.' He rose to his feet and looked about him wildly. 'And now they're hunting us!'

Desperately I pulled him back down, and as I did so I heard Eliot breathe in and hiss at us to lie still. I stared at the path before us; there was movement coming from the undergrowth beyond, and I saw a group of men walk out. They were dressed in Russian uniforms, but I could not see their faces, for they stood with their backs to us. Then one of the men turned and seemed to sniff the air. He looked towards the rock where we all lay hidden, and I heard Private Haggard mutter and groan. I too, staring at him, felt a sickness in my heart, for I was looking at the man I had shot in the skull the night before! I could recognise his wound, just a mess of blood and bone, and how the blighter was still alive I couldn't tell. Yet he was! His eyes were gleaming and shone very pale.

'No!' Haggard suddenly screamed. 'No, not me, not me!' He aimed his rifle, and with a single shot blew away a second Russian's face. He broke from the Sergeant Major's attempt to restrain him and started to scramble over the rocks towards the shrine.

Eliot swore. 'Quick!' he shouted. 'We must run as well.'

'Run? From an enemy? Never!' I cried.

'But they are infected!' Eliot screamed. 'Just look!'

He gestured, and as I stared I saw, to my horror, that the Russian felled by Haggard was slowly rising to his feet. His jaw had been shot away and hung from the skull by a single thread of sinew; I could see his throat, frothy with blood, as it contracted and opened, for all the world as though hungry to be fed. He took a step towards us; his comrades, who had gathered behind him, now began to inch forward in a single pack.

'Please,' Eliot begged again. 'For God's sake, run!' He reached for me suddenly and pulled me by the arm; I tumbled, picked myself up and, as I did so, one of the Russians broke from the pack and came stalking towards me like some hungry wild beast. I raised my gun to fire, but my arm seemed turned to lead. I stared into the Russian's eyes; they were burning with a look of the most terrible greed, yet somehow they were still as cold as before, so that the effect was one of the utmost ghastliness. Despite myself I took a step backwards, and at once heard from my adversaries a queer rustling, whittering sound, so that had it not sounded so damnable I would have called it laughter. Suddenly the Russian bared his teeth, then literally leaped up as though to tear out my throat. I put up my hands to push him away and then, from behind my shoulder, I heard a pistol shot, and the Russian fell back dead with a bullet drilled neatly between his eyes. I looked round to see Eliot standing there, the revolver still in his hands.

'I thought you weren't prepared to use a gun?' I asked.

He shrugged. 'Cometh the hour,' he muttered. He looked down at the Russian, who was starting to twitch as the other had done. 'Now, Captain,' Eliot whispered politely, 'now, Sergeant-Major– will you please, for God's sake, come with me and *run*?'

We did so, of course. Writing that down now, in the comfort of my Wiltshire study, I know it sounds bad, but it was not the men we were fleeing – rather their hellish disease. By George, though, infected as they were, they could still not half move. For as Eliot, the Sergeant-Major and myself, having found the steps by the side of the shrine, began to scramble our way up the mountainside, so also did the Russians start to follow us. The going on these steps was easier than it had been on the previous rock-face, and we all made pretty fair speed; but remorselessly our enemy followed us. I suppose they were bred to it, for your average Ivan is a hardy brute – and yet our pursuers had little true agility, for even as they scaled the rocks they seemed clumsy and doltish, and one would almost have said that their energy came exclusively from their desire to capture us. Certainly, glancing down at them, they seemed scarcely human at all, so hungry and eager their faces gleamed, like a pack of *dhole* – the Deccan wild dog – smelling our blood.

Inexorably they started to catch up with us; at length the nearest was scarcely an arm's reach away. By now I had had enough of showing him my back; I paused, to turn and face things out.

'No,' Eliot shouted desperately; again, he pointed east towards the mountain peaks. 'It's almost dawn!' he cried.

But the Russian was too close to flee from now. Again cold, burning eyes were staring into mine; the Russian almost hissed with venom, and he tensed and crouched as though ready to leap. At that same moment, however, the first ray of sun spilled up into the sky and the peak of the mountain was lost in a blaze of red. The Russian paused; he fell back; and all the others slowed down as well and then stopped.

At the same moment I felt a bullet whistle past me an inch from my nose. It bit into the rock, and splinters showered out between our pursuers and myself. I looked up to see Haggard standing on the edge of an outcrop, his rifle aimed, ready to have a second shot.

'What the hell are you doing, man?' I bellowed. 'Just get on up the path!'

But Haggard, so frayed his nerves had become, ignored me – the only time a soldier has ever disobeyed my command. 'No, sir!' he screamed. 'They're vampires! Vampires, sir! We must destroy them all!'

'Vampires?' I glanced at Eliot and shook my head, a gesture which Haggard observed and, I'm afraid, didn't take too well.

'I saw it before,' he screamed, 'when they came and took Lady

Westcote away. Lady Westcote and her lovely daughter; they must have fed on them, and now they're going to feed on us as well!'

Of course I tried to explain. I shouted up to him that there was a terrible disease, and I appealed to Eliot to confirm my words, but Haggard, waiting, began to laugh. 'They're vampires' he repeated, 'I tell you, they are!' He fired once more, but he was shaking badly now and again he missed. He took a step forward to get a better aim, and as he lowered his rifle his foot somehow slipped. I shouted out to warn him – but he was already gone. He fired and the bullet went harmlessly up into the sky; at the same time Haggard was waving his arms despairingly as pebbles gave way beneath his feet, and then he began to drop down the cliff-face until he landed with a sickening thud amongst the bushes by the shrine. These served to break his fall and must have saved his life, for I could see him struggling to lift himself; but his limbs were all shattered and he couldn't move.

Our pursuers meanwhile had been huddled together watching us with their cold, burning eyes. They had been quite motionless from the moment when the sun had first risen in the east; but now, watching poor Haggard's fall down the cliff, they seemed to tense and quiver as though with a new sense of life. They were all watching him as he struggled to pull himself free from the bushes; then they began to cluster together even closer and from all of them I heard the strange twittering sound which I had earlier taken to be their laughter. They began to retreat from us, back down the cliff; they went even more slowly and clumsily than before, as though the sunlight were water to be struggled against – but still they went. I watched helplessly as they reached the shrine and fanned out in a circle around Haggard who lay, his limbs twitching, amongst the bushes where he had fallen. He screamed and again tried to lift himself, but it was hopeless. The Russians, who had been watching the poor fellow rather as a cat might a mouse, now began to move in towards him – and then one ran forward, and then a second, until all of them were clustered round him with their heads bent over his bleeding wounds.

'My God,' I whispered, 'what are they doing?'

Eliot glanced at me, but he made no answer, for we both knew the legends of Kalikshutra and could see now that they had not been legends at all. They were drinking his blood! Those fiends – I could hardly think of them as men any more – they were drinking Haggard's blood! One of them paused in his meal and sat back on his haunches; his mouth and chin were streaked with red, and I realised he had torn Haggard's throat apart. I fired at them, but my arm was shaking and I didn't get a hit. Even so, the Russians backed away. Haggard's body was left lying by the shrine; it was covered in deep red gashes and his flesh was white, quite drained of blood. The Russians looked up at me; slowly, they began to return to their meal; I left them to it, for there was nothing I could do.

I turned and began to continue up the path. For a long time – a long time – I did not look back down.

On our ascent of the mountain face that terrible day, I do not intend to dwell. Suffice to say that it very nearly did for us. The climb was hellish, the altitude high; and we were drained, of course, by the horrors we had seen. By the late afternoon, when the rock-face was finally starting to level out, we were all pretty much at the limits of our endurance. I found a sheltered ledge, which would protect us equally from the blast of the winds and the prying of hostile eyes; I ordered that we pause there a while and take some rest. I settled down, and almost before I knew it was sound asleep. I woke up suddenly, without opening my eyes. I felt as though I had been out for only ten minutes, yet my sleep had been so dreamless and profound that I knew myself to be quite refreshed. I would not wake the others yet, I thought. It was still only the afternoon, after all. Then I opened my eyes to find that I was staring into the pale, full gleam of the moon.

It was chillingly beautiful, and for a moment the scene fairly took my breath away. The great Himalayan peaks ahead of me, and the valleys far below, mantled in shadows and shades of rich blue; the faint wisps of cloud below us, like the breath of some mountain deity; and over all, flooding it, the silver light of that burning moon. I felt myself to be in a world which had no place for man, which had endured and would endure for all time – cold, and beautiful, and terrible. I felt what an Englishman in India must so often feel – how far from home I was, how remote from everything I understood. I looked about me. I thought of the mortal danger we were in, and wondered if this strange place was to be my grave, whether my bones would lie here lost and unknown, far from Wiltshire and my dear, dear wife, crumbling gradually to dust beneath the roof of the world.

But a soldier cannot dwell on such maudlin thoughts for long. We were in deadly peril, that was true enough, but we would not escape it by sitting on our hands. I woke Cuff and Eliot, and once they had risen we continued on our way. For an hour we saw nothing worthy of comment. The path continued to flatten out, and the rocks began to give way to scrub. Soon we were walking through jungle again, and the vegetation overhead had grown so thick that not even the moonlight could penetrate it. 'This is very strange,' Eliot said, squatting down to inspect a vast flower. 'There shouldn't be flora of this kind at such an altitude.'

I smiled faintly. 'Don't look so disturbed,' I replied. 'Would you rather we had nothing to conceal our approach?'

And then, just as I said this, I saw the glimmer of something pale through the trees. I made my way up to it. It was a giant pillar, long shattered and overgrown now with creepers, but of a beautiful workmanship and decorated down the sides with a stone necklace of skulls.

Eliot inspected it. 'The sign of Kali,' he whispered. I nodded. I drew out my gun.

We went as stealthily as we could now. Very soon we began to pass more pillars, some flat on the ground and almost completely overgrown, others still massively erect. All had the same necklace-like decoration of skulls. The trees began to fall away and above the pillars I saw a lintel start to rise, bone-white beneath the darkness of the creepers and weeds. It was decorated in the florid Hindoo style, with the stonework twisting like the coils of a snake, and as I stared

41

at one of the loops so it began to move, and I saw that it was indeed the body of a cobra, coiled and heavy, the guardian spirit of this death-like place. I watched it slip away into the darkness; then I walked forwards and began to feel marble under my feet; ahead, I could see the stone lit silver by the moon, and when at length I left the shadows of the trees I saw all around me great courtyards and walls, still standing despite the jungle's tightening grip. Who had built this palace, I wondered – and who abandoned it? I was no expert, but it seemed to me that it was centuries old. I crossed the main courtyard. Columns stretched away from me in rows, and supported further columns on their roof. I guessed that they formed the palace's heart.

As I drew nearer to them I realised that they had been sculpted in the form of women – shameless and sensual, as so often seems to be the case, regrettably, with the ancient statuary of India. I will pass over their appearance, save to mention that they were quite naked and impossibly lewd. But it was their faces, oddly, which disturbed me the most. They had been carved with extraordinary skill, for they wore expressions of the utmost wickedness in which desire and delight seemed equally mixed. They were all facing the temple's far end, as though staring at the giant statues I had glimpsed from outside. I hurried on past them. At length the columns came to an end, and I saw a small courtyard just in front of me. Giant figures loomed against the stars. I walked on, and as I did so I felt a stickiness underfoot. I kneeled down and thought I could smell the odour of blood. I touched the stones, then raised my fingers to the light of the moon. I had been right; my fingertips were indeed red!

I walked forward to inspect the giant statues more closely. There were six of them arranged symmetrically on rising steps, three on either side. They were all women staring upwards, as the faces on the columns had been, at an empty throne. Just before this throne, the most damnable thing of all, stood a further statue, of a little girl. I climbed towards it up the steps. They too, I realised, felt sticky underfoot.

Eliot followed me. Suddenly, I heard him stop and I turned round. 'What is it?' I asked.

'Look,' Eliot replied. 'Do you recognise her?' He was pointing at the nearest statue to us. Now that we had climbed the steps we could see her face, lit silver by the blazing moon. It was a coincidence, of course, for the temple was clearly centuries old, but I saw at once what Eliot had meant – the statue's face was the very image of the woman we had captured, the beautiful prisoner who had subsequently escaped.

I turned back to Eliot. ' A great-great-grandmother, perhaps?' I joked.

But Eliot didn't smile. His head was angled, as though he were trying to pick out some sound.

'What is it?' I asked. For a couple of seconds, he didn't reply.

'You didn't hear anything?' he answered at length. I shook my head and Eliot shrugged. 'It must have been the wind,' he said. He smiled faintly. 'Or the beating of my heart, perhaps.'

I took a step forward to climb to the empty throne and Eliot promptly froze again. 'There,' he said, 'can you hear it now?' I listened, and this time I realised I could indeed hear something faint. It sounded like drums – not as we have them in the West but rather the *tabla* with its hypnotic, limitless beat. It was coming from beyond the empty throne. I crept up towards it; I put my hand on its arm and, as I did so, I felt a shudder of overwhelming dread so physical that I almost staggered back. Looking down, I realised that the throne was absolutely drenched in gore, not just blood but bones and intestines, and lumps of flesh.

'Goat?' I asked, looking at Eliot. He bent down and looked at what appeared to be a heart. His face froze as slowly he shook his head.

The *tabla* beat was clear now and picking up in pace. Beyond the throne was a crumbling wall; I approached it and, kneeling down, peered through a gap in the masonry. I gasped at what I saw. For I was staring at the ruins of a mighty town, overgrown – as the palace had been – by creepers and trees, and yet filled, it seemed, with inhabitants. They were shuffling and stumbling away from us, past the cracked arches and pillars of the town, towards some gathering which lay beyond our sight behind a further wall. In the distance I could see the haze of flames, and I wondered what their significance could be, for I remembered that the disease-afflicted creatures had a great horror of light. The whole scene was dominated by a colossal temple, the same tower I had glimpsed through the jungle earlier, and I could see even at a distance how its exterior was a mass of statuary, for it was silhouetted against the stars and its base was lit orange by the blaze of the flames.

I saw that Eliot was testing the wind. 'It's all right,' he said, 'the breeze will be against us.'

'Beg pardon, sir?' asked the Sergeant-Major.

'I mean,' explained Eliot, 'that they shouldn't be able to catch our scent. You have seen how they sometimes pause to smell the air.' He stared at both of us. All reluctance, all self-restraint seemed gone from his face now, and his eyes burned with the keenness of the seeker after truth. He turned and stared out at the looming form of the tower. 'The hunt is on, my friends,' he announced. 'Let us go, and see what we can find.'

On we crept, then, for perhaps a quarter of a mile. Occasionally we would see figures shuffling below us, but we kept well hidden and we were neither spotted nor smelled. The tower was looming impressively now and we began to hear other instruments over the drums – *sitars* and flutes, wailing like the ghosts of the ruined town. The drum beats too were quickening, as though rising to some climax that we couldn't glimpse, for the great wall continued to block out our view and I grew more and more eager to see what lay beyond. As the pace of the *tabla* increased, so we began to move faster ourselves until at last we were running across open ground. The ruins had fallen away now and there were fewer creepers and trees, so that we were, to all intents and purposes, almost wholly exposed. Once I thought we had been seen, for a group of hillsmen, shuffling like the rest, turned and I could make out the glint in their eyes; their stare, however, remained dead, and it was clear they had failed to make us out; we waited until they had moved on, and then we scrambled on towards the wall ourselves. It must once have formed the rampart of the ruined town; it was a mighty structure still, if a little broken-down, and it was with some effort that we clambered up its side. At length, however, we reached the top, as the beat of the *tabla* grew ever more fierce and the *sitar*'s wail seemed to rise up to the stars. We heard a great cry from a multitude of voices, somewhere between a cheer and a sob, and then, following it, a grinding, creaking sound. I crept forward and pressed my eye to a gap in the wall.

I crouched there in silence. Stretching away from the wall on which I stood, upwards of a hundred people were gathered – silent and utterly motionless. Their backs were turned to me, and they stood facing what seemed to be a wall of fire. The flames rose fitfully from a crack in the rock and a single bridge, narrow but ornately carved, arched high above their reach. From the bridge, a path then snaked up a steepish cliff towards the temple. This seemed built up from the very rock and loomed ghastly and massive over all of us. The riot of its statuary was more distinct now and had been painted, I saw, in black and violent shades of red. For some reason the very sight of it dampened my spirits, and as I stared at its summit I felt my heart begin to quail.

A particularly vivid spurt of flame writhed up from the abyss, and against the orange of the fire I could make out a hellish form. It was a statue of Kali. Her face was beautiful, and therefore all the more grim, for it was suffused with an incredible cruelty so vivid that I almost thought the statue to be real, and not only real but staring at me. Everyone in the crowd, I realised, was gazing at it, and I too studied it, trying to fathom what secret it held thus to capture and besot such a multitude. It had four arms, two raised up high with hooks in their grip, and two below, holding in each one what appeared to be an empty bowl. The feet, I saw, were attached to a metal base, and the base in turn to a mass of cogs and wheels. I heard a cracking sound; the statue began to move; and I saw that it was the machine which was serving to turn it round. The crowd moaned – and a devilish noise it was, for it seemed to speak of anticipation and greed. At that same moment, I felt Eliot tap me on the back.

'Unless I'm much mistaken . . .' he said.

'Yes?'

He pointed. 'Isn't that Private Compton over there?'

I looked. At first I couldn't understand what Eliot was talking about, for I could see only a group of savages, their faces frozen and dead, their clothes tattered and streaked with blood. Then my heart leapt up into my mouth. 'Good Lord,' I whispered. I stared at the man who had once been my soldier, gore-stained and dead-eyed as he was. 'But look here, Eliot,' I said, feeling utterly appalled, 'is there nothing we can do for him at all?'

Eliot stared at me, his bright, keen eyes betraying the depth of his despair. 'I am sorry, Captain.' He paused. 'There is nothing, certainly, that I can do as yet. This disease seems more deadly than I had ever dared to imagine . . .' His face was darkened by a sudden look of stern warning. 'You must put him from your mind, Captain – he is not your soldier any more. Do not even approach him – for I suspect that a bite, even a scratch, may prove fatal.'

I glanced back at Compton. It was perfectly true – there was nothing there; *nothing*; he might almost have been dead. And then, no sooner had I thought that, than I watched him start to change. It was no improvement for the better, however, for his face began to twist and his teeth to gnash, and his expression grew into one of imbecile savagery. He began to moan, as the whole crowd was moaning by now, and I wondered what this might possibly mean or portend. The music was reaching a most frenzied pitch and the crowd seemed roused to a fever of its own. Then, piercing even the general din, there came a scream of a kind I hope never to hear again, for it reached deep into my blood and chilled my very soul. The crowd fell silent, but hunger, I could see, was burning deep in their eyes. Again the scream rent the night; it was nearer to us now. Slowly the crowds began to fall away. The rhythm of the *tabla* beat faster, and yet more fast.

From the darkness a procession was making its way, a line of wretches tethered one to the other by neck chains and ropes. Two men led it, both in Russian uniforms, but their faces were as dead as those of Compton, and one had bullet wounds across his stomach; I recognised him as a soldier we had downed by the Kalibari Pass and left for dead. Yet now here he was again, and leading a chain-gang of those who must once have been his comrades-in-arms. For one of the prisoners was yelling in Russian; he screamed at his guards, and I realised that it was he who had been screaming before; now though, if anything, his despair seemed even more profound and I wondered what it was that could inspire such dread. The guard cuffed him across the face; the wretched man sobbed and fell silent; and a stillness settled over the whole ghastly scene. The procession had halted now, next to the statue of Kali. I inspected the row of prisoners. There were other Russians, and hill-folk too – men, women, even a child of seven or eight.

'Sir,' whispered the Sergeant-Major. 'The very rear!'

I looked, then I swore beneath my breath, for I could make out the soldiers I had left to guard the Kalibari Pass. They were tied together like cattle by the neck. One of them glanced at Compton, but no trace of recognition crossed Compton's face in return, and there was nothing to be distinguished there but degeneracy and greed.

Suddenly, a woman's voice seemed to whisper from deep within my mind. It was the damnedest thing; I am half-tempted now to think that I imagined it all, but Eliot and Cuff both claimed later that they had heard the voice as well, chanting as I heard it chant, and speaking with the same melodious tone. What was it? How had it happened, that we should all experience the very same thing? I do not readily stick my neck out, but any old India hand, if he is honest, will admit that once or twice he has experienced things he couldn't understand, and I believe that our hearing this voice was just such a thing. I like to think of myself as a level-headed chap; and the reader, I trust, will not lightly mark me down as a charlatan or crank. *However* – dread word! – I believe that what we heard was a mind-reader's voice, a mind-reader furthermore of the utmost skill and power, for her chant was as lovely as any sound I have heard, and I found that I was rooted like a tree to the spot. I remember thinking

47

vaguely that we should head off pretty sharpish, for I had this nervous feeling that the voice had discovered us, and I was afraid that our place of hiding was revealed; Eliot too, I know – from speaking to him later – felt exactly the same. But I couldn't move – nor could Eliot – nor could Cuff.

I closed my eyes, and a woman's face seemed to fill my thoughts; she was dark-eyed and lovely, with a necklace made from drops of the finest gold. She was the woman who had been our prisoner and escaped – and yet, in a strange way, she was also the goddess whose statue we had seen. Don't ask me how I knew this; I just had a sense of it, and pretty soon I was prickling with the most ghastly feelings of animal lust. And all the time, as these feelings were building up and I was attempting to cool them down, so this hellish woman was chanting; it was her voice I had been listening to, I realised now, and I wasn't surprised, for the chant was as lovely and unnerving as her face. Suddenly I recognised a word she sang interspersed among all the rest: 'Kali.' Faster and faster the chant rose, and the *sitars* with it, and the beat of the drums. My eardrums ached and seemed fit to burst. One last sound filled my brain, and I felt a shiver of terror and delight pass through my blood. 'Kali!' The music peaked on the final syllable, peaked and fell away. Then there was silence. I pressed my ears. I opened my eyes.

The Russian prisoner had been untethered. He was being dragged towards the statue of Kali, and once there he was lifted like an offering before the goddess's face. Meanwhile, one of the other guards was lowering the statue's upper arms; these were not fixed, I saw now, but could be cranked up or down and then positioned at will. I saw the guard polish the gleaming steel hook ... and I suddenly understood what was happening, the full repulsive magnitude of it. I wanted to turn away but I could not, for it was as though the voice were still chanting its honeyed poison through my soul. And so I stayed where I was – stayed frozen, and watched. The Russian's hands were bound fast together and his wrists placed over the point of the hook. The guard pressed them down; the Russian screamed and then screamed again as the guard moved his wrists up the curve of the hook, greasing the metal with the poor wretch's blood. He was left there, sobbing and whimpering, as a second prisoner – a young native girl – was brought forward by the guards. The same hellish routine was repeated with her, and then the guards cranked up the goddess's arms so that the victims were left hanging like carcasses of meat. The poor girl moaned and tried to stir, but the pain of the steel in her wrists was too great, and she slumped with the agony and hung motionless again. Behind her the orange flames writhed and twisted up into the night, but she and the Russian and the statue were still, a dark silhouette of unparalleled horror.*

Then I heard the machinery start to grind and creak. The goddess turned. As it did so, the Russian and the native girl writhed and screamed, for the jolting that was sent through their wrists must have been well-nigh unbearable. The statue shuddered and came to a halt and a low moan of disappointment went up from the crowd. My knuckles whitened as I clenched my pistol. How I longed then for a gatling or a Maxim! But I was helpless, and there was nothing I could do but lie there and watch. The *sitar*, I realised, was droning again now, and its notes hung heavy in the air like the mood of dread. The statue jolted suddenly; as it did so, the *sitar* was joined by the drums, and as the statue began to move round and round so the pace of the *tabla* increased in time. The victims hanging from their hooks were twisting uncontrollably now; their screams were terrible to hear as the pace of the statue's revolutions began to lift them up into the air, for all the world like some grisly fairground ride. There was a stirring from the crowd: everyone pressed forward and then suddenly I caught the flashing of a sword in someone's hand. It sliced down, and blood was sent arcing in a spray through the air; as

---

*I am indebted to my friend Francis Younghusband for pointing out to me the existence in former times of similar practices elsewhere in India. In the Deccan, for instance, victims were bound, not to the image of a goddess but to the proboscis of a wooden elephant. Those who are interested may care to read Major-General Campbell's *Narrative*, pp. 35–7.

it fell the monsters – I could no longer bear to think of them as men – lifted their faces to welcome the shower. Still the statue whirled round and round, and still the hapless victims twisted and screamed. A second blade flashed, and then a third, until soon they were falling like sparks of fire, dyed red by the flames and by living blood.

'We must go,' I said, trying to rise to my feet. 'We must go.' But still we couldn't move; we seemed trapped there by some infernal power, watching as the bodies were sliced to ribbons, seeing Compton, our own man – a British rifleman! – washing his face in innocent blood. At least now we could be sure that the wretched victims were dead, for their bodies were starting to disintegrate. A portion of guts slipped out from the Russian's belly, some sent flying out into the crowd, others caught in the bowls that the statue held. After a while the pace of the machine's revolutions began to subside; at length it creaked and shuddered, and came to a halt. From both hooks there was now suspended only a dripping mess of offal; certainly nothing that resembled a human form. The carcasses were unhooked and slung forthwith into the fire of the abyss. The dishes held in the goddess's lower arms, however, were removed with the utmost reverence and their contents poured into a giant golden bowl. The dishes were then replaced, and the statue cleaned. In the meantime, two new victims had been chosen from the line of waiting prisoners and were dragged forward, their wrists already bound. 'No,' I whispered, 'no.' But it was true; it was my soldiers who were being led towards the statue's waiting hooks.

I heard a footstep behind me, and I turned and looked round. A creature was standing at the foot of the wall. He hadn't seen us, but he seemed to know that we were hidden there, for he was smelling the air as though expecting to pick up our scent. I remembered the impression I had received of the mind-reader searching for our hiding-place, and I felt certain then – call it superstitious nonsense if you will – that our presence had indeed been noted from afar. I pressed myself back against the wall and gestured to my companions to do the same. We lay there frozen, and the creature below us started to shamble away. Then I heard a scream ... and a second scream. Despite myself I looked round. I must have gasped at what I saw, for my men were dangling from those infernal hooks and the statue was starting to creak slowly round. I froze again, but it was too late now – the creature had seen me. I could see now that he was followed by a veritable pack of his pals and this, I admit, made me feel our time was up. I emptied my revolver and my companions emptied theirs, but still the brutes came shuffling on. I laid one out with my fist and caught a second on the chin, but it was then that I heard the most terrible cries coming from behind my back, and I turned to see my soldiers just a mess of blood and guts, sliced into ribbons and screaming out their last. At the same moment I felt a thud on the back of my head, and I remember wondering if I had just bought it as well. I staggered and collapsed. A gruesome-looking chap stared down at me; he stank abominably and it reminded me of something. Then his image swam. I murmured my dear wife's name to myself. Then there was a blackness, and oblivion.

Letter, Professor Huree Jyoti Navalkar to Colonel Arthur Paxton.

9 June, 1887.

Colonel,

You must continue your advance with all possible speed. It is imperative – I repeat *imperative* – that you attack with fire. The inhabitants are in the grip of a terrible disease: light terrifies them. Therefore, when you arrive, you must torch the city. Trust me, I swear it, there is no other way.

I shall proceed ahead of you. Moorfield and his men, I am afraid, are in deadly peril. It may already be too late for them.

If they – or indeed I, or anyone – should approach you and yet not seem to recognise you, then kill us. A bullet through the heart. *Do not approach.* A single bite is sufficient to transmit the disease. There is no known cure. Tell all your men.

God's speed, Colonel.

S.S.

Extract, With Rifles in the Raj (continued).

❦

A DESPERATE STAND

A dungeon cell – 'Sri Sinh' – making a stand – a desperate retreat – a peculiar vision – the brahmin's curse.

I woke to the dripping of water on stone. I opened my eyes. All was darkness. I tried to stir. I heard the clank of chains from above me, and I realised that my wrists were manacled to a cold stone wall.

'Moorfield. Thank God!'

It was Eliot's voice. I tried to make him out, but the darkness was total.

'What happened?' I asked. 'How is Cuff?'

'He is alive, I think, but not conscious yet. You looked as though you got a nasty blow yourself.'

'It's nothing,' I answered. 'How about you?'

'I'm afraid I didn't quite match your performance. One of the brutes stuck a spear into my leg.'

'What rotten luck! Not too sore, I hope?'

Eliot laughed faintly. 'Well, I don't suppose we will be walking anywhere much, so it scarcely matters, I suppose.'

'Nonsense,' I answered. 'We must escape at once.'

Eliot laughed drily.

'Got any ideas?' I inquired.

He didn't answer.

'Eliot?' I asked.

'There,' he said suddenly.

'What?'

'Listen.' I froze. There was nothing but a faint dripping of water. 'Did you hear it?' he asked.

'What, the water?'

'Of course,' he said impatiently. 'It's coming from the far side of the cell.' He paused. 'Where the Sergeant-Major has been chained.'

I told him straight up that I didn't get his drift.

'The water must be coming from somewhere,' he explained. 'A subterranean source. If so, then the masonry will surely be weaker along the stretch against which it flows.'

I frowned. 'Then why would the creatures have chained him there?'

'I don't know,' answered Eliot, 'but is it really necessary to worry about that now?'

Well, of course, the moment Cuff came to we told him to give his manacles a tug. 'Very good, sir,' replied the Sergeant-Major. We heard him pulling and straining, and then he swore.

'No joy?' I asked.

'Not yet, sir,' he replied. 'But I don't intend to be beat by some savage's wall. Give me time, sir, and we'll see what we can do.'

He began to strain again, and pant, and still we heard him muttering and swearing to himself. 'I thought it was a long shot,' muttered Eliot at last.

'You don't know Cuff,' I replied. 'He's the strongest beggar I've ever come across.'

'Very kind of you to say so, sir,' gasped the Sergeant-Major, and at that moment we heard a great rending from the wall, and a clanking of chains, and Cuff fell forward with a thud on to the floor.

'Everything all right?' I asked.

'Yes, thank you, sir,' he answered. 'Rarely felt better.'

'Good work.'

'Thank you very much, sir.'

By great good fortune I had some loose matches in my pocket. I informed the Sergeant-Major of this lucky chance, and he reached for the matches and lit one against a brick. In the brief spurt of light I saw how his chains had been wrenched off completely from the wall; he was starting to pull at his wrist, and as the veins in his neck and forehead began to bulge the manacle suddenly snapped and gave. Then the match went out.

I heard the Sergeant-Major move across the cell and start to pull at Eliot's chains. This time, however, it seemed that the metal was too strong for him. 'Light another match,' I said, whispering, for by now the suspense of our situation was playing the devil with my nerves. 'See if you can find anything that might be of help.'

'Very good, sir.'

He removed a second match, and again there was a spurt of light. He looked round the cell, which I observed now was a rough-stoned, evil-looking place. He peered into the darkness of the far corner and then, just as the match was flickering to nothingness, I heard him gasp. 'What is it, Sergeant-Major?' I asked, as I saw him bend down. 'Found anything?'

'Yes, sir,' he answered. 'I rather think I have.' He walked over to me and took out a third – the final – match; he lit it and then held something up to the wash of the flame. It was a key.

'What the deuce . . .' I whispered.

The Sergeant-Major returned to Eliot. He fitted the key and twisted it; the manacles slipped from Eliot's wrists. 'Extraordinary,' I muttered, staring at him. Then the match went out. At the same time from beyond the cell we heard footsteps coming down towards the door.

'Cuff, Eliot,' I ordered through my teeth, 'back against the wall!' I heard them move; I prayed they were placing their wrists by the chains, but I had no time to check with them, for by now a key was scraping in the dungeon door, and the next thing I knew early-morning light was blinding me.

I blinked. A creature was standing in the doorway. There were several other human forms on the steps behind him, but it was this particular monster which made me frown and brace myself. He was pale, as all the others had been, and his eyes I couldn't see, for he kept them half-shut, but I knew at once that he was a different breed of thing from the creatures by his back. He seemed as chill as a statue carved from ice and yet, although his face looked flinty and cruel, there was also a softness in it, like a spoiled woman's perhaps, and it gave me the impression of an awful, shameless power. For all that, he reminded me of someone I had seen before and I frowned as I studied him, racking my brains. Then I remembered – his was the face I had seen up on the wall, staring down at me just before I went out cold. Eliot, I sensed, recognised him too, for I heard him start and then try to recompose himself. The creature took a step forward and I was certain now of who he was, for I recognised his stench. I remembered the priest, the old *brahmin* I had shot in the leg, and recalled that he too had stunk in the very same way.

The creature walked further into the cell, and three other figures followed him. Their eyes were as dead as all the others' had been; but their leader opened his own eyes wide now and I saw that they were not dead at all but almost twinkling. He scanned the wrists of Eliot and Cuff; for a moment I thought we were found out, but then the creature bent down by my side and I saw him draw forth a stake from his cloak. He stared into my face and drew the stake up, so that I imagined he was preparing to drive it into my heart. Then he winked at me; he turned; he threw himself against one of the figures behind his back.

The two forms rolled across the floor, and the others moved to join in the fray. But they were slow, and I saw how the man with the stake was forcing his adversary into the light where his movements were growing gradually ever more dull.

Eliot too, I realised, had thrown off his chains; he was wrestling with one of the creatures and calling out to Cuff to join him in the fight. 'Don't let them draw your blood,' he called, as he pinned his adversary against the sunlit steps.

Then I heard a scream, long and gurgling, and saw a veritable geyser of blood spouting up against the roof. One of the creatures lay dead, a stake through his heart, as his blood splashed upwards and then seeped across the floor. His slayer rose to his feet and took the stake from the dead monster's chest; he crossed to where Cuff had pinned his opponent to the wall. 'Into the sunlight,' said this extraordinary man.

55

Cuff pushed the creature forward; sluggish before, it seemed paralysed now. 'Yes, yes,' said the strange man, 'go on, through the heart.' He gave Cuff the stake. 'Eliminate all this damned vascular activity.' Cuff did as he was instructed and again a fountain of blood burst up across the cell.

'And now,' said the Indian, crossing to Eliot, 'let's get it done with. Step back, Jack. This is a painful business for we vegetarians, I know.' Eliot smiled and stood up as the Indian went about his grisly business. Once it was over, he rose to his feet. He shook Eliot's hand; then he turned to me. 'As you would say, Captain,' he said, stretching out his arms, 'bloody good show!'

I frowned. It scarcely seemed possible. 'It's not ...' I paused. 'It's not Professor Jyoti?' I asked.

'Very good.' The Indian wiped makeup from his face and, looking now, I couldn't imagine how I had ever failed to recognise him. And yet I had been wholly deceived, and my look of astonishment must have been writ very clear, for the Indian – let me call him Babu no more – laughed out loud.

'You old dog,' I whispered. 'How did you manage it?'

Professor Jyoti tapped the side of his nose. 'Know your enemy,' he said.

'But ... I mean ... look here ... in God's name ... how?'

The Professor drew himself up as far as his height would allow. 'Because knowledge,' he replied, 'is the business of Sri Sinh.'

I stared at him in amazement and, yes, I grant you, not a little shame as well. 'Good Lord,' I whispered. I realised how grievously wrong I had been about the man. Even now, thirty years on, the memory of my initial scorn makes me blush, for without a doubt the Professor was one of the bravest fellows I have ever met, and I have known quite a few in my time. He told me as he unlocked my wrists that he had been undercover in Kalikshutra for several days, and that the people had taken him to be one of their own. He had seen us fighting on the wall and had ensured, when we were taken, that we were not infected with the fatal disease. Furthermore, judging that Sergeant-Major Cuff was the strongest of us, he had left him chained where the wall was least secure, and secreted the key in the darkness by his feet.

'I could not have freed you then,' he explained, 'because as you have seen these diseased wretches are strongest at night. In the daytime, however, it is quite a different kettle of fish. Fortunately' – he slipped the chains from off my wrists, then glanced around the cell – 'everything turned out as well as could be hoped.'

'But, Huree,' said Eliot, 'if you have been amongst these people all this while, how have they failed to discover you? We have seen them; their disease enables them to smell out human blood.'

Professor Jyoti laughed. 'So many times I have told you, I think, that folklore leads where science must follow.'

Eliot's eyes glimmered bright and hawk-like. 'Go on,' he said.

'Can you not smell me? Do you not think I am stinking pretty bad?'

'Yes. You smell like the brahmins in the foothills often do.'

'That is because I have sat at their feet, and learned from them.' The Professor removed a pouch that had been slung from his belt, and opened it. As we peered into it, the stench from its contents rose up in a blast. I caught a glimpse of what seemed to be crushed vegetable matter, moist and white, before I could stand it no more and had to look away. Only Eliot continued to study it. He dipped his finger into the mess, then held it up to the light. 'What is it?' he asked.

'It is jolly rare, and most highly prized by the sages of the East. It would be called, I suppose, in English, Kirghiz Silver.'

Eliot frowned. 'Does it have a scientific name?'

'Not that I have heard of.* Indeed, I think only the brahmins know of it.' The Professor bobbed and smiled. 'Put it on your brow.' Eliot did so. 'There,' said the Professor. 'Now these creatures cannot smell

---

*I have been able to find no record of such a plant. The Kirghiz Desert, however, is the home of garlic. I wonder if Professor Jyoti's plant was a variant of that noxious-smelling bulb?

you. It is an old legend but, as I have proved to my satisfaction, none the less true for that.' He opened up his bag again. 'All of you,' he said, 'you must smear it on too. No, no, thicker,' he instructed, as I dabbed it on my cheek. 'For otherwise . . .' He paused. 'Otherwise, I think, we have no hope of escape.'

Well, by now we were all unchained and ready to give the attempt our best crack at least. Before we left, however, Eliot insisted on inspecting us all. I asked him what he was looking for. 'Bite marks,' he replied, as he scanned down my chest.

'But surely,' I said, 'if the disease were in our blood, we would know about it now?'

'Not at all,' answered Professor Jyoti. 'It depends on the strength of the victim. I have known one man hold out for almost two weeks.'

'Two weeks? Good Lord! Who the devil was that?'

'Don't you remember?' asked Professor Jyoti. 'Colonel Rawlinson mentioned him to you, I believe.'

'Of course!' I said, snapping my fingers as it came to me. 'That agent, the one who—'

'Shot himself through the heart. Yes, Captain.' Professor Jyoti nodded, and stared deep into my eyes. 'He was my brother.' He bowed his head, and turned and left the cell. I did not try to follow him, but I felt for the man. So his brother too had been as brave as he. A remarkable pair, I thought. Yes, a remarkable pair!

We joined the Professor at last when Eliot had passed us all fit. Our cell was deep in the ground, and as I climbed the steps towards a daylight I had feared I might never see again, I recognised at once where the savages had brought us. Behind was the ruined temple through which we had come the night before; just ahead, the giant statues and the empty throne. It reeked of gore and flies were swarming over it. I stared up at the throne and saw how fresh the blood and intestines seemed, far fresher than those I had touched the night before. We all of us, I think, put our hands up to our mouths.

'What is it?' the Sergeant-Major asked eventually.

Eliot looked at him. 'It is the remains of the victims sacrificed last night,' he said, speaking very slowly. 'Look.' He was pointing at a large golden bowl. 'Remember it? They used it to gather the remains. It is an offering to Kali.' He turned to the Professor. 'Am I right, Huree? That empty throne – it is Kali's, is it not?'

Professor Jyoti bobbed his head. 'So we must assume.' He pointed to the statues of the six women on either side. 'Observe these figures, though. According to the legends of the hill-folk, they are the guardians of the goddess's shrine. They protect it when their mistress is absent, but they are not otherwise seen. So this is very good. It would suggest that Kali herself is not here.'

'Steady on, old chap,' I protested, 'you're talking about this woman as though she might almost be real.'

'Real?' The Professor smiled and spread his arms. 'What do we mean by real?'

'Damned if I know. You're the Professor, you tell me.'

'If she exists – *if*...' – his voice trailed away – 'then she is something terrible. Something, perhaps, beyond the reckoning of man.'

We all stared at him in silence; then the Sergeant-Major cleared his throat. 'And this lady,' he asked, 'if she isn't here ...'

'Yes?'

'Well then, sir – where would she be?'

'Ah.' The Professor shrugged. 'That is a different issue altogether. But not here, and that is all that matters to us for the present. Not here.' He laughed suddenly. 'So come – let us make use of our advantage. Let us leave this place as soon as we can.'

And off we set. The place seemed deserted, but as before we were careful as we went, for if we couldn't be smelled we could still be seen. We kept up a cracking pace and Eliot, I noticed, was soon lagging behind. 'What's the matter, old chap?' I asked him.

'Oh, nothing,' he said, 'it's just this damn leg of mine.' I glanced down at it. The spear seemed to have gone pretty deep, and I guessed the wound was giving Eliot quite a bit of pain. But he assured me he was fine and so we carried on, Eliot slowing his pace down more and more. At length he collapsed and, looking at his wound again, I realised it was grimmer by far than he had ever let on. It was clear he wouldn't be walking much further for a while.

We had a brief council of war over this. Eliot told us to press on, like the gallant chap he was, but we were none of us having that. We knew that Pumper couldn't be far off now; if we could only hold out, then all might still be well. Our major problem, of course, was our total lack of firepower; but it was at this point that the Professor came up trumps again. He told us that he had stumbled across a great supply of explosives and arms, brought up by the Russians and no doubt intended for use against the Raj but now abandoned. It was agreed at once that we should attempt to recover them. Only one slight drawback, however, attended this plan. The arms cache was back by the ruined city wall.

Back therefore we had to turn – and an agonising trip it was, to be sure. We went as carefully as ever, but this time we caught glimpses – as we had not done previously – of pale-faced creatures gathered in the shadows. We would keep out of their way and trust that they had not caught a return glimpse of us, but I didn't like it and nor, I could tell, did Professor Jyoti. He kept glancing up at the sun, which was high in the sky now. 'It is past noon,' he muttered to me at one stage. 'The sun is starting to decline.'

'It has a way to go yet,' I replied.

'Yes,' said the Professor, staring round, 'and so do Colonel Paxton and his regiment.'

At length we reached the stretch of wall where the arms had been abandoned. Thank the Lord, they were still there. We began to gather them together, and as we did so Eliot, who had been posted as look-out, gave us a cry. 'We've got company,' he shouted. 'Over there.'

I looked up. Amongst the shattered stones of the city behind us, about thirty figures had gathered and were watching as we dug. I looked to my right, and then to my left; more of the blighters, watching us again. It was clear what their plan was – they were cutting us off from our routes of retreat, so that we would have nothing behind us but the mighty abyss. I looked at the bridge and saw, to my astonishment, that it was unguarded; I studied the tower beyond it, and again saw no trace of anyone. 'The tower,' I asked Professor Jyoti, indicating it, 'ever observed anyone moving up there?'

The Professor frowned. 'No,' he said slowly, 'but that doesn't mean it's empty.'

True enough, I thought – but that would be a risk we would have to take. We had no other choice.

I shared out what we needed from the cache of arms: weapons, explosives, ammunition. The rest I ordered to be dragged to the abyss; there was no fire rising from its depths now, but it seemed quite deep enough to serve our needs – and so it proved, for once the weapons had gone over the side we neither saw nor heard them land. We retreated to the bridge; as I have said it was a beautifully carved thing, but I knew it would have to go, for by now a crowd was forming all along the base of the wall and I was afraid they might rush us at any time. Fortunately, the engineering experience I had picked up in the Punjab stood me in good stead; pretty soon I had the bridge loaded with explosives, and we all dropped back a bit, where the cover was better, and waited for the action to get under way. Nothing happened, however. The afternoon sun continued to decline, and the crowds watching us remained by their wall. With each hour that passed, however, their numbers increased.

All too soon, the western peaks were touched with pink. I was growing impatient. I did not want to wait until darkness for the fight to begin; I wanted to see action before then, so that I could give the beggars a bloody nose and warn them of what they might expect from us. As I glanced across the far side of the abyss, my eye caught the statue of Kali on her hideous machine and an idea struck me. 'Professor,' I said, 'give me some covering fire. Cuff and I are going to toss that foul instrument of torture into the abyss. If that doesn't draw them out, then nothing will.'

The Professor frowned, then nodded. He lowered his rifle, and as he did so the Sergeant-Major and I ran back across the bridge. As we hurried to the statue, I heard the crowds behind us starting to stir.

I glanced round; only a few were crawling forward, but as Cuff began to heave at the statue and our intention became plain, so we heard a low moan and the whole line began to move.

'Quick!' Eliot shouted across to us; we heaved again, but still the statue wouldn't topple, and suddenly three or four broke from the line and began shambling towards us.

'This will have to be our last try!' I shouted out. I could hear footsteps behind me now, but still we heaved, and then the Sergeant-Major bellowed out a great oath to the sky, and there was a rending of metal and earth and wood. The statue teetered over the abyss's edge; the sun touched the gleaming hooks, so that they were dyed red one final time, and then they were falling – and the statue with it, and all that damnable machinery. I watched it go, and then I smelt the stench of rotting flesh behind me, and I turned to see dead eyes staring into mine. I felled the creature with a good left hook; he began to rise again, but I shot him through the heart and he lay there twitching like a landed fish. One down, I thought; how many more to go?

We began to retreat, and the crowds now were no longer keeping their distance but were trying to cut us off from the bridge. I almost thought we wouldn't reach it, for the blighters were literally snapping at our heels, and it was a hellish close thing. As we crossed, a swarm of our pursuers lurched after us, and as we gained the far side, so I heard the fizz of gunpowder snaking past my feet. We all ran on, then dived and blocked our ears; up went the bridge; down went our pursuers into the abyss.

It had been a good job, though I say it myself, and we had won ourselves a breathing space. The crowds fell back from the shattered bridge, and those who remained we picked off easily. But it was growing very dark now, and I knew that night-time would see our troubles really begin. Soon the stars were burning in the sky, and we made out movements again by the city wall. Fortunately, my field-glasses had survived the past few days intact and I was able to get a pretty good view of what was going on; I had soon worked out what their game-plan was. 'They've chopped down trees,' I muttered, 'and they're bringing them up. For God's sake, we must stop them before they reach the abyss.'

Well, we put up a bloody good show. As the creatures began to draw near to us, we gave them all the fire we could and managed to halt them in their tracks for a while. But they wouldn't stay down; I had never fought such an enemy before, and in the final count we were outnumbered a hundred to one. The beggars were soon swarming by the edge of the abyss; they laid down a tree, and began to swarm across that. We dropped our guns, and gave the tree on our side all the muscle-power we had; it was a hell of a job, but we did it, and the tree and its load was toppled into the abyss. But we knew there would be more, and that sooner or later they would get across; I began to think it might be time to retreat, for the tower would be easier to hold than open ground. I gave the order; we started to prepare ourselves to withdraw, with Cuff carrying Eliot and the ammunition box, and the Professor – who was too fat to run – accompanying him. Meanwhile I held to my position, giving the brutes opposite us all I had, but it was desperate now, for I might as well have been a mosquito attempting to halt an elephant's charge. There was a mighty crashing as a second tree thudded on to our side of the abyss. I watched as countless numbers of the brutes began to crawl across the trunk. 'Time to head off,' I thought to myself.

I retreated in good order up to the tower. Behind me, a mob of the creatures had crossed the abyss and were howling and baying in the most blood-curdling manner. Just outside the tower I was met by Sergeant-Major Cuff, who led me through a courtyard and into the tower itself. We found ourselves in a long, low room with the appearance of a temple sanctuary; it was dominated, as the palace had been, by an empty throne. Doors behind it led away into the dark; but one on the side of the room had a faint glow of light, and it was towards that exit that we turned. We ran up steps, as the passageway grew ever more narrow and close; as we ran I heard our footsteps answered by those of our pursuers, who must have seen where we had gone and who were now below us, sealing us in. The light though was getting stronger, and at length I saw it to be a torch held by Professor Jyoti, who was waiting crouched in the passage-way.

'A most extraordinary find, this,' he said, beaming at us. 'Have you seen these carvings? They must be centuries old.' He swept his torch along the wall, and I had a vague glimpse of yet more obscene images – women in assorted states of undress, feeding on what seemed to be human remains. Apt enough, you may think, in view of our own plight; and I confess that for a moment the images quite took away my breath, so vivid they were. But this was scarcely the time to be studying them – the footsteps behind us were drawing ever nearer, and when I turned I could see the gleam of pallid eyes.

'Where's Eliot?' I shouted.

The Professor pointed. 'Just up ahead. That's where we must make our stand.'

'Good,' I answered, for I could smell the reek of our pursuers now, and I knew they must sink us if we had too far to go.

Ahead of us the steps grew suddenly steep. I peered up them and felt fresh air against my face, and caught the gleam of stars. 'Hello?' I heard Eliot's voice call down. 'Who's there?'

'Only us, sir,' answered the Sergeant-Major. 'Bit of company behind us though.' He stood aside as the Professor climbed the steps. Our pursuers were almost on to us now; 'Quick, sir!' shouted Cuff, but having lost so many of my men so terribly, I was damned if I was going to risk another one's life. Nor was this mere idle heroism; the Sergeant-Major had the ammunition box with him, and I knew that if that were lost then we would all be done for.

'Go on, man!' I shouted. Still the Sergeant-Major wouldn't budge. 'Dammit, I'm giving you an order!' I bellowed, and only then did he begin to climb. As I tried to follow him, however, I felt cold fingers clasping round my leg, and when I tried to kick them away I lost my balance and fell back into the dark. I felt myself crash into someone, and then I was hitting the stone floor. I opened my eyes ... I saw a face. It seemed without lips, for the flesh round the mouth had rotted away, but it still had teeth, and they were open, and the stench of its breath as it pressed down towards my throat was like that of a sewer or an opened tomb. This was all the matter of a second, you must understand; before I had time even to put up a struggle, I heard a great bellow of rage and the thud of feet landing next to my head, and the creature by my throat was rising up again.

'You bastards!' I heard the Sergeant-Major roar. 'You bastards, you bastards, you bastards!'

The creatures were making for him; he was finished, I thought, for he didn't have the space or the time to use his gun, but he did have the ammunition box and so he flung that instead. The box, as I have mentioned, was of a fair old weight, and the rage with which Cuff hurled it served to dash the first rank of the creatures quite down onto the ground.

'You bloody fool!' I shouted. 'You brave, bloody fool! Now get up those steps!'

The Sergeant-Major nodded. 'Very good, sir,' he barked, and up he went.

I followed him, scrambling away as fast as I could, for I didn't want to be pulled down a second time. But the creatures weren't moving. When I glanced back round, those on the ground were still lying there. I could make out their eyes watching me with their imbecile stare, and I could see human forms – a multitude of them, stretching back down the passageway. I felt a sudden tremor of the most terrible fear. It wasn't the creatures, however, who had unsettled me; rather I had been struck by the queerest sense that they shared my fear with me; and that there was something approaching far more dreadful than they. And then, even as I was struck by this feeling, the creatures stirred and turned and bowed low to the ground. I peered down the passageway, but the light seemed to have grown suddenly much more dim, as though blackness were seeping up from the depths. This will all sound pretty crackpot, I know, and even now I'm not quite sure what it was that I saw. But at the time I had no doubt: I was witnessing bad magic. For as the darkness rose, so it seemed to draw in the light, much as blotting paper will absorb spilt ink. What lay within that darkness, I had no wish to see. I clambered up the steps and breathed in fresh open air.

'Captain, look.' Professor Jyoti was pulling on my arm excitedly. I stared about me. We were on the temple's very summit, on the curve of a dome. Below us rose walls crowded with stone and wooden statuary. Some of the wooden statues had been broken up to form a barricade – by Eliot, I guessed, for he seemed tired and pale, as though overworked, and his leg was still damp with blood. But at least now, I thought, he wouldn't have to use it again. This dome would clearly be our final stand.

'Captain, *look.*'

The Professor was beckoning to me. I hurried to the edge of the dome and peered down at the scene below. A line of redcoats was marching from the jungle. At the front of the column blew a Union Jack, and the faint strains of 'The British Grenadiers' rose to me on the mountain breeze.

'But damn it,' I muttered, 'they will be too late.'

'What do you mean?' asked the Professor.

I glanced at the steps leading back into the dark. 'The ammunition – we have lost it.'

'*Lost it?*' The Professor stared at me, then back at the advancing line of British troops. I turned to Sergeant-Major Cuff, who was standing guard by the steps. 'Any sign of movement yet?'

'Yes, sir, they're massing.'

I turned to Eliot. 'Light the barricades. Let old Pumper know we're here . . .'

'Sir!' It was Cuff. 'They're coming up now!'

I rushed to the steps. Cuff was heaving off some statue's head; he rolled it to the edge of the steps and let it drop. It was the damnedest bit of bowling I ever saw, for the deck was quite cleared and for a while all was still. Then I saw human forms moving again, down in the darkness, and I caught the glint of eyes at the base of the steps. Cuff had a second lump of stone in his hands. I glanced round at the barricade. The flames were starting to take. I turned back to the steps. The creatures were almost at our feet. 'All right,'

I whispered. I lowered my arm. 'Now!'

Down rolled the stone, and again the creatures were cleared from the steps. We were out of bowls though now, for there were no more statues' heads to be taken; a slab was loose, however, and we shifted that so that it blocked the way, but I doubted it would hold off the enemy for long. I glanced down over the temple's edge; flames were rising from the jungle, and Pumper's men were advancing on the abyss. Even as I watched they cleared the bridgeheads, but it looked like being a tight thing, for the flagstone was already shifting under the Sergeant-Major's feet and the fire we had lit was taking time to spread. We all of us gathered round to hold down the slab as the flames behind us began to crackle and lick, and minutes, precious minutes, slowly passed. Suddenly there was a shiver from below our feet, and the slab of stone cracked from side to side. Hands reached upwards and we all fell back.

The barricade now was a regular blaze, and so we hurried to take up our places behind it, for we knew that the enemy hated fire. And for a while indeed they seemed to be repelled by it; more and more of the creatures were massing by the steps, but still they hung back, and all the time Pumper's redcoats were drawing nearer, and my hopes began steadily to rise and rise. Then suddenly the enemy were at us. We fired; our remaining bullets were rapidly spent, and even though the stones in front of our barricade were slimy with gore, the creatures still rolled forward like the tide of a flood. We were swinging flaming brands at them now. One I caught in the face, and I watched his eyeballs shrivel and melt; another was torched like a bag of straw. From below us I heard a crackle of rifle-fire, and I knew that Pumper must have reached the foot of the temple. If only we could hold out! If only we could make it stick. Still the enemy came at us. I was weakening now. We all were. If the enemy turned our flanks, then we would surely die. Screams were ringing everywhere as the creatures were engulfed by the tongues of our flames, but I knew that their sheer weight of numbers was starting to tell. I looked at the far flank. The body of a burning man twisted and stumbled against the flames, but behind him were more men and I knew it was over, for our flank had been turned. Then the creatures paused; suddenly even the screams died away, and I could hear nothing but the crackling of the flames. A lull settled across the whole deadly scene. Far below us I heard British rifles again, but I was not tempted to hope this time, for I knew that death was waiting for us. I stared into the flames; I composed myself; I prayed I would not go unworthily.

And then I felt the fear again. I struggled against it, but like a dark fever it had me in its grip and seemed determined to wring out my very soul. It is a painful thing for a man to know that his bravery is failing him; yet after all, I told myself, what is bravery but the overcoming of fear? I tightened my grip around my club of burning wood; I walked to the edge of the barricade. If I had to die, then I would do it as nobly as I could, eyeball to eyeball. I would not allow my terror to conquer me. I raised my club. I rounded the barricade. . . .

There was no one there. Or rather – there was no one there who remained alive. Of corpses, however, there was a multitude. In the flames, across the dome, heaped down the steps – there lay our enemy, already putrefying. I stared around me in amazement; then I turned back to my comrades to tell them we were safe, but they too were gone and I was quite alone, exposed on that ancient and dreadful place. I stared into the fire; it seemed a regular inferno now, almost as though it were feeding on the dead, for I saw how the corpses were burning like wood, and the smoke from their flesh rose up in greasy streaks of black. Indeed, the smoke seemed almost like tongues of flame, and as I watched these tongues I saw that they were a veil, and that behind them were standing six human forms.

I staggered back, I freely admit, for I was bewildered and stunned. I knew that I must be sick, and I wondered if it wasn't my old malaria affecting me, yet I did not seem feverish; on the contrary, I had never before felt so gloriously clear-headed. I looked up at the human forms again; they had walked from the fire, and were staring down at me. They were women of an absolute loveliness, and one was the woman we had thought to make our prisoner. She smiled at me and

I felt the most beastly lust, at once glorious and cruel. My soul seemed quite opened to them; I took a step forward, but as I did so they all turned from me and bowed their heads, and I saw that the object of their adoration, raised high as though supported by the blaze of the flames, was a throne. I understood. They did not speak to me, I heard nothing put into words, but I understood. We would live. We had stumbled into one of the dark places of the world – but we would live. Strangely, I felt my terror start to seize me again. As though drawn, I looked up at the throne. I could see now that a woman was seated there. Two other shadows were standing on either side: one seemed to have a face much like Eliot's – although it could not have been Eliot himself, of course – while the other figure, though European, was like nobody I knew at all. I had no eyes for either of them, however, only for the seated figure who seemed to me the most desirable thing I had ever beheld. I struggled to summon to my mind's eye an image of my wife, but she would not come; there was only my desire; my infernal, beastly lust. It seemed to be quite burning me up. And yet, no – it was not only lust that I felt, for there was the terror too, intermingled with it, and it was tightening around my head. As I looked up at the throne and the shadowy form one last time, I knew that my consciousness was melting away. I felt darkness rising behind my terror's grip. I closed my eyes. Then there was nothing more left to feel.

What had happened? I cannot pretend to know. When I woke I had no recollection of anything that had occurred after our flank seemed to give, and neither, it turned out, did my comrades-in-arms. They too had lost consciousness in those final minutes, and when we awoke we knew only what Pumper Paxton could tell us. We had been found, he reported, laid out cold in a pile behind the barricades, the fires still blazing and the corpses of our assailants littered everywhere. For a while it had been feared that we might die ourselves, for we were all in comas of a remarkable depth, and it was a couple of days before we woke again. By that time

Kalikshutra had been left far behind, and when I tried to recollect it a great wave of terror and blankness intervened. Only recently has the memory of what occurred returned; I have set it down here for the very first time.

A mystery, then, the events of that strange time must remain. Who had the dark figure on the throne been? Who the man with the face like Eliot's, who his companion on the throne's other side? Why had they spared us? Had they even been real at all? I am well aware that I may sound a bit 'touched', and perhaps I was, for our time in the mountains had been harrowing enough. I cannot in my heart believe that I was the victim of a mere hallucination, if for no other reason than that I survived it to tell the tale. The final judgement, however, I must leave to my reader. Let him judge my account and my character for himself.

I was to see no more of Kalikshutra. Our mission, in one sense, had been a success, for we could now be certain there were no Russians there, nor likely to be in the future again. It seemed the Raj too was content to leave the kingdom well alone, for Pumper, as it turned out, had been absolutely forbidden to annex the place. I grew pretty hot about this, feeling as I did that Kalikshutra could only benefit from the introduction of British rule, for of the vileness of its native practices there could be no possible doubt. But I knew that Pumper could scarcely disobey his orders; indeed, he told me in strictest confidence that the future of Kalikshutra was the subject of some pretty top-level discussions back in London. And so it was that we put the place behind us; and if truth be known, I wasn't too upset to see its back.

Only one footnote to this tale now remains to be told – and that the saddest and most ghastly of all. It happened that we were approaching the ravine that would lead us on to the Thibetan road. As we passed the statue of Kali, I saw that a figure was crouched in front of it, his clothes streaked with ashes and his head bowed to the dust. Slowly, he looked up and round at us. It was the *brahmin*, the old fakir. He rose to his feet unsteadily and pointed at us; he began to scream and then he walked forward, shrieking all the time, and as he drew near to Pumper and myself I suddenly saw a terrible brightness in his eyes. It reminded me of the woman we had taken prisoner, and when I stared at his skin beneath the ash I saw that it gleamed as the woman's had done.

'He has the disease!' I shouted.

'Are you sure?' Pumper frowned, and when I said that I was, he ordered the *brahmin* to keep away. But the *brahmin* kept coming, and though he was ordered back a second time he would not halt, and Pumper had no choice but to beat him away. In the heat of the moment, as it were, he struck the *brahmin* across the face and the old man went staggering back into the dust. It looked bad and Pumper was appalled by what he had done, of course; he moved forward to go to the *brahmin*'s aid, but Eliot held his arm and pulled him back.

'Give him money,' he said, 'but for God's sake, you and your men must keep away from him.'

Pumper nodded slowly. He shouted the order to his column, and as they marched past he threw a purse of rupees at the priest. But the old man flung them into the dirt. He had risen to his feet by now, and he watched our progress with his burning eyes. As we advanced into the mouth of the ravine, the scream of his curse echoed after us. There was not a man, I think, who did not shiver at the sound.

I asked Eliot what the *brahmin* had been saying to us. He frowned and looked uncomfortable, and as he spoke I began to feel pretty bad myself. The *brahmin*'s village, it seemed, had fallen prey to the disease; in his eyes, it was we who had brought the wrath of Kali down.

'And his curse?' I asked.

Eliot looked me in the eye. 'Colonel Paxton should beware.'

'Of what?'

Eliot frowned, and then shrugged. 'Of a wretchedness such as the *brahmin* has known.'

This worried me for a day or two, and I asked Pumper to watch his back. But he was an old lion and scorned my fears; as the days went by, I too found the *brahmin* slipping from my mind. We reached Simla. I was kept there for a while by the pen-pushers, and

I had nothing much to do but kick my heels. I saw quite a bit of Pumper, naturally, and also Eliot, whose gammy leg was by now starting to mend. He had decided to return to England, I think, for his faith in his own research had been badly knocked by his experiences, and he told me he feared the disease in Kalikshutra was incurable. It disturbed me that he thought so, for I had seen for myself how fast it could spread, and I wondered if it would always be confined to the Himalayan heights. I remembered the *brahmin*. A couple of times, I had thought I saw him. I told myself that I had been mistaken or imagining things, but then one evening Eliot reported that he too had met him face to face in the bazaar. He had slipped away, but Eliot was certain it had been him. The medical authorities were informed, and a search begun. It turned up nothing – not a trace of the *brahmin* or the sickness was found.

Even so, I warned Pumper to be on his mettle. He did agree to carry a gun at all times, but more in a spirit of compromise, I think, than from any conviction he might really be in danger, and I had the sense that he was humouring me. The days passed; still the *brahmin* wasn't found, and I began to worry that I had been a bit of a fool. Pumper started to drop his guard. He was ribbing me by now, and one evening at the Club he got me to agree that the danger must have passed. He had a good laugh about it and I joined in, and I'm afraid we both ended up rather merry that night. We staggered out at quite a latish hour, and since Pumper's digs were nearer to the Club than mine, he offered to rustle me up a bed for the night. I agreed; Pumper's house was more pleasant than my quarters anyway, having as it did the family touch, and I was quite content to be staying there. The *tonga* rattled up the drive and stopped outside Pumper's bungalow; we both clambered out and paid the driver off. All seemed quiet within, so we paused on the verandah and gazed out at the stars. Suddenly, from inside the house we heard a scream, and then a shot rang out.

We hurried inside, of course, as fast as our legs would carry us. We were met by a terrible sight: Mrs Paxton standing there with a smoking gun and lying on the floor, quite dead, the *brahmin*. I bent down over the corpse. The bullet, by some miracle, had gone clean through the heart, and as I rolled the body over I looked up with a smile. 'He's gone,' I said.

But Mrs Paxton was shaking uncontrollably now. 'No, no,' she sobbed, 'you don't understand.' She dropped the gun, then turned and pointed to an open door. 'It's Timothy. He's ...' She swallowed. 'He's ...' She burst into tears. *'He's dead!'*

We hurried into Timothy's room. The boy was laid out on his bed. His throat had been torn away, and the mosquito net was spattered with blood. 'No,' Pumper gasped. 'No!' He knelt down beside Timothy's bed; he reached out to stroke his boy's hair, then he bent his head forward in the most terrible grief. It quite tore at my heart to see this brave man weep like a babe, and I knew there was nothing I could possibly say. Mrs Paxton had joined him now, and he rose to hold her in his arms. Suddenly, though, I saw her freeze.

'I saw him move,' she cried out. 'I tell you, I saw him move!'

Both Pumper and I stared at Timothy's face. He wore a smile now, which he had certainly not done before. 'Well, I'll be ...' Pumper whispered to himself. Then suddenly Timothy opened his eyes.

'Oh, my dear God,' laughed Mrs Paxton, 'he's alive, he's alive!'

'Get Eliot,' I said.

'But why?' asked Mrs Paxton. 'You can see he's all right.'

'Is he?' I asked. We all turned to look at Timothy. He had half-risen up, and the wound to his throat was still bubbling blood. But it was the look of hunger in his eyes which was most terrible, and the way that it seemed to pinch his white face. 'Get Eliot,' I repeated. Mrs Paxton sobbed and turned, and ran out of the room. Pumper and I followed her, bolting the door after us.

Eliot turned up twenty minutes later. I went into Timothy's room with him, and I saw the immediate look of despair on his face. 'Leave me,' he said. I did as he requested and then, a few minutes later, Professor Jyoti arrived as well.

'I was informed,' he said and then, without any further explanation, he followed Eliot into Timothy's room. We heard muffled voices; the two of them seemed to be arguing. Then the door opened again; Eliot came out and spoke to Mrs Paxton. He requested permission to operate; she gave it wordlessly, and Eliot nodded. He looked quite terrible, and I could tell that he didn't hold out much hope. He closed the door behind him and I heard the key being turned in the lock.

An hour later he came out again, his shirt covered with blood and failure writ large across his face. 'I'm sorry,' he said, and by George, he looked it. He walked across to Mrs Paxton, took her by the hands and pressed them. 'There was nothing I could do.'

He asked the Paxtons not to go into the room, but Pumper insisted. 'He is ... was ... my boy,' he said. I accompanied him in. The room was absolutely spattered with blood. Timothy lay spreadeagled on his bed; he had the look of an anatomist's specimen, for his chest had been sliced open and his heart removed. Pumper stared at the corpse for an eternity. 'And this was necessary?' he finally asked.

Professor Jyoti, who was standing on the far side of the room, bobbed his head fractionally. 'I am sorry,' he whispered.

Pumper nodded. He stared into Timothy's face, which did not seem a little boy's at all; it was still pinched and white, and sharp with cruelty. 'Do not,' said Pumper, 'let my wife see this thing.' Then he turned and left the room, and went back to Mrs Paxton. The body he ordered to be removed to the morgue. And this was the true ending of our mission to Kalikshutra.

The next day, my orders at last came through. As I travelled back down towards the plains, I did my best to put the whole ghastly business of the past month from my mind. Ahead of me was my regiment, and I would soon have little time for dwelling on it anyhow. New adventures awaited me, and fresh challenges.

Letter, Dr John Eliot to Professor Huree Jyoti Navalkar.

Simla,
1 July 1887

Huree –

What have we done? What have I done?

I am a doctor. A preserver of human life. You have persuaded me to become a killer.

Yes – I shall return to England. Your talk of vampires – of cruel demons, and bloodthirsty gods – how could I ever have listened to you? 'Such things exist,' you said. No! And again, I say, no!

In India, perhaps, one can believe in such things – but then, as you have often reminded me, I am not an Indian. So I shall go – as no doubt all we British should – back to my own world, where I can be certain of what is, and what is not. Where I can practise according to my own dictates. Above all, Huree, where I can expiate my fault – *where I can save, and not destroy, human lives.*

I leave for Bombay tomorrow. My passage on the London steamer is booked. I doubt we shall ever meet again.

I am sorry, Huree, we part in this way.

I remain, though,
    Your unwilling friend,

JACK.

WHAT HAVE WE DONE?

PART TWO

PART TWO

Letter, Dr John Eliot to Professor Huree Jyoti Navalkar.

Surgeon's Court,
Hanbury Street,
Whitechapel,
London.

5 January 1888.

My dear Huree,

You will see that I am now securely established in London. I trust you will note the address and perhaps, despite the nature of our parting, take advantage of it to write to me. I do not have much opportunity now for the type of arguments we used to enjoy. I have never been of a particularly convivial nature; and yet sometimes I find myself lonelier in this mighty city of six millions than I ever was amongst the Himalayan heights. Of my two oldest friends, one, Arthur Ruthven, is dead – the victim, it would seem, of a cruel and pointless murder – certainly a tragic waste, however he was killed. I miss him deeply, for he was a brilliant man. The other friend, Sir George Mowberley, you may have read of in the newspapers, for he is now a Minister in the Government – almost, as far as I am concerned, as upsetting a fate as poor Ruthven's. I mourn them both.

I cannot regret my isolation too greatly, though. I have little enough time on my hands as it is. My practice is exceedingly vast; so vast, indeed, and overwhelming, that I find myself almost numbed by it. My rooms, you must understand, are situated in the most outcast corner of this great city of outcasts. There is no form of wretchedness or horror that its streets do not breed, and I have been able to feel nothing for a month now but anger and despair. I was arrogant in my motive for journeying abroad – why did I feel I had to travel to the East to relieve the burden of human suffering when here, in the richest city in the world, there is misery on a scale so terrible?

To you, I can confess my response to this place. With others, however – yes, and with myself as well – I am as cold as ice. There can be no other way. How else shall I survive what I see on my rounds? A man dying of smallpox in a cellar, his wife eight months pregnant, their children creeping naked in the filth. A small girl, dead for two weeks, found buried beneath the ordure of her brothers and sisters. A widow with scarlet fever, still selling her body in her tiny attic room, while her children shiver in the bitter winds outside. Not even amongst the slums of Bombay did I witness such scenes of wretchedness. Emotion, in these conditions, would be like a candle-flame in the gale – even anger, I am afraid, is an indulgence I can scarce afford. But fortunately I am by nature, as you remember, a passionless creature; the powers of logic and reason that I draw on now in Whitechapel have always been the predominant features of my mind. For all your efforts, Huree, I remain untouched by the teachings of the East. Perhaps you will think my years in India wasted. But I cannot help what I am. There can be no reality for me beyond that which I observe – observe and sometimes, perhaps, deduce.

What though, you will no doubt ask me again, of those things I glimpsed in Kalikshutra? Do I doubt their truth? Do I think I can explain them logically? Not yet, I admit – but I am working hard – and one day I will, I am confident. One thing for sure, Huree: I do not accept your explanations. Demons? *Vampires?* What has science to do with such fantastical ideas? Nothing. I say it again – I have no interest in impossibilities. The physician who dabbles in such things must soon sink to the level of a medicine man. I will not become such a degraded thing, a witch doctor performing ghastly rituals to appease horrors and spirits he cannot understand. The memory of poor Paxton's son still haunts me, you see – the pain in his eyes, the blood that spurted from his skewered heart. What had he become, Huree? The victim of a terrible and inexplicable disease, yes – but not a ghoul, not a creature to be destroyed as he was. No doubt he *was* beyond the reach of my help; and yet I am haunted by the knowledge that I did not seek to cure him, but to kill him instead –

to *murder* him. When I did so, I betrayed my entire life's work.

For I repeat – I am an optimist, and a scientist. These continue to be my proudest boasts. The mysteries I work on must be capable of answers; the data I research must be observable. You remember my methods – I search out, I study, I deduce. I remain what I have always been, a rationalist, and my lifetime of research stays as valid as before. I have not given up, you see – far from it. I have set up a small laboratory in my rooms and, using the equipment I have there, I process the data that I gathered in the hills. I enclose with this letter a copy of a short article I have written, setting down some of my preliminary thoughts. You will observe that I have not yet abandoned my interest in these white blood cells I was studying before, and the puzzle of their remarkable longevity. I still have a long way to travel, of course; but I very much doubt it will be vampires that I find when I finally track the solutions to ground.

Write to me again. You will have noticed from this letter how keen I am to continue our arguments. Reply soon, and be as rude as you like.

JACK.

Letter, Miss Lucy Ruthven to Sir George Mowberley.

12, Myddleton Street,
Clerkenwell,
London.

12 April 1888.

Dear George,

Yes, it is really me, Lucy, your ever-dutiful ward, and no, I am not dead, or debauched, or utterly ruined, as your dear wife warned I would be, but perfectly happy and well. Tell Rosamund as much. I am sure she will be delighted. We all know how *fond* of me your wife has always been!

But you at least, dear George, do not hate me, I hope. It is perfectly true that it is now many months since I left your home; and that I have scarcely behaved as a pious ward should. But I am trying now to make some amends – even at the cost of appearing ridiculous, for what I have to tell you will seem very strange, especially since I am not, as you know, inclined to superstitious fears. Will you laugh, then, George, when I tell you that last night I had a terrible dream, so awful that I still cannot banish it from my thoughts – or will you realise how fond of you I must be, to tell you of it, and to risk your scorn?

You will need no reminding, of course, that it was exactly a year ago today that poor Arthur's body was found floating in the Thames. George, I saw it all last night – saw it in my dream, and it was horribly real.

His corpse was bobbing amongst the filth of the river, and as I looked I could see how drained and pale his dear face was. We were all gathered, his family and friends, on the river shore; we were dressed in mourning, and behind us was a coffin on an open hearse. One of the undertakers held a long pole in his hands, with a hook upon its end; he reached with it for Arthur's body; once the corpse had been dragged up through the mud it was borne, still naked, and laid upon the hearse. We all stood gazing upon Arthur's face; and then the reins were shaken and the hearse began to move away down a gloomy side street. I could not bear to look upon the carriage, nor the undertakers. For some reason they filled me with dread, as though the blackness into which they were passing was that of death, and they and their hearse were its emissaries. All of us, all the mourners, remained absolutely still as the carriage rumbled away from us and the horses' hooves began to fade into the dark.

And then, as I watched the hearse, I saw that you were following it – you and Rosamund, arm-in-arm. Rosamund was looking very beautiful, more lovely even than she usually does, and yet her face beneath her dark hair was as pale as death, as pale indeed as Arthur's had been. Your face, George, I could not see; your back was turned on me and I knew, as you went, that you were passing into the most deadly danger. I struggled to warn you, but no sound would come from my mouth; and still you walked on. At length you and Rosamund were wholly swallowed by the dark; and soon, even the rumbling of the hearse was gone. Only then could I scream; and screaming, I woke up. The horror, though, remained with me; nor has it faded yet.

I cannot suppress the dread that my nightmare was a warning – that you and Rosamund are somehow walking into some deadly peril. You will reply that it is the anniversary of Arthur's death which explains this agitation of mine, and no doubt it is – yet even so, dear George, do not forget that the murder of my brother remains unsolved to this day, and that my fears, however expressed, are perhaps not altogether vain. So please be careful – if not for your own sake, then for Rosamund's. I do not love her; but I would seek to spare her poor Arthur's fate. I could not wish that on anyone.

I long to see you – but unfortunately cannot for a while. The new season at the Lyceum begins in two nights' time, and I am to appear in the opening performance! As Mr Stoker (our theatre manager) has often told us, there is still a lot of work to be done. But later, George, I would like to see you, if I might, and repair whatever bridges need to be repaired. I feel we have been apart for far too long. My quarrel was always with your wife, never with you.

Perhaps you might even come and see me perform at the Lyceum? Whether you do or not, though, dear guardian, I remain your loving, if perhaps over-superstitious, ward,

LUCY.

Letter, Lady Rosamund Mowberley to Miss Lucy Ruthven.

2, *Grosvenor Street,*
Mayfair,
London.

13 *April* 1888.

My dearest Lucy,

I trust you will forgive me for writing to you at a time when I know your attentions will be fully focused upon your impending first night, but I am in a state of such distress that I cannot refrain from making contact with you. I beg you, please, to read this letter and not to cast it straight aside. You will soon appreciate, if you only finish this paragraph, that I have had little choice but to approach you over the terrible business I must now relate. This morning I received a letter. It was hand delivered. My name had been printed in capitals on the envelope, and the writing inside was in capitals as well. The letter was unsigned. I therefore have no way of knowing who sent it to me. And yet its message was an extraordinary and terrifying one. 'I HAVE SEEN G. MURDERED,' it read. When I tell you that my dear George has been missing for a week now and that furthermore, even before his disappearance, he had seemed the likely target of a dangerous conspiracy, then you will understand why I fear the worst. I have asked a man to investigate this mystery for me, not a policeman, not even a private detective, but an old friend of George's, possessed of remarkable powers which I have witnessed for myself. You will remember him, I am sure: his name is Dr John Eliot, and he may very well shortly be visiting you. I therefore feel it would be for the best if I give you a full account of my meeting with him, not only so that you may be prepared for his style of investigation, which is very distinctive, but also so that I may give you the facts surrounding George's disappearance just as I gave them to Dr Eliot himself.

I visited the Doctor this morning. The weather was more than usually icy and raw, and even those most prosperous stretches of London seemed unwelcoming as I journeyed through them on my way to his address. Beyond the City, however, I seemed to have entered a circle of Hell, and not even the most blissful of climates, I think, would have ameliorated the scenes of horror I witnessed there. George had warned me that Dr Eliot had what he once mocked as 'the missionary spirit' – yet surely even missionaries must shrink before entering such a place, where shivering creatures huddle in rags and young girls bare themselves without a hint of shame. Certainly, as a married woman of only tender years myself, brought up in the country and hence unused to such sights, I was greatly relieved when at length we attained our destination. As I stepped out, I was choked by poisonous fumes and the stench of rotten fish and vegetables. The pavement onto which I stepped was ankle-high in mud. This Dr Eliot, I thought as I pulled myself free, must be as singular a man as my husband has always claimed he was, to choose not only to practise but also to live in such a place.

It was with some relief, then, that I stepped into his surgery. Its silence, after the din of the crowded streets outside, was most welcome, and the air, though touched with the faintest tang of blood, seemed otherwise relatively fresh and clean. I asked the attendant who had let me in to inform Dr Eliot of my presence in his hall. 'If you want Dr Eliot,' she replied, 'you will have to go up and disturb him yourself. When he is at his studies, there is no other way of gaining his attention. Up the stairs, first on the left.' Then she turned and hurried away, and as I called out to thank her a wailing of children from the room beyond drowned out my words. I had a brief glimpse of bodies on rickety beds, and then the door was slammed shut. Time, I thought, was clearly precious in such a place, and realising this I grew even more reluctant to disturb Dr Eliot in his period of study. But then I contemplated the urgency of my mission, and the distance I had come, and I resolved at once to climb the stairs. On the landing, I knocked on the door to which the nurse had directed me. There was no answer; I knocked again. Still there was no reply, and so I gently turned the handle and pushed the door ajar.

The study, for such it clearly was, seemed a pleasant place. A fire was flickering in the grate, and thick rugs and deep armchairs completed the impression of a cosy cheerfulness. Books were piled everywhere, and various ornaments of a foreign, not to say exotic, character were hanging from the wall. Of Dr Eliot himself, however, there was no sign, and so I pushed the door fully open, walked inside and looked around. The study's far end, I could see now, was quite distinct from the remainder of the room. Indeed, it seemed a virtual chemist's laboratory. Test-tubes and pipings were everywhere, and a flame was rising from a burner on the desk. Crouched over this same desk, with his back to me, was the figure of a man. He must have heard my entrance, but he did not look around. Instead, I observed with some surprise that he was aiming a syringe into his arm. He jabbed the needle down, and the syringe began to fill up with a flow of purple blood. Then, gently, the needle was removed again and the blood added to some substance on a dish.

'Please take a seat,' said Dr Eliot, still not turning round. I did as he instructed. Five minutes I sat there waiting for him, as he studied his dish and scribbled down notes. At length, I heard him mutter impatiently and push back his chair. 'It is no good,' he said, turning to face me for the first time. His face was very thin, but seemed animated by the most remarkable energy, and his eyes were bright with intelligence. 'I am sorry to have kept you waiting so needlessly,' he said. He turned off the bunsen flame, and at once it was as though the flame behind his face and eyes had been extinguished too. He crossed to me and slumped into the armchair opposite. Of his former alertness there now appeared not the faintest trace. He seemed utterly sunk in lethargy.

'Now,' he said, scarcely able to keep his eyelids open, 'what can I do for you?'

I swallowed. 'Dr Eliot, I am the wife of a dear friend of yours.'

'Ah.' He widened his eyes at this. 'Lady Mowberley?'

'Yes,' I said. I smiled nervously. 'How did you know?'

He hooded his eyes again. 'I have very few friends, I am afraid, and even fewer who have recently been married. I am only sorry that I had to miss the happy day.'

'You were in India, were you not?'

He nodded with just the faintest inclination of his head. 'Until six months ago. I did write to George upon my return, but he has clearly been occupied with affairs of state. I gather he is now an important man.'

'Yes.' There must have been something in my voice, some catch perhaps, for Dr Eliot looked at me with sudden interest and leaned forward in his chair. 'There is some problem?' he asked. 'Lady Mowberley, tell me, is George not well?'

I struggled to compose myself. 'Dr Eliot,' I replied at length, 'I very much fear that George may be dead.'

'Dead?' His voice scarcely registered the shock he must have felt, but his expression was suddenly as alert as before and his eyes glittered as he studied me. 'But you only fear it?' he said at last. 'You are not certain?'

'He has been missing, Dr Eliot.'

'Missing? For how long?'

'For almost a week now.'

Dr Eliot's brow darkened. 'You have reported this to Scotland Yard?' he asked.

I shook my head.

'Why ever not?'

'There are circumstances, Dr Eliot. Very particular ... circumstances.'

He stared deep into my eyes, then nodded slowly. 'And so – because of these circumstances – you have come to me?'

I nodded. 'Yes.'

'May I ask why?'

'George always talked of you. He spoke very highly of your powers.'

Dr Eliot frowned. 'By powers,' he said, 'I suppose George meant those tricks of observation with which I used to impress him and poor Ruthven at university?' He did not wait for me to reply, but suddenly shook his head. 'I have no use for them now,' he said. 'No,

87

no! They were a childish waste of time!'

'Why childish,' I protested, 'if they might restore George to me?'

Dr Eliot smiled sardonically. 'I fear you have an over-inflated opinion of what I might be able to achieve, Lady Mowberley.'

'Why do you say that? I have heard stories of you, heard how you solved mysteries that had baffled the police.'

Dr Eliot rested his chin on his finger-tips; he seemed returned now to his former state of lethargy. 'We were great friends, your husband, Ruthven and I,' he said. 'But after Cambridge, we all went our separate ways. Ruthven became a brilliant diplomatist, Mowberley dabbled in his politics, and as for myself . . .' He paused. 'As for myself, Lady Mowberley – I discovered that I was not as great a genius as I had always thought. I soon discovered that the tricks which had so impressed Mowberley were not quite so brilliant after all. In short, I began to learn some modesty.'

'I see,' I replied, even though I did not, and indeed felt utterly dismayed by his words. I asked him what had taught him this modesty.

'A professor at Edinburgh, Dr Joseph Bell,' he replied. 'I was studying with him, to further my research. Professor Bell had a skill very like my own, for he could read clues to a person's character from a single glance, and he would use this talent to explain to his students the principles of diagnosis. To me, though, he taught a different lesson, for he knew that my deductive powers were very great and so he warned me instead of the opposite – that deductions may be logical, and yet not always correct. He would challenge me to display my skills, and though I was often proved to be right, so also I was sometimes very wrong. "That is the lesson for you!" he warned me. "Always beware of what you have missed. Beware of what you have failed to recognise, beware of what you have not dared to think." He was quite right, Lady Mowberley. Experience has taught me this much – answers are never more treacherous than when they seem most correct. In science there is always that which is unfathomable – how much more so then in human behaviour.' He paused, and fixed me with his stare. 'That, Lady

Mowberley,' he said at length, 'is why I have confined my recent studies to medicine.'

Dear Lucy, imagine how crestfallen I was! 'So you will not help me, then?' I asked.

'Please,' he answered, 'do not be upset. I have merely been warning you, Lady Mowberley, that my ability to aid you must be doubtful in the extreme.'

'Why? Because you are out of practice?'

'In the field of criminal detection – yes.'

'But such a skill might be recaptured, surely?'

Dr Eliot rested his chin on his fingertips. 'Really, Lady Mowberley,' he said after a slight pause, 'you would be best advised to turn to the police.'

'But it *might* be recaptured?' I insisted, ignoring him.

Dr Eliot made no reply to this at first, but continued to fix me with his glittering stare. 'Possibly,' he said at last.

I felt then, dear Lucy, that he was sorely tempted, and I resolved to tempt him just that little bit more, for it seemed to me that his reticence might in truth be vanity and that all he needed was some chance to display his powers. 'What can you see in me?' I asked him suddenly. 'What can you read from my appearance now?'

'As I have warned you, my reasoning may be faulty.'

'No, Dr Eliot, your results may be but not your reasoning, surely?'

He smiled faintly at this.

'So,' I pressed him, 'what can you tell?'

'Oh, nothing much, beyond the features which struck me as obvious when I first saw you sitting here.'

I looked at him in surprise. 'And what would they be?'

'Oh, merely that you are from a wealthy but non-noble family, that your much-loved mother has recently died, and that you hardly ever venture out from your home, having a morbid fear of High Society. All that is clear enough. In addition, I would hazard the suggestion that you have journeyed abroad within the past year or so, possibly to India.'

I laughed. 'Until your last comment, Dr Eliot, I was afraid that you were cheating and that my husband had written to you describing me.'

His expression was one of the utmost disappointment. 'I was wrong, then?' he asked. 'You have not been abroad?'

'Never.'

He slumped back in an attitude of despair. 'You see then what I mean? My powers have faded hopelessly.'

'Not at all,' I assured him. 'Your previous descriptions were utterly correct. But before you explain them to me, I would be interested to know why you thought I had been abroad?'

'On your neck,' he replied, 'I noticed a couple of blemishes which seemed to me very like mosquito bites. I have often observed that such bites, if they were ever once septic, will endure as faint marks on the skin for a couple of years. Obviously, if my diagnosis had been correct you would at some stage have had to have been abroad. India I guessed because of your necklace and earrings. They are of a very distinctively Indian make; I would not have thought that such jewellery was common here in England.'

'Hearing such an explanation,' I replied, 'I almost feel that I should have been abroad. However my life, I am afraid, has been far too mundane for that. The blemishes you noticed are merely an allergy to the filthy London air.'

'You were brought up away from the metropolis, then?'

'Yes,' I replied, 'near Whitby, in Yorkshire. I spent my first twenty-two years there, and have only been in London since my marriage to George some eighteen months ago.'

'I see.' He was studying the marks on my neck again, and frowning. I trusted that he was not too mortified. 'And the jewellery?' he asked at length.

I reached up to touch my necklace. You have surely seen it, dear Lucy? – the most beautiful thing, formed of wondrously crafted droplets of gold, but of a value to me far greater than its price. 'The jewels were given to me,' I said, 'by my dearest George.'

'A wedding present, perhaps?'

'No, sir,' I replied, 'they were a birthday gift.'

'Indeed?'

'I saw them in the window of a shop. I was on George's arm at the time and he must have remembered my enthusiasm.'

'How perfectly charming.'

I realised, of course, that I was boring him. His eyes were hooding over once again, and I was afraid that I would lose the advantage I had gained when I persuaded him to offer those other deductions which proved so remarkably exact. 'The previous points you made,' I asked hurriedly, 'could you tell me how you arrived at them?'

'Oh, they were simple,' he replied.

'My lack of noble blood is evident then, I suppose?'

Dr Eliot chuckled to himself. 'Your breeding, Lady Mowberley, is exquisite in every way. One thing, however, betrays you. You wear a brooch with the Mowberley coat of arms, and a bracelet round your wrist with the very same design. Clearly the ornaments have not been recently made. Therefore they must be heirlooms, a part of George's inheritance and not your own, and yet you seem most attached to the memory of your own family. Why then do you not wear jewels inherited from them? Probably, I would suggest, because such jewels do not bear a coat of arms, and you are seduced by the novelty of wearing ornaments that do.'

'Dear me!' I lamented. 'You seem to have a low opinion of my character.'

'Not at all,' laughed Dr Eliot good-humouredly. 'But was my reasoning exact?'

'Perfectly,' I replied, 'though I blush to confess it. You made it seem quite simple. However, I do not understand how you knew of my attachment to my family's memory. Perhaps you were informed of that by George?'

'Not at all,' answered Dr Eliot. 'I merely observed your umbrella.'

'My umbrella?'

'You will permit me to compliment you again, Lady Mowberley, when I observe that your dress perfectly reflects your wealth and taste. Your umbrella, however, seems out of place. It is clearly old, for its handle has a couple of cracks which have been expensively repaired, and the initials carved into the wood are not your own. It is ridiculous to assume that you cannot afford a new umbrella – therefore the one you carry must have some sentimental value, and when I observe the thin strip of black still tied in mourning round the handle, the probability is hardened into fact. Whose umbrella had it been, then? A woman's, clearly, and someone older than you, for the umbrella itself seems almost antique. I deduced, therefore, that it must have been your mother's.' He paused suddenly, as though embarrassed by the rational coolness of his tone. 'Please accept my apologies, Lady Mowberley, if my words have caused you pain.'

'No, no,' I replied. I paused fractionally, to compose myself and be certain that no catch would betray me when I spoke. 'I have had almost two years now,' I told him, 'to grow accustomed to my loss.'

'Indeed?' He frowned. 'That is a great pity, then – your mother never saw you married.'

I shook my head. And then – I was feeling a little emotional, perhaps – I told him the full story of my marriage to George: of how we had been pledged to each other since he was sixteen and I was twelve, he as the son of a peer of the realm, I as the daughter of a wealthy self-made man. 'For George's family, you must know,' I told him, 'had lost much of their wealth, and for the sake of my own they were prepared to overlook the meanness of my birth.'

Dr Eliot smiled sardonically at this. 'I am quite sure they were,' he said. 'But – forgive me if I seem to pry – you were content with this arrangement yourself?'

'Oh yes, indeed!' I replied. 'You must understand, Dr Eliot, that George has been my sweetheart for as long as I can recall. When my mother died, to whom else could I turn?'

'But George, surely, had left Yorkshire a long time before? Had you seen him at all since then?'

'Not for six or seven years.'

'A period which you had spent entirely near Whitby?'

'Yes. My mother, Dr Eliot, had grown very sick in that time. She needed me to attend on her, for she was nervous and infirm.'

He nodded gently. 'Yes, well,' he replied, 'that would explain it, I suppose.'

I looked at him in surprise. 'Explain what?' I inquired.

'You will recall,' he said, a faint smile on his lips, 'how I observed that you did not seem fond of High Society?'

'Yes,' I replied, remembering that he had indeed. I frowned for a moment, and then I smiled ruefully. 'But of course – you deduced from your knowledge of my secluded youth in Yorkshire that I would be ill at ease amongst the salons of the metropolis. How very simple.'

'Yes, exceedingly so.' Dr Eliot smiled. 'Except, of course, that when I made my observation I knew nothing of your youth.'

'You did not? But ...' I stared at him, startled, as I realised the truth of what he had just said. 'But how then did you know?' I asked.

'Oh, it is even simpler than you presumed.' He gestured languidly. 'Your arm, Lady Mowberley.'

'My arm?'

'Your right arm, to be precise. There are splashes of mud on your shoulder and sleeve. Clearly you have been leaning against the side of a hansom cab. A lady of your position, however, might surely have been expected to ride in a carriage of her own. The fact that you do not admits of only one explanation – you do not consider the expense of maintaining such a vehicle worthwhile. Evidently, then, you are not in the habit of making many excursions or calls.'

'Remarkable!' I exclaimed.

'Commonplace,' he replied.

'It is quite true,' I admitted – and you will know this all too well for yourself, dear Lucy – 'that I have not yet adjusted well to city life. It is all so different from the country existence I knew as a child. My allergic response to the filthy London air, and my natural shyness, have combined to render me a virtual recluse.'

Dr Eliot bowed his head. 'I am sorry to hear it.'

'I have very few friends in town, and no one in whom I could confide or trust.'

'You have your husband.'

'Yes, sir,' I nodded, and then lowered my head. 'I had my husband.'

Not an emotion could be traced across Doctor Eliot's gaunt, impassive face. Fingertip to fingertip, he arched his hands and then slumped back into the depths of his chair.

'You will understand, of course,' he said slowly, 'that I cannot promise anything.'

I nodded wordlessly.

'Very well then,' he said, gesturing with his hand. 'Please, Lady Mowberley. Draw up your chair, and give me the facts surrounding George's disappearance.'

'It is an extraordinary tale,' I told him.

He smiled faintly. 'I am certain it is.'

I cleared my throat. Relieved and full of sudden hope as I was, I felt nervous too – nervous, dear Lucy, as I feel nervous now, for what I told Dr Eliot then I must repeat in my writing to you, and I am afraid that the details may cause you great pain. My story touches on your brother's death. Do not blame George for having kept the details from you, dearest Lucy, for his motives, I am confident, will grow clear from my account. Indeed – I only tell you the details now because I fear that a similar horror may have overtaken him. But read on – you have the courage, I know, to learn all which has hitherto been kept from you.

'My husband,' I told Dr Eliot, 'had always had great ambitions to rise in politics.'

'Ambitions,' Dr Eliot murmured, 'but not the application, as I recall.'

'It is true,' I admitted, 'that George sometimes found the day-to-day business of political life tiresome. But he had hopes, Dr Eliot, and noble dreams, and I always knew that were he given the chance he would make a great name for himself on the national stage. But although George struggled manfully to advance his own career, his hopes always seemed doomed to frustration, and I know he felt his failure very keenly. He would never admit it to me, but I know that his despair was compounded by the parallel success of your mutual friend and contemporary, Arthur Ruthven. Arthur's career in the India Office, I need hardly tell you, was a glittering one, and although barely thirty he was already spoken of as one of our most brilliant diplomatists. Clearly the precise details were kept from me, but he was responsible, I knew, for numerous missions of great delicacy and trust.'

'Always within the India Office?' Dr Eliot interrupted me.

I nodded.

'Very good.' He shut his eyes again. 'Proceed.'

'Arthur Ruthven,' I continued, 'was a very good friend – you will hardly need me to tell you that. He was perfectly aware of George's desire to rise in the Government, and I am sure that he did his best to help. Do not misunderstand me, Dr Eliot. Arthur was always the soul of propriety. He would have done nothing unworthy of his position of trust. But he may have had words with his Minister, he may have dropped the occasional hint. Nothing more than that, I am certain – nothing more. Suffice it to say, however, that some two years ago, shortly before our wedding, George finally entered the Government.'

'In the India Office?' Dr Eliot asked.

'Yes.'

'What were his responsibilities?'

I frowned. 'I am not certain. Does it matter?'

'If you don't tell me,' he replied sharply, 'how can I possibly decide?'

'I do know,' I said slowly, 'that he has a Bill to pilot through the House this summer. Obviously he has never talked about it much to me, but I believe it is related to the Indian frontier.'

'Indian frontier?' To my surprise, Dr Eliot seemed suddenly awakened by this news. He leaned forward and his eyes, I noticed, were glittering again. 'Elaborate,' he said impatiently. 'Which aspect, exactly, of the Indian frontier?'

'I couldn't say,' I answered helplessly. 'George never talks to me about his work. I am his wife, Dr Eliot, after all.'

He slumped back into his chair with a sign of evident frustration.

'But this parliamentary Bill,' he asked, 'for which George has the responsibility – do you know if he was working on it with Arthur Ruthven?'

'Yes,' I said. 'I am certain of that much, at least.'

'George as the Minister and Arthur as the diplomatist?'

'Yes.'

'Good.' He folded his hands again. 'Then that is suggestive.'

I frowned. 'I don't understand you,' I said.

He gestured disdainfully. 'Clearly, Lady Mowberley, if Arthur Ruthven's fate *has* overtaken your husband – forgive my bluntness, but we must consider the possibility – then we shall need to establish what it is which might link the two men. They were both working on this Bill and it is concerned with the Indian frontier. That is a topic of some sensitivity, I would have thought. You see, Lady Mowberley, what a fruitful line of inquiry at once opens up?'

'Yes.' I nodded and I thought further. 'Yes, I am sure you are right.'

He looked at me with interest. 'Why, you have evidence of it yourself?'

I swallowed. 'You are seeking for something which links the two men. Well, Dr Eliot, there is something. Whether it relates to George's work, I do not know. George himself seemed to imply that it did, but I believe it was as great a mystery to him as it is to me now.'

'Ah,' said Dr Eliot, with something like contentment. He lounged back in his chair and closed his eyes again, then swished one hand lazily. 'Continue, Lady Mowberley.'

I swallowed, as well I might. Prepare yourself, Lucy, for what you must now read, for I am afraid that it will not be easy for you. 'It was just over a year ago,' I said slowly, 'when Arthur came round to our home for a light dinner.' I then described to Dr Eliot what we had discussed that night: chiefly, dear Lucy, it had been you, and your determination to go back to the stage. You will remember how opposed your brother had been; and yet by the end of that evening he was laughing admiringly at your enthusiasm, and talking almost as though he would encourage you. 'I see that Lucy is determined to be a New Woman,' Arthur said, 'and clearly will not be turned aside. For obsessions are irrational and almost daemonic things, and we delude ourselves if we think they are a malady alone of the young.'

'Indeed,' murmured Dr Eliot, who had been lolling with eyes closed as I gave him my account. 'I remember at college Ruthven had a famous obsession of his own.'

'And what was that?' I inquired.

'He was a great collector of ancient Greek coins.'

'And so he still was when I knew him. Indeed, he often claimed within my hearing that his collection was quite unsurpassed.'

'Amusing,' murmured Dr Eliot faintly.

'Yes. We all found it so, I believe. Arthur himself readily admitted that there was an absurd aspect to his enthusiasm, especially in one otherwise so sober and reserved. "But there is nothing I would not do," he told us that night, "in pursuit of a coin from the age of the Greeks. I have the honour of my collection to uphold. Indeed, it seems that I have grown notorious, for see" – he reached in his bag – "I have only today received a personal challenge."'

'"A challenge?" I remember George exclaiming. "What the devil do you mean?"'

'Arthur smiled faintly, but did not reply. Instead, he placed on the table a red wooden box. He opened it, and we saw that inside was a small piece of card with writing on it. "What is it?" I asked in astonishment.

'"See for yourself," said Arthur, handing it to me.

'I took it. The card was of the highest quality but the writing was clumsy, and the ink of a strange quality, for it was a dark purple and flaked when touched. The message, however, was even more strange – so strange, indeed, that even now I can remember it perfectly. *Sir, you are a fool*, it read. *Your collection is worthless. You have allowed the greatest prize of all to slip through your hands*. It was signed simply, *A rival*.

'George took the message from my hands and read it for himself. He began to laugh, and soon we had all joined in – Arthur the loudest, although it was clear, I think, that his pride had indeed been touched. We asked him how he intended to respond to his insolent challenger. Arthur shook his head and laughed again, but I was certain he intended to follow the mystery through. How, I wasn't sure, for I didn't press him, but behind his laughter I had recognised pique and resolve.

A week later, I asked him if he had discovered his challenger's identity; he shrugged the question aside, but he smiled in that close way he always had and it was clear that the mystery had been preying on his mind. Two weeks later, Arthur Ruthven disappeared. A week after that, his corpse was found floating in the Thames off Rotherhithe, naked and wholly drained of its blood. Arthur's expression, George reported to me, had been one of the utmost horror.'

I paused. Dr Eliot, his eyes half-closed, had laced his fingers together as though in prayer. 'Your account,' he said at last, 'implies a link between Arthur's disappearance and his earlier receipt of the peculiar box.'

I nodded. 'Yes,' I said, and cleared my throat. 'When Arthur was pulled from the water, his hand was found to be clenched. The fingers were straightened out and a coin – a Greek coin – was discovered in his palm.'

'Suggestive,' observed Dr Eliot, 'but not conclusive.'

'The coin was certified to be of great value.'

Dr Eliot stared at me impassively. 'You informed the police?'

'I did.'

'And their response?'

'They were very polite, but . . .'

'Ah.' Dr Eliot smiled faintly. 'You did not have the box, then?'

'It was never found.'

'Ah,' nodded Dr Eliot again. 'That is a shame.' He narrowed his eyes. 'But perhaps, Lady Mowberley, since you obviously feel it worth your time to be here, you have some further evidence yourself?'

I lowered my eyes. 'I do,' I whispered.

'Tell me.'

Again, dear Lucy, I had to compose myself. I swallowed. 'Some months ago,' I said softly, 'a parcel came, addressed to our house. Inside there was a box ...'

'And the box was the same as that which Arthur had received?'

'In almost every way.'

'Remarkable,' said Dr Eliot, rubbing his hands. 'There was a piece of card too, then, addressed to George?'

'No, sir,' I replied. 'It was addressed to me.'

'Ah.' He narrowed his eyes again. 'Intriguing. What was its message, Lady Mowberley?'

'An insulting one.'

'But of course.'

'Why, "of course"?'

'Because the message to Arthur had been insulting as well. What did your message say, Lady Mowberley?'

'I am reluctant to reveal it.'

'Come, come, I must have all the facts.'

'Yes.' I swallowed. I closed my eyes, then repeated the message from memory. '*Madam, you are blind. Your husband does not love you. He has countless women apart from you.*' I choked, and sat in silence. At length I opened my eyes again.

'You are quite right,' said Dr Eliot softly. 'That is indeed insulting.' He paused. 'Do you have the message and box with you now?'

I nodded. I reached down and then handed the box across to Dr Eliot, who had risen to his feet. He took it gingerly, and crossed to a light where he studied the box with careful attention. 'It is clearly of no great workmanship,' he said. 'I would judge it has been used to transport merchandise – yes – see here ... there are words below the paint, in a Chinese script.' He glanced up at me. 'I would guess it to be from the docks,' he replied.

I shook my head. 'What would a person from the docks have to do with George or myself?'

'Well, now,' said Dr Eliot, 'that is the mystery, is it not?' He smiled faintly and opened the box to take out the card. As he studied it, his smile faded and grew into a frown. 'Whoever wrote this,' he said at last, 'is a better pensman than she pretends to be, for the cursives are quite inappropriate to what is otherwise a clumsy hand. I say she, for the style of writing is a feminine one. Also, the ink – you will have guessed, of course – it is clearly an admixture of water and blood.'

'Blood?' I exclaimed.

'Undoubtedly,' he replied.

'But ...' I swallowed. 'You are sure?' I shook my head and swallowed again. 'But, yes. Yes, of course you are.'

Dr Eliot furrowed his brow. 'There is clearly an intention expressed here, not only to insult but to frighten you.' He studied the card again, then shrugged faintly and returned it to the box. 'You showed this to your husband, I presume?'

I nodded wordlessly.

'What was his response?'

'Outrage. Utter outrage.'

'He denied the message's accusation?'

'Absolutely.'

'And you – forgive me for asking this, Lady Mowberley, but I must – you believed him?'

'Yes, sir, I did. Why should I not have done? George had always been the best of husbands, and the most transparent of men. If he had been betraying me, I would have known of it.'

Dr Eliot nodded slowly. 'Good,' he murmured, 'very good.' He sank back into his chair. 'So proceed, Lady Mowberley. What happened next?'

'Three days after the receipt of the box, George too disappeared.'

'Indeed?' Dr Eliot's face grew dark and intense. 'That must have been a terrible shock to you.'

'I was terrified, I freely admit.'

'You went to the police?'

'No, sir, I could not bear to, for I was afraid to admit that he might be truly gone. And indeed, after I had passed two sleepless nights, he returned to me – white-faced, glazed-eyed, but still my own sweet

George, perfectly alive. Some great mystery, however, had clearly engulfed him, for whenever I pressed him on the reasons for his sudden disappearance a shadow would cross his face, and he would ask me to forget that he had ever been gone. He found it hard to sleep, Dr Eliot; sometimes, when he believed I was asleep myself, he would cross to the window and stare out at the street. At other times, whenever he did chance to dream, he would toss and turn and mutter strange names. Finally, some three weeks after his initial disappearance, he disappeared again. This second time he was gone for several days, and I was almost frantic when he finally returned. I demanded to know what was happening but George continued to obfuscate. He did imply, however, that the mystery was related to his Government work. How or why he didn't say, but I received the impression of some great conspiracy, centring on the Bill he had to steer through Parliament, and requiring all his attention and time. He asked me not to worry, and promised that one day he would reveal the full truth to me. In the meantime, I would have to tolerate his occasional absences and his lengthy hours at the Ministry. He asked for my understanding and support.'

'And you gave it?'

I nodded. 'But of course.'

'The absences continued?'

'Sporadically.'

'And his work in the Ministry?'

'Has been brilliant, I believe. You may not be aware of George's reputation now. He is remarkably young to have reached the position he holds. His mysterious behaviour, however it relates to the progress of his Bill, is clearly proving to be of great benefit to his political career. And yet . . .' I paused and gazed into the eyes of Dr Eliot, which gleamed bright from his otherwise pallid face. 'And yet,' I repeated in a low voice, 'I remain afraid.'

'Well,' said Dr Eliot briskly, 'that is not to be wondered at. Remind me again – he has been absent now for over a week?'

'A week and a day.'

'That is unusual?'

'Yes. Before now, he has never been absent for more than three days at a time.'

'And that is why you have broken his injunction and come to me to seek for help?'

'There are other reasons.'

'Indeed?' he exclaimed.

I nodded. 'I will be frank, Dr Eliot. I fear the worst – yet I am also afraid lest you should think me mad.'

'Go on,' he said. 'If it is any comfort to you, Lady Mowberley, you strike me as being eminently sane.'

'That is very kind of you,' I replied, 'although there have been times today when I have doubted it myself. This is what occurred to me last night. I retired late to bed. Once my maid had undressed me, I dismissed her and sat alone awhile, wishing that George were with me and wondering where he might be. At length, I rose and crossed to the window. It was a blustery night outside, and I sat staring at the rain-swept skyline of London as though searching for some clue which might lead me to George. Dimly, I became aware of footsteps sounding from the cobble-stones below. I looked down. Illumined by the gas lamp I saw two figures, a gentleman and a lady. I saw that beneath his cloak the gentleman was in evening dress; he was swarthy-skinned, with a dark, bushy beard, and so I guessed him to be a foreigner. The lady's face I couldn't see, for she was standing with her back to me, swathed in a hood and a flowing black cloak. At length she turned and took the gentleman's arm; they both began to walk on down the street. As she went, however, the lady turned and glanced up, as though looking at me. I had no chance to make out her face, since it remained in the shadow cast by her hood, but for one second the street light caught her skin and it gleamed, Dr Eliot, I swear that it gleamed! Then she turned and was gone; but I was left with a feeling of the most abject horror. I cannot explain it. But it was real – vividly real. I felt simply that I had seen something horrible.'

'And this something horrible had been what? – the woman?'

'I know that it sounds ridiculous.'

'Yes,' he mused, 'but intriguing as well.'

'You do not think me mad?'

'On the contrary.' He smiled faintly. 'You have more to recount?'

'Yes.'

'Then do so. You retired to bed?'

'Yes. I took my medication ...'

'Ah.' He interrupted me at once by holding up his hand. 'This was for your nerves?'

'Yes.'

'What would this medication have been?'

'It is opiate-based, I believe.'

Dr Eliot nodded slowly. 'I am sorry, Lady Mowberley. You were saying, I believe, that you had retired to bed?'

'Yes. I slept well; I always do. Then, at four, the chiming of the church clock awoke me. I slipped back at once to sleep, but this time my dreams were bad. I woke up suddenly again, I opened my eyes – and my blood froze in my veins. The woman – I knew at once that it was the same one I had seen on the street – was staring at me. She was in my room. She still wore her cloak, but her hood was thrown back and her face was the most beautiful I had ever seen. At the same time, it was also the most terrible.'

'In what exactly did this terror lie?'

'I couldn't say. But it filled me with fear. Staring at it, I was absolutely paralysed.'

'Did you speak to her?'

'I tried. I couldn't though. I can't explain it, Dr Eliot. I am afraid you will think me very weak.'

He shook his head. 'Describe the woman.'

'She was ... I don't know what age – young, I suppose, but – no ...' My voice trailed away. 'What I want to say, I suppose, is that she seemed almost *beyond* age. She was dark-haired – long-haired too, I would have guessed, although it was hard to tell for her tresses were concealed below her shoulders by her cloak. Her face was very pale. It almost seemed as though it were lit by a flame from somewhere within her. Her lips were red. Her eyes were dark, and very bright.'

'Dark and bright simultaneously?'

'Yes.'

Dr Eliot shrugged faintly. 'And so what did this remarkable woman then do?'

'Nothing. She just stood there staring at me. Then she smiled suddenly, and turned. She left my room and I saw her, through the open doors, gliding towards the stairway.'

'Did you follow her?'

'Not at first. I felt, as I told you, paralysed. At length, though, I summoned up all my resolve and rose from my bed. I crossed to the doors and walked on until I was standing at the head of the stairway to the hall. The woman was below me, at the foot of the stairs. She had pulled her hood up again. Then the door to my husband's study opened and the foreign gentleman walked out. He had papers under his arm.'

'The foreigner, describe him.'

'Large, black-bearded, as I said, dark-skinned.'

'And what did he do? He approached the woman?'

'Yes. She seemed to speak to him, though I didn't hear her words, and they both of them turned to look up at me. Their faces were quite blank, and their eyes gleamed terribly . . .'

Dr Eliot's frown increased. 'And so what happened next?'

'The woman took the gentleman's arm. He still had the papers. They turned and walked away across the hall, disappearing from my view. I hurried down the stairway and saw them as they walked through the open front door. I ran across the hall and out into the street, but though I looked both ways I could see no trace of them. It was as though they had vanished on the early-morning light. I returned inside and woke the servants. We inspected the contents of the house carefully, but there was no sign of any burglary. Even in my husband's study, no drawer or cabinet seemed to have been forced. Everything was exactly as I remembered it.'

'You mentioned the open front door. Had that been forced?'

'Not that I could see.'

'A window, perhaps?'

'I don't think so. Certainly not obviously.'

'So how do you think they entered, Lady Mowberley?'

'I confess, I am baffled. Indeed, in the hours following the episode I began to believe myself the victim of some hallucination conjured up from my troubled brain, and I worried, as I told you, that I might be turning mad. Then, however, came the morning post. Amongst the letters was one without a stamp. I read it at once. I am afraid – yes, afraid, Dr Eliot – that I am not mad at all.'

I had the letter with me. I pulled it out, and handed it across. Dr Eliot read it and his face darkened. Yes, Lucy, it was that same printed message that I have told you of before: 'I HAVE SEEN G. MURDERED.' Dr Eliot studied the letter, then he rose and crossed to a lamp on his desk. 'I thought as much,' he said, turning back to me. 'This letter was surely posted by a woman.'

'How can you tell?' I asked him, rising to my feet.

He pointed out some smudged marks on the back of the letter. 'This is powder,' he said. 'The letter has been written on a table which has also been used for the application of cosmetics. You will observe that the marks are quite pronounced. I would judge that the writer of this letter is in the habit of applying a great deal of powder to her face.' He turned to the envelope and held it to the light. 'Yes,' he said, pointing to a mark by the edge. 'See the sheen? This is grease-paint. The evidence is irrefutable.'

Irrefutable, dear Lucy. I am prepared to accept that the Doctor is right. What class of woman, then, should I suspect of writing the letter to me? One, I dread to mention; the other, of course, you represent yourself. Lucy – I am desperate and so I must be blunt. I know of no actress save yourself, and certainly of no actress who would also be an intimate of George. Did you write me the letter? You do not see me as your friend, I know, but George you love, and it is in his name that I appeal to you. If it was not you who wrote to me, then I must fear the very worst – both that George is dead, and that before his murder he was betraying me. I cannot believe such a thing of him, however. *I cannot*. Therefore, again, I appeal to you. Did you write the letter? And if you did, will you please – please, dear Lucy – help Dr Eliot?

For I must tell you now that he has agreed to take on the case. I have mentioned your name in association with the letter, and so I suspect he will shortly be visiting you. Do not feel threatened by him. Even if it was not you who wrote the letter, I am certain you will be able to afford him some assistance. I have given you all the details of this mystery, as I understand them, both because I think that it is time you knew the truth and because you will be better able to help with the case. Do not reject my appeal, dearest Lucy – both for George's and your own sake.

I am, although you do not believe it, your very dear friend,

ROSAMUND, LADY MOWBERLEY.

Postscript. I add this late at night. Dr Eliot called round this evening. I was surprised to see him. He had told me on my visit this morning that it would take him some time to sort his surgery out, but not as long, it would seem, as he had originally thought. 'Llewellyn, my colleague at the surgery, has been away for three weeks', he told me as the footman took his hat. 'The least he can do is to act as my locum for a couple of days.'

I looked at him in surprise. 'That is all the time you think you will require?'

He shrugged. 'We shall have to see.' Then he began to stare around the hall. I guessed that he wished to inspect George's study, so I indicated it to him and followed him as he walked through the door. For several minutes he stalked around the room, rather like a bloodhound sniffing out its prey. 'Well,' he said at length, 'I can find no trace of a forced entry through the windows, but this' – he indicated the surface of the desk – 'is of some interest.'

I stared at it, but could see nothing out of the ordinary.

'I am assuming,' said Dr Eliot, 'that you have forbidden the servants entry here since last night?'

I agreed that I had. 'I wanted to leave it as I found it,' I told him.

'Excellent,' he exclaimed. 'The over-zealous housemaid can be the bane of an investigator's life. Now observe closely, Lady Mowberley. There is a very thin layer of dust on the desk. It is even everywhere, except for here.' He pointed. 'You see? A rectangle which exactly fits this red-lined box – here.'

He had stalked across the room to another table, on which one of George's Government boxes had been placed. 'Clearly,' he said, 'this was moved last night and must therefore have been the object of your intruder's attentions. What is in it?'

'George's papers,' I replied.

'Relating to the Bill on the Indian frontier?'

'Presumably.'

'Well then, let us see.' Dr Eliot pressed down the catches on the box. 'Locked,' he muttered. He peered down at the box. 'Again, no sign of it having been forced.'

'Perhaps the intruder was alerted by his companion before he could open it?'

'Perhaps.' Dr Eliot furrowed his brow. 'Do you have the key?'

'I do not.'

'Very well.' He felt in his pocket. 'I trust the India Office will forgive me for this.' I observed that he had a small piece of wire in his hand which he fitted in the lock. He twisted and jiggled it and at last, after several failed attempts, I heard the lock give. Dr Eliot smiled. 'The thieves of Lahore swear by this little tool,' he said, slipping the 'key' back into his pocket. Then he opened the lid of the box. He stood back, and I gasped. For, Lucy – imagine my horror – there was nothing there! The papers were gone!

Dr Eliot, however, seemed positively gratified. 'We had to expect this, of course,' he said as he glanced round the study again. 'I doubt we will find much more of interest here. Lady Mowberley, I would like to see your bedroom now, if I may.'

Still stunned by the magnitude of the crime we had just uncovered, I led him upstairs. Again, Dr Eliot prowled around the room. By my *cabinet de toilette* he paused and frowned. Then he picked up my bottle of medicine. 'This is for helping you to cope with the London air?' he asked.

I told him that it was.

'It is full,' he said, almost accusingly.

'Yes,' I replied, 'I have only just begun it.'

'When?'

'Last night.'

'Do you still have the bottle that you had finished before that?'

'The maid would have thrown it away.'

'Could you retrieve it?'

I rang for the housemaid and ordered her to bring the empty bottle up to me. 'You surely don't suspect,' I asked Dr Eliot as we waited, 'that someone might have been drugging me?'

He looked round at me. 'It is suggestive, is it not, that you should have been woken by your mysterious woman on the very night that you had changed your medicine?'

'Dr Eliot, what are you implying?'

He ignored my question. 'You had always slept soundly,' he inquired, 'before last night?'

I agreed that I had. 'But why would anyone have been drugging me?' I persisted.

He shrugged. 'There are clearly things in this house that are of value to someone,' he replied.

'George's papers?'

He shrugged again but his thin lips, I observed, had lightened into a smile. I asked him if he were any nearer a resolution of the mystery.

'There are possible glimmerings of light,' he replied, 'but I may yet be wrong – these are early days, Lady Mowberley.' At this moment the servant girl returned with the empty bottle. Eliot took it eagerly; he held it up to the light, then asked if he could also take the bottle I had just begun. I had plentiful supplies of the medicine, so I readily agreed and asked if there was anything else I could do. 'No, no,' he replied, 'I have seen all I wished to see.' He turned, and I accompanied him back to the hall, but as he prepared to depart he suddenly paused. 'Lady Mowberley,' he said, returning to me, 'there was indeed a further question I wanted to ask. Your birthday – it would not have been a few days after George's first disappearance, would it?'

I looked at him in astonishment. 'Why, yes,' I replied. 'The day after he returned, in fact. But, I don't understand – why . . .'

He cut me off with a wave of his hand. 'I will keep you informed of developments,' he said again. Then he turned and headed back down the street. This time he did not look round and I watched him until he had disappeared. I wondered what trail he could possibly have found.

As I still wonder now. I am staring down from my bedroom window at the street below. It is empty. The church bells have just sounded two o'clock. I must to bed. I hope I shall sleep. Certainly, my brain feels tired enough. The mystery seems to me, if anything, to have grown even more baffling. But perhaps, dearest Lucy, it will seem clearer to you. I can only hope so. I trust we shall have good tidings very soon. Good-night. Think of George – and me – in your prayers.

ROSA.

Letter, Hon. Edward Westcote to Miss Lucy Ruthven.

Gray's Inn,
London.

14 April 1888.

My dearest Lucy,

I cannot bear to think of you miserable. It is some terrible mystery, I know – and yet, my dearest, there must be no secrets between us. You have made me the happiest man in the world – yet you, by contrast, seem nervous and upset, and it pains me to the very depths of my soul. Is it Lady Mowberley? Has she been guilty of some fresh snub? Or are the phantoms from your past rising up again? You spoke of Arthur last night, in your dreams. But your brother is dead – just as my mother and sister too are dead. We must look forward, my love. What is gone is gone for ever. We have the future now.

Above all, my dearest Lucy, you mustn't allow yourself to be distracted tonight. Only think! A first night at the Lyceum! Appearing on stage opposite Mr Henry Irving – there are not many actresses who can boast of such a thing! You will be the toast of London, I am sure! I shall be so proud, darling. Good luck, good luck, good luck, and good luck again, darling Lucy, your ever loving

NED.

Narrative composed by Bram Stoker, early September 1888.

I have not the slightest difficulty in recollecting the events which I must here narrate, for they were so striking in themselves, and so remarkable in their conclusion, that I believe anyone would have been impressed by them. I, however, had additional reasons for committing the adventure to memory, for it so happened that I was searching for a good story at the time, with the intention of turning it into a play, or – who knows? – even a work of prose. For the circumstances of early April, I should reveal at once, were very particular.

The celebrated actor for whom I am theatre manager, Mr Henry Irving, had just returned from a most successful tour of the United States. Having conquered America, he was now preparing to receive once again the homage of London in that great temple to his art, the Lyceum Theatre. To open the summer season, Mr Irving and I had decided that the Lyceum would present *Faust*, a most spectacular production, and an evergreen favourite of the London crowds. It was not, however, an original production; nor were the plays we had scheduled for later in the season. Mr Irving himself was well aware of this, and in his conversations with me confessed that he regretted it. Many were the nights – many, indeed, still are the nights – when we would meet over a beefsteak and a glass of porter to discuss possible new roles for Mr Irving to play. In those early April weeks, however, we could find nothing suitable. At length I proposed that I write a new piece myself. Mr Irving, I regret to say, laughed at this suggestion and branded it 'Dreadful', but I was not discouraged; indeed, it was from that moment that I began to cast around for a possible theme. To that end, I began to record in my journal such unusual events or ideas as occurred to me, and it is those same jottings that I draw upon now.

I must confess, however, that for several weeks I continued uninspired. My dear wife was sick at the time; add to such a domestic crisis the pressures attendant upon any manager before a theatrical run, and the failure of my literary exertions will, I hope, seem excusable. Our season was due to open on the 14th; as that day drew nearer, so my hours grew less and less my own. At length, however, the 14th arrived, and as so often happens in the eye of a storm, I found myself surprised by a sudden calm. I sat in my office, knowing that I had done all I could and wondering all the same if it would prove to be enough. But I could only wait and hope for the best. It was then that Dr Eliot sent in his card.

I glanced over it. The name it announced meant nothing to me. But such was my state of mind that I welcomed any distraction, and so I asked for Dr Eliot to be shown into my room. He had clearly been waiting by the door, for he entered at once as though he had some urgent matter to pursue. Although his resolve was clear enough, however, so also was his calmness; indeed he seemed absolutely imperturbable, to an extent remarkable in one so young, for he could not have been more than thirty years of age, yet I could fancy at once what a power he would have over his patients. He took a seat by my desk and stared straight into my face, as though trying to penetrate the depths of my thoughts.

'You have a Miss Lucy Ruthven here,' he said abruptly, 'as one of your actresses.'

I acknowledged that we did. 'She is to play in the performance of *Faust* tonight.'

'A major role?'

'No, but not a small one either. She is exceedingly young, Dr Eliot. She has done very well to have gained such a part.'

He looked at me shrewdly. 'You admire her talent, then?'

'Oh, yes,' I agreed, 'she will be a wonderful actress.' I paused and flushed suddenly, for it seemed to me that my enthusiasm might be misinterpreted, but Dr Eliot appeared not to observe my confusion. 'I need to speak to her,' he said. 'I assume she is not in the theatre at present?'

'No,' I replied, 'she will not be here until after four. However, if you wish to leave her a note I could show you to her dressing room.'

Eliot inclined his head. 'That would be very kind of you.' He rose and followed me out from my study, and I led him down the stairways and narrow theatre corridors. 'I have had great difficulty in finding Miss Ruthven,' he said, as he clambered after me, 'I had been informed that she is legally the ward of Sir George Mowberley. However, it would appear that she does not choose to live with him.'

'No,' I replied. 'But you must understand that she only became the ward of Sir George on the sad occasion of her brother's death. You heard, perhaps, of that poor gentleman's murder?'

'Yes, yes,' said Eliot hurriedly, as though keen not to discuss such a topic. 'But it is still strange, is it not,' he continued, 'that Miss Ruthven does not live with Sir George at present? What age is she now?'

'Only eighteen, I believe.'

'Then you are right, that is young indeed.' He paused. 'I called at the Mowberleys' last night. At the mention of Miss Ruthven, it seemed to me that Lady Mowberley grew somewhat cold.' He paused again and glanced up at me. 'I was afraid that there might be bad blood between them.'

This had been said in an inquiring tone of voice, and I nodded in response. 'I believe you may be right,' I replied. 'It is likely, I suppose, that Lady Mowberley did not approve of Miss Ruthven's intention to go on the stage.'

'I must confess,' said Eliot, 'that I am a little surprised myself. I knew her brother quite well, you see. They are of very good family.'

'Yes,' I answered, somewhat aggrieved, 'and that is why she acts here at the Lyceum, where Mr Irving has done so much to improve the status of the acting profession.'

'Please,' he said hurriedly, 'I did not mean to be insulting. But you must acknowledge, Mr Stoker, that it is rare for a girl with such a background to wish to join the stage.'

'I am not certain, Dr Eliot. Many may wish it. Few have the courage to act on such a wish.'

He considered this. 'Yes,' he murmured at length, 'you may be right.'

'Dr Eliot,' I told him, 'Miss Ruthven is a girl of great character and purposefulness. She has, I might almost say, a man's mind – and yet she also has a woman's heart and natural purity. She will adorn the stage, just as she adorns her family name. Have no fears for her, Dr Eliot. She is a remarkable person in every way.'

Eliot nodded slowly. I flushed again, and swallowed; then I turned and hurried on down the corridor. Eliot, following me, made no further comment. It was with some relief that I saw the dressing rooms ahead. 'Here we are,' I said, taking my keys from my pocket. Then I saw that the door to Miss Ruthven's room was fractionally ajar. 'You are in luck,' I told him. 'She is already here.'

'Then it is strange,' answered Eliot, 'that she chooses to sit in the dark.'

I saw now that he was quite right, that the room did indeed appear to be in darkness. I frowned and glanced down at my keys. For some reason, we both paused outside the door. I felt a strange presentiment – of what, I cannot say – not fear exactly, but uncertainty, perhaps ... and talking to my companion later, I know that he had experienced a very similar emotion. I observed a faint flush upon his sallow cheeks. He glanced at me, then leaned against the door. 'Lucy,' he called out, knocking gently. 'Lucy!' Slowly he pushed open the door. I followed him into the dressing room.

He reached for a lamp and I saw the spurt of a match. The room was lit by a soft orange glow. Eliot held the lamp up high. He was staring at something behind me, and his brow seemed very dark. I turned round and started, for reclining in a chair was the figure of a man.

He was young and very beautiful, with delicate features and curling dark hair. His eyes were closed; indeed, so perfectly still he sat, and so pale were his cheeks, that I would have thought him a corpse were it not for the faint dilation of his nostrils which flickered as though in appreciation of some gorgeous scent. Slowly, the young man opened his eyes. They glittered. Indeed, I found myself quite hypnotised by their stare; it reminded me somewhat of Henry Irving's, though colder and more unsettling, for it seemed expressive of a great despair and pride such as not even an actor could simulate. The young man must have observed my discomfiture, for a faint smile touched his full red lips and he rose languidly to his feet. His dress was rich, and perfectly cut. A long cloak fell about him. 'I am afraid I have rather surprised you,' he said. 'Permit me to apologise.' His voice was wonderfully musical, and hypnotic just as his eyes had been. 'I have come to call on my cousin,' he went on as he stretched out his hand. 'My name is Ruthven, Lord Ruthven.' His hand, when I shook it, felt as cold as ice.

'This is a great pleasure, then,' said Eliot, shaking Lord Ruthven's hand in turn. 'I was a friend of Arthur, your elder cousin.'

A faint shadow seemed to cross Lord Ruthven's face. 'I never knew him,' he murmured at last. 'He is dead, is he not?'

'In most regrettable circumstances,' answered Eliot.

'Yes,' said Lord Ruthven, 'I heard of it.' He narrowed his eyes, then shrugged faintly. 'I have lived abroad all my life, and only returned to England recently. It is the privilege of the well-travelled man, that his relatives mean very little to him. And yet sometimes' – he glanced around the dressing room – 'even relatives can surprise. For instance,' he continued, picking up an envelope from the desk, 'I find I have an actress in my family. Why, it is more than surprising. It is positively romantic!' He opened the envelope and removed a theatre programme – marked, I observed, with the Lyceum crest. Lord Ruthven handed me the programme and I saw that Miss Ruthven's name had been underlined in red. 'It was sent to me today.'

Eliot looked up from the programme, which he had been studying over my shoulder. 'Indeed?' he asked, then frowned. 'By whom?'

'It was unsigned.'

'And the envelope? Had that been written on?'

Lord Ruthven raised an eyebrow. 'No,' he said slowly. 'It was left at my club.' He smiled faintly. 'Why your interest, sir?'

Eliot shrugged. 'I was merely wondering who might have sent it, that was all.'

'Oh, but there can be no mystery there. It was surely sent by the fair young Miss Ruthven herself. Indeed' – Lord Ruthven turned back to me – 'that is why I am waiting here. I have decided to attend the performance tonight and shall require a private box. Perhaps, since my cousin is not here herself, you might assist me instead?'

'I am afraid,' I said, 'that what you request is impossible, my Lord. It is the opening night of the Season; there are absolutely no boxes to be had.'

'Is that so?' He spoke quite calmly; there seemed no menace in his tone that I could identify, yet all the same – I know not how – I felt myself suddenly terrified. Drawn to stare into his eyes again, I saw Lord Ruthven smile mockingly at me. I am a large, strong man and not a coward, I hope, but I found myself suddenly shaking like a leaf. Lord Ruthven's beauty seemed blinding, and yet ghastly too, like that of a snake, deadly and cruel. It felt almost as though he were feeding on my strength. I dabbed at the sweat as it rose on my brow.

'I am sure,' I said at last, in a low voice, 'that some accommodation might be made.'

'Good,' said Lord Ruthven pleasantly. He rose to his feet, and as he did so my sense of terror melted away. He crossed to the door. 'Where will the ticket be kept for me?' he asked.

'By the Private Entrance, my Lord.' I glanced round at Eliot, who was sitting at the table writing a note. 'You could tell Miss Ruthven to leave any message for you at the same place, Dr Eliot.'

'Dr Eliot?' Lord Ruthven's pale features seemed lit by a sudden spark of interest. 'That is your name?'

'Yes,' Eliot replied. He furrowed his brow. 'Why, does it mean anything to you?'

Lord Ruthven did not answer. He smiled, though; and not until the smile had frozen away did he shrug and turn. As he did so, he brushed against one of Miss Ruthven's costumes. To my surprise I saw his face grew suddenly animated: his cheeks flushed, his eyes blazed and his nostrils began to dilate again. It was almost as though he were breathing in some perfume from the dress; but when he had gone, and I held the costume to my own nostrils, I could smell nothing. I turned to Eliot and shrugged. 'He seemed quite mad,' I commented. Eliot made no answer; instead he stared at the doorway through which Lord Ruthven had just disappeared, and then round at Miss Ruthven's dressing room. He frowned and returned to his writing, and I did not want to disturb him, for I was in a hurry now to return to my office. Eliot did not take long to write his note; once he had finished it he turned it over and held it to the light, as though inspecting it, then left it propped against the mirror lamp. We returned to the corridor and walked in virtual silence back through the theatre. I showed Eliot the Private Entrance and parted from him there.

I then rapidly forgot all about him, for no sooner had we made our farewells than the floodtide that is an opening night began to rise again, and soon it had swept me utterly away. I had no time to contemplate the curious business of the afternoon; when I passed Miss Ruthven I did pause to wonder what arrangement she had reached with Eliot, but I did not stop to ask her. One thing I did know, however, and that was that Eliot would not be attending the performance; when I had asked him, he had told me that he had no great taste for plays, or indeed anything fictional at all.

Faust, however, as it was performed on that opening night, would surely have enraptured even Eliot. It was a consummate triumph; and if the chief plaudits went as ever to Mr Henry Irving and Miss Ellen Terry, then those given to Miss Lucy Ruthven were not far behind. She was a revelation, if not to me then to the audience, and the talk after the show was all of her. By the Private Entrance I saw

Lord Ruthven; I wondered what he had made of his cousin's display. He was standing talking to Oscar Wilde, but he paused in his conversation as I went by him and smiled faintly at me.

'Bram!' Wilde called out, noticing me too. 'Dear man! Your young actress, Miss Ruthven – this is her first leading role, I hear? I refuse to believe it! Only years of practice and careful subterfuge could have enabled her to appear so *triumphantly* unspoiled.'

I bowed my head. 'And you, Lord Ruthven?' I asked. 'Did you enjoy your cousin's performance?'

'Oh, exceedingly so.' His eyes glittered as he nodded his assent. 'She was charming. I quite disagree with you, however, Mr Wilde. She had that rare type of freshness which is not a pose. It will fade, of course, for a girl of such beauty and evident intelligence will soon grow to value style above truth, but meanwhile' – his eyes glittered again – 'it was a delightful display.' He paused, and glanced over my shoulder. 'But talking of Lucy,' he murmured, 'here comes another admirer now.'

I glanced round and saw Eliot coming up the stairs. 'Admirer?' I asked with a frown.

'I had assumed so.' Lord Ruthven smiled. 'Why else do men come calling on actresses?'

My frown deepened as I looked round for Eliot again. He had reached the top of the stairs by now and was standing there, clearly debating which door he should take. I made my excuses to Lord Ruthven and Wilde, then pushed through the crowds to Eliot. He saw me coming and walked across to meet me. 'Mr Stoker,' he asked, 'which route am I permitted to take?'

'To Miss Ruthven's dressing room?' I inquired. 'This way. We will go across the stage.'

'There is no need to escort me. I remember the way.'

'No, no,' I said, 'it is not in the least inconvenient.'

He shrugged. 'It is very kind of you.'

I led him down to the stage. 'You missed a wonderful perform-ance tonight,' I remarked, wondering how to broach what I had to say.

'So I hear,' he replied. There was a slight pause. 'I gather that Miss Ruthven has had a great triumph.'

'Yes,' I said shortly.

Eliot smiled. 'She seems to be quite the favourite of the hour.'

'Yes,' I said again, even more abruptly; then I paused, and stopped in my tracks and turned to face him. 'Dr Eliot . . .' I began.

'Yes?'

'I feel I should tell you . . .'

'Yes?'

'I feel I should tell you . . .' I said again. I swallowed. 'Miss Ruthven – her heart . . . well, I must be blunt – it is already given.'

He stared at me and his frown slowly lightened into an expression of amusement. 'My dear fellow,' he said, starting to walk across the stage again, 'you mistake the nature of my interest in Miss Ruthven.'

'Indeed?'

'Yes, I assure you.' He chuckled. 'My brain exists purely to think and calculate. It has never been concerned with the fairer sex. Why, it is a virtual machine. You may rest assured, Mr Stoker, that I am not a rival to anyone.' He studied me, the look of amusement still lingering in his eyes. 'But tell me, if you are able, who is the lucky man?'

I frowned. 'What is your business with Miss Ruthven?' I asked. 'Are you here to help her?'

'If I may. But why do you assume that she requires my help?'

'Because . . .' I sighed, and shook my head. 'She has seemed preoccupied recently, Dr Eliot – almost afraid.'

'Has she now?' Again the flush of interest returned to his cheeks. 'And you feel it is related to her love affair?'

'I did not say that.'

'No, but you implied it.' He waited, then shrugged. 'If it is of any relevance, then no doubt Miss Ruthven will inform me of it herself. And here is my chance' – he paused, and smiled – 'to find out.'

For by now we had reached her dressing-room door. It was wide open. Eliot knocked as he walked in. 'Lucy?' he asked. 'I hope I am not disturbing you?'

She looked up. She was sitting by her mirror, almost hidden behind great bouquets of flowers, and had been fixing a hat on her braided golden hair. There was still so much of the child in her face that her blue eyes at first seemed as nervous as a fawn's; but when she recognised us, her fresh cheeks glowed with happiness. 'Jack Eliot!' she whispered. 'Is it really you? Jack!' She held out her hands. Dr Eliot kissed her white-gloved finger-tips. 'But it is so wonderful to see you again,' she laughed, 'after – oh! – so many years!' She stepped back and curtsied elegantly. 'I must seem very grown-up to you now, do I not, dear Jack?'

'Terribly so,' replied Dr Eliot. 'Quite a crone.'

Miss Ruthven laughed and turned to me. 'You see, Mr Stoker, he has not laid eyes on me since I had pigtails and dolls, and ugly teeth.'

Eliot shook his head. 'No, no, Lucy, do not malign yourself.' He turned to me. 'She was as beautiful as a child as she is lovely now.'

'Oh, pooh,' answered Miss Ruthven, 'don't try flattering me, Jack Eliot! I remember you well enough. He was always a cold fish, Mr Stoker. Women were much too giddy for him.'

Eliot smiled faintly. 'I told you that?'

'Yes, quite solemnly, and I can only have been twelve.' She turned back to me. 'Did you know that Arthur ...' – she paused, and her laughter died away on her lips – 'Arthur was my brother, Mr Stoker ...' She composed herself and a faint flush of colour returned to her cheeks. 'Arthur called Jack the Calculating Machine.'

Eliot bowed his head. 'How flattering.'

'And you still have your old calculating powers, do you, Jack?'

Eliot stared at her. Her voice had sounded suddenly remote and strange. Gently she reached up to a necklace round her throat. There was a pendant hanging from it and she stroked it as though it was a lucky charm, and all the time she stared unblinkingly into Eliot's eyes. Her own seemed deep, and very wide. 'Jack,' she whispered. 'Jack. I hope you do still have your powers. Because we need them. I am afraid there is something rather dreadful going on.'

Eliot's face remained wholly impassive, then he slowly raised an eyebrow. 'We?' he asked.

Miss Ruthven nodded. 'Yes, we,' she whispered. She held out an arm. 'Ned,' she called and a young man stepped out from the doorway beyond the wall of flowers. He seemed very young, as young as Miss Ruthven, and as handsome as she was beautiful, with fine features and curling black hair. 'Jack, Mr Stoker.' Miss Ruthven smiled as she took the young man's arm. 'Allow me to introduce Edward Westcote. He is the dearest boy in all the world.' She looked into his eyes. 'I must tell you; it can be a secret no longer. We are married, dear friends. We are living together as husband and wife.'

I was stunned, I freely confess, and for a moment I hardly knew what to say. Eliot, however, did not seem surprised in the slightest – indeed, appeared almost to have been expecting some such announcement. 'My congratulations,' he said. 'Mrs Westcote.' He kissed – I can call her Miss Ruthven no more, so let her be Lucy henceforth – he kissed Lucy on her cheeks. Then he shook Westcote's hand.

'Congratulations,' I echoed.

'Mr Stoker,' Lucy asked anxiously, 'you are not angry, I hope?'

'No, no,' I said. 'I am delighted for you. It is just that . . .' I paused. 'I am surprised, I suppose, that you have kept it secret from me.'

'But, dear Mr Stoker, nobody knew.'

'Why, though? I would not have minded.'

A faint shadow passed across Westcote's face. 'You would not,' he said, holding his wife's arm, 'but there were others, Mr Stoker.'

'Indeed?' asked Eliot, angling his head. He stared at Westcote unblinkingly, then at Lucy. 'I cannot believe that Arthur would have objected.'

'He did not,' Lucy answered.

'Then why the need for secrecy?'

Lucy glanced at her husband, then at me. 'You will remember, Mr Stoker,' she said, 'that for several months, some time back, I was very ill.'

I nodded. 'Yes. You had just begun here, as I recall. The delay it inflicted upon your career was a great pity.'

'And yet I was here long enough to have met Ned.' She looked up at her husband and blushed prettily. 'When I fell ill, he proved to be my constant nurse. My resolve to become his wife was forged during those long months of seclusion. My brother – and yes, you are quite correct, of course, Jack – my brother Arthur did not object at all.'

'Then I fail to see what the problem was.'

'Arthur was killed, Jack. He was murdered before our engagement had even been announced.'

Eliot stared at her. 'I am sorry, Lucy,' he said at last. 'Very sorry.'

'I know, Jack.' Again, she reached to stroke the pendant which was hanging from her neck. With her other arm, she clung tighter to her husband. 'After his death – you will know this, perhaps – George Mowberley became my guardian.'

Eliot frowned. 'But again ... I do not understand. George was always the most tolerant of men, and he adored you. He could not have objected either, surely?'

'No.' Lucy paused. 'But Lady Mowberley did.'

'Ah.' Eliot nodded slowly. 'I should have guessed. But why does she ...'

'Why does she hate me?' Lucy interrupted with sudden passion. 'I don't know, Jack, but she does. At first she seemed very kind, as she is to almost all the world, but then, when I fell ill, she wouldn't even visit me – not once, not for all that time I was sick. And when I was recovered and she had learned about Ned, again she was cold, even angry with me. She refused him entry into her house.'

Eliot glanced at Westcote. 'What did she have against you?' he asked.

'I don't know,' Westcote replied. 'I have never even met her.'

Lucy shook her head. 'It was not Ned she was hostile to, but me.'

'It seems most strange,' said Eliot thoughtfully. 'Lady Mowberley struck me as being a charming woman.'

'And so she does almost everyone.'

Eliot's frown deepened, and he stared up at the couple as they clasped each other's arms. 'Very well, then. I can understand that her opposition was distressing to you both. Did it truly matter, though? Surely it was George who was the guardian?'

'It is Lady Mowberley who is rich. She controls the purse-strings. Jack, you remember how deeply in debt George always was?' Lucy smiled faintly. 'He is not prepared to risk contradicting his wife.'

'Ah.' Eliot thought, then nodded slowly. 'Yes, that sounds plausible.'

'Oh, it is,' agreed Lucy, 'utterly. And so you see, Jack, we really didn't have a choice in the matter. If we were to be married, it had to be done in secret. It *had* to be. And we had already waited for almost two years. And we were so *absolutely* in love. We simply couldn't have waited another day.'

Eliot smiled faintly. 'Of course not.' He glanced at Westcote. 'And what about you, sir? Do your parents know?'

Westcote's brow darkened faintly. 'My father is in India,' he said after a pause. 'I have not yet had the chance to inform him. Naturally, in due course, I shall do so.'

Eliot studied him attentively, angling his head in the distinctive way he had, so that he looked rather like a kestrel observing a vole. 'And your mother?' he asked slowly.

Westcote swallowed. 'My mother ...' he said, and then his voice trailed away and he swallowed again. He looked up. 'My mother, I regret to say, is dead.' Lucy moved closer to him and pressed his hand; Westcote continued to stare straight ahead. 'She disappeared some two years ago with my sister. They were kidnapped by native tribesmen in the Himalayas. My sister's corpse was never found, but my mother's was. She had been left unburied on a mountain track; she had been drained of her blood, and her throat had been cut. It was the most terrible thing, Dr Eliot. Terrible!'

'I am sorry,' said Eliot after a pause. 'Forgive me for asking. I should not have done.'

'You were not to know,' Westcote replied.

'No,' said Eliot. 'Of course I was not.'

'Indeed,' Westcote went on, staring down into the eyes of his wife, 'it was the pain of my loss which drew me closer to Lucy. You seem an old friend of hers, Dr Eliot. You will know then that she is an orphan, and that her own father too disappeared and was killed. Forgive me, my dearest Lucy, for touching on such a theme, but that is after all why we are here, is it not?'

Lucy met his ardent gaze, but made no reply.

'Lucy!' Westcote sounded almost desperate now. 'You *are* going to tell me, aren't you?' He turned to us. 'There is some danger threatening her, I know that there is. Her father was killed, drained white of his blood just as my own dear mother was. Then her brother, last year, suffers the very same fate. It is not too much, I think, to talk of a curse – a curse on the House of Ruthven. And now Lucy has some secret dread, and she will not talk to me of it, even though I am her husband and would die for her!'

Lucy continued to stare deep into his eyes. 'My darling,' she whispered, 'I was wrong to keep it from you.' She reached up to stroke his tousled hair; then she kissed him gently and turned back to us.

'Ned is quite right,' she said, her voice very soft and low. 'I have seen something terrible.' She gestured towards Eliot. 'He knows what.'

Eliot's face remained impassive but his eyes, I saw, were glittering and alert.

'It was very clever of you, Jack, to deduce that it was I who had written to Lady Mowberley that George might be dead.'

Eliot shrugged. 'It was simple.' He reached for a letter left on Lucy's dressing table and I recognised the same one he had written that morning. He turned the sheet of paper round. 'You see, Lucy. Powder. Your own letter to Lady Mowberley had the very same marks.'

Westcote was staring at Lucy in astonishment. 'You wrote to her?' he asked. 'You wrote to that . . .' His indignation prevented him from finding a word. 'But Lucy – why?'

Lucy stared round the room and then, smoothing out her skirts, she sat down. I turned to leave, for I sensed that she was preparing to make some private revelation, but she held up a hand and asked me to stay. 'I want you to understand why I have been upset just recently, Mr Stoker. And especially over the past few days. I know I have not been easy company.'

She looked up into her husband's eyes. 'But it is not myself I am afraid for, dearest boy,' she said. 'Do you truly think I would have hidden such a thing from you? No, Ned – never. But I am afraid – terribly afraid – for George Mowberley.'

Eliot stretched out his long fingers. 'Ah yes,' he murmured, 'George.' He clasped his fingers together again, then rested his chin on them and stared at Lucy imperturbably. 'So, then,' he said. 'His murder. Tell me what you saw.'

'Murder!' I exclaimed.

Eliot nodded slowly. 'It was murder, was it not, Lucy, that you claimed to have witnessed?'

Lucy stared past us. She began to stroke the pendant at her throat, then she nodded slowly. 'I think so,' she said.

'Only think?' Eliot frowned.

'There was no body, Jack.'

He raised an eyebrow. 'Intriguing. Then what did you see?'

'He was at a window.'

'Where?'

'It looks out over Bond Street. I was walking there two days ago. I had dreamed the night before ... about my brother's death – and that George was threatened by the same ghastly fate. That will sound stupid, Jack, I know, but I had been very affected by the nightmare, for it had seemed exceedingly real. I had even written George a letter, describing it to him, and then I decided very late that a letter would not suffice. I had to see him.'

'Very well,' said Eliot, 'but why in Bond Street?'

'There is a jeweller's shop. It is run by an old valet of George's. When my relations with Lady Mowberley were particularly bad, I often used to meet George there.'

'What number?'

'Ninety-six.'

Eliot nodded, and gestured at Lucy to continue with her tale. She was still stroking the pendant, but her voice now was unhesitant and perfectly clear. 'It was quite late,' she said. 'We had been rehearsing hard. When I arrived at Headley's – that is the name of the jeweller's shop – I found that it was closed. I stepped back to look up at the top storey of the building above the shop, for that is where Mr Headley and his wife have their rooms, and I wanted to see if I could make out a light. But their windows were dark, and I was just about to turn and walk back up the street when my eye was caught by movement from the storey below. I glimpsed the figure of a man silhouetted against the window frame. He saw me; he staggered forward and pressed his face against the pane. He seemed very pale and his eyes were staring terribly, but it was George, I know it was, I have no doubt in my mind. He seemed to be calling out to me, but then I saw hands pull him back and some cloth was pressed over his mouth. He struggled free and I saw that his chin was covered with blood, but then the cloth was clasped to his mouth again and I saw him slump. Then the light went out. I saw nothing more. I hammered and hammered on the door that led up to the floors above the shop, but there was no response, and so I turned and called out to a policeman.'

'A moment, please.' Eliot held up a hand. 'You remained standing by the door all this time?'

'Yes,' said Lucy.

'No one could have left through the doorway without your knowing it?'

'No.'

'And there is no alternative exit from the building?'

'No, none at all.'

Eliot nodded. 'Very good. That is a matter of obvious importance, then.' He folded his hands. 'Now – you were telling us how you called out to a policeman, I believe.'

'Yes,' said Lucy, her eyes burning bright. 'I told him what I had seen. He listened to my story politely enough, but he must have thought that I was being hysterical, for there was no urgency in his actions, and as he questioned me, I could detect the hint of doubt in his voice. He came back with me to Headley's, however, and using a piece of wire he unlocked the door to the flats above. Pushing past him, I hurried up the stairs and came to a second door. I rattled it, but it was locked. I called out to the policeman to hurry, but as I did so I heard the sliding of a bolt and the door was opened to me. A servant – I say a servant but his voice, when he spoke, seemed a gentleman's – asked me if he could be of any help. For a moment I was struck dumb; the servant's eyes seemed unspeakably cruel, like a rattlesnake's, and his breath was revolting, so vile that it seemed almost to stink of chemicals. He asked me again if he could be of any help; but by now I had recovered my sense of urgency, and I slipped past him to see if I might surprise the murderer. But the room into which I had come was deserted, without any sign of violence or bloodshed at all, and indeed seemed the very image of undisturbed luxury. Only an opera cloak flung untidily over the back of a *fauteuil* seemed out of place; and that was scarcely proof of a brutal killing. I began to worry that I had behaved rather foolishly.

'The policeman, who had joined us by now, was clearly of a similar mind. He informed the servant of what I had seen, but as he described it, he made no attempt to make it sound even faintly plausible. A broad smirk spread across the servant's face. "I am afraid," he said with a low, hissing chuckle, "that the Master is absent at present, but the Mistress is here. I could inquire of her, if you wish, whether she has committed a murder recently?" He tittered again, and his whole body seemed to twist and writhe with his amusement; then he turned and, beckoning the policeman, led him through a door. I was left in the front room alone.

After a few minutes the door opened again and a woman came in. How can I describe her? Her dress was beautiful – red velvet, cut low. Her dark hair was braided and very long. Her face was so lovely, it was almost painful to see. I felt ... strangely drawn to her. She had ... something – a power – an overwhelming attractiveness ...' Lucy closed her eyes. For a long while she said nothing. 'She filled me with terror,' she whispered at last. Her voice trailed away.

'Up until that moment,' she continued eventually in a distant voice, 'I had begun to doubt that I had seen George's murder at all. But Jack – when that woman came in, I knew for certain that I had not been hallucinating but had indeed seen something terrible. And then – when I received Lady Mowberley's letter ...' Her voice trailed away; she frowned and shook her head. 'I knew,' she repeated simply. 'I knew.'

'Knew what?' asked Eliot, impatience in his voice.

Lucy looked up. 'The woman that I met in that room – it was the same woman who has been haunting Lady Mowberley.' She looked round at Westcote and me. 'Lady Mowberley saw her last night,' she explained, 'after she had broken into her house.'

'But how can you be sure it was the same woman?' asked Eliot as impatiently as before.

'In the letter, that description of her ...' Lucy shook her head again. 'You remember that Lady Mowberley could not define the qualities of her intruder's face? – not exactly – she could only say that it was the most extraordinary face she had ever seen? Well' – she nodded her head – 'that was exactly how I felt too. As I said, it was beautiful, Jack – oh, how beautiful – but there seemed the most potent sense of danger in her eyes as well, and fascination, and evil, and greatness too, and oh – how can I describe it? I can't. I just can't.' She clenched her hand and raised it to her lips, in clear frustration at her failure to define what she had seen. 'But I could feel her almost seducing me,' she whispered softly. 'Yes, seducing me. In the end, I had to force myself to tear my gaze away.'

There was a lengthy pause, then Eliot folded his arms and leaned back against the wall. 'There are many striking women in London,' he said.

'No, Jack, but listen, I haven't told you all.' Lucy unclenched her fingers, and turned back to us. 'There was a second person Lady Mowberley saw last night: a foreign gentleman, a dark-skinned man, from India perhaps, or Arabia.'

'Ah,' said Eliot with sudden animation and surprise, 'you never saw such a man yourself?'

'Yes,' said Lucy, 'I did. The policeman had just returned into the front room. He told me that he had searched everywhere in the flat but had found no trace of a struggle, still less of a corpse. He apologised to the mistress of the house, and suggested that we make our retreat forthwith. Then we heard footsteps coming up the stairs outside . . .'

'*Up* the stairs?' asked Eliot, interrupting her.

'Yes,' said Lucy.

'You are certain?'

'Absolutely.'

Eliot frowned. 'I am sorry,' he muttered. 'Continue, please.'

'There is very little else to say. The gentleman came in through the front door. He was dressed in evening clothes, though without anything to cover them, and it was clearly his cloak which had been left on the *fauteuil*. He listened to the policeman's account of what I had seen, and appeared most surprised, and then we left. I had no reason particularly to suspect him. It was only when I received Lady Mowberley's letter that my doubts began to harden into fear. Jack – I *had* seen George up there. I *had* seen him killed!'

Eliot had been listening all this time with his eyes half-closed. 'I agree,' he murmured, 'that it all seems most suggestive. However, tell me – the foreign gentleman's response to your own presence in his front room: did he seem unsettled by it in any way?'

'Not at all,' Lucy replied. 'He appeared remarkably calm. Indeed, he seemed almost to be mocking me. His self-possession was perfectly loathsome.'

'Loathsome?'

'Yes. That was how he struck me.' Lucy repeated the word with insistence. 'Loathsome.'

Eliot nodded. 'And did he speak to you at all?'

'The merest pleasantries.'

'Ah.' Eliot's brow darkened and his eyes opened wide and as beady as before. 'Then this does indeed seem a most baffling case,' he agreed. 'I take it, dear Lucy, that you wish me to pursue it as far as I can?'

'But of course, Jack. Arthur is dead already – in what strange circumstances, I have only recently fully learned. The thought that George should have been tempted to the same awful fate ...'

'Very well.' Eliot nodded and glanced at his watch. 'If you have nothing more to say, then, I should depart at once ...'

'Oh, but Jack, I do!'

Lucy had reached out to hold him and Eliot looked round in surprise. 'What is it?' he asked.

'Tonight – I saw them again – they were here tonight.'

'In the theatre?' I exclaimed. 'Not the lady and the foreigner?'

Lucy nodded. 'I am certain it was them. They were seated in their own box, on the right, the one nearest to the stage – that was how I could distinguish them. The woman was not there for the second half, but the gentleman stayed for the entire performance. He left though, very hurriedly, during Mr Irving's speech of thanks at the end.'

Eliot turned to me. 'Would you have a record of the person who had hired that box?'

'Naturally,' I replied. 'The details would be in my office.'

'Then let us go there at once.' Eliot turned to Lucy. 'Have no fear,' he said, holding her hands. 'I will do all I can to resolve this case.' He kissed her; gathering his coat, he then left the room and I followed him. We began to walk down the corridor towards my office, but as we went we heard footsteps from behind and, turning round, saw Westcote coming after us.

'Dr Eliot,' he asked, 'I must know – is Lucy in great danger, do you think?'

Eliot shrugged faintly. 'It is too early to be certain,' he replied.

'If there is anything I can do, any danger that must be run ...'

Eliot nodded. 'Then stay with your wife. Be with her at all times. Be prepared for anything.'

Westcote stared at him hesitantly. 'And that is how I can help her best?'

'I am certain that it is.' Eliot smiled and clapped Westcote upon the shoulder. 'Good luck,' he said. 'Be worthy of the woman you have married.' And then he turned, and I accompanied him, and we heard

Westcote go back down the passage to his wife.

'You truly think Miss Ruthven is in danger?' I asked, once we had reached my office.

'Mrs Westcote, you mean.'

'Yes, of course.' I corrected myself. 'Mrs Westcote.'

Eliot took the ledger that I had handed to him, and shook his head. 'I think not.' He frowned. 'But then this case is not as simple as I had earlier assumed it to be.' His frown deepened, and then he shook his head again and stared down at the ledger where I had opened it.

'Here,' I said, pointing, 'this was the box. Good Lord! Dr Eliot! What on earth is the matter?'

For Eliot had turned the most deathly shade of pale. His eyes were fixed on the entry in the ledger and his lips had parted in amazement. 'And yet,' he murmured, rising to his feet, 'it must surely be a coincidence . . .'

His eyes dimmed and he seemed lost in his own private reverie. I looked down at the ledger to see what had caused him such astonishment. The box had been reserved in the name of the Rajah of Kalikshutra. 'A Rajah!' I exclaimed. 'So Miss Ruthven was right. He was an Indian.'

'Yes,' said Eliot, looking back at me. 'Or so it would seem.'

'Does Kalikshutra mean anything to you?'

'A little,' he replied. He glanced down at the entry in the ledger again, his face now as impassive as it had been before. He shrugged, then slammed the ledger shut. 'It is late,' he said. 'No doubt I will have a lengthy day ahead of me tomorrow. I must go, Mr Stoker. I thank you for your time.'

'I will come with you,' I replied. I locked up my office and then accompanied Eliot out into the street. We walked together up Drury Lane, looking for a hansom, but it was later than I had thought, and even around Covent Garden the streets were almost empty. We walked on down Floral Street, and as we did so I became aware that a carriage was following us – black, with a coat of arms on its door, its wheels rumbling along the cobbled stones. As it drew level with us, there was the rap of a cane upon the window and the vehicle shuddered to a halt. The window was opened and a pale hand beckoned to us. Eliot ignored it; he continued to walk down the street.

Lord Ruthven leaned out from the carriage window. I watched him smile. 'Dr John Eliot,' he called out. 'I believe that your surgery is very starved of funds?'

Eliot looked round at him in surprise. 'And if it is,' he said, 'what concern is that of yours?'

Lord Ruthven held out an envelope, and dropped it. 'Read this,' he said. 'It may prove to be to your advantage.' Then he rapped with his cane on the carriage roof. The coachman shook out the reins, and the vehicle began to move away from us.

Eliot watched it as it rounded the next corner and disappeared, then he bent down and picked up the envelope. He opened it and read the message inside; then he handed it to me. From the address embossed at the top of the sheet, I recognised the name of a street in Mayfair. 'Visit me,' Lord Ruthven had written. 'We have much to discuss.' I looked up at Eliot. 'Will you go?' I asked.

He made no answer at first, then he shivered and wrapped his coat tight about himself. 'I have enough mysteries to concern me as it is,' he muttered at last. He took the letter from my hand and began to walk on down the street.

'If I can help you . . .' I called out after him.

He didn't look round.

'You know,' I called out again, 'I would do anything to preserve Miss Ruthven from danger.'

'Bond Street tomorrow,' he said, still without glancing round. 'Nine o'clock.'

'I will be there,' I promised.

'Good-night, Mr Stoker.' He walked on. The darkness rapidly swallowed him.

The next morning in Bond Street, I expected to find him by the jeweller's shop. Instead he was standing by the doorway to the right of Headley's, which I realised was the entrance to the floors above. Eliot smiled when he saw me, and came out to take my arm. 'Stoker,' he said cheerily, but his grip as he held me was very tight, and he pulled me with some force to prevent me from walking further down the street. 'Not past the front of the jeweller's shop,' he said, still in a voice as cheery as before, rather as though he were suggesting breakfast. Indeed, his whole manner was that of someone inviting a friend up to his rooms. He pushed open the door and ushered me through; then, perfectly coolly, he followed me in and locked the door.

'Where did you get the key?' I asked in some surprise.

'Lahore,' he replied. His smile had faded completely now; he looked up the stairs and his face was perfectly inscrutable again. 'Do you notice anything interesting?' he asked.

I stared about me. 'No,' I replied.

'Not the carpet?'

I looked down and studied it carefully. 'There seems nothing unusual,' I commented at last.

Eliot fixed me with his piercing gaze. 'I did not say unusual, I said interesting,' he replied. 'Well, it can wait.' He turned and began to walk up the stairs.

I followed him. 'What are we doing?' I asked.

Eliot had stopped by a door on the first-floor landing. He still had the key in his hand. He fitted it into the lock, and only then did he glance round at me. 'Don't worry,' he said, 'I have had the flat watched all night. There is no one in.'

'For Heaven's sake, though,' I whispered urgently, 'this is burglary. Think what you are doing, Eliot!'

'I have thought,' he answered as he turned the key, 'and there is no other way.' He opened the door, and hurried me in. Quietly, he closed the door behind us and turned to face me. 'Do you believe that Lucy was telling the truth?' he asked.

'Of course,' I replied.

'Then we are justified in what we do, Stoker – I fear that there may be some great evil abroad. These are deep waters we are in. Believe me, we have no choice but to break in to this place.' He looked about him. The room was just as it had been described to us. It was opulent, decorated with great refinement and taste, and yet there was a lushness – almost, dare I say it, a *decadence* about it – so that its beauty seemed overheated, like that of an orchid too ripely in bloom. I felt oddly nervous and Eliot too, glancing around the room, seemed to flinch. I followed his gaze. He gestured towards the front wall where there were two bay windows looking out on to the street. 'That is where George would have been standing when Lucy saw him,' Eliot murmured. Taking a small eye-glass from his pocket, he walked along the edge of the wall and fell to his knees. Having studied the carpet with minute attention, he frowned and shook his head, then moved across to the second window. Again, he bowed his head and studied the floor. I joined him. The carpet was thick and brightly coloured, but I could see at once that it was quite unstained. Then suddenly I heard Eliot breathe in sharply. 'Here!' he whispered, pointing at the wainscot. 'Stoker! What do you make of this?'

I looked. There was a spot of something, so tiny that it was scarcely visible to the naked eye, and above it a couple more spots. Eliot peered at them. He scratched at one, then held his finger up to the light; the nail's edge was coloured a rusty brown. He frowned, then dabbed at the nail with the tip of his tongue. 'Well?' I asked impatiently. Eliot glanced round. 'Yes,' he replied, 'it is certainly blood.'

I turned pale. 'So Lucy was right,' I whispered. 'The poor fellow was murdered after all.'

Eliot shook his head. 'But she saw his face quite damp with blood.'

'Yes,' I said slowly. I frowned. 'So what is your point?'

'That whoever the blood on that cloth had come from, it could not have been from a serious wound to George.' He pointed at the panelling. 'These tiny stains are hardly consistent with the flow of blood that would have been necessary to soak a piece of fabric. The very fact that the marks are still here suggests that no serious wound was inflicted at all.'

'But why?' I asked.

'Because,' said Eliot impatiently, 'the stains were not wiped away. They were overlooked, not just by Lucy but by whoever lives in this flat. Observe the carpet. Lucy was quite right. There are no marks of blood there – or at least, none that can be distinguished. No,' he said, shaking his head and rising to his feet, 'these traces of blood only make the case more intractable. On the one hand, they prove that George could hardly have bled to death. But on the other, they suggest that Lucy was not imagining things when she saw him smothered by a cloth damp with blood. It is all most perplexing.'

He looked about him, then rose to his feet. He crossed to the door on the far side of the room, opened it, and I followed him through into the passageway beyond. Like the front room, this corridor was richly furnished, and the rooms which it led to seemed as luxurious as the rest. I was struck, though, by the absence of a bedroom, and commented on this peculiarity to Eliot.

'Clearly,' he answered, 'this flat is not employed as a place of residence.'

'Then as what?'

Eliot shrugged. 'It must serve its owners as a convenience stop, a place of rest or refuge in the centre of the capital. Where their principal abode lies, we cannot yet be sure.'

'It must be somewhere exceedingly refined.'

'Oh?' Eliot looked at me sharply. 'Why do you think that?'

I stared at him, surprised. 'Well, only because the expense that has been lavished on this flat is so remarkable,' I replied.

'Yes,' he agreed, 'it is more than remarkable, it is baffling, and it is precisely that which leads me to doubt that our suspects live openly anywhere.'

'I don't understand you.'

Eliot gestured impatiently. 'Look around. Yes, Stoker, you are right – money has been spent with great abandon here. But why on this place? Why on a flat above a shop? Even if it *is* Bond Street. Surely they could afford somewhere better than this? It all seems most implausible. Unless ...' He paused and stared about him again, and his face seemed to lighten as though with a sudden flush of hope. 'Well,' he said slowly, 'it is clear that we shall find no dead body here. Perhaps there are other avenues we can search more profitably.' He clapped me on the arm. 'Come, Stoker. I need your help in an experiment.'

We returned to the entrance door which Eliot opened. 'You will notice,' he said, pointing down, 'how very thick the stairway carpet is. I observed it at once. It was that to which I attempted to draw your attention downstairs.'

'I am sorry,' I replied, 'but I still fail to see its significance.'

Eliot looked surprised. 'Why, Stoker, a thick carpet muffles the sound of feet!' he exclaimed. He glanced up at the floor above. 'Now – perhaps you would care to ascend to that balcony there, and then come back downstairs, past this door and then on down the next flight of stairs. But, please! – tread as quietly as you possibly can.'

'Quietly?' I replied. 'I am not a light man on my feet, I am afraid.'

'Exactly,' said Eliot, shutting the door in my face so that I was left alone by the balcony. Seeing his point at last – I am afraid you will think me a little slow! – I did as he had requested. Once I had finished my descent I waited by the front door, but then, when Eliot did not reappear, I climbed back up the stairs. As I did so I walked with my normal tread, and at once the door to the flat was flung open. 'Excellent!' exclaimed Eliot, coming out to join me. 'Now that you are walking like an elephant again, I can hear you perfectly, but during your descent there was not so much as a tiny creak. Most suggestive, I think you will agree.'

He locked the door to the flat after him, then climbed the stairs to the second floor. 'You think that it was the Indian, then, who was the murderer?' I asked, following him.

'We are merely amassing possibilities,' answered Eliot. 'But we have destroyed our Rajah's alibi, for although he was heard *ascending* the stairs, that does not prove that he came in from the street. Yes, I think he could have quite easily hidden himself while Lucy fetched the police, and then retreated back down to the front door as quietly as he could.'

'But what would he have done with the corpse?' I asked.

'That is the mystery,' Eliot replied. He removed his eye-glass from his pocket again, and bent down. He studied the carpet carefully, but after a few minutes he shook his head and stood up again. 'There are no traces of blood. They could have been washed away subsequently, of course, but I think even so we would notice the marks. No,' he said, shaking his head again, 'this narrows down the possibilities.'

'You have a theory, then?' I asked.

'It would certainly seem,' he replied, 'that we are approaching a solution.' He paused suddenly and his nostrils widened, as though struck by the scent of a possible trail. When he looked up at me, I saw that his eyes were gleaming like burnished steel. 'Come, Stoker,' he said, turning and making for the stairs. 'Let us go now and visit the jeweller's shop.'

We did so at once. As my companion pushed open the door, a small, white-haired man came up to him. 'Can I be of assistance, sir?' he asked, rubbing his hands as though soaping them.

Eliot glanced at the shopkeeper with great *hauteur*, then perused the shelves and cabinets. Several seconds passed. 'I believe,' said Eliot at length, drawling slightly, 'that you are Mr Headley, the jeweller to Lady Mowberley.'

'Yes,' replied the man uncertainly. 'I have that honour.'

'Very good.' Eliot turned his gaze upon him. 'Some time ago, I dined with her and Sir George. It was in honour of her birthday. Lady Mowberley was wearing some striking jewels which were purchased, I believe, from this very shop. They had then been presented to his wife as a gift from Sir George.'

Mr Headley frowned and scratched his head. 'If you would care to wait, sir, I will consult my books.'

He began to shuffle towards the counter, but Eliot shook his head. 'No, no,' he said impatiently, 'there is no need to look. You will remember the jewels, I am sure. They were quite distinctive. Earrings and a necklace, from the region of India named Kalikshu-tra.' Eliot pronounced the last word with great emphasis; when he spoke again, there was an edge to his voice. 'You will remember them,' he said slowly. 'I am certain you will.'

The shopkeeper looked uneasily between the two of us. 'They were never my property,' he said at last.

Eliot frowned. 'But they were in your shop window, were they not?' He paused, then slowly nodded his head. 'Yes, I seem to remember Lady Mowberley being quite definite on the matter. She had seen them in your display whilst out walking with Sir George, and he came here subsequently to purchase them. I am certain it was this shop.' He narrowed his eyes. 'It could have been no other. You were after all, were you not, Sir George's valet?'

The old man had started to twist his hands again, clearly agitated. 'It is quite true,' he said in a querulous voice, 'that Sir George and Lady Mowberley saw the jewels in my display. But I repeat, sir – they were not mine to sell. By the time Sir George came back here, they had been returned to their place of provenance.'

Eliot shook his head impatiently. 'Place of provenance? I don't understand.'

'They had been loaned to me.'

'By whom?'

The jeweller swallowed. 'By a man who wished to enter into business with me.'

'So he is the one with the jewels from Kalikshutra?'

'Yes, but if you are interested I have jewellery from other regions of India, and indeed from all around the world . . .'

'No, no,' interrupted Eliot, 'it must be Kalikshutra. If you don't have the jewels, then I must go to the man who does. How am I to get in touch with him?'

Mr Headley frowned. 'Who are you?' he asked with sudden suspicion.

'My name is Dr John Eliot.'

'A friend of Lady Mowberley, you said?'

'And is there any reason why I should not be?' Eliot replied. A look of sudden alertness had blazed up in his eyes, for I could tell this last comment had interested him greatly. But he did not pursue its implications; instead, he leaned forward on the counter and, when he spoke, did so in a tone of perfect affability. 'We are both of us, Mr Stoker and myself, keen collectors of artefacts from the Himalayas. Stoker, please give Mr Headley your card.' Eliot paused as the old man inspected my address; then, without saying a word, he pushed a guinea over the counter and into Mr Headley's hands.

'Now,' said Eliot, when the jeweller had taken the coin, 'we are keen to trace your colleague. Perhaps, first of all, you could tell us what your own relationship is with him – just so that we know how we ought to proceed.'

The old man creased his brow. 'He came to me – oh – about six or seven months ago, it would have been.'

Eliot nodded. 'Good. And what did he propose?'

Again, the old man frowned, and looked suspiciously between us as though still not certain of our purpose with him.

'Please, Mr Headley,' said Eliot. 'What did he propose?'

'He proposed,' replied the old man, 'he proposed ... an agreement.'

'Well, naturally,' said Eliot coldly, 'it would hardly have been a marriage. Come, Mr Headley, you are not being straight with us.'

'All in good time,' muttered the jeweller, blinking up at us defiantly. 'He told me – this colleague of mine – he said he had top-grade jewellery. I didn't believe him at first – you get all kinds of nonsense in my line of trade, as I'm sure you can appreciate – but as it turned out ... well, sir, you've seen some of it yourself hung around Lady Mowberley's throat – beautiful, it was, really beautiful. He had a small shop, he said, down by the docks ...'

'Where, exactly?' Eliot asked.

'Rotherhithe, sir.'

'You have his address?'

Mr Headley nodded, bent down and pulled out a drawer. 'Here, sir,' he said, handing up a card. Eliot took it. '"John Polidori," he read. "Three Coldlair Lane, Rotherhithe."' He looked up at the old man. 'He is Italian, then, this Mr Polidori?'

'If he is,' replied the shopkeeper, 'then he speaks English better than any foreigner that I've ever heard.'

'There was a John Polidori,' I said, 'who was Lord Byron's personal physician for a while. He wrote a short story which we adapted once for the Lyceum.'

Eliot glanced at me. 'You are surely not suggesting he might be the same man? How old would he be now?'

'Oh, no,' I replied, 'Lord Byron's Polidori killed himself, I believe. No, I'm sorry, Eliot, I only mentioned it because of the coincidence.'

'I see. How fascinating you are, Stoker, with your theatrical reminiscences.' Eliot turned back to the old man. 'Now,' he said, 'we have been quite distracted. Where were we? Yes. This Mr Polidori came to you. He had jewellery.'

'Yes.'

'So what did he want with you?'

Mr Headley smiled. 'He had a problem. He had the goods – but that was basically all he had. I mean, who's going to go down to Rotherhithe? Not your real nobs, not your gentlemen with money to spend. If you're going to set up shop in a serious way, well, sir, it's got to be Bond Street.'

Eliot nodded. 'And so that was where you came in?'

'Yes, sir. He'd supply the goods to me, and I'd display them.'

'And the jewels from Kalikshutra – why didn't he leave you to sell those particular items yourself?'

'As I mentioned, sir, he has a shop of his own. That's the address, on that card you've got.'

'Very well,' said Eliot, his eyes starting to gleam again. 'What of it?'

'Sometimes, with certain customers, he'd want them to come and visit him.'

'Why?'

'It was those who he thought had a special interest in jewellery – collectors, if you like. He preferred to deal with them direct.'

'And so you would point them in his way?'

'If you like, sir. It was good business; he always gave me a decent return.'

'And Sir George? He was one of those you pointed down to Rotherhithe, then?'

'Yes, sir. Quite specific about it, Mr Polidori was. "Get me Sir George," he said. "Whatever he comes in and asks for – tell him you haven't got it. Send him down to me."'

'You didn't find this surprising?'

'No, sir, why should I have done?'

'Because Sir George, so far as I am aware, has never been a collector of jewellery in his life. Why would your colleague have been interested in him?'

Mr Headley smiled faintly beneath his moustache. 'He may not collect it for himself,' he said, 'but there's plenty of others he collects it for.' He winked. 'If you get my meaning, sir.'

'Yes,' said Eliot shortly. He did not smile in return. 'Yes, I think I do.'

The old man looked suddenly worried. 'You won't take what I just said the wrong way, I hope, sir,' he stammered.

'Wrong way?'

'Well ...' The jeweller swallowed. 'I do realise, sir, that Lady Mowberley must be worried, and I do feel for her, really I do.'

'Indeed, Headley? And why is that?'

The old man frowned. As he looked up and stared into Eliot's face, he seemed suddenly quite hostile again, and when he spoke his voice was measured and cold. 'I think, sir,' he said slowly, 'that if you need to ask ...'

'Yes?' pressed Eliot impatiently.

'Then I shouldn't tell you.' Mr Headley was unblinking, his face set like a stone. 'Not if you don't know already, sir. I am sorry' – he paused, then spoke the word with offensive dullness – 'sir.'

Eliot raised a hand to reach into his pocket.

'Don't you go trying with your bribes,' the old man said. 'You won't get me that way again.'

Eliot slowly lowered his hand again. 'Very well,' he said. His face, I was surprised to observe, seemed suddenly good-humoured and almost relieved. 'At least tell me this, then,' he asked.

The jeweller stared at him, but didn't reply.

'You have seen Sir George recently? Within the past week or two?'

Still the old man made no reply.

'I must be honest with you,' said Eliot. 'I am indeed working for Lady Mowberley. I am sorry that I felt it necessary to deceive you. But she wishes only to know if Sir George is still alive – nothing more. She is a wife, Mr Headley – you are married yourself, I know. So please' – he stared straight into the old man's eyes – 'I appeal to you. Have you seen Sir George during the past two weeks? Please, Mr Headley.' He paused. 'Lady Mowberley is very concerned.'

The jeweller looked away. He stared out at the street, then he turned back to face Eliot.

'When?' Eliot asked.

Still Mr Headley did not blink.

'Out on the street? You saw him there?'

The old man shrugged.

'Good.' Eliot paused. 'When?'

The jeweller sighed. 'Two days ago,' he said at last.

'Thank you, Mr Headley.' Eliot paused, then smiled. 'You must be very fond of Sir George,' he observed.

'Always have been,' the old man replied gruffly. 'Ever since he was a babe.'

Eliot nodded. 'Yes,' he said, 'it is a relief to witness.'

'A relief, sir?'

'Yes, Mr Headley, a relief.' He turned to me, and his face did indeed seem mobile with precisely that emotion. 'Come, Stoker. We have completed our business here.' He glanced down at the card which he still held in his hand. 'I shall call on Mr Polidori in due course. But for now' – he raised his hat – 'good morning to you, Mr Headley. You have been of great assistance. Thank you for your time.' And with that, he turned and left the shop.

I followed him out into the street. 'Well, Eliot,' I asked impatiently, 'what did you make of him?'

'That he was honest and loyal.'

'Yes, loyal to Sir George, certainly. But were you expecting him not to be?'

'I wasn't sure.'

'Why, what did you suspect?'

Eliot paused in his walk and turned back to gesture at the building we had just left. 'Remember,' he said, 'that the Headleys not only occupy the shop but also live on the second floor. Anything out of the ordinary that happens in that building is bound, in the due course of time, to come to their attention. That much was clear even from Lucy's narrative.' He turned and began to walk again, speaking as he did so in a low urgent voice. 'Now,' he said, 'suppose that Headley had been suborned. Suppose that he had been part of a conspiracy against Sir George. How much blacker would our case seem then! For it is evident, I think, that whatever it was that Lucy witnessed in that flat, it was not some sudden catastrophe but rather an episode in a sequence of events, stretching back probably for several months. Headley himself must have been aware that *something* was going on – it staggers credibility to think that he was not.'

'But why then would he not reveal it to us?'

'Because, as we have just agreed, he believes he is being loyal to Sir George himself – which in turn implies that he has not thought Sir George to be in any danger during this time.'

'Yes, of course.' I remembered what the old man had been hinting at. 'He seemed to be saying that Sir George was having an affair.'

Eliot nodded. 'I cannot say I was surprised by his suggestion. When Lady Mowberley first came to me, the suspicion struck me immediately. George was always ill-disciplined with the fairer sex. Naturally, I have not imparted this theory to Lady Mowberley herself.'

'So what are you saying, Eliot, that you still think it possible?'

'Oh, more than possible, I would think it certain he has been having a romance of some kind.'

'So why then was he killed?'

'I do not believe that he was killed.'

'But . . .' I stared at him in astonishment. 'Lucy said – she saw him being . . .'

'No, no,' said Eliot, shaking his head as he interrupted me, 'it is quite impossible. You saw the carpets with your own eyes. No blood-letting took place in that room, no slicing of anyone's throat. And yet we have a mystery. George was seen there by Lucy from the street, but when she entered the room he was gone. Where to? What had happened to him?'

'I confess, I am baffled.'

'Surely not, a man of your keen wit?'

I thought. 'I have it!' I cried. 'Sir George was throttled, and his corpse hidden away in the Headleys' flat!'

'Very good,' replied Eliot, a thin smile on his lips, 'but unlikely. We have just agreed on Headley's loyalty to his old master. He would be unenthusiastic, I suggest, about harbouring anyone who had Sir George's corpse in tow.'

'You are right, of course.' I shrugged and shook my head.

'Come, Stoker, think! Two solutions present themselves immediately.'

'They do?'

'Yes, as clearly as day.' Eliot glanced at me, and his glittering eyes were those of an expert with a challenge worthy of his skills. 'The first, I regret to say, is by some way the least likely of the two, but it is possible, I would conjecture, that the Rajah is Sir George himself. The idea struck me during Lucy's narrative. Yes, yes,' he said hurriedly, seeing me open my mouth to object, 'I have already agreed it is improbable. Lucy saw the Rajah and spoke to him. She is remarkably observant, and knows Sir George well; she would not be a person easily deceived. Also – it leaves unexplained what she saw at the window of the flat. However, we are agreed that Sir George has been conducting an affair; if we are correct, he would then have the motive for disguising himself. Our theory would also explain the Rajah's presence at the theatre last night – he had come to see his ward's first night. So I am unwilling to discount the idea altogether. I would prefer first to observe the Rajah for myself.'

I shook my head. 'I am not convinced, Eliot. The difficulties of the theory seem to me far to outweigh the advantages.'

'Yes,' he replied, 'I agree with you. But we must wait. Who knows what time and careful observation may yet unearth for us?'

'You mentioned a second possibility.'

'Yes.'

'What would that be?'

'Ah,' said Eliot, his gaunt face seeming visibly to darken before my eyes, 'we move now into darker territory.'

'Are you able to tell me?' I asked, for I had detected a hint of reserve in his voice.

'Not every detail,' he replied, 'for there are aspects of this affair which touch on great matters of state, and if they do indeed lie behind Sir George's disappearance – as I fear they may – then we are up against a dangerous and terrible conspiracy. That is why I cling to the hope that the Rajah may yet prove to be Sir George; the alternative, that the Rajah of Kalikshutra is indeed who he claims to be, is too grim to contemplate.'

'But why?' I asked, both appalled and intrigued. 'What is this plot which you seem to suspect?'

'You will remember,' he answered, 'that my interest in this case was first attracted not by Lucy, but by Lady Mowberley. She has suggested to me – and this is what I find so disturbing – that Sir George's disappearance is linked to Arthur Ruthven's death.'

'Good Lord,' I exclaimed. 'Linked, Eliot? How?'

'By a very peculiar circumstance. Both men were insulted by anonymous messages. The first was almost comical. Arthur, who I believe held more rare coins than any man in London, was told that his collection had been surpassed and rendered worthless. The second message, which came some time after the first, was more obviously offensive. Lady Mowberley, who has loved her husband from a tender age, was informed that George was an adulterer.'

'That much at least, then, was true.'

'The truth of the insult is irrelevant. What matters is the point of correspondence between the two messages.'

'They seem quite different to me.'

'On the contrary,' replied Eliot, 'they are very similar. Do you not see, Stoker? They both challenge their target to prove himself.'

'How do you mean?'

'Arthur Ruthven's case is clear enough, I take it? Good. Then let us look at George's. Stoker – you are a married man. Imagine the following scenario. Your wife is told that you are unfaithful to her. What would you do?'

'I would try to persuade her that I was still true to her.'

'Of course you would – you would seek to prove yourself. But consider further – it is your wife's birthday in only a few days' time. What else might you do?'

'Buy her something, a wonderful gift?'

'A scintillating reply! Exactly so!'

'Jewels. Of course. He bought her the jewels.'

'As he does all his women. You remember that Headley told us so. They clearly knew and worked on that.'

'They?'

'Yes,' he answered, 'they.' He paused, and his thin face grew dark and intense with thought. 'The forces behind this conspiracy,' he murmured, 'how cunning they have been! How deeply laid their plots!'

'You think, then, that this Polidori . . .'

'Oh, he is clearly a scoundrel.'

'Why?'

'All this rigmarole about shops in Rotherhithe, and fabulous jewellery! If he owns such priceless works, and is not dishonest, then why did he not just buy up Bond Street himself? Why this preposterous skein of arrangements? No, no, it is patent villainy! Clearly his aim was to lure George down to Rotherhithe, to a quite specific place, namely' – he glanced down at the card – 'Three, Coldlair Lane. But why?' His frown deepened. 'Why, Stoker, why?'

'You had a theory, you said?'

He glanced at me; then, as though suddenly decided on something, he took me by the arm. We had reached the environs of Covent Garden by now; I was led down a narrow alley, away from the bustle of the vegetable stalls, where the yellow mists that were rising from the Thames served further to muffle our voices and forms. 'You will remember,' Eliot said, in an even lower voice than before, 'how the jewellery lent by Polidori came from a region of India?'

'Yes,' I answered, 'from Kalikshutra.'

'Very well, then,' nodded Eliot, 'here are some interesting facts. Sir George Mowberley is the minister responsible for the ordering of our Indian frontier. Arthur Ruthven, before his disappearance and death, was the senior diplomatist handling the bill. Kalikshutra, I know from personal experience – for I was until recently resident there – is the most troublesome kingdom on the whole frontier. You yourself, Stoker, will recollect how poor Edward Westcote's mother was murdered there. You will agree, I am certain, that the coincidences seem rather to be mounting up?'

'You believe there is an attempt to suborn the process of the bill?'

'Let us say, it seems possible.'

'But Arthur Ruthven – he was found murdered . . .'

'Yes – his body drained white.'

'Then surely – I am sorry to have to say this – shouldn't we expect Sir George to have been murdered as well?'

'Not necessarily. Not if he proved more amenable.'

'Amenable?'

Eliot sighed. For a long time, he stared into the swirlings of the fog. 'I mentioned,' he said at last, 'that I was in Kalikshutra myself.' He closed his eyes and his gaunt face seemed suddenly very tired. 'There is a terrible disease there,' he murmured. 'Amongst other symptoms, it attacks the mind . . .'

'Good Lord, what are you saying?' I exclaimed.

Eliot shrugged. 'I wonder – I wonder . . .' His voice trailed away, as though dampened by the taste of yellow fog in his throat. 'Is it not possible,' he asked eventually,' that Sir George has somehow been enslaved by this disease? After all, it might explain what Lucy witnessed from the street. George was not being killed; rather, when the cloth was placed over his face it was further to reduce his already weakened self-control. It would then have been an easy matter for the Rajah to have led his victim up the stairs, where the two of them could have waited motionless.'

'Because Sir George had been placed under the Rajah's power?'

'Exactly. Reduced to the state of a zombie, if you like.'

I considered this possibility. 'Yes,' I said, nodding slowly, 'yes, that would almost fit the facts.'

Eliot frowned. 'Almost?'

'The cloth – the one that was placed over Sir George's face – you are suggesting that it might have been chloroform, or something of that kind?'

Eliot stared at me. 'Yes,' he said shortly. 'Something of that kind.'

'But on the wainscot – those spots that you found – you said they were definitely spots of blood.'

'Yes.' Eliot frowned again and turned away. He was angry, I could tell, that on this one small point, at least, my thinking had proved to be ahead of his own. 'I did acknowledge,' he reminded me, with a slight sharpness in his voice, 'that our case remains incomplete.' He began to walk towards the bustle and din of the Strand and I followed him, having almost to run before I joined him again, so lengthy were his strides. He glanced up the Aldwych at Wellington Street. 'Why, Stoker,' he exclaimed, 'here we are, returned to the Lyceum. I have already kept you too long from your work.'

Clearly, I had annoyed him more than I had realised. 'What will you do now?' I asked.

'As you have only just pointed out yourself, there is still much to be investigated.'

'I cannot be of any more assistance to you?'

'Not at present.'

I thought I was being dismissed and so, bidding him farewell, I turned and began to walk on to the Lyceum. But he called after me.

'Stoker!'

I looked round.

'Will Lucy be in the theatre this afternoon?' he asked.

'She should be,' I replied. 'Why, what do you need from her?'

'The pendant from her neck.'

I stared at him in surprise. 'Her pendant? Why?'

'You did not observe it closely, then?' He chuckled, and rubbed his hands. 'Well, it may just prove to be a fancy of mine. We shall see.'

147

He raised his hat. 'Good day to you, Mr Stoker.'

'I am keen to remain of assistance,' I called out after him.

'I am sure you are,' he replied. But he did not look round, and was soon lost in the swirl of the traffic and the fog. I began to push my own way through the crowds. Beyond them, the Lyceum was waiting for me.

I threw myself at once into the theatre's affairs and was soon fully preoccupied, even to the exclusion of that sea of wonders across which I had been sailing only a few hours before. Mr Irving, as was so often his wont after a triumphant first night, was low and irritable; he suffered from that reduction of spirits which must afflict any great artist after an effusion of his powers, and I did not find him easy company. Instead he haunted me like a ghost and, black-clad as he was, I came to dread his tall lean figure almost as a harbinger of woe – or at the very least, of a stream of orders and complaints! I was soon feeling quite exhausted. I had therefore almost forgotten about Eliot when he surprised me, late in the afternoon, as I was in the process of inspecting the private stalls.

I was glad to see him, especially since there seemed an expression of gratification on his face.

'You have had some success?' I inquired.

'I believe so,' he replied. 'I have been at work this afternoon in my laboratory.'

'Indeed?'

Eliot nodded. 'I analysed traces from two bottles of medicine that Lady Mowberley has been using. One, which she is taking now, is perfectly harmless. The other, however, which she had finished and thrown away, had been heavily doctored with opiates.'

'She was being drugged, you mean?'

'There can be no doubt at all. The fact that she had finished the medicine and was drinking from a new bottle explains, evidently, why she woke to her intruders. We must assume, I think, that they had been present in her house on other nights as well.'

'But to what purpose?'

'That, I am afraid, I cannot speculate on.'

'It relates to matters of state, then, you think?'

'Stoker, you are a discreet man. I must request you not to press me any further on this matter.'

'I apologise,' I replied. 'My curiosity, I am afraid, is only a measure of how intrigued I have become by this case.'

Eliot smiled. 'So I may take it, then, that you are keen to assist me again?'

'If I can be of any use.'

'You are free tonight?'

'After the performance.'

'Excellent. You might order us a cab, and have it wait for us in a side street by the theatre exit.'

'Why,' I asked him, 'what do you expect?'

Eliot gestured with his hand as though to wave the question away, and as he did so I caught the glint of something silver in his palm.

'You have seen Lucy, then?' I asked. 'I assume that is her pendant you have with you there.'

Eliot held out his hand and opened his palm. 'Look at it closely,' he said.

Studying it, I saw what I had failed to before – that it was a coin, of wonderful craftsmanship and seemingly very old. 'Where is it from?' I asked.

Eliot looked up at me. 'From the clammy hand of Arthur Ruthven's corpse,' he replied.

'You don't mean to say ...'

'Yes. He was holding it when they fished out his body from the Thames.'

'But why? You think it has some significance?'

'That,' said Eliot, rising to his feet, 'is what I hope to find out now. No, no, Stoker, stay where you are. I shall see you tonight. And please – do not forget to order the cab.' Then, before I could reply, he had slipped through the curtains at the back of the seats and vanished again. I rose to follow him, but as I left the stalls I almost collided with Henry Irving, in a fury over some damaged scenery, and I had to go at once and sort the wretched business out. I contented myself afterwards with ordering the cab; otherwise, of course, I could only wait.

Time, though, slipped by fast. It was soon evening, and the actors were putting on their costumes and paint. I myself donned my tails and stood, as was my custom, at the head of the stairs by the Private Entrance, ready to greet our audience. There was a steady stream of the brightest stars in the firmament of London Society – and as I welcomed them, so I felt the thrill which has never faded: that of being manager of the Lyceum Theatre and the great actor whose domain it is. And yet I felt distracted; all the time, even as I chatted and smiled with my guests, I was wondering what exploits the night would hold for me, what conspiracy of dark secrets we might uncover. Increasingly, it was the cosy world of the theatre which began to seem the stranger and more remote, so that the crowds of bejewelled women and shirt-fronted men appeared mere shadows to me, spectre-like and insubstantial when set against the vividness of my imaginings. I fancied that I saw, all the time, the strange woman whom Lucy had described, with her extraordinary beauty and mystery-filled eyes; I fancied that I saw the Rajah, deadly and cruel. And then suddenly – borne on the stream of people up the stairs – I did see him! The Rajah – I was certain it was him! He wore evening dress and a long flowing cloak, but he was distinguished by the turban which was wound about his head, for its material was of a marvellous richness and studded, just above the brow, with a jewel of a size I had never seen before. As he walked, I observed how people frowned or blanched and made way for him.

Without thinking, I approached him to greet him in my capacity as the evening's host, yet as I stared into his face I found that my words seemed to fade and die in my mouth. He filled me – I cannot explain how – with the most remarkable sense of revulsion and distaste. His mouth was exceedingly full and moist, but twisted too, so that the corners seemed to rise in a lascivious sneer. His eyes were perfectly dark. His features were hard, like stone, yet there was a softness about them too which seemed to hint at intemperance and lechery. His complexion was one of extraordinary pallor. In short, I never met a man I loathed so immediately; it was all I could do not to raise my fist and offer him a blow. The Rajah seemed to sense my hatred, for he smiled at me, baring his teeth – which were pearly-white and peculiarly sharp – so that the cruelty in his expression only seemed enhanced. Despite myself I took a step backwards; the Rajah smiled again as though with bitter mockery and then, with a swirl of his cloak, he was gone. I followed him, to mark where he sat: it was in the same box he had taken before. Once I had noted this, I returned to my office, much perplexed. I wondered what Eliot would make of it.

As the performance began to draw to its conclusion, I hurried outside to inspect our cab. It was stationed where I had instructed it to wait, in a dark alley where it could not easily be made out. I tipped the driver and ordered him to be ready to leave at any time; then I turned again and walked back down the street. Just as I was about to re-enter the Lyceum, I felt a hand on my arm and I spun round. It was Eliot.

'Thank God,' I exclaimed. 'The Rajah – he is here!'

'Excellent.' Eliot rubbed his hands together. 'I rather thought he might be. Come, let us go inside. The wind is rather chill for the time of year.'

I led him back to the foyer, from where we would observe anyone leaving the theatre. 'I have had a most interesting time,' Eliot commented as we walked inside. 'Our case is very near completion now.'

'Indeed?' I asked. 'Your business with the coin was satisfactory, then?'

'It was,' he replied, 'exceedingly so.' He felt in his pocket and, withdrawing the coin, held it to the light. 'You will observe the lettering, Stoker. It is in Greek.'

He handed the coin to me and I slowly spelled the letters out, for they were very worn. 'Kirkeion.' I looked up. 'A town? I have never heard of it,' I confessed.

'Nor should you have done, for its fame has not survived into modern times. The coin, however, is undoubtedly authentic. Its value is literally incalculable.'

'Who told you this?'

'The expert I consulted at Spink, which – as I am sure you will know, Stoker – is the pre-eminent valuing house for coins in London. As such, Arthur Ruthven was a well-known figure there. All the dealers were familiar with him. I spoke to the one who had dealt with him last.'

'And what did this dealer report?'

'He recollected the interview very well. Arthur, it seems, had appeared agitated in the extreme. He kept pressing the dealer for any rumours he might have heard, hints of rare coins in circulation. The dealer could think of nothing, but when Arthur remained insistent he recalled that a couple of strange coins had been brought in – silver, very ancient, from a completely unknown town.'

'Goodness!' I looked down at the coin in my hand. 'The same as this?'

'In every point. The dealer was most excited when I showed him the coin you are holding now. He brought out the two original coins, which had remained unsold since the day when Arthur inspected them – the price being, as I think I just mentioned, astronomical. When I saw them, it was clear at once that the dealer was perfectly correct – they were indeed from the very same source.'

'And what was that source, do you think?'

'The immediate source, you mean?' Eliot smiled faintly. 'Can you not guess?' Again he felt in his pocket, and this time drew out a notebook. 'A card had been attached to the case in which the two silver coins were kept. Any further inquiries were to be addressed to the name on that card. The dealer kindly wrote it down for me.' Eliot flipped open the notebook. 'Here it is.'

'"John Polidori"', I read out. '"Three Coldlair Lane." But my goodness, Eliot, this is extraordinary.'

'On the contrary,' replied Eliot, 'it is not extraordinary at all. It merely confirms me in my initial suspicion that both Arthur and

George were deliberately lured to Rotherhithe.'

'Then we must head there at once!' I exclaimed. 'Eliot, what are we waiting for?'

He clapped me on my arm. 'I am glad you are with me, Stoker,' he replied, 'but first, we must show just a little patience. This Polidori, whoever he may be, is not the only fish we have to catch. You say the Rajah is here, in the Lyceum? Very good, then let us wait for him.' And indeed, at this very moment a burst of applause began to thunder from the auditorium. 'The play is finished?' he asked.

I glanced at my watch. 'So it would seem,' I replied.

'Then quick,' he said urgently, 'we have not a moment to lose.' We hurried back out into the street, and ran through the traffic to the dark alleyway where our cab was waiting hidden. 'Forwards,' whispered Eliot to the driver, 'so that we can watch the crowds as they leave the Private Entrance. But be sure to remain in the shadows.' The driver did as he had been instructed, and we saw the first wave of theatregoers as they flooded out into the street.

'Will you be missed tonight?' Eliot asked me.

'Doubtless,' I replied.

'Mr Irving was content to release you, though?'

'He was not content,' I answered with a smile, 'but Mr Irving must sometimes be withstood. Otherwise, he would drain my whole life away.'

Eliot smiled at this and turned to make some reply, but at that moment he froze, then seized my arm. 'There,' he whispered, pointing and I stared where he gestured. I saw the Rajah descending the steps, and again I observed how the crowds made way for him, so that he seemed like Moses parting the sea. Eliot leaned forward. 'He seems to have George's build,' he murmured, 'but his face ...' His voice trailed away, and I detected a trace of that revulsion which I had experienced myself.

'You felt it,' I asked him, 'a strange disgust?'

Eliot glanced at me. I had never seen his brow so dark. But he made no reply, and instead leaned forward to whisper into the cabman's ear, 'Follow him.' The hansom creaked forward. I saw that the Rajah too had climbed into a cab. This startled me, for I had thought that he was bound to possess a carriage of his own, such had been the wealth on display in his flat. Eliot, however, seemed quite unsurprised and merely asked our driver to keep the hansom always in sight. 'And if you stay hidden all the time,' he added, 'then there's a guinea for you on top of the fare.' Our driver touched his cap. We watched the hansom as it clattered past. For almost a minute, we stayed where we were. Then the driver flicked his whip and we too began to rattle down the street.

Once away from the bedlam of crowds and carriages, we made good speed. As we approached the turning to London Bridge, Eliot began to lean forward in his seat, his face alert and his body tense. But the hansom ahead of us did not turn, and instead continued to rattle onwards along the river's north bank. Eliot slumped back despondently into his seat. 'It seems my calculations are a little awry,' he said. 'We are undone, my good Stoker. I had been certain that our Rajah would be heading for Rotherhithe and the mysterious Polidori. But now, see! – we have passed the final bridge across the Thames, and still we have not turned south. I am a bungler, a hopeless bungler.'

'Do you wish to halt the chase?' I asked.

Eliot shrugged irritably and waved his hand, then peered out through the mists at the object of our pursuit. The cab was still only a dim silhouette, but it was slowing now, for by this time we had passed beyond the City into the East End and the road was starting to grow uneven beneath the wheels. The streets were narrowing too, and the mist hung in white wreaths above the slimy paving stones, so that any light – be it from a street lamp or from a public bar – drizzled and died, and cast no illumination. Soon, indeed, there were no lights at all, only boarded-up windows and tenement entrances stifled by rubbish, and if we saw faces then they seemed like those of the damned in hell, for they would stare pale-faced and dead-eyed at us, and sometimes they would shriek as though with hatred, or laugh horribly. I was starting to grow uneasy now but Eliot, whose eyes were always fixed on the hansom cab ahead, seemed rather to be relaxing his disappointment and returning to his former state of eagerness. 'Stay back,' he whispered urgently to our driver, for the cab ahead of us was slowing down. It turned by the entrance of a dark narrow street and disappeared from our view.

Slowly, we approached the entrance ourselves. Eliot peered out from the cab. The street ahead of us was empty. Eliot waved our driver on. We began to bump along the pitted, greasy stones. There were a few lights now in the windows above us, red and faint, and silhouettes would occasionally pass behind the blinds. Ahead were shadows slumped against the wall. As we passed, some would rise, but most stayed where they were and scarcely seemed human in their misery at all. Eliot glanced back at them and there was a terrible anger, I noticed, on his face. But then he looked round again and I too, straining my eyes, saw what seemed to be a forest of trees ahead of us, and our cab began to shudder to a halt. 'The shadows again,' Eliot ordered in a whisper, for by now we had left the street and the closeness of the buildings behind. Instead, we were stationed on a quayfront which stretched away to our left and was piled with sacks and merchandise. Ahead of us, black masts rose like gallows against a full, yellow moon. Beyond the ships, silent and dark, I could make out the Thames as it flowed towards the sea.

'Over there,' whispered Eliot, pointing.

I looked. The Rajah had left his hansom and was walking away from us, along the edge of the quayside buildings. He turned up a narrow alleyway and was lost to our sight; at once Eliot climbed from the cab and I followed him. We paid the driver and then began to walk, taking care not to be seen, along the route we had just watched the Rajah take. By the turning to the alley, Eliot beckoned me to lower my head; we crept forward and stationed ourselves behind a stash of crates, from where our view up the street was relatively unobscured. We could just make out the Rajah, almost indistinguishable in his black cloak from the muddy paving stones. He was talking to a woman, leaning over her, then suddenly taking her in his arms.

At once, Eliot tensed. 'Look!' he whispered. I stared up the street. The Rajah, who still had the woman tight in his arms, had begun to kiss her across her neck.

'Do we really need to watch this?' I whispered. 'I see nothing that betokens any danger here.'

But Eliot, to my astonishment, seemed utterly absorbed, and his face in the moonlight looked frozen and grim. I couldn't fathom what it was he feared might happen. Certainly, I had little doubt on the matter myself. The Rajah's kisses were longer now, and he was slowly opening the woman's blouse. He held her against the wall; he lifted her up; he rubbed his cheeks across her naked breasts. Eliot reached out, as though to alert me to some anticipated horror; but I had seen quite enough now, and I looked away. Suddenly there was a gasp and a moan; and then, to my surprise, I heard Eliot chuckle quietly in my ear. I looked round again. The Rajah and his whore were engaged in the act of copulation, and I could see no cause for merriment in such a sordid scene. Eliot, however, seemed perfectly delighted. 'Thank God,' he told me. 'I had really feared we might have seen something worse.' He glanced back at the alleyway, and chuckled again. 'I think now,' he whispered, 'that we may very well need a boat. See if you cannot hire one. Then wait in it for me.'

I opened my mouth to demand an explanation, but Eliot waved me away, returning as he did so to his observation of the Rajah and the whore. I left him as stealthily as I could, but also, I admit, with some considerable disquietude. My faith in Eliot's powers, however, remained very great, and I did as he had instructed me, finding an old riverman with a boat for hire, albeit at a highly extortionate rate. I then lay concealed for upwards of half an hour, crouched by the steps that led down to the boat, waiting for Eliot to reappear. A soft drizzle began to fall. The moon was blotted out by wisps of black cloud.

Suddenly, I saw Eliot searching for me. I leaped to my feet and waved to him; he saw me and changed his course, running along the quayfront until he had reached the steps. 'Quick,' he said, joining me in the boat, 'they have started further up, but they have oars like us, so we should catch them.'

'Them?' I asked, as we began to pull out between two giant ships towards the open river beyond.

'Yes,' nodded Eliot, 'the boat is piloted by one of the ugliest brutes you have ever seen. I am afraid he will give us quite a race for our money. He looked very strong.'

'I was once accounted,' I told him, 'a very strong rower myself.'

'Excellent, Stoker!' he exclaimed. 'Then take your place. If you do not object too much, I shall conserve my energies for the case in hand.' And so saying, he scrambled forward to the very prow of the boat. From there he searched the waters with his piercing gaze, for we were now pulling away from the docks and out into the flow of the great river itself. 'There!' Eliot exclaimed suddenly, and pointed. I saw a tiny boat, not too far ahead of us, journeying against the current towards the river's far bank. 'They are heading for Rotherhithe,' said Eliot, with a huntsman's glee. 'I was certain they would!' He glanced round at us, his thin, eager face animated by a desperate energy. 'Faster!' he encouraged. 'Faster! We must cut them off before they reach the shore.'

It looked like being a close-run thing, for our quarry was still a long way ahead of us. But we were gaining on the boat, and when a tug loomed suddenly out from the waters ahead of us and illumined the darkness with the beam of its lantern, I was able to distinguish the forms of the men we were pursuing with some clarity. The Rajah was sitting with his back to us, but once or twice he would glance round, and I saw how the dreadful cruelty that I had noticed before now seemed quite vanished from his face, for his expression appeared one of apprehension and almost fear. His fellow in the boat, however, who was facing us, seemed quite without emotion of any kind. As Eliot had said, he was a creature of remarkable strength and ugliness. His face was exceedingly pale, so that even in the shadows cast by the far shore it seemed to gleam as though lit by some inner light; his eyes, however, were so dead and expressionless that they gave the sockets the appearance of being without eyeballs at all. He was, in short, a ghastly sight, and on the darkness of the waters he seemed like the ferryman of the dead. This then was our quarry as we battled against the river's greasy flow, with ahead of us the lurid glow of London, red even against the falling rain, while on either side, brooding down upon us, stretched nothing but darkness and a silent gloom. No one in the whole great city was aware of us; yet we battled on the river that flowed through its heart, and a stranger chase it can never have seen.

By now, we were drawing very close. 'They seem to be heading for that wharf,' cried Eliot, 'but I think we have them! They will not reach it!' He had to shout, for a merchant-vessel was ascending the Limehouse Reach behind us and the noise of its engines was growing deafening. I glanced round; the vessel towered above us, and already the waves from its passage were making our own boat hard to handle. I struggled with my oar as we bobbed and fell; and then suddenly I saw Eliot mouth something, and he leaped forward and threw us both down. At the same moment, I heard the whistle of something as it passed over my shoulder; I looked up, and saw that the oarsman in the far boat had risen to his feet and held a gun in his hands. He aimed again; the Rajah seemed to be shouting, and then he tried to seize the oarsman's arm, but the creature shrugged him away and pointed the revolver towards Eliot's head. But at the moment when he fired their boat was hit by a wave, and the shot was bad. Our riverman yelled something in my ear, but I couldn't hear it, for the merchant-vessel was almost on us now and the noise from its engines was terrible. The riverman swore loudly and pushed past me. He reached for something from beneath the tarpaulins, and I saw that he held an old revolver in his hand. He steadied his arm and aimed at the creature, who had by now shrugged himself free; then I heard him fire. At that very moment, however, our boat was buffeted by a great surge of wash; we were all knocked forward, and in the confusion I failed to witness the effect of the shot.

When I looked up, however, it was to see the creature sprawled over the prow of the boat, an arm trailing in the water and red blood flowing in a stream from his head. The riverman grinned toothlessly. 'I was in the South Seas,' he yelled into my ear. 'Pirates. You learned to shoot on the waves out there.' The wash that had hit our boat now smashed into theirs; the creature was knocked forward, and he slid into the murky darkness of the waters, where he bobbed face-down like jetsam on the waves. At the same time, the Rajah had scrambled to his feet and was staring appalled at the floating corpse. The riverman had aimed the revolver again.

'No,' screamed Eliot, pulling down his arm, but the riverman had already fired, and we saw the Rajah shriek as he clutched at air, then fell into the waves. A fresh surge of wash caught his body, so that it was almost carried to the steps by the wharf – while our own boat, now that the merchant-vessel had passed us, was starting to drift backwards again in the river's current. 'Look,' said Eliot.

I stared at the wharf, and saw what seemed to be a bundle of rags washed on to the bottom of the steps. Then it began to move, and I realised that it was a human form. Slowly it rose to its feet, and turned round to look at us: it was the Rajah. Eliot frowned and his knuckles, as he gripped the side of the boat, were exceedingly white. The Rajah turned his back on us and began to climb the steps. When he reached the top, he did not glance round once. Instead, he slipped into the shadows and was swallowed by the dark.

Eliot's aquiline features were frozen and grim. He made no comment, however, until we had reached the foot of the wharf ourselves, and he had stepped from the boat and helped me out in turn. He crouched down by the edge of the steps. 'We owe you a debt of gratitude,' he said to the riverman.

'Two guineas should about cover it,' the man replied.

Eliot nodded. He felt in his pocket, then taking out the coins he tossed them into the riverman's palm. 'The corpse must be found, of course,' he murmured.

The man grinned. 'It will be,' he said. He cackled. 'And then it will never be found again.'

'See to it.' Eliot turned back to me. 'Come, Stoker, we still have pressing business of our own.' He began to climb the steps. I glanced round at the riverman again. I watched him drift off, then followed Eliot to the top of the steps.

'What now?' I asked him.

Eliot, who had been staring at the streets which led from the wharf, glanced round at me. 'What now?' He smiled. 'Why, Stoker, we approach the solution to this mystery.'

'But we have lost him.'

'Who?'

'Goodness, Eliot, who do you think? The Rajah!'

'Ah, yes, of course.' He smiled again. 'Very well, then, let us go and track him down.'

'You know where to find him?'

Eliot pointed at a mean-looking street just ahead of us. He walked towards the entrance and gestured up at a sign that had been fixed on a wall. I read it: '"Coldlair Lane." Good Lord!' I turned back to Eliot. 'So your suspicions were correct.'

He nodded. 'So it would seem. And yet I fear, Stoker, that I have been led badly astray on this case. There is a dimension to it that I still cannot understand.'

'Only one dimension?'

He looked at me in surprise. 'Why, yes. The outline of the case is surely clear by now?'

'Not to me,' I replied.

'Then let us make it so.' He began to stride through the filth of Coldlair Lane. 'We have a call to pay on Mr Polidori.' I joined him as we walked the length of the street. It was filled with rubbish, but seemed otherwise quite abandoned by human life, for the windows had been boarded up and there were chains and locks on most of the doors. 'Ah,' murmured Eliot, stopping at length, 'here we are.' He rapped on a door which had a number '3' scrawled on it in thick white chalk. Eliot waited, then stepped back into the centre of the road; I joined him there. We were facing a shop front; a sign fixed above the window read 'J. Polidori, Curiosities'. The window itself seemed full of nothing but junk; it was dark and dingy, and certainly quite without any jewellery. Eliot pointed to the window of the floor above. 'Can you not see,' he asked, 'the faintest flickering from beyond the blinds?' I stared, but could make nothing out; the rooms seemed to be in darkness. 'There!' cried Eliot again, and this time I did catch something, an orange glow as though from a spark. Eliot marched across to the door and began to hammer on it. 'Please!' he shouted. 'Let us in!'

He turned to me. 'There is a subtle and horrible crime afoot. When the door is opened to us, we must act with great coolness. We may then, I am confident, baffle our opponents' plot.' He turned to look back through the window, then glanced round at me. 'Here he comes,' he whispered. Now I too could hear footsteps from inside the shop. They stopped; a bolt was slid open, and then the front door creaked ajar.

'Yes?'

It was the stench I noticed immediately, the burning tang of acid. I remembered what Lucy had told us of the servant's breath.

'Mr Polidori.' Eliot spoke now with perfect politeness. 'I was given your address by a friend. I gather we may share common' – he paused – 'interests.'

The door remained ajar. 'Interests?' a soft voice hissed at length.

Eliot glanced up at the window above the shop. 'We have come a long way, my friend and myself.'

He had gestured at me while saying this. I tried not to look too baffled, but his approach I confess had caught me rather off guard, for I had not the faintest idea what 'interests' he had meant. Polidori, however, seemed to understand, for after a short pause he opened the door. 'You had better come in, then,' he muttered. He waved us through, and we stepped into the shop.

Polidori bolted the door, then turned round to face us. He was very pallid and his neck lolled strangely, but he was otherwise rather handsome – of an age, I would estimate, not over twenty-five. There was, however, something peculiarly unsettling about him which I cannot explain, unless it was the strange restlessness evident in his expression and stare. Locked in the small shop with him, I felt myself instinctively tense and prepare for the worst.

'Upstairs?' asked Eliot.

Polidori bowed his head. 'After you,' he said in a silky tone.

He gestured towards a rickety staircase and we began to ascend it. I had to bow my head, so small was the stairway, and as I climbed I felt a great sense of horror and revulsion rising up in me – quite disproportionate to my circumstances, for I am not an easily frightened man. The cause, however, may well have been more physiological than anything else, for mingled with the stench on the shopkeeper's breath I began to smell a second odour, heavy and sweet, borne on brown smoke from the room above. As I ascended I became aware of strange imaginings, crawling like insects on the margins of my brain; I tried to brush them aside but felt, even as I did so, a terrible temptation to yield to them, for they seemed to promise strange delights and great wisdom, and a refuge from my fear. I remembered Eliot's warning, however, and struggled to remain as alert as I could.

At the top of the stairs was a drape of purple silk. Eliot brushed it aside, and I followed him into the room beyond. It was filled with the brown smoke I had smelled on the stairs, and it took me some seconds to see beyond the haze. The walls, I could dimly make out, were covered with threadbare tapestries, and in the far corner of the room was a metal brazier; occasionally it would spark and wink, and I realised that it had been the glow of its charcoal we had seen from the street. A pot was simmering over the heat; an old Malay woman was tending it, and when she looked up I saw that she was hideously shrivelled and old, with eyes that seemed like lustreless glass. Suddenly, however, she began to rock on her seat, laughing loudly; a man who had been curled up on a sofa nearby to us looked up suddenly, and also began to laugh. He burst into conversation, very urgent and gushing but monotonous too, as though he had the secret of all existence to convey but without the words that would express it adequately.

'Blood,' he dribbled, 'in blood lies the generation, and the life, *in blood* . . .' His voice trailed away, and his face twitched horribly before lapsing into stillness. In one hand he clutched a dark bamboo pipe; he held it up to his lips, and I saw a red glow in the bowl as he pulled on the smoke. All across the room now I could make out similar spots of glowing and fading light as the victims of the poison fed on their drug, perfectly oblivious to us and to all the world. They lay twisted and numb in fantastic postures, and they seemed to me – staring at them through the smoke – like the victims of some explosion of volcanic ash, embalmed in their death throes for all posterity to witness and to shudder at. Such then did it mean, I thought, to be a subject of the mighty monarch Opium!

'I have had the very finest of our house prepared for you, sir.'

I turned round. Polidori, with a malignant grin, was offering me a pipe. His teeth, I observed now that they were bared, seemed very sharp. When he curled his upper lip, he assumed the character of some cunning beast of prey.

'No?' he said at length mockingly. He turned to my companion. 'How about you then, sir?' Again he curled his lips. 'Surely you will breathe in our smoke' – he paused – 'Dr Eliot?'

Eliot, far from appearing startled at this mention of his name, remained perfectly composed. 'I gather, then, Mr Polidori,' he said, 'that you have been alerted already to our interest in you?'

Polidori's face and body seemed to twist with the joke. 'I saw Headley this afternoon,' he nodded. 'He mentioned your and Mr Stoker's call.'

'Good,' replied Eliot coolly. 'Then you will know the purpose of our visit here.'

Polidori grinned. 'You want Mowberley.'

'I see we understand each other perfectly.'

'Not so, I'm afraid, Dr Eliot.'

My companion raised an eyebrow. 'Oh?'

'He is not here.'

'I know that he is.'

'What makes you so sure?'

Eliot shook his head. 'If you won't lead me to him, I will find my own way.' He walked forward, but as he did so Polidori grabbed at his wrists, pulling Eliot so that the two men's faces were pressed close together, and I saw Eliot wince from the stench of Polidori's breath.

'Release him,' I ordered. 'Release him!' Polidori glanced round at me, and after a long pause stepped back from Eliot. His smile, however, if anything grew only more broad.

My companion, in turn, remained as cool as before. 'You will see,' he said courteously, 'that we are quite determined.'

'Oh, quite!' grinned Polidori, baring his teeth.

'Where is your mistress?'

'My mistress?' Polidori suddenly laughed. He stooped his shoulders, and began to twist his hands round and round as though in a lather of servility. 'My mistress,' he moaned, 'oh, my beautiful mistress! Lusted after by all the world!' He straightened suddenly. 'I don't know who you mean.'

'Whoever she is, whatever she is' – Eliot paused – 'you do.'

'Tell me, then.'

'You have lured two of my friends – you know their names – to this den of vice. Your purpose has been to break them – to win the secrets of their diplomatic work. What interest could you have in such an end? Nothing. Therefore – by a process of perfectly logical deduction – you must be working for someone else, someone with an interest in the parliamentary bill.'

'Oh, Dr Eliot, Dr Eliot,' Polidori moaned, 'you are so terribly ... *clever!*' He spat out the last word; as he did so he sprang forward again, but Eliot cried out to me in warning, and before Polidori could seize me I had caught him by the arms. Polidori froze, a mocking sneer of contempt on his lips.

'Now,' said Eliot patiently, 'I have no wish to make this unpleasant. I am not interested in tracking your' – he paused – 'what word should I use, if not your mistress? – your *accomplice* down. Merely tell me where you have Mowberley; then we can all leave each other well alone.'

'Oh, how exceedingly considerate of you.'

'I warn you now, I shall call in Scotland Yard if there is no other way.'

'What,' sneered Polidori, 'and destroy the reputation of the noble minister?'

'I would prefer not to,' replied Eliot, 'but whatever else he loses, I must at least preserve his life.'

'It is not in danger.'

'So you admit he is here?'

'No.' Polidori paused, and when he smiled he bared his teeth again. 'But he has been, Dr Eliot.' He stepped back slowly, his eyes still on us and his hands upraised. Without looking round, he handed the pipe down to the old Malay crone; dully, she lit it for him and Polidori, placing the stem between his lips, drew on the smoke, three or four puffs. He closed his eyes. 'It is very good,' he murmured, 'oh, so very good indeed. Men would come a long way for it.' He opened his eyes again suddenly. 'And they do, Dr Eliot. Believe me – they do.' He smiled slowly and his lips, when they parted, were veiled by a yellow film of saliva. He licked it away and his eyes, which before had seemed clouded, were suddenly cold and piercing again. 'You are too clever, Dr Eliot. There is no conspiracy. Men must have their opium – even ministers in the Government.'

'No.' Eliot shook his head. 'You have lured him here.'

'Lured him?' Polidori sank back in a chair. The mist seemed to roll across his eyes again. 'Lured him,' he repeated, 'lured him, lured him.' He blinked up at us with an expression of sudden urgency. 'I must have wealthy men,' he laughed. 'Men of means. West End gents.' His laughter now was nothing but a stream of high-pitched giggles. 'So yes – I lured them, Dr Eliot.' He began to mumble again, repeating the phrase as he had done before. Slowly, he leaned forward and pointed an unsteady finger into my companion's face. 'But if they took the drug – if they took it – then that was their own responsibility.'

His eyes, wide with a look of moral solemnity, suddenly creased and he subsided into spluttering giggles again. He lay in his chair and began to mumble at empty space. Eliot observed him with detached interest. 'See,' he observed, 'how numb the muscles in his cheeks are growing. The stupor he is sinking into is clearly profound.' He glanced around the room. 'This may prove easier than I had dared to hope.'

He began to inspect each body where it lay, but at length I saw him stand and frown. He turned to me and shook his head.

'Perhaps he is with the Rajah,' I suggested.

'Who?'

I stared at him in surprise. 'Why, Sir George, of course. Isn't that who we are searching for?'

Eliot laughed shortly at this – almost rudely, I felt. 'Well, of course it is,' he replied, and turned his back on me.

I felt angry at this sudden brusqueness. 'I am very stupid, I am sure,' I told him, 'but I fail to see why you must treat my suggestion with such utter scorn.'

Eliot turned back to me at once. 'I am sorry, Stoker, if I have caused you offence. Your contribution, however, was a laughable one, and we have no time to waste on debating it. And yet ...' His eyes narrowed as his voice trailed away. 'And yet,' he repeated, 'your line of reasoning was not, perhaps, as foolish as it at first appeared. No ...' With sudden energy, he crossed to the wall and began to move along it, pressing it with his hands.

'What are you doing?' I asked.

He glanced round at me. 'With the Rajah, you said. Well, clearly, I laughed because there *is* no Rajah ...'

'What?' I exclaimed.

'No Rajah,' he repeated, 'but there is a Queen. Would she ever live in such squalor as this?' He gestured with his arms and then, even as he did so, his gaze strayed to the brazier in one corner of the room. At once he crossed to it and pushed it aside, then struck at the wall which lay beyond. As he did so the old hag who had been staring into the coals looked up at him and began to shriek. Eliot ignored her as she clutched on to his coat, gibbering with fear; I crossed and tried to calm her, but her fingers would not be prised free from the hem. She stared at the wall as though menaced by it; Eliot was stripping it of its dirty, smoke-stained hangings, and revealing behind them a rough wooden door.

'She is coming,' chattered the Malay, 'coming for her blood! O Queen, Queen of pain and delight!' She choked suddenly and her face was twisted by a rictus grin, hideous like a skull's. 'Oh, my goddess,' she mumbled, letting slip Eliot's coat as she raised her hands to her eyes. 'My goddess of life – my goddess of death.'

Eliot glanced at me. As he did so, I saw his gaze stray from my face and a frown crease his brow. I glanced round and saw Polidori was watching us. He was still slumped in his chair, but his eyes were open again and perfectly unclouded. Eliot unbarred the door and pushed it open; at once I felt cool night air against my skin, a blessed relief from the fumes of the smoke and its poison in my lungs. Eliot took a step forward; then he glanced round at Polidori again. He was still watching us, his eyes as bright and unblinking as a cat's. Eliot took my arm. 'For God's sake, come on,' he whispered. He turned, and did not look round again. I followed him through the doorway to find we were on a bridge. Below us, I saw water; ahead, a wall of brown and dirty brick. I glanced round again; Polidori's eyes were still watching me. Violently, I slammed shut the door.

I could feel a soft, cold drizzle washing my brow. Already, away from the fumes of the opium, my energy and courage were returning to me. I looked around again. The bridge we were on was wooden and old; it spanned a narrow stretch of water which clearly had once been used by merchant vessels, for there was a warehouse built on the opposite side. But there was only one tiny boat moored there now, and when I looked at the entrance out to the Thames I saw a row of spikes embedded in the walls, so that access was barred to any larger craft. The warehouse too seemed utterly disused; its wall was streaked with black and its windows, like those of Coldlair Lane, had been boarded up. I stared at it, and felt despair; it was clearly uninhabitable – we would find no one inside.

Eliot, however, had already crossed the bridge and was picking the lock of a heavy wooden door. At length he stood back, and the door creaked ajar. To my surprise, I saw a crack of red light. Eliot glanced at me; then he passed inside and I followed him.

And at once we both stood still again. I had been through many strange things that night, but nothing that compared with the sight before me now – and indeed, I almost wondered if I were not still in the opium den, trapped in the coils of some smoke-borne dream. For what we saw appeared a vision – it was impossible to believe we were in a warehouse at all. Instead we seemed to be in the hallway of some fantastic palace, and yet, no . . . hallway is not the right word, for it was scarcely a hall but something far stranger and vaster than that – almost, I thought, like a floor suspended in space, for above me the ceiling was obscured by dark, and the only walls I could distinguish were behind us and ahead. There were ebony doors in the centre of both these walls, and alcoves stretching away on either side. In every one was a statue and these figures, I saw, had each been sculptured in a different fashion, suggestive of a wide range of cultures and historical times, so that here an Egyptian or there a Chinese might be seen. Yet there was something similar about the statues, indefinable at first, and unsettling; I scanned them and realised suddenly that no matter how varied the styles in which their faces had been portrayed, the same expression was on all of them – sensual, and beautiful, and very cold. It was almost as though the statues were of the same woman; that was clearly impossible, yet even so it was very strange.

I stared at the line of faces, and then I shivered and looked away for, foolish though it will sound, I had felt almost as though their eyes were staring at *me*! I peered instead into the shadows on my left and right. These waited beyond the light of the gas flames which spurted above each alcove; I could not see what the darkness concealed. On its margins, however, the delicate lines of stairways stretched up and down in impossible sweeps; impossible, I say, for they appeared to be unsupported by any structures I could identify, but to have been spun instead from purest gossamer, and patterned in filaments through the naked air. I could see no limit to them, neither above nor below – an obvious illusion, for the warehouse had not been especially large – and yet the effect was really quite remarkable. I turned to Eliot. 'Just think,' I said, 'how much money has been spent on this place.'

He did not reply at first. He was staring, I realised, at one of the statues. It had clearly been fashioned by an Oriental hand, for it had the form and the garb of those Hindoo works of art which I have often admired in London's museums. Yet this goddess, in truth, was of a quite different order of craftsmanship from anything I had seen before. Its face wore that mocking voluptuousness which it shared with all the other statues' faces, and the effect was both repulsive and thrilling; merely staring at it, I felt my flesh begin to tingle. With an effort of will, it seemed, Eliot broke away from the statue's gaze. 'We must hurry,' he said, turning to me. 'We shouldn't linger here.' He crossed to the door ahead of us.

He opened it and passed through; I followed him. Ahead, stretched a long corridor carpeted with rugs of vivid patterns and colours; the walls were red, inlaid with gold, and the doors which led off the corridor at regular intervals were again made of ebony. At the end of it, far distant from us, there appeared to be a door; and then suddenly, seeming to reach into my blood, I heard the sound of strings. I had never heard music of such beauty before. It drew me . . . it was quite irresistible. There seemed something unearthly about it, almost frightening. I began to hurry down the corridor. Eliot sought to restrain me; he held me by the arm as he tried each ebony door, but they were all locked and I was quite content that they should remain so. There was only one door that I wanted to open, and that was the door which would take me to the music.

Yet no matter how rapidly I progressed down the corridor, I seemed to come no nearer to it. This was an illusion, of course – it must have been: it was likely that the opium fumes were still in my head and playing tricks on me. I paused and shook my head, to try to clear them, but the ebony door remained tantalisingly distant, and when I glanced back over my shoulder I saw that the door I had come from now seemed just as far away. I glanced at Eliot. His face was very pale, and beads of sweat were glistening on his brow. He tried another side door; the handle would not turn. He tried again with the next door; the same result. He stopped hurrying and leaned against the wall, wiping his brow. He stared about him and I observed on his face, normally so composed and restrained, a frantic disbelief. He cupped his hands around his mouth. 'Mowberley!' he cried out. 'Mowberley!'

At once the music stopped. I blinked. Clearly the sound of Eliot's voice had banished my opium dream, for the ebony door seemed much nearer now. I walked towards it and opened it.

The room beyond was snug and painted pink. It might almost have been a little girl's nursery, for a fire was blazing merrily in the corner and I saw next to it what appeared to be a doll's house, and a stack of children's books. In the centre of the room, however, was a large desk piled with manuscripts, and on the wall were pinned various maps and charts, some very old and clearly objects of study. By the far wall four men were gathered with musical instruments, violas and violins. As we walked in, they started and twitched, but they did not look up at us; instead their heads lolled forward onto their chests and their eyes, although open, stared at nothing. Their expressions, it struck me suddenly, were very like that of the helmsman we had pursued across the Thames.

'Who are *you*?'

It was the clear, high voice of a very young girl which had come from behind the piles of manuscripts on the desk. I glanced at Eliot, who seemed as surprised as I.

Together we walked to the side of the desk. I could see now that there was indeed a little girl sitting there. She was a most exquisitely beautiful child, with long blonde hair tied by a ribbon and delicate features like a china doll's. She wore a charming pink frock with a pinafore, and her white-stockinged legs, as she sat at her chair, swung to and fro. She was holding a pen, which she raised to her lips, and as she stared at us her wide eyes were almost comically solemn. She could not have been more than eight years old.

'You are not meant to be here, you know,' she said, with that self-possession so typical of children her age.

'I am very sorry,' replied Eliot courteously. 'We are looking for a friend.'

She digested this information. 'Not Lilah?' she asked at length.

'No,' answered Eliot, shaking his head. 'We want my friend. George Mowberley.'

'Oh, *him*.'

'Do you know where he is?'

'Oh, *he'll* be downstairs,' said the child, her nose wrinkled in faint disdain.

'Could you perhaps take us to him?' Eliot asked.

The young girl shook her head primly. 'Can't you see, I have my work to do?' She laid her pen down neatly on the desk, then swung herself down from her chair on to the floor. She looked up at us. 'But I will call Stumps. He can show you.'

She crossed to a bell-pull and, reaching up on tip-toes, gave it a tug. Then she pointed to a door behind her desk – not ebony like the one we had come through but painted pink and white like the rest of the room. 'There now,' she said, 'he will be waiting outside.' She swept back her hair almost coquettishly, then returned to her chair. Before she could pull herself up, Eliot had taken her in his arms and lifted her on to it.

'Thank you very much,' she said dutifully. 'And now I must continue with my studying.'

'Of course,' said Eliot. 'Goodbye.'

'Goodbye.' But the child had not looked up; she was already engrossed in some book on the table, and her mouth began to move as she sounded the words. Eliot smiled faintly as he looked on her, then gesturing to me we went out from the room. As I closed the door, I heard the stirring of music again. I wanted to pause and listen, but Eliot pulled on my arm. 'Unless I am much mistaken, here comes our guide now.'

I gazed where he pointed. We were standing on a balcony, and stairways – much like those I had seen before – were stretching up and down before us. But there was a crucial difference, and I was now more certain than ever that I had earlier been the victim of some fleeting opium dream, for whereas previously the stairs had seemed like structures from a vision, there was nothing very strange about the ones before me now beyond the incongruity of their presence in a warehouse – which was remarkable enough, to be sure, but not impossible. I supposed that the owner of the place had a taste for the grotesque and bizarre; certainly, the servant approaching us supported such a view. I would estimate he was no more than three foot tall, and his face seemed almost to have been melted away. There were two small holes where his nose should have been, and his lower jaw was stunted so that his tongue lolled over his black, broken teeth. Flakes of skin were oozing on his scalp. His limbs were short and fat like a baby's and yet, despite his page-boy's uniform, he was clearly of a considerable age. I shuddered at the sight of him; but then I saw his eyes, which were deep and expressive with a sense of pain, and I felt almost ashamed.

He stood before us and grunted something. Because his lower jaw only reached the roof of his mouth, he was hard to understand, but was clearly asking us what we required.

'Sir George Mowberley,' said Eliot. 'Can you show us where he is?'

The dwarf stared at him and seemed to frown, though it was hard to be certain, so twisted was his face. He pointed back down the stairs and gestured at us to follow him. We did so, walking slowly, for his pace was very slow. Half-way down, I was startled to observe a panther watching us. I tensed, but the panther merely yawned and with lazy nonchalance began to lick its paws. In the hallway at the foot of the stairs, I saw what seemed to be a python coiled around a chair; in a further room, we startled two small deer. 'What is this place?' I murmured. 'We appear to be in a zoo.'

Eliot nodded slowly; but he made no reply. He was clearly tense; his face looked rigid and drawn, and he kept glancing over his shoulder as though expecting to be surprised. We saw no one, however,though I too, infected perhaps by Eliot's mood of apprehension, began to feel possessed by a sense of dread.

The dwarf stopped at length by a door. 'Here,' he breathed. The effort of articulation appeared to cause him pain. He opened the door for us and Eliot thanked him. My dread was thickening into horror now. I could feel it as a cloud, rolling through my mind.

Eliot squeezed my arm. 'Are you all right?' he asked. His forehead was clammy; his eyes seemed to be faintly protruding, as though with terror, and I wondered if my own eyes were looking the same. In a strange way, however, it comforted me to know that he felt as I did.

I nodded. 'Come, Eliot,' I said. 'Let us face the worst.'

I had half-expected, I suppose, in the room beyond, to find some hallucination of the kind that had confronted me before. Instead there was just a heavy, velvet-red darkness. It took my eyes some seconds to adjust to it. Gradually I realised there were candles burning, tiny pinpricks of light flickering in an arc. Beyond them I saw the vague silhouettes of furniture, and beyond them the folds of curtains, rich and soft like the darkness itself, so that it was quite impossible to distinguish them apart and I felt enclosed, as though trapped within something heavy and alive. The air was thick with incense and opium smoke, and the perfumes of exotic, pollen-laden flowers. I felt quite drained of my energies. It was as though the darkness were feeding on me and I longed for some relief from it. Only ahead of me, where the arc of the candles met at the wall, had the darkness been banished and the curtains drawn back. There was a picture on the wall, illuminated. It seemed vividly pale against the red of the paintwork. It was of a woman. She had the face – I could tell at once – of the statues I had seen in the alcoves above. In this picture, however, she was represented as dressed in the very height of the latest fashion. She had the most ghastly beauty. I had to lower my gaze. When I did so, I saw for the first time a body spread like an offering on the floor. It seemed to be the Rajah. His clothes were sodden; there was a wound to his leg; his face was smeared with streaks of blood.

Eliot crossed to him and turned him over. I followed him and saw, by the Rajah's head, a large silver dish I had not noticed before. It was filled with a thick, dark liquid. I touched it with my finger and held it up to the candle-light. 'Eliot,' I whispered, 'I think it is blood.'

Eliot glanced up at me. 'Indeed?' he asked.

I shivered, and looked about me. 'There is something about this place,' I muttered, 'which seems ...'

'Yes?' Eliot inquired.

I shrugged. 'Almost supernatural,' I replied.

Eliot laughed good-humouredly at this. 'I think we should exhaust all natural explanations,' he said, 'before turning to a theory such as that. And indeed' – he turned back to the body whose pulse he had been taking – 'this is not a case, I feel, which defies the laws of nature.'

Something in his tone alerted me. 'You have a solution, then?' I cried.

'In the end,' he replied, 'it was very simple.' I stared down at the Rajah's face; it was the same, but ... I can only say – it was not the same. The features were those I had seen before on the steps of the Private Entrance, but the cruelty had been softened and quite removed and the cheeks, I could see even through the streaks of blood, were now rosy and plump, not pallid at all. 'I don't understand it,' I said. 'It *is* the Rajah's face, but it seems so remarkably – impossibly – changed.'

'I agree,' nodded Eliot, 'it was a miraculous disguise that he wore. Even I when I first saw him failed to penetrate it.'

'Who is it, then?' I asked.

'Why,' replied Eliot, 'Sir George Mowberley, of course.'

'Is he ...'

'Oh, yes.' Eliot nodded. 'Perfectly alive.' He briefly inspected the wound to Sir George's leg. 'It must have been the bullet,' he murmured. 'Nothing serious. But we should remove him from here as soon as we can.' He glanced round and, as he did so, the candles guttered as though suddenly disturbed. At the same moment the room seemed to pulse about me; again I felt as though some force, some entity, were draining me, so that the touch of my tongue felt like leather, and I imagined that my bones were being turned into ash. My eyeballs were dry and burning, as though all their moisture was being sucked out, so that even my sockets began to ache. Feeling drawn, I turned to look at the picture on the wall. Eliot too was staring at it.

'Can you feel it?' I asked.

He turned. His face seemed shrunk to the contours of his skull. Suddenly, though, he laughed and shook his head.

'What is it?' I asked in some surprise.

'Why, Stoker,' he replied, 'this is like a set from one of your plays – do you not think? A haunted house, with accompanying tricks? No, no' – he shook his head again – 'there is danger here, but not from any supernatural agency. The enemies we confront may be devilish, but alas, they are no less human for that.' He bent down. 'Come,' he said, lifting Sir George's arms, 'we must not be discovered here. Our conspirators will not be pleased to find us stealing their prize. Let us get moving at once.'

I took Sir George's feet and helped to lift him up. With my other hand I opened the door; I had not remembered shutting it but I kept my mouth quiet, for I had no wish to suffer further mockery. Even so, in my imagination the darkness seemed still to be draining me; I wondered when my limbs would start to rustle, so withered and dry my body felt. Eliot too, I thought, was struggling with his burden, as though much weakened; and though he smiled at me reassuringly, his face was rigid and pale again. We left the room; as we did so, we both simultaneously turned to stare at the painting one last time. The woman's form glimmered; then a mist of darkness seemed to roll across the room and the candles were extinguished one by one as we watched them, until the whole room was dark. 'For God's sake,' muttered Eliot, 'let us get out of here.' We staggered down the corridor. From upstairs, I could still hear the faint strains of music. We hurried away from it. At the end of the corridor was a large hall; and at the end of the hall, two heavy metal gates. They were both open. We passed through them, and felt rain against our brows. We had reached the street at last.

'This way,' said Eliot, pointing towards the flickering of a gas lamp. He kept glancing over his shoulder as we went, but no one followed us, and as we reached the main street I knew that we were safe, for a large crowd was gathered on the pavement of the road. I was surprised to see so many people together, for it was early in the morning; the crowd stood in the shadows away from the lamp, where the darkness was still pitch, and at first the object of their interest was impossible to make out. There was a policeman bending down beside a crumpled silhouette. Eliot asked him what had occurred; the constable replied that a woman had been assaulted and left for dead. At once, of course, Eliot offered his services; as he bent down, I saw him frown suddenly and reach for one of the victim's wrists. 'Quick!'

he shouted. 'That rag, give it quickly!' He tied it around the wrist, and I saw a purple stain slowly spread across the cloth. Eliot looked up at the policeman. 'Didn't you see,' he asked, 'that her wrist had been cut?'

'So were the others!' shouted a woman from the crowd. 'They all had cuts to them like that, they all did, some to their throats, some to their bodies, and some to their wrists!'

'Others?' Eliot asked.

'All around here,' nodded the woman. Others from the crowd shouted out their agreement with her. 'The police don't do nothing for us!' 'They don't care!' 'They keep it all hushed!'

The constable swallowed; he looked very young. He told Eliot in a low voice that he didn't know anything about the case. Rotherhithe wasn't his beat. He had come from the north docks, to investigate the reported sound of gunfire on the Thames, and though he had found no evidence of the gunfire, he had come across the woman, and he was doing his best – and as he'd already said, it wasn't his beat. He stared down nervously at the woman's blood-stained wrist, and swallowed again. 'Will she live?' he asked at length.

Eliot nodded. 'I think so,' he said, 'but she must be got to a surgery at once.' He stared up at the policeman. 'Presumably, if you are from the north docks, you have a launch here now?'

The constable nodded.

'Good,' said Eliot, rising to his feet. 'Then you will take us across. I can treat her best in Whitechapel.'

The policeman nodded, then suddenly frowned. 'Excuse me, sir, for asking, but what are *you* doing here?'

'Us?' Eliot shrugged. 'We have been' – he smiled faintly – 'enjoying the nightlife of the docks.' He gestured down at Sir George whose leg wound, I observed, he had been careful to conceal. 'And some of us, I'm afraid, have been enjoying it rather too much.'

The policeman nodded slowly. 'Yes, sir.' He grinned suddenly. 'So I see.'

'Be obliged if you'd keep it to yourself,' said Eliot briskly. 'And now let's not waste any more time. Come on. We need to get this poor woman into your boat, and then into a bed.'

And so it was that we were soon crossing back to the north bank of the Thames, and on to Whitechapel. Once there, a couple of policemen helped to carry the injured woman into the surgery; Eliot, before accompanying them to treat her, asked me to take Sir George upstairs. 'And for God's sake,' he whispered, 'keep that leg wound covered.'

I nodded. I transported my burden without mishap, and stayed by his side for upwards of an hour. At length Eliot joined me again. 'She will pull through,' he said, sitting down beside Sir George. 'I have got her asleep in a bed downstairs.'

'And him?' I asked, gesturing at Sir George.

'Him?' Eliot smiled. 'Oh, he has been misbehaving badly. We must send him back to his wife at once.'

'But is he really all right, do you think?'

'I am certain of it. But let me just examine him, and treat his wound which, as you can see ...' – he exposed it – 'is really just a scratch ...' He paused for a moment to stare at Sir George's face; then he smiled faintly and shook his head; then he frowned, as though embarrassed, and returned to dressing the wound. But there had been affection in his smile, and such affection in a man as cold as Eliot, I thought, must be worth a good deal.

'You are very close to him?' I asked.

Eliot shook his head. 'Not now. But once. We were drawn as opposites so often are. Myself – and Ruthven – and Mowberley.'

I nodded and stared at Sir George's face again. 'When did you know?' I asked at length.

'What – that he and the Rajah were the same man?'

'Yes.'

Eliot smiled grimly. For a while, he continued with his work in silence and I had begun to think he wouldn't answer me. 'George was always ...,' he said suddenly. 'He was always ...' He shook his head. '*Fond of women.*'

'Yes, you said.' I nodded slowly. 'The prostitute in the alleyway, then?'

'Exactly so.'

'But ... excuse me for any indelicacy ... but – there are many men who ... well ... might not a Rajah have – you know – as well?'

'Yes,' said Eliot shortly. 'Of course. But I had convinced myself that if the Rajah were indeed not Sir George, then his purpose with the prostitute would have been something quite other than sex.'

'Indeed?' I stared at Eliot in surprise. 'In the name of God, what?'

'I do not wish to say.' His face froze. 'It was a folly of mine.'

'But surely ...'

'*I do not wish to say.*' This was spoken with a sudden iciness and my expression must have been one of surprise, for Eliot immediately touched my shoulder in a gesture of apology. 'Do not press me on this topic, please, Stoker,' he asked. 'It is a matter of some embarrassment to me. You will remember – my mention of the Kalikshutran disease ... it is something I have attempted to put from my mind; yet it is clear I have not entirely succeeded, for I sometimes find myself suspecting its existence where it could not possibly be. Suffice it to say, though, that my imaginings were proved false and I knew – *I knew* – from that moment on – that Sir George was our man. When I saw him on the boat, the expression on his face once he had seen *me* ... I was certain.'

'There is one thing, though,' I said, 'which I still don't understand.'

'Indeed?'

'Yes.' I studied Sir George's face again. 'How *did* his features seem to change so much? How was it that we failed to recognise him?'

'Ah.' Eliot nodded slowly. 'You will remember, Stoker, in Coldlair Lane, I mentioned that the case was perfectly clear to me save for one detail alone. Well – you have just touched on the detail which still baffles me. I confess – I cannot answer your question.'

'Have you no theory?'

Eliot frowned. 'Perhaps ...' he murmured.

'Yes?'

He shook his head. 'No,' he said at length, 'it is impossible.'

'Tell me,' I pressed him.

'I was merely going to comment,' he said, 'on the coincidence.'

'Coincidence?'

Eliot nodded. 'You will remember that Lucy, when she saw Mowberley's face at the window, imagined it to be daubed with streaks of blood. Tonight also, when we discovered him ourselves, his face was again daubed with streaks of blood.'

'Goodness, Eliot!' I exclaimed. 'You are perfectly right! What do you make of it?'

'I confess,' Eliot answered, 'I can make nothing of it at all.'

My disappointment must have been evident in my face, for Eliot smiled. 'We must wait, I am afraid,' he said, rising to his feet, 'for Mowberley to regain his consciousness. Perhaps then some light may be shed on the matter. And to that end, Stoker, I wonder if I could press you for one last favour.'

'Of course,' I replied, 'you know I am keen to be of service in this case.'

Eliot had crossed to his desk. Now he sat down by it and began to scribble a note. 'Mowberley must be restored to his home and his wife,' he said. 'Lady Mowberley has borne his absence very bravely. We cannot keep him from her any longer. Therefore, Stoker' – he turned in his chair – 'I was wondering if you might deliver the Minister on your way back home.'

'It will be no trouble at all,' I replied.

Eliot nodded. 'I would come myself,' he murmured, 'but I have left Llewellyn alone here for too long as it is.' He returned to his note. At length he finished it, sealed it up and handed it to me. 'If you would be so kind, deliver this as well to Lady Mowberley.'

'You must promise me, in return, to keep me informed of any developments.'

Eliot smiled. 'But of course, my dear Stoker. To whom else could I possibly turn? But I doubt this case will trouble us much more. No, I think we can consider our solution to be found.'

And on that note, I left him. I had much to ponder, though, as I sat in my cab, for I could not be so certain that the mysteries were indeed resolved. I thought of all I had recently experienced and heard, until, exhausted as I was, the various images from the past few days began to blend in my mind. I saw Lucy; the Rajah; Lord Ruthven and Sir George; I was chasing them with Eliot in a boat down the Thames; then I was with them all in Polidori's den. And then I thought of the portrait in the perfume-clouded room; and all of a sudden I was jerked back awake. I shuddered at the memory – why, I couldn't say – save that the woman's beauty had seemed so impossibly great that I wondered if it was that which was unsettling me. We still did not know who she was, nor what her purpose was in Rotherhithe – yet Eliot could talk as though the case were solved.

I shook my head. I was reluctant to doubt a man of such extraordinary powers – yet I suspected it would not be long before I heard from him again . . .

Letter, Dr John Eliot to Lady Mowberley.

Surgeon's Court,
Whitechapel.

16 April 1888.

Dear Lady Mowberley,

I have had some success in our case. I am delivering George into the capable hands of Mr Bram Stoker and he in turn, I hope, will have delivered him to you by the time you read this note. The outline of the mystery is now fairly clear; the full details, however, must await George's recovery, which I am certain will be rapid and without undue complications. He has much to tell you. However, you must demand the whole truth from him. As I recall, he is inclined to bluster.

You mentioned, when you visited me, that if there was anything you could do for me in return then I had only to ask. Perhaps you will regret that offer, for I do indeed now have a request. Please, Lady Mowberley – might you not be reconciled with Lucy Westcote? I do not know the nature of what has come between you, although I can hazard a guess. Perhaps all that is required for a reconciliation is that one of you should make the first move?

I shall call on you during the next week, to see how George progresses.

> Until then, I remain, Lady Mowberley,
> Your servant,

JACK ELIOT.

Letter, Lady Mowberley to Dr John Eliot.

2, Grosvenor Street

24 April

Dear Dr Eliot,

Words cannot express my gratitude. George has told me every-thing. It has been very painful for me – as you yourself must have known it would be. Your skill in teasing the solution out, and your courage in resolving it, cannot be praised too highly. George will write to you himself when he is more fully recovered. At the moment, he is still very weak.

I cannot, of course, refuse your appeal with regard to Lucy. It is true that I feel uncomfortable with her. She is a very headstrong young woman and I cannot approve of her conduct, which is altogether too *Parisian* for me. What seems proper to the London fast set, I am afraid, appears very immoral to a stick-in-the-mud like myself. My quarrel, however, has never properly been with Lucy but with the young man to whose abode she fled. The nature of his offence I am sure you can guess. Your appeal for reconciliation must therefore be directed towards Lucy herself. I am always willing to entertain her. Indeed, more than that – I am willing to persuade George to release her inheritance, for I know that she has been short of finances and that it is I who have been largely responsible for that.

Maybe I was mistaken – but I did it for the best. Before you judge me too harshly, you must visit Lucy and extract the full story from her. I repeat, however – and you may tell her so yourself – that once George is recovered he will set about releasing money for her. I am certain that it can be arranged with the lawyers, so that she need not wait until she comes of age.

Dear Dr Eliot – again, I thank you from the bottom of my heart. I am, sir, your most devoted and beholden friend,

ROSAMUND, LADY MOWBERLEY

Dr Eliot's Diary (kept in phonograph)

24 April. – Much to record. In the morning, received a letter from Lady Mowberley which seems very promising. Since I had a morning free, I decided to act on it at once. Around nine, took the tram to Covent Garden. On the way, curious sensation of being watched. Clearly irrational, yet couldn't shake the impression off. Maybe I have been working myself too hard. Need more sleep, perhaps? A false economy to deny myself, if the patients suffer as a consequence.

Arrived at the Lyceum. Lucy not yet there, but Stoker was in his office and gave me her address. He flushed at the first mention of her name. Poor fellow – I believe he is very much in love with Lucy. I wonder if he is quite aware of this himself?

The address he had given me was in Clerkenwell. I headed there at once. The street was not dingy, but nor was it fashionable; I recalled what Lady Mowberley had written, that Lucy was short of funds, and as I waited for her in the hall I could see signs all around me of economy. And indeed, when Lucy came hurrying down the stairs to greet me I thought I detected, even through the warmth of her welcome, traces of embarrassment, as though she were ashamed of being seen in such a place, especially by an old friend of her brother's like myself. I was therefore confident she would welcome my news; but to my surprise, she merely laughed and shook her head. 'We are perfectly happy here,' she insisted. 'I should be angry with you, Jack, for so misjudging me. The quarrel is not over any inheritance.'

'Then what is the cause?'

She stared at me defiantly. 'I don't know – ask Lady Mowberley. I told you, Jack, her hostility has always seemed quite motiveless to me.'

'Well, then,' I answered with a shrug, 'you have no reason to reject her offer of peace.'

'But I told you, Jack, we don't need the money.'

I looked around. 'Is that so?' I asked.

Lucy flushed. 'We have my earnings, and Ned's allowance while he studies for the Bar.'

'But surely, Lucy, you can find some better place to live? The Westcotes, for instance, Ned's family – they must have a town house ...'

My voice trailed away as I observed Lucy's expression; she had turned deathly pale. She shook her head, then tried to smile. 'I'm sorry,' she said. 'It is just your suggestion of the Westcotes' house – Ned has so conditioned me with his own horror of it that I seem to grow upset at the very mention of the place.'

'Horror?' I asked, surprised.

Lucy shrugged. 'Ever since his mother and sister disappeared. Ned claims that the tragedy has touched the house. I don't know how, but he is quite insistent about it. He cannot bear to go through the door. We went once – it is in the woods by Highgate – and we just stood there by the gates, then turned and hurried back. It was very strange, Jack. I felt it too – a sensation of ... yes ... horror. Almost physical. I knew at once what Ned had meant.'

I bowed my head. 'I am very sorry, then, for having brought the matter up. It was most insensitive of me.'

Lucy smiled. 'You weren't to know.' She took my hands, and looked around her. 'And anyway,' she murmured, 'this may not be Highgate but it is very snug.'

'Yes,' I said slowly. I glanced up the stairs. 'Exceedingly so.'

Lucy cocked an eyebrow. 'And what is that supposed to mean?'

I shrugged, then smiled.

Lucy hit me with feigned frustration. 'Really, Jack, I'm surprised at you. I had always thought you were a Socialist. Shouldn't you be pleased to see us living in a slum?'

I smiled again faintly. 'It wasn't you so much I was thinking of.'

'Oh?'

I bowed my head; then slowly I raised it to stare into her eyes. 'I was thinking,' I murmured, 'more of your child.'

Lucy's face froze. 'You know,' she whispered.

'It wasn't so hard to guess.'

'No,' she said at last. A smile touched her lips. 'It never is with you.' She laughed suddenly. 'Damn you, Jack, and there I was – nervous all this time that the baby might cry and give the game away. I needn't have worried. How did you know?'

'Oh, come, Lucy, a year's illness and seclusion, a hurried marriage, a young girl leaving her guardian's home – you could write it up into a melodrama and have it shown at the Lyceum.'

'You missed out the wicked step-mother.'

'But has she really been so very wicked?'

'Of course.'

'Why?'

'She refused to see Ned.'

'Well, can you blame her?'

'Jack!'

'Just remember – they are not quite so ... progressive ... perhaps, in Yorkshire.'

'And what is that supposed to mean?'

'You are the actress,' I told her, 'you are the one who is paid to see through other people's eyes. Just try, Lucy. Lady Mowberley comes to London, after a lifetime spent in Whitby. Her husband's ward demands to go on the stage. Then almost at once, this ward is bearing some strange man's child. I think, in the circumstances, she's entitled to feel a *bit* of moral outrage.'

'Well ...' Lucy frowned, then shrugged. 'Perhaps. Just a little bit.'

I took out Lady Mowberley's letter. 'And now she wishes to be reconciled with you.' I handed it to Lucy.

She read it through a couple of times, carefully. 'But she still won't see Ned,' she murmured at last.

'No,' I replied, 'but surely you can see why?'

Lucy shook her head.

'Because by blaming him, she removes the need to blame you.'

'Do you really think so?'

I nodded. 'Give her time, Lucy. She will come round. But first of all, you must give her a chance yourself.'

Lucy smiled at me slyly. 'If I didn't know you better, Jack, I would think you admired Rosamund.'

'But you do know me better, Lucy. I am merely acting on what I have observed.'

'Oh?' Lucy arched an eyebrow. 'And what have you observed?'

'That there is no reason I can make out for you two not to be friends.'

Lucy continued to stare at me; then she shrugged and folded the letter away. 'Well,' she murmured, 'you may be right.' She glanced up the stairs. 'But there is my baby now as well.'

'I don't see why that should be a problem. It is only your husband she seems to have proscribed.'

Lucy nodded slowly. 'Oh, Jack,' she said suddenly, 'he is the most beautiful child. I cannot regret what has happened, you know.'

'Of course not. No one is asking you to.'

'After Arthur ... well – I missed him so badly, you know. The mystery of his death, the horror of it, so like our father's end ...' She swallowed and paused. 'Apart from Ned, Arthur was all I'd ever had. I could never believe that he had really gone.' She shook her head; then she turned and began to hurry up the stairs. She glanced back at me. 'Well, come on, then.'

'What?'

She stopped, and almost stamped her foot. 'Oh, Jack, you are impossible! Even if you don't want to see Arthur, you could at least pretend you do.'

'Arthur?'

'Oh, Jack, for goodness' sake, *my baby*!' She held out her hand. 'You've got to come upstairs and say he's wonderful.'

I went with her uncomplainingly. The youthful Arthur, it turned out, was fast asleep. Admiration much easier as a consequence. He is indeed, as his mother claims, a most beautiful and *placid* child, rather as I remember his namesake, though without the moustache. I was about to mention this, when the doorbell rang. 'Don't make him cry,' said Lucy, 'or I shall be cross with you.' Down below, the housemaid was answering the bell. Lucy left me, closing the nursery door behind her and then hurrying downstairs. For several minutes I heard the murmur of conversation. I couldn't tell who the visitor might be. Then I heard footsteps coming up the stairs. Lucy opened the nursery door again. 'In here,' she whispered. There was a figure behind her and I blinked with surprise. It was Lord Ruthven whom Lucy was ushering in.

He seemed less anaemic than before – definite colour in his cheeks, and more animation in his general bearing. Very good-looking and very young, though he somehow makes me feel nervous and overawed – remarkable *power* in his presence. Not sure why – not in the habit of being impressed by aristocrats.

Lord Ruthven walked across the room to the crib. He bent over the sleeping Arthur and smiled with delight as he studied the child; then he closed his eyes and breathed in deeply, almost as though savouring some pleasurable scent. (*Mem.* His response to Lucy's costume in the dressing room – very similar. Interesting.) At length he opened his eyes again. 'Dr Eliot,' he murmured, speaking for the first time since entering the room. 'What an unexpected pleasure!'

Lucy was clearly surprised that we knew each other. I told her of our earlier meeting, but when I mentioned the programme she had sent to Lord Ruthven her look of bemusement grew only more profound. 'But I sent out no programme,' she exclaimed. She turned to him. 'It must have been someone else who sent it to you, I'm afraid.'

'No matter,' replied Lord Ruthven. Gracefully, he reached for Lucy's hand and raised it to his lips. 'It is the result that matters, not the cause.'

'Do you really believe that?' I asked.

'When I am feeling particularly idle, yes.' He arched an eyebrow in a manner that was clearly a Ruthven family trait. 'You disagree, Dr Eliot? As I remember, the provenance of my programme was interesting you before.'

'It seemed curious,' I replied, 'in the circumstances.'

Lord Ruthven stared at me keenly. 'Indeed?' he asked. 'And what circumstances would they be?'

I wondered, remembering how both Arthur Ruthven and Lady Mowberley had similarly been contacted anonymously, even though the coincidence in Lord Ruthven's case was not exact. 'Have you ever heard of a John Polidori?' I asked.

I had not really expected him to; for the briefest moment, however, a shadow seemed to pass across Lord Ruthven's face, and then his expression was perfectly composed once again. 'No,' he said nonchalantly. But he was lying, I could tell that he was, and he himself seemed to know that I knew. He stared at me icily; then, as I opened my mouth to press him further, he reached for Arthur and, picking the child up, held him close to his chest.

Lucy had moved forward with an involuntary start. 'You have woken him,' she said.

But Lord Ruthven made no apology. 'He is happy to be awake.' And Arthur did indeed seem perfectly content. He made not a sound, but stared instead into his Lordship's eyes and reached up to stroke his pale, smooth cheeks.

'I am not usually an admirer of children,' Lord Ruthven murmured, 'and indeed have always had the greatest respect for Herod. This child, however ...' He paused, and a flicker of pleasure curled the corners of his lips. 'This child ...' he smiled again – 'he almost persuades me to change my mind.'

'You are just showing off, my Lord,' said Lucy briskly, 'and pretending to be more wicked than you really are, when you say you dislike children.' She turned to me. 'It is only since the opening night of *Faust* that we have become acquainted, my cousin and I, but the very first time he visited me, Jack, he seemed to know at once that there was a child in the house. I hadn't told him. He must be almost as clever as you.'

'Oh, hardly,' murmured Lord Ruthven. 'Perhaps, though' – he smiled – 'it is just that I have a nose for them.' He puckered his nostrils. As he did so, Arthur choked and began to cry, but Lord Ruthven fixed him with his stare again and at once the baby's sobs trailed away. 'You see,' said Lucy, 'the power that he has? Wouldn't he make Arthur a wonderful nurse?'

Lord Ruthven laughed. There was something cold in his amusement, and almost mocking, I felt. 'I must be going,' I said. I turned away, and after kissing Lucy on her cheeks began to walk down the stairs.

'Dr Eliot.'

Lord Ruthven's voice had been almost a whisper. My first instinct was not to look round again, to pretend that I hadn't heard his call. But I was intrigued by Ruthven, despite myself.

He was standing at the top of the stairs, Lucy's baby still in his arms. 'When are you going to visit me?' he asked.

I shrugged. 'I am still not clear what you want to discuss.'

'Your paper, Dr Eliot.'

'Paper?'

Lord Ruthven smiled. 'You published it earlier this year. "A Himalayan Testcase: Sanguigens and Agglutination." That was the title you gave it, I believe?'

I stared at him in surprise. 'Yes, it was,' I agreed, 'but I hadn't realised ...'

'That I was interested in such matters?'

'It is a rather obscure branch of medical research.'

'Indeed it is. And your paper is particularly obscure, for to the complexity of the subject you bring the radicalism of your views – if I understood them correctly, that is. But then ... it is always the radical which is most intriguing, is it not?'

'An interesting sentiment from a member of the House of Lords.'

Lord Ruthven smiled faintly. 'We must talk, Dr Eliot.'

I considered this request. 'The last time we spoke, you mentioned funds for the surgery . . .'

'Yes.'

'And in return . . .'

'In return, all you have to do is to dine with me.'

'I am busy, I am afraid . . .'

'There is no urgency. Sunday, the third weekend in May. That should give you time to clear your diary, I hope?'

'Yes,' I shrugged, 'I'm sure . . .'

'Good,' said Lord Ruthven, interrupting me. 'Come at eight. You have my address.' He nodded, then turned and was gone before I even had time to agree. But I shall go anyway, of course. Even a small donation to our surgery would be invaluable. And besides – Lord Ruthven seems an interesting man. I am sure his company will prove stimulating. Yes, I shall certainly go.

During my return to Whitechapel, I continued to have the sensation of being watched. It persisted as far as Liverpool Street. I was struck there, amidst the crowds that were thronging Bishops-gate, by a woman of remarkable beauty, seated in a carriage. She seemed to be studying me. Her hair, however, was not dark but blonde, and her features undoubtedly European. Powerful attraction towards her – like nothing I have ever known. Greater even than the desire I felt for the woman captured by Moorfield at the Kalibari Pass. A feeling too – very strong – like the one we all experienced on the Kalikshutra wall: my mind being probed. Ridiculous, of course.

Must catch up on my sleep. Shall retire to bed shortly.

Bram Stoker's Journal (continued).

. . . My interest in the case seemed not to abate, but to grow with the passage of time. Eager to discuss it further, I would sometimes invite

Eliot to share a meal with me. He would answer my invitations only irregularly, for quite apart from the pressures of his work he was by nature, I think, a solitary man. Nevertheless, we would sometimes meet, and on such occasions I would press him to recount any developments.

He told me that Sir George was recovering gradually, but that he had not himself paid his friend a visit yet. Of the prostitute we had rescued, he had more certain news. Her name was Kelly – Mary Jane Kelly – and she was not in fact from Rotherhithe at all but from a tenement half a mile from Eliot's own surgery. He told me that he had sent an orderly to the address; he had found a man there, claiming to be the woman's husband but seemingly unconcerned by his wife's condition. He had been abusive and drunk. In the circumstances, Eliot was determined to keep his patient for as long as he could. Funds were low, though, he told me. 'She cannot stay with us indefinitely,' he sighed. 'A wretched business – as it always is.'

One evening he sent me a note, informing me that Kelly was due to be interviewed by the Rotherhithe police the next day. Naturally I was eager to witness such a session, and so arranged my affairs that I was able to attend. Arriving at Whitechapel the following morning, I went straight up to Eliot's rooms. He was huddled amongst his tubes and bunsen flames, but seemed pleased to see me despite being disturbed. 'I was certain you would come, Stoker,' he exclaimed, rising to greet me. 'Our adventure is not yet quite at an end.'

He led me downstairs to a private room, where we were shortly joined by an officer from Rotherhithe. Eliot rose and left us, and when he returned he had Mary Kelly by his side. She seemed nervous, but much recovered nonetheless, and agreed to describe what she could remember of her assault. Eliot, I observed, was watching her with sudden uncertainty; and I noticed how she seemed distracted by the bustle of the street outside. Opposite the window was a rubbish tip; stray dogs were nosing amongst the litter for scraps, and the patient could scarcely keep her eyes from them. When Eliot pressed her, however, she assured him that she still felt

SLAVE OF MY THIRST

perfectly well. And so the interview began.

Her story was a simple one. She had been drinking in a pub by the Greenland Dock, where she had fallen into conversation with a sailor who had told her of a friend who was looking for a girl. Kelly, being short of funds, had agreed to accompany him. The sailor had led her to a hansom waiting outside; the door was opened to her, and Kelly had clambered in.

At this point in her story, however, she began to shake. She staggered to her feet and crossed to the window, pressing her face against the pane of glass. Again, I observed how she was staring at the dogs. Eliot attempted to lead her back to her seat, but she shrugged him away. She asked that the dogs be allowed to sit with her, and when Eliot refused her demand Kelly pressed her lips together and wouldn't say a further word. Instead, she continued to stare out at the dogs on the tip. Eliot, I could tell, was growing worried now; he clearly thought it best, when the patient's recovery was still so fragile, to humour her whims, and so he ordered that a dog be brought in for her. Kelly greeted it with delight and, sitting down again, settled it on her lap. After a couple of minutes, she continued with her tale.

Inside the cab, she told us, the sailor's friend had been waiting for her. This friend, however, had not been a man. At once I saw Eliot lean forward in his chair, and I too listened to Kelly's description of the woman with particular care. It did not, however, match either Lucy's or Lady Mowberley's, for the woman Kelly had seen had been a negress – though again, of a beauty which had struck Kelly literally dumb. Indeed, when Eliot pressed her on this point, she agreed that the woman's loveliness had *frightened* her. The negress had then – I blush to record it – stripped her of her clothes and fondled her in a most lewd and offensive manner; Kelly had been too nervous even to object. The negress had also brought out a jar – made of gold, Kelly said, and wonderfully decorated. The negress had held her wrist and sliced it with a knife; the blood had begun to spill into the jar. At this point Kelly had screamed; she had opened the carriage door and leaped into the street. The carriage hadn't stopped. Kelly had lain where she had fallen; slowly, her consciousness had slipped away.

At this point she fell silent. The policeman tried to press her on a few further points but she refused to answer him, stroking and fondling the dog instead. At length, the policeman sighed and rose to his feet. Eliot called for an attendant to remove Kelly back to her bed, but when she came Kelly wouldn't be budged from her chair. Instead she clung to the dog, moaning to herself, then suddenly staring at the wound to her wrist. She began to scream unintelligibly, and to rub at the scar. 'My blood,' she shrieked, 'my blood, it's been stolen, it's all gone!' She ripped at her bandages and a thick stream of blood began to drip on to the dog. Kelly stared at it, fascinated, as the dog began to whine and to lick at the blood, twisting and writhing on the woman's lap. Eliot tried to remove the animal, but Kelly clung to it desperately, then shuddered and moaned and threw it to the floor. The dog yelped with fear; but as it tried to run from the room, Kelly seized it by the throat. 'My blood,' she screamed at me, 'don't you see, it's been given my blood!' With her bare hands, she ripped apart the poor dog's throat. It thrashed desperately, but before anyone could lay his hands on Kelly, she had severed the artery with her nails, and the dog expired with a frothing howl of pain; as the blood pumped out Kelly rubbed her wrist against it, as though seeking to absorb the flow into her scar. By now the attendants had seized her; she was removed from the room, but as she was led away she broke free and threw herself against a far wall, scrabbling against it desperately as though attempting to pull it down with her fingernails. The patient was seized again, and tranquillised.

Eliot stayed almost an hour by her side. When he rejoined me, he could only shake his head. 'Mental illness is not,' he confessed, 'my speciality, and yet I am reluctant to see the woman removed to an asylum. She was so close, I felt, to recovery.' He sighed, and slumped into a chair. 'I should never have let her be questioned. I am entirely at fault.'

He mentioned one possible line of inquiry. It seemed that the angry crowd we had encountered in Rotherhithe had been perfectly correct, and that Kelly might not have been the only victim of the mysterious negress. Other women too, and sailors from foreign ships, had indeed been reported missing, with no subsequent trace of them ever being found. A prostitute, however, had been discovered in Rotherhithe – like Mary Kelly almost drained of her blood, and now accounted clinically insane. Eliot tapped his notebook. 'I have the address of the asylum where she is kept. If Mary Kelly's symptoms persist, it may be worth my while visiting there.'

'And I shall accompany you,' I said at once.

Eliot smiled. 'Naturally,' he replied. 'But first we must see how poor Kelly improves. Do not worry, Stoker, I shall keep you informed. For now though, if you will forgive me – I have a lot of work to do.'

And so I left him, much perturbed and more puzzled than I had been before I arrived . . .

Letter, Sir George Mowberley to Dr John Eliot.

> *The India Office,*
> *Whitehall,*
> *London.*

> *1 May 1888.*

Dear Jack,

You're a damn nuisance, aren't you? Always beware of thin, clever men – wasn't there some chap who said that once? Shakespeare probably, it usually is – and anyway, even if he didn't, he should have done. Because, thanks to you, Jack Eliot, I am now in a pickle of rare proportions, what with the scratch to my leg and my amatory exploits exposed, and Rosamund angry and upset with me – well, I say she's angry, but she isn't really, because if truth be told she's being an utter brick. In fact, it's forgiveness all round *chez* Mowberley, which is pretty good of Rosa and sensible too, I suppose, because at the end of the day, it's a simple fact of life, isn't it, that men have needs and women don't? You're a scientist, Jack, you'll back me up on that. I mean, hang it all, it's biology. The female nurtures and builds up the home, while the male goes out and makes his way in the world. That's all I've been doing – making my way in the world. I know I've been a brute – an utter pig – but as God is my witness, it didn't seem like that at the time.

I know it's hard to explain to you, because you're such a damned cold fish and you've never had much time for the weaker sex, but these past few months I've been pretty much head-over-heels – bewitched, besotted, bowled first ball. Don't worry, Jack – I'm not really cross with you for spoiling things, because I know you've done me a bloody good turn, and I am grateful, really I am, marriage being a sacred bond and all that rot – still, I'd like to try and explain it to you if I can, just so you don't think I'm a total ass. Damn it! Now, who's that? Some civil servant just come in through the door, droning on about something official, confound him to hell! Shall resume later.

Later. Well, that's that sorted out. Or not, as the case may be, because actually, between you and me, Jack, all these niggling details leave me rather cold – don't have much time for them, more of a broad strokes man myself. That's what I'm here for, after all, the broader picture – details are for clerks and bureaucrats, pen-pushers, don't you know? It was Lilah who helped me understand that. I suppose you've been told I'm working on a pretty big Bill, future of the Empire at stake, etcetera, etcetera, all very hush-hush? Yes, Rosa would have told you. Anyway, it's savagely complex, and before I met Lilah I was getting really quite swamped, but now I've got it all nicely in hand, and it's three cheers for me for having sorted it out. I've made quite an impression, though I say it myself. Actually, you know, politics has turned out to be quite a lark. Amazing to think I ever found it difficult. But sorry, Jack, I'm heading off beam. Where was I? Oh, yes – my affair with Lilah, and how it all began.

Well, oddly enough, it was Rosamund's fault. No, not *fault* exactly, that's the wrong word, of course, but she would keep on about this jewellery she'd seen in the front of Headley's shop, and once she'd made her mind up – well, you know what women are like – nothing else would do for her. But here comes the catch – this jewellery turns out to be bloody fancy stuff, Indian, I think, and can only be bought in Rotherhithe. Rotherhithe! Not where a gentleman cares to be seen. But because Rosa's upset with me, and because it's her birthday soon, and because I'm sped by the wings of love and all that bilge, to Rotherhithe I head – and a ghastlier hell-hole I've never seen. Can you believe that people choose to live in such a place? Seems extraordinary to me. But anyhow, feeling like some true-hearted knight on a quest, I pick my way through all the turnip-heads and dung, reach the shop, go in, knock up the owner, ask for the jewels – and do you know what? – I'm informed, quite coolly, that the jewels have just been sold!

Well, Jack, I was not pleased. In fact, I would go so far as to say that I was positively miffed. So I think, damn it, Rosa will just have to put up with some other gift; I've wasted enough time on these jewels as it is, there is an Empire out there and it doesn't run itself. I storm out – or rather, I'm in mid-storm, because before I've left I have a sudden stroke of luck. The shop door opens and a woman comes in. She's a stunner, Jack, a rare old eyeful, like no one I've ever seen before. Expensive-looking, damnably exotic, none of your prissy English miss about her – she's got dark hair, red lips, all the fittings. But I can't remotely do her justice because I'd have to be a poet, which I'm not, being totally unendowed on the description front; so all I will say, Jack, is that if you saw her, even you might turn your head. She was bewitching – what else can I say? To gaze was to fall like a weight beneath her spell. And I did gaze – goodness, did I gaze. Suddenly, it was springtime, and there were bluebirds twittering, and, oh God – you know – all the works.

Now, when bluebirds get a-twittering, you don't hang back. We fell to chatting, me all gallant and her all shy, but I could see the come-hither in her eyes and I knew my luck was in. It wasn't that I'd forgotten Rosa – damn it, I still love her and all that – but as I said, I just couldn't help myself. And it was almost as if Fate had meant this beauty for me, because suddenly up pops the shopkeeper and it turns out she's the one who bought his jewels, and when she finds out I want them she offers them to me, and I settle a price, and it's all dandy as hell. Her carriage is outside. I get in with her, and we head off to her abode. It's not far from the shop, and it's ... well ... you've seen it, Jack, it's a pretty stunning place. Not really to my taste, you understand, a bit too flamboyant and clever for me, but then she's from foreign climes, so not her fault, I suppose, it's just the way they breed them out there.

Anyway, she sits me down and gets out the jewels, and all the time servants are scurrying here and there, bringing me cushions, and champagne, and God knows what else, and I'm generally feeling like some Oriental despot. I mean to go but I don't, I simply can't move and then, before I know what I'm doing, I'm having her, there on the cushions, and it's as though I'm entering Paradise, because I've never known a woman as perfect as her, who moves as she moves and does the things she does. Sorry to go into the details, old man, but it's important you understand the effect she had, and anyway, you're a doctor, you know about these things. It *is* Paradise, Jack, what she gives to me. I told her this at the time, and she laughed and said that the Muslim heaven was full of girls, but she hadn't realised that the Christian heaven was. I told her, in that case I was planning to convert at once. She accepted this proposal quite solemnly. 'The meaning of Islam is submission,' she said. 'From now on, I shall be your religion. Therefore, first, you must submit to me.' Aren't women charming, with their little whims and ways? And it paid too, you know, because as a reward for my submission I was allowed to enter Paradise again, where I stayed all night and the following day. Wonderful woman, Jack – wonderful!

But I don't want you to think that it was just beastly animal lusts and all that. We talked too and even her voice was magical. Really, I could have sat there all night just listening to it – actually, come to think of it, that's exactly what I did. Her real name was something foreign and unpronounceable, and when I tried to say it it only made me spit – so we settled for Lilah as a compromise. She was a Far East trader, she said, which explained what she was doing living by the docks, but do you know, Jack, when she also claimed she had royal blood I wasn't in the least bit surprised? She had that air, if you know what I mean. I tried to find out where her royal blood came from, but she just laughed and said her homeland was all the world. I would think, though, that she is from India or Arabia – somewhere hot, anyway, where the skins are not as pale as ours and the passions a good deal more flammable. For she's proud, Jack, proud as the devil, and with her servants at least she likes to crack a pretty nifty whip. My good self, by contrast, you'll be glad to hear, she honours and obeys like a perfect slave. Damned flattering, as you can imagine. She's clearly found something she is drawn to in me – the natural authority of the public man, perhaps? You will laugh, Jack and think I am boasting, but it is surely a fact of life, is it not, that an important national figure like myself must accrue an aura of power? It is to this, I am sure, that Lilah responds, for she is after all, only a woman, and a foreigner to boot, while I am a Minister in Her Majesty's Government. Above all, Jack – and this is my proudest claim – I hold the title of an English gentleman, and what foreign girl could ever rival such a boast? It is my birthright, after all, to order and command. Lilah, I think, is merely recognising this.

And indeed, in some strange way, she has helped me to understand it for myself. It is the queerest thing, but I never felt half so confident before I met her, whereas now, as you're probably aware, I am spoken of as a possible future Foreign Secretary. Foreign Secretary! – me, George Mowberley! – whom you and Arthur Ruthven used to laugh at so! Well, Jack, the last laugh is with me, for I have found talents in myself I had only half-suspected before, and in a sense, I suppose it's all down to Lilah's help. I don't mean that she advises me on policy, or makes suggestions herself, or anything of that kind – that would clearly be ridiculous, for she may be bright but she's a woman all the same. And yet, you know, Jack, it is perhaps the very fact that she *is* a woman which has helped me so much, for though she may not understand diplomacy or politics, nevertheless she listens to my explanations with such sweet and tender concentration, and is so wonderfully absorbed in all I have to say. When I talk to Lilah, I find I'm thinking more clearly than I've ever done – problems melt away, while ideas and solutions start to crowd on me. Don't scoff, Jack. I know it's your favourite habit, but before you start off just ask yourself this: why has my Bill been such a swimming success? Before I met Lilah, there'd been problems with it – I've already told you that, I think. But then, actually, such a confession wouldn't have surprised you much at all – I've always been a bit of a duffer in your eyes. Don't deny it! But I can assure you, Jack, my days of dufferdom are long gone now, and what's more I'm not embarrassed to tell you so. Only a matter of months, old boy, since I met Lilah, but my work is now the toast of the Cabinet. Did you realise that? Or that the press like to call me 'a glittering star'? Me! Only just thirty! Have you ever heard of such a thing? Were you or Arthur ever called 'a glittering star'? I think not. And yet, without Lilah, who knows? – I might just have gone ahead and packed the whole business in.

So you can see now how important she has been to me. I told Rosamund right at the start that my absences were caused by the pressures of work. Well, Jack, it was the simple truth. Not the whole truth, I admit, but the truth all the same – *I work at my best when Lilah's by my side.* I can't get round that. And remember, it wasn't just my career I've had to think about – I was dealing with the future of the British Raj itself. Pretty weighty stuff, you know. So really, Jack, what else could I have done? Only what I did. I began taking my papers down to Rotherhithe. I got cracking on the spadework for the Bill. Gradually, over the months, Lilah grew more and more indispensable. An hour with her, it seemed, was worth a whole day's work elsewhere. It was tricky of course, before the Easter recess, getting down to see her for any longer than a night, but once Parliament had risen I hied off pretty sharp and booked in for a stay. Oh, yes, I can hear you ask, in your always-suspect-the-worst-of-George tone of voice – and what have I been getting up to all this time? Well, I won't deny it, Jack, that there may have been the odd bout of carnal pleasuring – I mean, damn it all, she's the most bewitching creature, the absolute loveliest, for God's sake! – but I did work too, in between, and what's more worked bloody hard and well.

I can prove it. Remember what Rosa saw? Me togged up in my Sultan's clothes? Well, I'd never have been in my study if I hadn't needed papers from my box. It wasn't the first time, either. Previously, of course, I'd had Rosa on that sleeping drug, so she never found me out and I was able to get away with it. I can see now that I behaved like a fathead over that whole affair, but it was tricky, Jack, damned tricky, because I thought if Rosamund saw me it would only make things worse. It was Lilah's plan, anyway – she had the drug amongst her merchandise, and I don't know how, she just persuaded me. Remarkable the things she can get me to do. I sometimes half-wonder if she's not a mesmerist.

Actually, while we're on the topic of Lilah's ideas, the darkie disguise was one of hers as well. I know I must have looked a rare old sight, but even so I don't think anyone ever recognised me. No, you did, I suppose – eventually – but no one else did, not even Lucy or Rosamund. We went out quite a bit, in fact – Lilah liked the occasional London jaunt, and that's why she bought the flat above Headley's shop as a base for our adventures in the centre of town. That's where the togging-up went on, so I could then cut my dash as the Sultan, you see. Didn't do the make-up, though – that was very much Lilah's side of ship. I never worked out what she used on me – damned effective, though, whatever it was – once she'd slapped the stuff on, I seemed a wholly different chap. I wasn't just that my skin was darker, but it gleamed as well, and the whole structure of my face seemed changed. Very odd. I used to look in a mirror and feel quite frightened of myself. Whenever I asked Lilah she'd just smile and look away, and if I pressed her she'd turn all Mystic East on me. 'Do not lift the veil,' you know, all that Arabian Nights sort of stuff. Actually, Jack, for a while I almost wondered if the make-up wasn't blood – it was a liquid, you see, quite red and sticky, and it had the same sort of smell, like an underdone steak. Of course it wasn't blood at all, but you can tell how similar it looked from Lucy's response when she saw the stuff all streaked across my face. Hell of a business, that was. Can you imagine? There I am, innocently indulging in a spot of adultery, and I glance out of the window and there's my ward looking up at me from the pavement outside. Pretty hairy, eh? Fortunately, Lilah's on the mark. She smears my face with the cloth, and I give Lucy one further horrified glance, and then I'm hoofing it up the stairs as fast as I can. I wait on the landing while Lucy and some doltish constable are let into the flat, and Lucy starts yelling murder and looking for my corpse. Well, said corpse is tickled pretty pink by this – you know me, Jack, a sportsman through and through, and besides I'm longing to see Lucy again, so I do a bloody risky thing. I sneak back down the stairs; I wait out on the street; then I saunter back up the stairs again and stroll into the flat. And the damned thing is, even though Lilah had only smeared the make-up on, Lucy can't tell who I am! In fact, she seems positively revolted by me!

Bloody amusing! And actually, even though she didn't recognise me at the time, it was splendid seeing the dear girl again. You know she's had a baby? Or maybe you don't, in which case I shouldn't have mentioned it. Oh, well – too late now. But anyway, the point about this offspring is that Rosa blames Lucy's lover for it, and so Lucy hates Rosa, and so the two of them refuse to see each other and Lucy never comes to visit me. Add to that all the time I've spent with Lilah and you'll see why I was glad to see her face again, because we've been virtual strangers for almost a year. I can't deny I've sometimes felt pretty rotten about it. I mean, hang it all, Lucy *is* my ward, and when you think about poor Arthur and all she's been through since his death, and her tender years and all that . . . well – I felt guilty, as I said. That was why I went to the Lyceum, you see. I couldn't miss her opening night. Stupid of me, really – especially going there on the second night as well. Talk about tempting fate – or rather, talk about tempting you, Jack – you and your mighty calculating brain, honed by years of puzzles and long-division sums. I suppose I must have been pretty easy meat. Ah, well – it's an ill wind that has no silver lining, or whatever the saying is. You know what I mean. I've learnt my lesson, Jack – I can see now what a total and utter fathead I've been. I can promise you this, though – there'll be no more visits to Lilah's for a while.

And that's a gentleman speaking, giving you his word. Dear

Rosamund – what a lovely, sweet and forgiving thing she is, and damn it, old man, what a lucky fellow I am, what with the warmth of the family hearth and all that. How could I ever have put it at risk? How could I ever have been such an ass? How could I ever have caused my dear Rosa such pain? Well, thank God for the straight and narrow, I say, and long may I continue on it! I can't say I regret Lilah, Jack – she was something too wonderful and different for that – but I have had my fill, I realise now.

Come and visit me, Jack. Call in on my office. It's damned impressive, and has the largest desk in the history of the world. But then, considering what's being run from it, I suppose, a largeish desk is pretty much required. But no, shouldn't boast – the point is that I'm pretty keen to see you, old man. It's been a long time, hasn't it? I would drive over myself right now, but I'm still a bit weak, apparently, and though I'm allowed to work at my desk – (my huge desk!) – I'm not allowed to travel. Damn shame, but there it is.

All the best, old man. And again, from Rosa and myself – many thanks.

> Until very soon, old fellow,
> Your devoted friend,
>
> GEORGE.

Dr Eliot's Diary.

7 *May*. – A hard week, with very little time for either research or thought. Able to work in my laboratory this afternoon, though, and then later read through Kleinelanghorst on cancerous cells. Interesting arguments, but where is his evidence? The same problem I have with my own theories – lack of consistent experiential proof. I seem to be going nowhere. I wish I had samples of the Kalikshutran blood. Then at least I would have something to work on. But as it is, I am hopelessly lost.

Better luck with the Rotherhithe affair, though even that is not entirely solved, and there are aspects of the mystery which still concern me. But at least George seems to have learned his lesson; I have emphasised to him that he should keep away from Lilah – and if he can only stick to his word and not go back to her, then any future danger should be minimised. He had written to me earlier in the week, and seemed remarkably recovered from all his experiences. It is appalling, though, to think he is a Minister – the more conceited he grows, the more stupidly he seems to behave – the same George Mowberley, then. And yet ... not altogether. For when I arrived at Grosvenor Street to visit him last night, I found that he was still, as he had claimed to be, exceedingly weak; indeed, so weak that I am astonished he has been attending to his work at all, for at Cambridge he would go to bed at the slightest excuse, and yet now he is slaving like some driven thing.

'It is his Bill', said Lady Mowberley in a private aside. 'He believes that it will make his career, and yet if it kills him what happens to his prospects then?' She asked me to have a word with George; I willingly obliged. But all my arguments were laughed away; George insisted there was nothing the matter with him, and when I continued to press the issue he challenged me to test his health and identify anything wrong with him. I did so, and could find nothing obvious, I admit. Yet how to explain his weakness, which remains so evident? On a sudden intuition, I checked him for any sign of scarring. The only scratch I could find was down the side of his neck, but George claimed it was a shaving cut and I see no reason to dispute his assertion. I could therefore only advise him, as a doctor, not to work too hard – at which he laughed, as well he might have done, for he is not used to hearing such advice from me.

When Lady Mowberley retired, George talked to me more about Lilah. His passion for her was evident, yet to my relief he did seem wedded to his resolution not to see her again. Much general breast-beating, and praise of his wife. I asked him how his work was progressing without Lilah's help. He shrugged and seemed offended, then muttered that I had taken his letter too literally – he was not really dependent on her presence by his side. He laughed rather forcedly. Then, when I asked him whether Lilah might not be from a region on the Indian frontier, he laughed a second time and spluttered most indignantly. 'Why the devil should she be?' he asked.

I explained; I pressed him on the matter of Kalikshutra. I asked him, for instance, whose idea it had been to name him as the Rajah of that kingdom on the Lyceum register – his own, or Lilah's? George frowned and thought. 'My own,' he muttered at length. 'Yes, definitely, my own, my own, my own.' This phrase repeated with increasing assertiveness. 'You see, Jack,' he added, as though worried that I was still not convinced, 'Kalikshutra is a kingdom covered by my Bill. I have been busy deciding what its status should be. Therefore, it's hardly surprising that its name was on my mind. Don't you think?' He glanced up at me; I made no reply. 'And also,' he said hurriedly, 'there were those jewels, the ones I bought from Lilah – you remember them? Well, they were from Kalikshutra too.'

I smiled faintly at this. George leaned forward. 'What the deuce are you implying, Jack?'

I shrugged. I didn't answer him at first. Instead, I asked him what he was proposing for Kalikshutra in his Bill.

He looked indignant. 'You know I can't tell you that.'

'Very well,' I replied, 'then I apologise. But all the same, George, I was just wondering ... the work you've been doing on Kalikshutra – did Lilah by any chance help you with that?'

George stared at me in silence for a second or two; then he shook his head and laughed again. 'For God's sake, Jack, I've told you, she's a woman – she doesn't actually *understand* politics.' He boomed uproariously at the very idea, and the conversation gradually drifted to other matters. Occasionally, though, I observed a faint frown on his brow, which I chose to interpret as a hopeful sign; if George had really never considered what I had suggested to him, then it was high time that he did. I hope that it will genuinely encourage him to stay away from this mysterious Lilah; I write that not just out of concern for Lady Mowberley's wounded feelings, but for George himself. I am not certain what it is exactly that I dread; there are many strands here, and perhaps I am afraid to see what pattern they may form. I have sometimes thought of Huree: he would have an answer – he would identify the pattern for me. But of course he would be wrong; and I can't waste my time with impossibilities. There is only one thing of which I am certain: this mystery is yet to be fathomed to its depths.

All this I was thinking in my cab last night, journeying back from the Mowberleys. Oddly enough, even as I was pondering the case I was struck by a sense I have had before that someone – or something – was watching me. Of course, I know that such a feeling is invariably irrational but nevertheless, so overpowering did it grow last night, that I leant out from the window and scanned the street behind me. I could make out nothing; it was dark by now, and even the gas lights were shrouded in curls of purple mist, while the street itself was full of traffic. I laughed at myself for being an idiot, and sat back again inside the cab. Nevertheless, when we reached the Whitechapel Road I paid off the hansom and proceeded to Surgeon's Court on foot. The noise of traffic soon died away; before the turning to Hanbury Street, I ducked inside a tenement door and waited to see who might follow me. No one came; I was preparing to return to the street when suddenly I heard the splashing of hooves and the slicing of wheels through the Whitechapel mud. A hansom passed me; as it did so, a curtain was drawn back and I saw a face at the cab window, staring at me. A second, and it was gone; but I had recognised it all the same. It was the face I observed before by Bishopsgate – the woman's, blonde-haired, exceedingly pale. I must assume, therefore, that my intuition had been correct, and that she had indeed been following me. I do not know why.

One suggestive point of correspondence, though. In Lilah too, and in the negress seen by Mary Kelly – a loveliness which is reported to chill the blood.

11p.m. – A visit from George. Entirely unexpected; it was late, and George himself was still looking very weak. He came straight to the point. He wanted to visit Lilah, to ask her if she was indeed from Kalikshutra. It seems, then, that my suggestions have indeed been bearing fruit. Disturbed, though, that George should even contemplate returning to Rotherhithe. I repeated all my warnings, then made him sit down and write a letter breaking off his relationship with Lilah for good. I told him to leave it with me – that I would see it posted. He left around midnight, with many words of thanks.

15 May. – My date with Lord Ruthven. A very remarkable evening, which seems to promise unparalleled opportunities for research. I was late leaving – a lengthy surgery – and it was not until nine that I finally arrived. Lord Ruthven's home is very splendid but not, I think, much lived in, for the furnishings seemed somewhat sepulchral for a man of his undoubted taste. I asked him if I was correct; he acknowledged that I was, explaining that he did not much care for the English cold. He spoke enthusiastically of Greece. And yet for a lover of sunnier climes he seems remarkably indifferent to the darkness of his home, for many of the rooms were lit by single candles, and even in the dining room the illumination was only fitful. Yet there were enough candles for me to see that, in this room at least, Lord Ruthven had spared no effort or expense, for it was magnificently decorated and the table itself was groaning with food.

'Please help yourself,' said my host, with a wave of his hand. 'I don't have the patience for anything formal.' I did as he instructed, while a servant girl of astonishing prettiness served us both wine. I am not an expert on such matters, but I could tell at once that it was very good, and when I asked Lord Ruthven, he smiled and agreed that it was the best. 'I have an agent in Paris,' he murmured. 'He sends me only the very finest vintages.'

I observed, however, that he did not drink much himself; nor, though his plate was full, did he really eat. Yet this did nothing to inhibit my own pleasure in the evening, for Lord Ruthven's powers of conversation were very great, and I cannot remember a more fascinating or witty host; certainly, not one so young and yet so brilliant. Indeed, there seemed something almost unearthly about his attractiveness, and listening to the magical tones of his voice, staring at his beauty lit gold by the flames, I felt that same shiver of uncertainty he had induced in me before – in the theatre, and standing on Lucy's stairs. Almost without realising it, I began to resist the pleasure that his conversation was giving me, and I was even careful not to drink too much of his wine, as though afraid that it might be seducing me. I began to ask myself what such a seduction might mean: what power Lord Ruthven might choose to exert if I fell; of what enchantments he might be capable.

And so I grew increasingly restive, and wondered all the more what his purpose had been in inviting me. At length, glancing at a clock and seeing how late it had grown, I asked him to explain his interest in my article, for my curiosity I told him could no longer be restrained. Lord Ruthven smiled. 'You are perfectly correct to be curious,' he said. 'But first we must wait for Haidée.'

'Haidée?' I asked.

He smiled again, but didn't answer me. Instead, he turned to the maid and ordered her to tell Lady Ruthven that Dr Eliot was in attendance in the dining room. The maid went; we sat in silence. I had assumed that we were waiting for Lord Ruthven's wife; but when Haidée at length came into the room, I saw that she was remarkably old, tiny and stooped, and very pale. She had clearly once been beautiful, though, and her eyes – which were very wide – were still as luminous and bright as Lord Ruthven's own. But they did not seem as cold; nor did Haidée, though her affinity to him was obvious, fill me with the same strange feelings of uneasiness and fear. She kissed my hand, then went to her chair, sitting there like a wax-work; yet for all her stillness, I found her presence a comforting one.

Lord Ruthven leaned forward and began to talk to me about my paper. He had mastered the principles well and seemed – which is more than can be said for my colleagues – to be enthused by them. In particular, he was intrigued by my theory of sanguigens, and the opportunities for classification presented by the apparent presence of antigenic substances in red blood cells. He asked me to explain the potential I saw in this discovery for transfusions; I did so, and when I mentioned the need to use compatible blood types he seemed to grow visibly tense. 'You mean,' he asked in a low, urgent voice, 'that the correct sanguigen, extracted from a donor, might combine with that of another man? That is what is required? The correct type of blood?'

I replied that my research was still in its infancy, but Lord Ruthven waved his hand impatiently at this. 'I quite understand your professional reluctance to speak in terms of certainties,' he told me, 'but let us just take for granted that we are discussing probabilities. A probability, after all, is better than nothing at all.' He leaned forward again, his stare unblinking, his pale hand resting on my own. 'I need to know this, Dr Eliot,' he said at last. He swallowed. 'If we could find the correct "sanguigen", the correct ... "blood group" – and if we combined it with my own blood, then would you expect them to be compatible?'

I nodded. 'That is what my theory argues.'

'How many different blood groups have you identified?'

'Four, so far.'

'Might there be more? Might there be very rare sanguigens?'

I shrugged. 'It is possible. As I said, opportunities for research have been limited. My paper has hardly set the scientific world on fire.'

'But it has interested me.' Lord Ruthven smiled. 'And I am a very rich man, Dr Eliot.'

'So you have said.'

Lord Ruthven glanced at Haidée. For a few seconds, there was no sound but the ticking of the clock. Haidée, who had been staring into a candle flame since first sitting down, slowly raised her eyes. She licked her lips with a quick, darting tongue and her teeth, I noticed, were very sharp.

'We are both of us,' she said, then paused, '... ill.' Her voice was silvery and clear, but very distant too, as though coming from a great depth. 'We would like you to help us find some cure, Dr Eliot.'

'What is its nature?' I asked.

'It is a sickness of the blood.'

'Yes, but how does it manifest itself? What are its symptoms?'

Haidée glanced at Lord Ruthven, who was gazing into his wine. 'I believe,' he murmured, still not looking up at me, 'that we suffer from a form of anaemia.'

'I see.' I studied him, observing his pallor. 'And hence your interest in receiving transfusions of blood?'

'Yes.' He inclined his head faintly. 'And hence in turn our interest in finding out to which sanguigen – which blood group – we belong.' Lord Ruthven looked up at me at last. 'Find out for us. Restore us to our health. Cure this sickness which infects our blood.' He paused. 'I can assure you, Doctor, it would be worth your while to have me in your debt.'

'I don't doubt it,' I answered, 'but really, a bribe is not necessary.'

'Nonsense. A bribe will always help. It is only vanity which makes you claim otherwise.' Lord Ruthven removed a paper from the inside of his jacket and glanced at it. 'How much would it cost to install the basic equipment your hospital needs?'

I considered carefully. 'Five hundred pounds,' I replied.

'You have it,' he said at once. He scribbled briefly, then pushed the piece of paper across to me. 'Present this to my bankers tomorrow. They will see that you receive the money.'

'My Lord, this is remarkably generous.'

'Then, please' – his eyes narrowed – 'respond to it with some generosity of your own.' Still staring at me, he reached for Haidée's hand and grasped it tightly. A shadow of pain seemed to pass across his face, but was gone as soon as I had noticed it.

'I will need samples of your blood,' I said, scraping back my chair.

Lord Ruthven nodded. 'Of course. Take it now.'

'I can't, I don't have the equipment, but if I come back tomorrow ...'

Lord Ruthven held up a hand to silence me. He reached down, and I heard the click of a case being opened and something removed from it. Then he sat upright in his chair again and laid down two syringes in front of me.

I shook my head. 'But the blood will clot ...'

'No.'

I looked at him in surprise. 'But I have no sodium citrate, I will need ...'

'We will not wait, Doctor. Listen' – he leaned forward – 'it is a feature of our sickness that our blood will always remain fluid.'

'Haemophilia?'

Lord Ruthven smiled mockingly. 'Our scars heal. Our scars *always* heal. But when blood is taken directly from the vein, removed as you will remove it through a needle's point, it never clots. If you don't believe me, Dr Eliot, you have only to put it to the test.'

I stared at him doubtfully, but he had already removed his jacket and was rolling up his sleeve. He pinched a blue vein and, staring at it, I saw him close his eyes as though in ecstasy.

'I will need a container, a flask to transport it in,' I said.

Lord Ruthven smiled, and gestured with a turn of his head at the maidservant. I glanced at her and saw she was holding two champagne bottles. I opened my mouth to protest, but Lord Ruthven raised a hand. 'These will be perfectly adequate,' he insisted, 'so please, not a word.'

I shrugged. His taste for melodrama was clearly something I would have to ignore. I took one of the bottles, laid it by Lord Ruthven's arm and then picked up the syringe. The flow of blood from his vein was very fast and as I withdrew the syringe I saw on his face an expression of deep pleasure. He watched unblinkingly as I decanted the blood into the bottle, then corked it. He picked up the bottle and stared through the thick green glass at the blood. 'How charmingly Gothic,' he murmured. He raised it to me. 'Your very good health.'

I repeated the process with Haidée. Her vein was much tougher than Lord Ruthven's had been. At my first attempt, the point of the needle failed to enter it. I apologised to her, but she seemed to feel no pain and instead merely smiled – sadly, I thought. At the second attempt I succeeded in drawing her blood; it seemed almost impossibly thick. When I decanted it into the second bottle, I saw how dark it looked, and glutinous.

I have kept the two samples separate and divided them in turn. One test-tube of each patient's blood I have stored in the cold room; the other I have before me on my desk as I speak. I wish to test Lord Ruthven's assertion that his blood will not clot. I shall leave it at room temperature until the morning. But for now, it is very late and I must withdraw to bed.

16 May. – Lord Ruthven was quite correct. It seems impossible, but all the samples of blood – both those in the cold room and those preserved at room temperature – have remained fluid. Am keen to analyse them. Will do so once my morning ward-round is complete.

1 p.m. – Separation of red blood cells and plasma far advanced. A curiously rapid process: it has taken, I would estimate, thirteen or fourteen hours rather than the customary twenty-four. Significant?

2 p.m. – Extraordinary results. The red blood cells, in both the residue at the bottom of the test-tubes and in the plasma on the surface, are dead; Lord Ruthven's self-diagnosis of anaemia is clearly correct, for the red cell count is remarkably low – around 20–15 per cent haemoglobin, I would estimate. In view of my patients' otherwise apparent good health last night, this reading was startling enough; but the greatest surprise came with my analysis of the white blood cells which, viewed under the microscope, have proved still to be alive. Not only alive but in great concentration as well, and subject to remarkable protoplasmic activity. It is inconceivable that red blood cells should be dead while the leucocytes remain alive – and yet this seems to be precisely what has occurred.

Have stored different samples of the leucocytes at different temperatures. Interested to know which will be the first to die. When I have the results, will return to Lord Ruthven.

Late. – Have been reading through my notes on Kalikshutra. Remarkable points of correspondence with the case in hand. I don't know what to think.

I wonder why Huree hasn't written to me.

18 May. – Two days gone. Leucocytes remain alive in all four samples. No sign of any degeneration.

19 May. – Samples as before. In Kalikshutra, the leucocytes were dead two days after extraction from the veins. At the time, I had thought that impossible; but it is clear now that I had not realised what impossibility might be.

Addendum. – Have wired Calcutta. Huree, it seems, is attending a conference in Berlin. There are aspects of this case he might find interesting. I shall see how the course of my research goes.

20 May. – Increasingly distracted in the surgery by thoughts of the blood samples upstairs in my room. Still no degeneration of white cells. Uncertain as to how I should proceed.

An encouraging talk with Mary Kelly, though. I hesitate to repeat the claim, but she seems well on the way to a full recovery. She has been telling me the story of her life – a sad one, as I had known it would be. A terrible waste, for she seems intelligent enough, and educated too. She talks of returning to her lodgings. I wish I could help her to something more than a single room in some squalid tenement. At least now, with Lord Ruthven's help, I can afford to give her the treatment she still needs.

Late. – A note from George, obviously written while drunk. He wants to visit Lilah again, and asks if I will accompany him. Have replied at once, telling him *on no account* to go to Rotherhithe.

21 May. – To George's office at Whitehall. To my surprise, am shown in. George rather sheepish and hung-over: he had written the note, he tells me, because he still wants to confront Lilah over the Kalikshutra business, but agrees it is best to let sleeping dogs lie. He gives me his word again. I mollify him by admiring his desk.

When I return to the surgery, Llewellyn informs me that Mary Kelly has something she wishes to tell me. When I visit her, however, she appears nervous and upset, and talks only of inconsequential matters. Something on her mind, though, that is clear enough.

Note, Miss Mary Jane Kelly to Dr John Eliot.

Dere Doctor Elliot, it's horrible. I wanted to tell you before but I can't, she'll know, or leestways that's how I feel. She's fading now. I haven't heard her voice for a long time. But she was there in the beginning in my blood, and that's what's making me afrade because I don't know what's been happening to me, and what she might know or hear me say or anything. I hope you understand.

But it is better now like I said. But sometimes I want the blood she took from me back again. I feel dizzy and can't control what I do. When I saw the dog that was what I felt, I couldn't control myself. Always animals. Again I am very afrade because I don't understand. Why do I have these thorts? They are very strong and I can't resist them, because I just know it, all my blood has been given to animals and changed, I know it, and I want it back. Sometimes when the feelings come and I think I am possessed, I can't help it.

But these thorts are fading too. I think I am better now sir. Thank you very much. Yours faithfully

MARY JANE KELLY (MISS)

Dr Eliot's Diary.

23 May. – A curious note from Mary Kelly. Reference to a mysterious 'she' – clearly the negress who had sliced her wrist. Subsequent questioning of the patient confirmed this assumption. Kelly very reluctant to talk about her assailant, though, and would only do so in the lowest of whispers, shaking all the time. Poor woman, she is clearly terrified and nothing I could say would comfort her.

It seems there are a good number of unpleasant imaginings abroad. At the moment I find that even I am distracted by irrational fears. Reluctant to identify them too closely, so leave them unformed on the margins of my mind. I remember what happened the last time I surrendered to superstition. Must not allow it to happen again.

The state of the blood samples is unchanged: the leucocytes remain alive.

26 May. – Mary Kelly talks of discharging herself. I find out later that a man, one Joseph Barnett, had visited her earlier that morning, for the first time since her admission here. Claimed to be her husband; doubtless something worse. I can only assume he is running short of funds.

Condition of the leucocytes unchanged.

30 May. – Mary Kelly discharged. Joseph Barnett arrived to help lead her away. I felt strangely saddened at seeing her go. Unprofessional, of course, to identify with any particular patient, but she seems to embody for me all the blighted potential, the wretched waste, that is inflicted on millions of my countrymen. She, and all those like her, deserve so much more.

Condition of the leucocytes unchanged.

The implications grow more and more unnerving by the day.

4 June. – George reported to have called on me while I was out. He wouldn't leave a message, but I can guess what his business was. According to Llewellyn, he will call again tomorrow.

1 a.m. – Around midnight, experienced the strangest prickling down the nape of my neck. Turned round. Lord Ruthven was standing behind my chair. I had not heard him enter. He bade me good evening, very coldly, and though he did not say I knew why he had come, and what his purpose was. I glanced back at the test-tubes stored on my desk, and all of a sudden shivered at the thought of Lord Ruthven's illness, and what it might be. The very idea of his blood, flowing and alive in his veins, filled me with horror. Hard to explain such a feeling, but it was very real.

Lord Ruthven himself exceedingly cool and restrained, but angry too – sense of some maelstrom beneath a great sheet of ice. He asked me very softly how my work was progressing; I answered him by explaining my research on his blood cells, but his anger seemed unappeased.

'Why should you be surprised, Doctor?,' he asked me coldly. 'I told you before that our blood would never clot, and as for the blood cells – well ...' He paused, and smiled for the first time that night. 'You saw such a thing in Kalikshutra, did you not?'

I stared at him, surprised, then asked him how he knew.

'I have read all your papers,' he replied, 'even the most obscure.' I should be flattered, I suppose. The article was printed only in India; Lord Ruthven must have gone to some effort to obtain it. 'So then, Doctor,' he pressed me, removing his coat and unbuttoning his sleeve, 'have you started your work yet on a cure for the disease?'

'Disease, my Lord?'

'Yes, yes,' he said impatiently, 'the same disease you described in your paper.' He stared at me in sudden disbelief. 'What?' he exclaimed. 'All this time and you haven't even recognised it in the samples of our blood? Why do you think I approached you at all?'

'But the disease described in my paper does not exist outside Kalikshutra,' I replied.

Lord Ruthven raised an eyebrow. 'Indeed?'

'If you have read my paper on the blood type I studied there,' I told him, 'then you will know that the leucocytes survived for only forty-eight hours. Yours have been active for over two weeks now.'

'Then it is clear, is it not, that my condition must be all the more advanced?'

'My Lord,' I told him, trying to make him understand, 'your cells are of a quite different order from any I have ever seen before. Yes, I admit there is a certain resemblance to those I studied in the Himalayas. But it is the differences which are more significant. Yours are not degenerative. Yours do not affect your appearance and mental health, which if anything appear to have been enhanced. *Your cells, in short, show not the slightest sign of dying at all.*'

Lord Ruthven looked up at me, his grey eyes hard as jewels.

'Do you not see,' I insisted, 'the implications of what I am saying?'

He sneered faintly. 'I understand them quite well enough.'

'Why, my Lord . . .'

'Enough.'

'But in the name of God . . .'

'Enough!'

'But you can't understand – I mean . . . we could be talking of virtual immortality.'

Lord Ruthven did not reply to this. But as I opened my mouth to repeat what I had said, I felt my tongue suddenly dry and stick to my throat. It sounds ridiculous, I know, but the horror seemed to submerge me again. Then Lord Ruthven smiled; he extended his naked arm. The terror ebbed away from me.

'I have paid you,' he told me, 'to undertake a programme of research. You will require a fresh sample of my blood. Take it.'

I did so. The sample is in the cold room now. Tomorrow I must intensify my analysis. I shall give Lord Ruthven any results I obtain as soon as I can, for I accept that through my delays I have indeed wronged him. But why my reluctance? Why – I must admit to the word – my dread? The behaviour of his blood cells is admittedly extraordinary; but there is surely a rational explanation for their state. What more exciting task in all medicine could there be than to identify it? Who knows what mysteries might then be solved?

I shall work on the sanguigens tomorrow afternoon.

Telegram, Dr John Eliot to Professor Huree Jyoti Navalkar.

5 June.

Come as soon as you can. Remarkable developments. Need your advice urgently. Have no one else to whom I can turn.

JACK.

Dr Eliot's Diary.

5 June. – Let me remind myself aloud of my methods. It is important that I do so, for I am afraid that otherwise I may plunge into wild and illogical conclusions. I must clear my head of all imaginings, all the fervid emotions to which I have of late been prey, and approach the data with the cold disinterest of the scientist. This is a singular affair, that is true enough – and yet it has always been the singular, in my experience, which has proved most fruitful when examined with care. Let me banish all thoughts of the fantastical, then; let me lay down the facts, and the bare facts alone. Deduction is nothing if it fails to be exact.

Very well. This morning, in the early hours, I began my analysis of Lord Ruthven's blood, and specifically my attempt to identify his sanguigen. I took a smear and placed the slide beneath my microscope. As before, I observed how the red cells were dead and the white cells still alive. I then took a sample of my own blood and added it to the slide. Results immediate. Phagocytosis of the type identified by Netchnikoff: my own blood cells, both red and white, attacked by the white cells in Lord Ruthven's blood, absorbed, and broken down. Sample then seemed to pulse, almost as though some charge were being generated; even with the naked eye, I could see the smear shimmer and expand on the slide. Agglutination of a kind, then; but better described, perhaps, as annexation, for my own cells have been utterly overwhelmed and destroyed.

I repeated the process with the weeks-old samples of leucocytes, both Lord Ruthven's and Haidée's: results the same. I then took samples of blood from Llewellyn and two of the nursing aides, whose blood types I had previously identified as being mutually distinctive; but with all three sanguigens, the cells were attacked and absorbed just as mine had been, and once the process was finished it was as though they had never been. The red cells in Lord Ruthven's blood, however, which previously had been quite dead, were now reanimated – a result so extraordinary, and so contrary to medical science, indeed all science, that I can still scarcely credit it. The proof, however, is incontrovertible: I have persisted with my experiments, drawing blood from all the volunteers I could persuade to help me, and the results have continued the same as before. Conclusion? It would seem that Lord Ruthven's condition is of a kind never before even suspected by medical science; his blood type, certainly, is something quite strange to me. But beyond that, I cannot – I will not – yet deduce.

I am reminded of the comment by my old professor at Edinburgh, Dr Joseph Bell. 'Eliminate the impossible,' he always told me, 'and whatever remains, no matter how improbable, must be the truth.' But what if nothing remains? Must the impossible then be acknowledged as the truth?

6 p.m. – I should abandon this whole course of research. It is possible there are things man should not attempt to know. I remember Kalikshutra, and the skewered body of the little boy. Once the impossible is instated as reality, what frameworks and boundaries will then remain? Where might we not end?

11 p.m. – I went at last, for all my initial determination not to go. Lord Ruthven received me in his study; despite the fine evening outside, the curtains were drawn and only a single candle flickered in the room. I could see at once, however, that he was flanked on either side by seated men and women, for their faces and hands seemed to gleam against the dark; they smiled as I walked in, their teeth ivory-white and sharp, and their expressions almost predatory. I waited to see if Lord Ruthven would request them to leave, but he did not, and in truth I was hardly surprised, for it was apparent – seeing them together now – that Lord Ruthven's ailment had afflicted the others too, for they all shared the same pale beauty and that same strange sense – which I think I now understand – of something terribly corrupted and wrong.

Lord Ruthven gestured at me to pull up a chair. I did so and then, in reply to his invitation, told him of the experiments I had been conducting all day. 'In short,' I concluded, 'I cannot be certain that your illness is wholly, or even largely, anaemia. If it is, then its form is like nothing I have seen. It is susceptible, furthermore . . .' Here, I paused. I stared up at the watching pairs of eyes. They glittered at me unblinkingly.

'Go on,' said Lord Ruthven.

'The anaemia, I was going to say – which is strictly speaking a deficiency of haemoglobin – is susceptible in your blood to an immediate cure.'

'And that is?'

Again, I paused. At length I smiled. 'Do you really need me to tell you?'

He made no reply.

'Tell us,' said one of his companions, her lips curled in a sneer.

I rested my chin on my fingertips. 'Blood,' I told her. 'Fresh human blood.' I stared again into Lord Ruthven's eyes. They were as cold as before, but no longer impenetrable. Instead, I could glimpse sadness and self-loathing there, and I knew my suspicions were surely correct. Yet even at that point I could not bear to accept them as the truth. I stared into the faces opposite me, searching each one for some sign of denial, but they remained as frozen as the masks of the dead and the silence of the room made my flesh start to crawl.

One of the crowd suddenly laughed. 'He confirms me in my opinion, I am afraid, my Lord, that doctors are always insufferably dull. You pay them money, and in return they tell you what you already know.' He yawned. 'Damme, how I long for some genuine surprise.'

Lord Ruthven held up a hand to silence him. He leaned forward. 'Doctor Eliot,' he murmured, 'you would agree, I presume, that a need for blood might be an illness in itself?'

I studied hard to preserve my impassivity. 'Yes, I would,' I replied.

Lord Ruthven nodded. 'Then might there not also be a cure for that need? Might there be a blood type that our cells would not absorb?'

'If there is,' I said slowly, 'then I am yet to find it, I am afraid.'

'But you might? If you continued your search?'

I observed him carefully. 'I would need,' I said at length, 'to know far more than you have been prepared to tell me so far. I would need the truth, my Lord.'

No reply to this. Again, the silence seemed to crawl against my skin.

'He can do nothing for us,' a woman said, and another nodded. 'He does not seem right to me,' she murmured. 'Not right at all.'

'Oh?' Lord Ruthven raised an eyebrow.

The woman nodded. 'He is mortal. What can he know? There is no cure.'

'How can we be certain,' Lord Ruthven replied coldly, 'if we do not try?'

The woman shrugged. 'You tried before, my Lord. You remember? With another doctor.'

'That was different.'

'Why?'

A shadow seemed to pass across Lord Ruthven's face. He did not reply. Instead, he gazed into my eyes and suddenly their gleam was engulfing me. As before, I felt terror reaching out to lap at my mind, then rise and submerge it. I surrendered, like an addict to his opium smoke, and as I did so I saw all my dreams laid out before me – the promise of great work achieved, medicine revolutionised, the whole course of biology and science changed ... if only I would help him ... if only I would work to obtain him a cure. And I felt sudden anger, knowing that he was tempting me, and so I shook my head and struggled to break free.

'Cure?' I exclaimed, finding my voice. I rose to my feet. 'Cure for what, my Lord?' I stared at him, frozen in his chair. 'What is this disease you can only hint at,' I asked, 'this thirst for blood which I would never have believed if I had not seen it smeared on a slide beneath my microscope's lens?' Silence. Again the glitter of eyes that seemed scarcely human, and suddenly I laughed, staring at them all – monsters from the darkness of folklore and myth, uncovered at last by the glare of modern science. The irony amused me. 'You are right,' I said, inclining my head towards the woman who had dismissed my work. 'I cannot help you.' I glanced back at Lord Ruthven. 'I am sorry.' Then I turned and began to walk from the room.

'Wait!'

I froze.

'*Wait.*'

I turned round. Lord Ruthven had half-risen from his chair. 'Please,' he whispered. 'Please.' And then suddenly, his beauty was contorted by a hideous rage, in which pride and desperation and shame were all commingled, and betrayed across his face like the passage of a storm. He at once shuddered, and clenched the sides of his chair; his features recovered their former calm, but when he spoke his teeth were bared like an animal's fangs. 'I am not accustomed to beg,' he whispered. The chill in his voice was paralysing. 'Do not doubt, Doctor, that I can push you, if I choose, into madness or death. Or perhaps' – he paused – 'into something far worse.' He smiled. 'Do not defy me.'

The woman had reached up to take his arm. 'My Lord, please.' She seemed afraid. 'Either let the man go or kill him and be done with it.'

Still Lord Ruthven's stare was unchecked.

'My Lord.' She pulled on his arm again. 'Do not forget.'

He frowned. 'Forget?'

The woman held his hand. 'Our mysteries will always overwhelm the mortal who glimpses them. You know that.' She raised his hand to her lips. 'Remember Polidori.'

Polidori. The name made me start. Lord Ruthven must have observed my gesture of surprise, for he smiled faintly. 'No,' he said. 'Polidori was greedy, presumptuous, over-reaching. This man is different; he is nothing like Polidori.'

'So you lied,' I said quietly. 'You do know him.'

Lord Ruthven looked up at me and shrugged. 'I was concerned for your safety, Dr Eliot.'

'How?'

He shrugged again. 'Polidori is dangerous and quite, quite mad.'

He smiled faintly. 'But you know that; you have met him yourself.'

There was a murmuring from the crowd. One of them rose to his feet. 'He has? Where?'

Lord Ruthven continued to smile. 'In Rotherhithe. Isn't that so, Dr Eliot?'

I nodded slowly.

He gestured at me. 'Dr Eliot here is quite the detective, you see. You were right, Dr Eliot. It was Polidori who sent me that programme for Lucy's first night, I am certain of that now. Just as it was also Polidori who lured my other cousin, Arthur Ruthven, to his death. And so you see why I warn you – *stay away from him.*'

I considered his words. 'Your hints,' I said at length, 'are intriguing in the extreme.'

Lord Ruthven raised an eyebrow. 'Indeed?'

I nodded. 'Arthur Ruthven's death, for instance – I had assumed it related to his work at the India Office. And yet you are claiming – what? – that it has to do with his relationship with you?'

'Both theories may be correct, do you not think?'

'How?'

'You have your secrets,' murmured Lord Ruthven, 'while I, Dr Eliot . . . I have mine.'

'So you won't tell me?'

He bowed his head almost imperceptibly. 'In due time, perhaps.'

'And the programme Polidori sent you – you will not reveal how that is dangerous either?'

Again, Lord Ruthven bowed his head.

'At least tell me, then, if Lucy is endangered.' As I said this, I saw how Lord Ruthven started. His face, though, remained frozen, and he made no reply. 'She is your cousin,' I went on. 'If Polidori's enmity towards you has already killed Lucy's brother, then you owe it to her, do you not think, to preserve her safety as best you can?'

'I thank you,' said Lord Ruthven coldly, 'for reminding me of my duty.'

'I am very fond of Lucy.' Lord Ruthven's lip curled at this, but I ignored his sneer. 'If there is indeed a conspiracy in Rotherhithe . . .'

'Then you would do well to keep clear of it,' said Lord Ruthven, interrupting me lazily and rising to his feet. 'Dr Eliot, I offer you that advice in the best of faith. Despite your rejection of my offer tonight, my admiration for you remains perfectly undimmed. You have chosen not to glimpse into the nature of our kind. Very well, then. Stay true to that resolution. Do not pit yourself against Polidori.' He reached out to take my hand and pressed it. 'Do not go to Rotherhithe.'

His touch was very cold, and I shivered despite myself. Lord Ruthven smiled; he released my hand. 'Please,' he whispered. He took a step back. 'Leave the good Dr Polidori to me.'

I continued to meet his stare; then, sensing that our interview had come to an end, I turned and walked towards the door. This time Lord Ruthven did not try to halt me. But by the door, it was I who paused and turned round again.'It is not just Polidori you are confronting,' I said. 'In Rotherhithe, down by the Thames . . . There is someone – something – much greater than him. Much greater, perhaps, my Lord, even than you.' Lord Ruthven stared at me; for a long time he made no reply, and I was afraid of how angry my warning might have made him. But at length he nodded very curtly, as though acknowledging my words, and I realised that he had seemed almost unsurprised by them. I turned, and left, and hurried from the house.

Heading towards Oxford Street, I passed by the front of the Mowberleys' house. Lights were still burning on the ground floor and so, remembering that George had called on me the previous day, I rang the door-bell and asked if he was in. He was not. I was about to press on when I heard, coming from a nearby room, the sound of Lucy's voice. I asked the butler to introduce me, and as I walked into the drawing room I saw – to my pleasure and surprise – Lucy and Lady Mowberley seated together. They both rose to greet me. 'Our matchmaker!' exclaimed Lady Mowberley, clasping Lucy's hand. 'You see, Dr Eliot – we are become perfect friends.' They pressed me to stay, but I was in no mood for conversation and so did not accept. Have agreed, however, to escort them both on a walk one afternoon.

I asked Lady Mowberley where George was. 'He is working late in his office,' she replied. I tried not to betray my unease, but she must have sensed something for I saw a shadow pass across her face. She did not press me, however, and indeed left Lucy to escort me back to the door.

'Is everything well?' I asked her in a whisper as we went.

She nodded. 'Yes, thank you, Jack, quite well.' She kissed me lightly on the cheek and smiled. 'You really are the most appalling busy-body.' She gestured back towards the drawing room. 'You can see for yourself the fruit of your good work.'

'Yes,' I said slowly. I paused by the door. 'Lucy ...' I wondered what I should tell her. As she waited she raised an eyebrow at me, and I was reminded forcibly of Lord Ruthven, so much so that the blood must have drained from my face, for suddenly I saw Lucy staring anxiously at me.

'Jack,' she said, 'whatever is it? You look awful.'

I composed myself. 'Lucy,' I whispered, 'be careful. For God's sake, be careful! Warn Ned, and look after your son and yourself. Above all – do not trust Lord Ruthven. Do not allow him near to your child.' She frowned and opened her mouth to question me, but I did not wait, for what else could I have told her? I do not understand the peril myself. Yet seeing Lucy's face at that moment, and knowing what might be at stake, I knew then that I could never abandon her.

And even now, when I have been able to examine my situation more rationally, I am certain that I have made the right choice – I cannot turn aside from my course, for all that I told Lord Ruthven that I would not pry into the nature of his kind. Heaven knows into what I am venturing; but there is too much at stake – perhaps too many lives. If I must journey beyond the bounds of science a second time, then so be it. Please God, though, I do not repeat the errors of the first.

Mem. I must talk to Huree as soon as I can.

12.30 a.m. – Llewellyn has returned late. He gives me a note, which George had left with him earlier tonight. I open it feverishly and read the following: 'Have gone to Rotherhithe. Don't worry, old chap – all for the best of reasons. Was wondering if you'd care to join me, but dammit, you're not here. Ah, well. All the best, your old chum George.'

He's an idiot – always was. Don't know what to do. This is rushing me faster than I had ever planned to go.

He will be in danger, though.

1 a.m. – No choice. I will have to go. Will walk out to Bishopsgate and find a cab.

Telegram, Professor Huree Jyoti Navalkar to Dr John Eliot.

6 June.

Lecture series in Paris arranged. Is situation critical? If not, will come when tour is finished.

HUREE.

Dr Eliot's Diary.

6 June. – Telegram from Huree waiting for me on my desk. *Is* the situation critical? Not confident. Not confident of anything any more. The evening of my visit to Lord Ruthven I would have been; but everything has changed. Even my resolution to face, if necessary, the impossible, seems comical now and not necessary at all. And yet it is hard to be certain. What *have* I been through? I must clear my mind. To forget is to surrender; to apply reason, to recall. Must not abandon my methods now.

So then. I set off for Rotherhithe around 1 a.m. Afraid, sitting in the cab, that it would prove either an embarrassing or a fruitless quest. Latter alternative seemed more likely at first, for once we had entered the tangle of streets that I remembered from my previous visit to Rotherhithe, I grew hopelessly lost, and when the cab driver became impatient I had to pay him his fare and watch him drive off. Continued my search on foot, but without any better luck. Strange, for my sense of direction is excellent and I was certain I had memorised where the warehouse stood; but although I could locate the High Street without any problem, the streets beyond it seemed to melt before my gaze. Searched for the entrance to the warehouse for upwards of half an hour, while the mist rolled in thicker and the street-fronts grew ever more unfamiliar and strange. At length abandoned my search, and returned to the High Street; from there, I made my way to Coldlair Lane. Found it without difficulty.

The shop-front was black, but the door on to the street had been left ajar. I walked through it; there seemed nobody inside. As I walked past the counter to the staircase, though, I began to smell the odour of opium again and then, mounting the stairs, heard an addict's cough as he drew on his smoke. I ascended carefully. Pulling the awning aside, I saw that the room was as full as before; bodies were hunched and twisted in the dark, and most of the faces seemed familiar. I peered through the smoke towards the corner. There, hunched by the brazier, sat the old Malay woman; I took a step towards her, and as I did so she looked up suddenly and bared her teeth. Yellow spit began to form round her lips; she sucked it in and, as though prompted, other addicts also began to stir and hiss, so that the collective noise was an unnerving one, much like a pit filled with restive snakes. A man by my feet began to mutter and groan; he reached for me, and when I kicked him away another stretched out to try to hold my leg, and then another, and another one.

I pushed at them with my cane, and for a moment succeeded in beating them off, but pain seemed to have almost no meaning for the poor wretches, so complete was their enslavement to their drug, and soon I was being pulled down on to the floor again. Soft white fingers gripped me around my throat; my head was lifted up, and I saw before me the old Malay woman. She had a pipe in her hands, and was extending it towards me. I shouted at her to keep away, but her expression was quite glazed and my words had no effect. As the stem of the pipe was placed by my lips, I clenched my teeth; I felt hands struggling to pull my jaws apart, but the addicts' fingers were moist with sweat and they slipped as they tried to gain a grip on my cheeks.

Suddenly the old Malay began to dribble again, and her lips formed a hideous grin; she pulled on the pipe, then bent low over me, and her spittle dripped slowly and fell on to my face, so that I almost gagged as her lips touched my own. Somehow, though, I kept my teeth still clenched tight; I longed to breathe, but I could not, for the Malay's lips remained pressed against mine and the thick brown smoke was filling my mouth. I began to thrash; more hands pressed me down, and still the Malay was holding me, her kiss implacable, and I knew that shortly I would have to inhale. I felt the room spinning; still I didn't breathe. The Malay's eyes began to fade; then her face; one final struggle, and then at last I breathed in. I waited for the taste of the smoke in my throat, but it never came. Instead I found I could breathe easily again, that the opium taste had been diluted by air. I opened my eyes and looked up. I saw Polidori. He was staring down at me, a smile on his lips.

'You just keep coming back, Doctor. How flattering. But you must excuse them' – he gestured at the shuddering bodies by his feet – 'if they get the wrong idea as a consequence.'

Slowly, I picked myself up. I breathed in deeply again.

Polidori studied me with mock concern. 'So what *have* you come for?' he asked at length.

'The same as before, I'm afraid.'

'Ah.' Polidori rubbed his hands. 'Then perhaps you have the makings of an addict after all.' He gestured with his arm. 'This way, please.'

He opened the door behind the brazier and I followed him out across the bridge. 'What a devoted and attentive friend you must be,' he said, opening the warehouse door to me. 'Hurtling after Sir George like this all the time, rescuing him.' He leered at me. 'A guardian angel.'

I paused before following him through the doorway. 'George is well, then?' I asked.

'Never better. Adultery is so improving for the health, don't you think?'

'You haven't harmed him?'

Polidori drew himself up as though cruelly wronged. 'Me?' he exclaimed. 'Harm Sir George? Why on earth would I do that?' He watched me as I followed him in. 'Besides,' he murmured in my ear, 'I wouldn't dare. Not harm the lover of her Ladyship.' He drew his face close to mine, his pale eyes wide; then he spluttered with laughter and kicked the door shut. 'This way,' he said abruptly, not looking round. I followed him across the hall and through a second door.

A corridor stretched ahead of us, just as I remembered it. *Mem.*, a curious effect on that previous visit – for several minutes, no matter how fast Stoker and I moved, we never seemed to draw closer to the door at the end. Talking to Stoker later, it was apparent that the illusion had affected us both. At the time I had suggested opium fumes as a possible cause; now, though, walking down the corridor a second time, I imagined myself inured to the effect of the smoke, for I reached the far door without difficulty. Indeed, I began to congratulate myself on the improvement to my constitution, for I had breathed in far more fumes this second time round, to no apparent ill-effect. But it was then that Polidori opened the door; I followed him through it; I looked around at the room beyond. And at once I knew I was affected after all.

For there was no nursery. Clearly, my powers of observation had deserted me – far from retracing my steps, as I had assumed, I had been brought down a quite different corridor. I was now standing on a staircase of spiralling iron, black and wonderfully ornamented. Beyond me lay a room in which even the air seemed rich with textures and different shades of light, and yet, no – to say 'room' is to misdescribe it, for it seemed something far beyond an architect's skills – almost, though I hesitate to say it, like a fantasy conjured from some decadent's dreams. I am aware, of course, of how unobjective I am sounding now; yet I can think of no other way to describe the room's effect on me, which was very powerful and somehow, at the same time, inescapably *real*. In part, I suppose, it must have been my own dream I was glimpsing, summoned from beyond my conscious mind by the opiates; and yet not entirely, I think. For the room was not all hallucination; something strange was out there before my gaze. I tried to study it but I found the effort hard. The dimensions appeared to be seeping from my stare, and even the colours of the walls seemed to change. I do not mean that they shimmered in the fashion of a mirage; rather that they seemed so deep, so intense, so *beautiful*, that I couldn't imagine anything more perfect, yet I only had to look away for a second to realise – when I glanced back at them again – that I had been blind before, for the beauty now had grown even more intense. The crimson of the curtains, the gold of the lacquer, the details of the tapestries and artwork, all seemed to deepen before my stare, as though promising some dark meaning, some tantalising secret just beyond my grasp . . .

Of course, I am sounding ridiculous now. Indeed, I am embarrassed to play back the phonogram – my clarity of thought must have been remarkably affected at the time. And yet I owe it to myself, I suppose, from the clinical point of view, to describe exactly what I felt and saw, so that I may judge the extent to which my perceptions had been drugged, or merely seduced by the beauty of the room. Certainly, from the very start, I found my senses betraying me into an emotional response of a kind that I am not accustomed to experiencing, for it is my reason which is usually predominant, yet standing there by Polidori I found it suddenly under siege. Staring around me, I felt my alertness and sense of danger flooding away; in its place there was left a strange, excited euphoria and the ache, deep within my bones, of still greater pleasures and revelations to come. It was the most wonderful pain I had ever known. I began to realise, what I had never before understood, how a man might surrender his reason and self-control. And at once I knew I had to fight – against the pleasure and against the beauty of the room, for they both seemed indistinguishable to me, equally seductive and dangerous, and when I steeled myself, I could remember this, and remain myself. But still I was drawn. Slowly, I began to walk down the stairs.

I wondered what power the room had, to disturb and enrapture me in such a way. Certainly, it displayed a wealth that seemed almost magical. Silk-fringed rugs were piled on the floor; the designs on the walls were of the most remarkable skill; the furniture was crafted from rich, fragrant woods. Lilac blossom filled the air, and from golden tripods rose the subtle perfume of ambergris, dizzying and lulling my thoughts even more. I paused and, as I had done before, sought to clear my mind; aware of how susceptible the human brain can be to the influences of sight and sense, I knew that my reason – in such a place, and endangered by unknown threats – had to be preserved, for in truth it was the only weapon I possessed. And so I braced myself, and then stepped towards a curtain which was drawn across the room. I reached to part it; and as I did so I shuddered, as though approaching some great mystery. 'Pass through it,' whispered Polidori in my ear. I glanced round at him; I had forgotten his presence entirely – somehow I no longer found it threatening; instead, my emotions were absorbed by some greater source of fear which seemed, like the presence of a god in an ancient sanctuary, to be waiting for me beyond the veil. I reached for the curtain again; I took it in my hand; I passed through it.

If the room had been beautiful before, now, past the curtain, it seemed a hundred times more so. I clenched my fists, determined that I would not be seduced by its delights – determined to cling to my reason, my analytic powers. I looked around and saw a child before me, seated by a table; she was frowning with concentration, staring at a chess-board. I recognised her from my previous visit with Stoker. She looked up at me suddenly. 'Hello,' she said. Not a trace of surprise was evident on her face. Before I could reply to her greeting, she had returned to her game. She moved a queen and took the remaining king from the board. With great care she placed it next to a line of other pieces; then, smoothing back her plaits, she smiled calmly and turned in her chair.

I followed her gaze and recognised George seated on a divan. He was poring over a map. I took a step forward and, as I did so, he started and looked round at me. 'Great Scott!' he exclaimed. 'Jack! So you came here after all.' He rose to greet me, but then checked himself, and just as the young girl had done, he turned away from me again.

They were both staring at something I couldn't quite make out; whether it was the shadows cast by the crimson gas flames or the heaviness of the incense in the air of the room, I hesitate to say, but certainly, for a second, I found myself the victim of an optical trick. I seemed to be observing a haze of gold and red, the deep red of blood, shimmering as water does when glimpsed through great heat. I blinked and rubbed my eyes, and the illusion was gone. Instead, there was a woman. She wore gold around her neck; her long dress was red, and I realised that these were what I must have just glimpsed. But now, even in the shadows where the woman still stood, I could make her out quite clearly. Despite myself, I gasped. Her appearance was radiant and extraordinary; I had never seen such physical beauty before. The woman walked forward into the light and stared into my eyes. I stayed frozen where I was.

I knew at once that this was Lilah. I remembered what George had written to me: 'even you might turn your head'. He had made this claim expecting I would not believe him – yet there I was, staring virtually transfixed. I fought against this attraction: I knew I could not surrender to it. Instead, I struggled to observe Lilah clinically. There was much to observe. She was dressed in the very height of the latest Paris fashion, her arms and shoulders bare, her scarlet dress tight around her waist and hips, and she moved with the grace of one born to such a style. Yet clearly she could not have been; and indeed, the very ease with which she wore European *haute couture* only emphasised how foreign – almost how unearthly – she seemed. 'Exotic,' George had called her, and so she was – so she would have been anywhere – but especially so now in London's darkest quarter, amongst the squalor of the docks, amongst the warehouses that stood by the filthy Thames. Her hair was raven-black and thick, and braided with gold; her skin a rich brown; her features delicate and yet remarkably strong; in her nose winked a stud of amethyst. She reminded me forcibly of the bandit that Moorfield had captured on the Pass above the road to Kalikshutra; yet striking though that girl had been, the woman before me seemed a thousand times more beautiful, and more dangerous. I felt this at once, this mistrust of her, for reasons I find it hard now to justify, it being my method to resist an instinctive response, lest the process of deduction should be prejudiced. And yet in truth, I found that instinct was all I had left to me – my powers of analysis seemed blinded and defied. Perhaps it was Lilah's very beauty which unsettled me, for its radiance was like the sun's, beyond all my attempts to survey it as a whole. Or perhaps it was the legacy of other, older fears: dark memories of Kalikshutra, and a statue I had seen there daubed with blood; legends of Kali the terrible ...

I was being ridiculous, of course – my imagination had run away with me. Yet that Lilah can have such an effect, even on a mind as cold and resistant to the sex as mine, is tribute enough to her powers of fascination, and I could see now why George should have fallen so helplessly for her. Nor were my initial thoughts of Kalikshutra entirely the prompting of superstitious fear; for it was apparent to me, seeing George surrounded by his maps, that my suspicions of Lilah had been very close to the truth. George himself, of course – before I could even open my mouth – at once began to assure me that this was not the case at all; he had put it to Lilah, he told me, asking whether she had an interest in the frontier, and she had said it wasn't true, and there it was, everything was fine, he was just getting on with his Bill because, as he had said, this was where he found he could work at his best, and really I shouldn't worry, *everything was fine.* He would appeal to Lilah occasionally and she would murmur a supportive response, her voice as enchanting and seductive as her face, with that same quality that Lord Ruthven's possessed – soft, and silver, and musical. So naturally, I found my darkest suspicions flooding back, as I wondered what nature of thing she might be, for she inspired in me, I cannot deny it, doubts greater even than Lord Ruthven had done. I began to rehearse in my mind all I had heard of her before, from Lucy, and Rosamund and George himself. And as I did so, I saw Lilah smiling softly at me.

It was almost as though she had been reading my thoughts. She stopped George with the faintest elevation of her hand, then began to ask me about the steps by which I had first tracked him to her lair. I was reluctant to say much, but it was soon apparent that George had told her the story anyway, and as I spoke I had the sense that she was toying with me. She would glance occasionally at the little girl who was still seated by her chess-board; as George praised my deductive powers and skills, Lilah would smile at the girl and the girl, solemn-faced, would peruse George and myself in turn. Her stare, I realised, was making George fidget. I finished speaking abruptly.

Lilah rested her fingers on the little girl's head. 'You see, Suzette,' she said, 'the Doctor is a real-life detective. He solves mysteries.'

Suzette considered this, studying me attentively. 'But when you have a mystery,' she asked me, 'how do you know when it finishes?'

I glanced at Lilah and Polidori. Polidori flashed me a grin, then bared his teeth. 'It's very hard,' I said, turning back to Suzette. 'Sometimes, mysteries never end at all.'

'That doesn't seem fair, then,' she replied, swinging her legs as though on a swing. 'If you don't know when a mystery ends, you might have got the beginning quite wrong as well. You might even have been in a different mystery altogether, and never realised it, and then where would you be?'

'In difficulty,' I replied – 'or worse.' I glanced round at Lilah again. Her expression was one of perfect serenity.

'Here,' I heard Suzette say. She was tugging on my sleeve and I looked down at her. She was holding a magazine in her hand. 'This is my favourite,' she said as she handed it to me. I looked at the title: *Beeton's Christmas Annual.* The child smiled at me and took it back, opening it at a well-thumbed page. 'In stories,' she said, 'detectives *always* know when the mystery ends.' She began to read out a title carefully. '*A Study in Scarlet: A Sherlock Holmes Mystery.*' She looked up at me. 'Do you know it?' she asked.

I shook my head. 'I don't have much time for stories, I'm afraid.'

'You should read this one,' said the little girl. 'The detective is very good. He might help you understand some of the rules.'

'Rules?'

'Yes, of course,' she said patiently, 'for when someone gets murdered.' She looked down at her magazine again, and repeated the title slowly and with relish. '*A Study in Scarlet*. That means a study in blood.' She looked up at me suddenly. 'And when blood is shed, there must be rules. Everyone knows that. How will you manage if you don't know what they are?'

'But blood hasn't been shed.'

'Not yet,' she replied.

'Will it be?'

'For God's sake!' muttered George, looking away. But Suzette ignored his protest and continued to stare at me, her eyes as wide and solemn as before.

'Well, I'm sure you must hope so,' she said at last, 'otherwise, what is the point of being a detective at all? You wouldn't have anything exciting to do.' She reached for her magazine, then climbed down from her chair and smoothed out her dress. 'So let us just hope that it's a matter of time.' She looked up at me; her eyes seemed exceedingly bright and cold. She reached for my hand and pressed it tightly. 'Just a matter of time.'

There was silence, then suddenly Polidori began to laugh. George stared at him with unconcealed distaste, then peered at Suzette with an even more visible shudder. 'Really,' he muttered, 'this is all pretty poor.'

'Poor?' Lilah asked. She had settled herself upon a velvet-lined chaise and was smoking a cigarette. It was delicate and long; its smoke curled as languidly as Lilah herself.

'Well, yes, confound it,' George spluttered with sudden fury, 'it is poor, damned poor! Just look at her! She shouldn't be reading murder stories! Dolls, ponies, that's what little girls are meant to enjoy, magical fairies, things like that. Not all this blood nonsense. I mean, dash it all, Lilah, you can't say it's normal!' Suzette continued to stare at him, quite unperturbed. George plunged his hands in his pockets and looked away. 'Gets at my nerves,' he

233

muttered to me, 'sitting there all the time, with her baleful gaze and her ghoulish chat. Worse than the Lord Chancellor. Puts me off my drink.'

Lilah raised a languorous hand. 'Please,' she murmured, 'you will upset the child.'

'Upset her?' snorted George. 'You need someone to do a damn sight more than upset her. You spoil that girl, you know, Lilah. I mean, look at her!' Suzette was watching him as impassively as before. 'Where the hell's her respect?'

'For you?'

'Yes, of course, for me!'

'Perhaps you should earn it, then,' said Lilah with a sudden iciness, extinguishing her cigarette and rising to her feet.

George ignored her. Indeed, he seemed not to have heard her at all. 'I mean, dash it all, I know she's an orphan,' he said, still staring at Suzette, 'and it's bloody good of you to have her as your ward, and God knows I'm as keen on charity as the next man, so well done, Lilah, yes, I mean that, well done, *but*' – he paused to draw in breath – 'the fact remains' – he narrowed his eyes, and breathed in again – '*the fact remains* . . . she is a little brat.'

Lilah shrugged faintly. 'So what do you propose?'

'Simple,' said George. 'Have her taken in hand.'

Lilah laughed, a strange, enchanting, inhuman sound. 'And you are volunteering yourself, I suppose?'

'Me?' George frowned. 'Goodness, no, what a comical idea! I meant a nanny! This is woman's work we're talking about now. That's what you've been lacking, my dear, a damned good nanny, one who can get Miss Suzette into a nursery and teach her the sorts of things that little girls should be made to understand.' He glanced at the child. 'A few of the feminine virtues, don't you know? Mildness, sweetness – obedience.'

Lilah turned, as though bored by the conversation, and began to sweep back her hair. 'As it happens,' she murmured, 'I may follow your advice. It has certain possibilities.'

'Glad to hear it,' answered George.

'But for now' – Lilah turned round again – 'I shall have to rely upon myself.' She held out her hand. 'Come, Suzette. You are annoying Sir George. It is time for bed.'

Suzette walked forward with a pert flounce, her hand still tightly pressing mine. 'I want you to come with me,' she said. I glanced at George, then accompanied her.

'She has never met a detective,' whispered Lilah in my ear, as I passed her by the door. 'You have an admirer.'

We walked into the hallway beyond, which was dark. I heard the click of Lilah's heels as she followed us out and then, as the door was shut behind us, everything fell black. Ahead of me, I could not see a thing. I looked round and caught a faint glimmer, like that of moonlight. It took me a second to realise it was Lilah's skin.

She clapped her hands. At once, flickering pale veins of light ran up through the darkness and I saw, looming ahead of me, what seemed a mighty pillar, and beyond it arches and yet more halls, all trellised by the same delicate lines of fire reaching like ivy out across the stone. The illumination was not strong and it took me time, keen-eyed though I am, to adjust to the light; but as I did so, I realised that I was standing before a massive stairway, and that the pillar I had glimpsed was the support for its spiral – about fifteen feet thick, I would estimate, with each step in turn more than twenty feet wide. I had assumed it was an illusion, either deliberately crafted or induced by the opium, for it seemed impossible in a warehouse that it could truly be there; but as I began to climb the stairs, following Lilah with Suzette still by my side, the stone beneath us echoed to our steps and I realised with a shock that it had to be real. I glanced about me again. The whole structure had been crafted from a dark purple rock, igneous and crystalline, and polished so that our figures were reflected in its gloom. My own form, shivered and distorted by the half-light, followed me like some spectre trapped beneath glass. The effect was unsettling, and no doubt deliberate.

I looked up at Lilah. She was still ahead of me but had paused, and was bending down stretching out her hand to something in the dark. 'Isn't he handsome?' she asked. I frowned. Two unblinking green eyes were staring up at me and I recognised the panther I had seen before. It yawned, and stretched, and rose to its feet. It watched me with a lazy disinterest; then began to pad down the stairs.

'Is it tame?' I asked.

'Not altogether,' whispered Lilah. For some reason, she laughed. 'But very beautiful.'

'And that will be a comfort, will it, when you are savaged to death?'

Lilah smiled slowly. 'Don't be so responsible.' She stared after the panther. 'I love my animals,' she murmured. 'More than humans, by and large. They demand less, and their dependence is so much more complete. Isn't that right, Suzette?'

The little girl stared up at her. 'Yes, Lilah,' she replied.

'Look.' Lilah gestured with her arm. I turned, and stared. By now I should have been inured to surprise, but nothing – not even the events of the past weeks – had prepared me for the sight before me now. Ahead there stretched a giant passageway, and it was filled with animals and flocks of birds. I could make out a lion, some pigs, a dozing snake; beyond them were yet other beasts and indeed, as far as I could see, the passageway went on until it vanished into darkness – an impossible sight. I turned to Lilah, to ask her what this hallucination was, but she raised her hand and pressed a finger to my lips. She lowered it again slowly; I thought that she intended to kiss me, for her own lips were parted and very close to mine; I could even smell the perfume that hung on her breath. But she smiled, and turned away from me to kneel down by Suzette. She stroked the little girl's cheeks. 'Leave us alone now,' she whispered. 'I have to talk with the Doctor.' Suzette didn't answer, but hugged her and then turned and began to run down the passageway. The birds rose, startled, and wheeled above her head. The animals shrank back against the walls. Suzette ran on. Her footsteps echoed on the naked stone; they seemed to fill the air, even when she could barely be seen any more. Then she was gone. A darkness began to rise like a fog from the distance. Soon the animals were only faint silhouettes, and the passageway seemed nothing but a deep gash of black. I turned to

Lilah. 'I think I need to clear my brain,' I said.

She reached out to touch me, as she had done before. She smiled. 'Affected by Polidori's opium?' she asked.

Her eyes, like Lord Ruthven's, were remarkably deep. I forced myself to break away from her stare. 'Perhaps,' I replied.

Lilah nodded. 'Come with me.' She took my arm. We continued to climb up the steps, and I observed how the light began to fade from the walls; yet I could still make my way, and indeed see more clearly now than I had done before. I looked up. Above me there stretched a great dome of glass and beyond it, quite unclouded, was a blaze of stars. 'The London air is so foul,' said Lilah, 'and so polluted with light. But as you see – with optics and angles – the effect can be nullified.'

'Remarkable,' I exclaimed. 'I would never have thought it possible.'

'No.' Lilah smiled faintly. 'I am sure you wouldn't.'

I continued to stare upwards through the dome at the sky. I could feel Lilah's eyes on me and I knew they would be cold, as cold as the stars. Still I didn't look round. 'It reminds me . . .' I said at last. I paused. 'It reminds me – the clearness of the sky – of the view from the mountains in Kalikshutra.'

'Does it?' The question hung in the air. Now I did glance at Lilah. She was no longer watching me, but had raised her head and was gazing in turn at the stars. She closed her eyes, as though in rapture, and then slowly she turned her face back to mine. Again I felt a powerful surge of attraction towards her – fear and desire in equal measure rose and struggled the one against the other, and when she reached for my hand I took it away, much too violently, from her. 'You don't trust me,' she said, as though almost surprised.

I very nearly laughed. She sensed my amusement and half-smiled herself. 'But why should you?' she murmured. 'You blame me for deceiving your friend.'

'And I am right to, am I not?' I replied coldly. 'You are deceiving him.'

'Well, yes, of course.' Lilah shrugged. 'That's obvious.'

I stared at her in surprise, for I had not expected to gain an admission so easily.

'Don't look so thunderstruck,' she murmured. 'I wouldn't have dared try deny it to you.'

'How flattering.'

'Do you think so?'

'Of course. You have clearly never told George.'

'True. But George is an idiot.'

'And a friend of mine.' I paused. 'Why shouldn't I tell him what you have just told me?'

Her eyes glittered; then she shook her head, turned away and began to walk up the stairs towards the glass of the dome. She paused for a long time, staring out at something that I couldn't see. 'I gather,' she said at last, turning back to me, 'that you work in Whitechapel, amongst the very worst slums.'

I shrugged faintly. 'I work in Whitechapel, yes.'

Lilah nodded. 'You must have sympathy for the poor, then, Doctor Eliot, for the disadvantaged, for the oppressed. You don't have to answer me, I know you do. George has told me so. "My friend Jack, the East End Saint!" That's what he calls you, you know. "The East End Saint." He thinks it's a joke.'

'I'm sure he does. What is your point?'

'That George finds most things a wonderful joke. His work at the India Office, for instance. His responsibility towards the people whose lives he is going to affect so casually, so *very* casually, with the stroke of a pen, the drawing of a line. The very idea that he can sway the lives of millions, a man like him . . . A joke – he finds it all a joke. And sometimes, Doctor Eliot' – she paused, and stared out through the glass again – 'sometimes, so do I.'

I watched her. She was, I realised again with a clarity that made me feel distant from myself, quite frighteningly beautiful. I wondered what was wrong with me, to be so distracted at such a critical time by a physical attraction, by an irrelevance. Keep to your methods, I told myself, stay true to them or you are nothing, you are dead. I walked slowly up the stairs to join her by the glass where she was gazing out at the mighty sprawl of London. We seemed impossibly high. I could see the city below me in blots of red and black, with the river like a snipping of gut through its heart.

'It angers me,' she said slowly, 'that I have to whore after a man such as George.'

She hadn't looked round at me; I studied her face. I remembered a profile I had seen before – the statues of a goddess, set high amongst the jungles and the mountain peaks. 'Are you ...' I whispered slowly. My voice trailed away. Slowly, Lilah looked round at me.

'I must know ...' I said. 'In Kalikshutra, the goddess Kali is spoken of as someone who is real ...'

'And so she is, in the souls of her worshippers, in the great flow of the world.'

'That is not what I meant.'

'I know.'

'Then tell me ...'

Lilah opened her eyes wide in a mocking innocence. 'Yes?' she asked.

'What are you?'

'Am I Kali, do you mean?' Lilah laughed. 'Am I Kali?' She seized my cheeks suddenly and pulled my face towards her own, exposing my throat to her kisses – three, four, five, kissing me as though intoxicated, then laughing again.

'You are misinterpreting me,' I said angrily, breaking away.

'There is no need to be embarrassed,' said Lilah. 'You have lived in India. You know that the gods have often walked the earth.'

I met her stare. 'And Kali too?' I asked.

'In Kalikshutra – perhaps.' Lilah smiled; then she shrugged and turned away from me. 'Of course, I am teasing you,' she said softly, staring out at the night. 'But not wholly. Kalikshutra is a haunted place, unearthly ...' Her voice trailed away; she turned again to look at me. 'You know that yourself, Doctor. The fantastic and the literal can be easy to confuse there. It is a place ... apart.'

'Yes,' I said coldly. 'I did notice that.'

'I am glad.' There was no irony in Lilah's voice. 'Because you see, Doctor, I am part of a myth myself. It is not just the Hindoo gods who reached the Himalayas. There are other beliefs, the customs that endure where Buddhism still survives, in Tibet and Ladakh, along the roof of the world. Divinity is believed to exist in human form, passed from successor to successor, so that when the holder dies the spirit is reborn in a tiny child. This child is found; he is proclaimed by the priests; he is brought up by them as the vehicle of God. In due time he will lead and protect his people as he has always done.' She paused, then turned round again to stare out at the night. 'That belief,' she murmured, 'exists in Kalikshutra too.'

I studied her. 'The form, though,' I said, 'is presumably not quite the same.'

Lilah glanced at me.

'The child,' I went on, 'the one that the priests search for, the reincarnation – in Kalikshutra, it is not a boy.'

Lilah bowed her head. 'Evidently.'

'You are their queen?'

'Their queen . . .' She smiled. 'Perhaps – and something more.'

I stared at her. 'I see.'

'Do you though, Dr Eliot?'

I frowned, for the question had been asked with a bitterness I hadn't heard from her before. I wondered suddenly if I had not been maligning her in my fears, and felt a prickle of guilt and embarrassment.

'How you can blame me?' she asked suddenly. 'You, Doctor Eliot, with your sympathy for the weak and the oppressed? Why shouldn't I try to deceive your friend, when an entire people is depending on my attempt.'

I didn't answer. I saw a shadow of anger pass across her face. 'One day,' said Lilah softly, staring past me, 'it would be good for Sir George to understand what it means to be weak, to be the object of someone else's casual insolence. Perhaps then he would not dispense people's destinies with such' – her lip curled – '*unthinking* regard.'

I felt abashed, for my friend and for myself. 'He is a kind man,' I said weakly.

'And that absolves him?'

I shook my head. 'You are the one who must decide on that.'

'No,' said Lilah. 'It is you who must decide. Will you tell him what I have told you tonight? Expose me? Now that you know what I am?'

'"Know what I am..."' My voice trailed away as I echoed her words. I paused; I turned back to the window and stared out at the sky; saw, to the east, the first hints of dawn. I remembered Huree's words: 'They weaken with the light.' I remembered my escape with Moorfield up the cliff; I remembered waiting on the temple for the sun. I glanced back at Lilah again. I studied her face. She seemed, if anything, even more lovely – more lovely, and proud, and radiant.

'You say,' I told her slowly, 'that I know what you are. But I don't. What I have seen here tonight...' I shook my head. 'It was something more than opium. Something I can't explain and which ... yes' – I met her gaze – 'I admit ... unnerves me.'

'Does it?' Lilah smiled and turned away. 'George told me how you went to Kalikshutra, and then were too afraid to stay.'

I ignored her jibe. 'So it *is* the same,' I said quietly.

'Same?'

'What I saw in the mountains, and the ...' – I searched for a phrase – 'the conjuring tricks here.'

'Conjuring tricks?' asked Lilah, raising an eyebrow at me. She laughed. 'There is no magic, Doctor. It may be that there are powers you don't understand, powers your science can't explain, but that does not make them conjuring tricks.' She shrugged, and laughed again. 'You are betraying your jealousy.'

'Perhaps.'

'I could teach you if you wished.'

I heard the echo of Lord Ruthven in her offer.

'Afraid again?' she pressed.

'Of your powers?' I shook my head.

'Of what then? Of your own ignorance?' She took my hands, she whispered very softly into my ear. 'Of your failure to understand what nature might be?' She stepped back, and I saw how her eyes seemed to flicker as though sparked by some charge. They caught me in the way that a lamp traps a moth. I seemed to be falling into her eyes, a great, great depth. Beyond them, I suddenly knew, lay strange dimensions, impossible truths, waiting to be fathomed and exposed to an unsuspecting world, with myself a Galileo, a second Newton perhaps. The temptation was sucking on me, pulling me like a weight. I knew I had to fight it.

With an effort I turned away from Lilah's stare. I looked out at London, at the orange glow of dawn. I saw the Thames dyed red between the darkness of its banks. I saw it flow. I saw the composition of its waters. The clarity was quite exceptional. The dye, I realised, was that of haemoglobin. I could see leucocytes as well, flowing in the plasma, pumped by a giant, invisible heart. The whole of London was a skinless, living thing. I saw how the streets were flowing red, a limitless network of capillaries, and I knew that if I only waited a little more, this vision would reveal some remarkable truth, some startling breakthrough in haematology, and all I had to do was wait – just a tiny moment more. I stared directly below me where the Thames flowed past, a ceaseless jugular lapping the wharf. I thought of how unnerving a sight it must be for the rivermen, the waters all around them turned to blood. I thought of the bodies they must have seen in the past, bleeding out into the current. Then I thought of Arthur Ruthven. I shut my eyes, I willed the vision to disappear.

When I opened them again, I saw Lilah's face. 'I didn't kill him,' she said.

I was quite unsurprised, I remember, by her reading of my thoughts. 'But you lured him here,' I said.

'No. Polidori did that.'

'At your behest.'

Lilah shrugged. 'He wasn't amenable.'

'And then? Once you had found that out?'

'He left. He was only with me an hour. It was apparent at once that he was unsuitable.'

'But Arthur was missing for a week before his corpse was found.'

Lilah turned away impatiently. 'I have told you, Doctor Eliot, that it wasn't me. Why should I have killed him? How would that have helped me? I remember at the time, I was afraid Arthur Ruthven's murder might serve to put off George. I repeat, Doctor Eliot – I had not the slightest interest in seeing him dead. Indeed, if anything, just the opposite.'

I frowned. I knew that her argument was a convincing one; it had troubled me before. Even so, how could I trust her? Her, or anyone? 'What about Polidori?' I asked.

'Polidori?'

'Arthur's body had been drained of its blood.' I waited, I knew I didn't need to say any more. 'Answer me,' I said, 'or I swear I shall have no choice but to tell George everything I know.'

Lilah narrowed her eyes; she inclined her head faintly. 'It wasn't Polidori either,' she said.

'How do you know?'

'I asked him, of course, when I heard of Arthur Ruthven's death. He denied the accusation at once – denied it vehemently. He wasn't lying.' She smiled at me. 'I can tell such things.'

'I am sure, but forgive me – it's hardly admissible evidence.'

'You think not?' Lilah shrugged. 'Then speak to him yourself.'

I nodded. 'I will.'

'Good.' Lilah smiled and reached out for my hands. 'I'm impatient to see you lay this matter to rest. I would like to feel you are trusting me.' She pressed her cheek against mine and whispered in my ear. 'Do you understand, Doctor? There is no reason why we shouldn't be friends.' She kissed me softly on my lips. 'No reason at all.'

I didn't reply, but turned to walk back down the stairs. She took my arm and wordlessly, we descended to the room where George sat poring over his maps, studying his plans, drawing up policies for the Indian frontier. Polidori was gone. I glanced at Lilah. She led me from the room to the bridge and the den, and the dirty shop below. That was where we found Polidori.

I asked him what he knew about Ruthven's death and he denied murdering him, of course, as Lilah had said he would. 'Why are you accusing me?' he kept asking, his eyes narrow with suspicion. 'Where's your evidence?'

Well, I wasn't telling him about my lines of inquiry, of course. I did mention Lord Ruthven, though, just to measure his response. He flinched visibly and glanced at Lilah, as though some unspoken secret between them had been breached. Lilah, however, remained perfectly impassive, and Polidori – turning away from her again – began to gnaw at the knuckles of his hand. 'What about him?' he asked.

'He said that you had lured Arthur to his death.'

Polidori giggled hysterically at this. 'Well, he would, wouldn't he?'

'Why?'

Polidori grinned. 'If you don't know that, you'd better ask him yourself.'

'No – I'm asking you.'

Polidori glanced at Lilah. 'It wasn't *me*', he said with sudden violence. 'I told you before, it wasn't *me*. *I* didn't kill him.'

A curious emphasis, as though accusing someone else – a partner perhaps, a confidante. But who? Lord Ruthven? – Polidori almost seemed to be implying so. But from what I can tell of their relationship, they are hardly partners; and besides, where is Lord Ruthven's motive for killing his cousin? He had none that I can see.

This case, though, is growing stranger by the day. I am reminded of Suzette's question – 'How do you know when a mystery comes to an end?' Especially when ... yes, let me say it – when the motives may not be reducibly human at all. But for now, let me continue with my own methods of investigation and approach – I am afraid of what Huree might lead me to do. Never forget the boy – *never forget the boy*. Let Huree come in his own time, then – I won't wire him yet. But perhaps it is already too late for such qualms?

And Lilah? What sort of game am I playing with her? Or rather – what is she playing with me? Again – reluctant to follow this line of thought too far. Must do so, though. There is clearly much she has yet to reveal.

Therefore haven't told George anything. Will keep what I have heard and seen to myself for now.

Letter, Lady Mowberley to Dr John Eliot.

2, Grosvenor Street.

20 June.

Dear Dr Eliot,

I am afraid that you will start to dread my letters, for they never seem to contain anything but requests and fears. I am relying once again, though, on your friendship for George – and on the repeated proofs you have offered of your consideration for me. Forgive me, then, for presuming on your kindness once more.

You will know, I think, that George has resumed his visits to Rotherhithe. He has been there three times in the space of the past fortnight, never for more than one night at a time, it is true, and always, he assures me, in the interests of his work. He has asked me, if I doubt him, to refer to you – apparently you accompanied him on his first visit back, and can vouch for the probity of his behaviour there? Well, be that as it may – I am not writing to you in the role of wronged wife. Let George get up to whatever he wishes. It is not his morals I am concerned for, but his declining health.

You see, dear Dr Eliot – he is fading away before my very eyes. You would be shocked, I think, if you were to see him now. He is pale and weak, but very hectic too, as though burning with some fever that is eating up his bones. I cannot believe that George has ever been thin before, but now he is a scarecrow, and frankly I am terrified. The worst of it is, you see, that he still won't admit there is anything wrong with him. His Bill is very near completion now, and he is working day and night at it. Even in those brief hours of sleep he has, he tosses and turns as though plagued by bad dreams. I believe his work is literally haunting him.

245

I wonder – would you have the time to examine him and perhaps, if you can, have a word in his ear? If you wish, we could meet beforehand to discuss his case. I know you are a busy man, but if you have the opportunity I could hold you to your promise to escort me on a walk. I know that Lucy would be keen to accompany us as well, for her husband is away at the moment attending to business at his family's country home, and so she is quite alone. I have seen much of her recently; I believe, thanks to your good agency, that we are now almost intimate. Her husband, however, I am afraid, I still cannot bring myself to forgive; doubtless you will find this strange, but the truth is, Dr Eliot, I have not brought myself even to lay eyes upon him yet. Doubtless he is a very charming young man – Lucy, indeed, appears very much in love – yet I cannot put it from my thoughts that he behaved irresponsibly towards her when they were not even wed. It is always the woman, is it not, who receives the blame in such a situation? For myself, I prefer to blame the man.

Let me know a date which would be suitable for our walk. We would have to go in the morning, of course, so that Lucy could be at the Lyceum in time for her performance – but that would not be a problem, I hope? Perhaps we could visit Highgate – it is a favourite stroll of mine, for although it is hardly countryside, it does at least offer some relief from the grimy London air.

Until very soon, I hope.

I remain your devoted friend,

ROSAMUND, LADY MOWBERLEY.

Letter, Mrs Lucy Westcote to Hon. Edward Westcote.

Lyceum Theatre.
27 June.

My dearest Neddy,

You see how lovelorn I've become. Barely half-an-hour until curtain up, and here I am scribbling to you. Quite the devoted wife. If Mr Irving finds me, he will be very cross, for he doesn't like his actresses to think of any man but himself – he tries to bleed us dry of our emotions, and would cheerfully make us his slaves if he could. Fortunately, while you are away I have Mr Stoker to defend me – he may not be as utter a hero as you, my sweet, but he is very kind, and just about brave enough to stand up to Mr Irving if he must. But I don't want to see him in any trouble – so as I write it, I shall just have to keep this letter out of sight, hidden beneath my cloak. There goes Mr Stoker now. He smiles at me. Such a nice man – though I do wish he would get rid of his appalling beard, and not laugh in quite so *muscular* a way. In fact, Ned, while on the topic of Mr Stoker, he has invited us to a dinner party at his home next month. Oscar Wilde will be going as well – it seems he was a suitor once to Mr Stoker's wife although I must admit, if the rumours are true, I find that hard to believe. Oh yes, and Jack Eliot is being invited too – you met him, I think? – yes, of course you did. He probably won't come, though, since it might mean having fun – but it would be nice if he did. The problem is, he tends only to enjoy the company of people if they're sick.

No – I'm maligning him. He came out for a walk only this morning, in fact, and while that may not sound *tremendously* daring, at least it's a start. Fortunately, the weather was pleasant and the views beautiful and I think Jack scarcely noticed the lack of consumptives or people with no arms. We did have Rosamund with us, though, and since it seems that George is ill again, he was able to talk about diseases with her – perhaps that's what kept him going. Rosamund was wonderfully charming yet again. Despite my best efforts, I find myself liking her more and more. If only she would agree to meet you, and forgive you your cruelty in marrying me, I think we would end up as perfect friends. Indeed, there is something about her which almost reminds me of you. If you were a girl – which I am very glad you are not, of course! – I think you might look rather like her. Do not be insulted, darling – for Rosamund is, as I have told you before, exceedingly pretty, with your own dark curls and brightness of eye. I would like to see you together, just for the comparison. Perhaps I will soon. I cannot believe that Rosamund will persist in her obduracy for long.

Mr Irving has just passed by, looking saturnine in his opera cloak. Not long now until the start of the play, and really I should put you aside, dear Ned, but there is something I have to tell you, you see. You probably guessed as much – you know me too well – for here I am, chattering away, just as I always do when I have something bad to confess. It *is* bad, I'm afraid, my love; and especially at the moment, when you are preoccupied with your family's affairs. Because you see, I have broken my word to you. I know I had promised you I would not, but this morning whilst out on our walk we visited your family's Highgate house. It was not intentional; I had failed to realise we were even close by until we rounded a corner and I saw it – the lane through the trees that leads up to your house. I wanted to go back; but Rosamund said that it was one of her favourite walks and begged to go on, and although Jack supported me once I had explained my qualms, I found myself suddenly filled with curiosity. I just couldn't resist it: my fear, my promise to you, they were suddenly nothing – I had to go on. And so we walked down the lane as far as the gates, and then – I don't know why – instead of passing them by, I led the way through. They were unlocked, you see, and I was afraid that perhaps there had been burglars, but I cannot pretend that was my true motive – as I said, I was curious, and that was all. I had to see the house. It suddenly seemed the most important thing in my life.

Well, Ned, you'll be glad to know the house is quite secure. The shutters are closed, the front door locked, and although we tried we couldn't get in. Should you not employ a watchman, though? Or at the very least, a gardener – the grounds are becoming terribly overgrown. I was thinking this as I looked about me, how wild and waste the whole place seemed, and then suddenly it came on me again – the dread . . . that same strange terror we had both felt before. Of my companions today, Rosamund appeared quite unaffected, but I think Jack – judging by the way he suddenly clenched his fists – may have felt it too; certainly, when I suggested that we continue with our walk he agreed with some haste. Rosamund came back with us but she lingered by the gates, pausing to breathe in the scent of wild flowers. She seemed positively charmed by the overgrown state of the garden and only left it reluctantly. She is a great admirer of Nature, of course, and misses it keenly; for my part, though, I found myself longing for crowded, bustling streets, and did not entirely recapture my nerves until we had hailed a cab and were heading back to town. Again, as on that occasion when I went with you, I could not explain the depth of my feelings. I fear though, Ned, that you are right; some shadow of evil has fallen on the place.

There – you see how acting can affect the brain – I am starting to write like a melodrama. I must stop scribbling anyhow, for Mr Irving has seen me and is baring his teeth in a threatening way – we start in five minutes. Forgive me, Ned (I certainly expect you to, now that I've acted so nobly in confessing all – I *do* feel guilty, though). I miss you, my love. Write and tell me when I can expect you back. Make it *soon*!

The audience has fallen silent. The drums are rolling. Mr Irving is twirling his moustache. No more time. But I love you, Ned. Even on the stage, I'll be thinking of you.

All, all love,

Your ever doting

L.

P.S. Arthur very well and beautiful. With Rosamund tonight. She quite dotes on him. She seems almost to *breathe* in his presence, much as Lord Ruthven does. Strange, is it not, how things can turn out?

Dr Eliot's Diary.

1 July. – A week that started pleasantly, but did not continue so for long. On Tuesday, a walk with Lucy and Lady Mowberley across Highgate Hill. Lucy seemed the very picture of good humour, although there was one curious incident which did occur. In the woods by Highgate Cemetery, we came across the lane which led up to the Westcotes' house. Lucy was reluctant to proceed at first, then enthusiastic; then, once in the gardens, unsettled again. The house was very impressive but entirely abandoned, and I was not surprised, bearing in mind what Lucy had told me before, that she should have been disturbed by the place. Even I felt an irrational distaste for it; but were it to be repaired and inhabited again, then I am certain these responses would rapidly fade. I can understand Westcote's association of the house with his bereavement; but to leave it deserted is merely to surrender to his grief. As it is, the place is a dispiriting one. It was noticeable how Lucy's own spirits rose again, the further we left the house behind.

Lady Mowberley, by contrast, was much harder to comfort and, indeed, seemed exceedingly nervous and upset. She described George's condition in terms which, at the time, I assumed to be exaggerated. I told her how important it was that I saw George for myself, and she then confessed her difficulty in persuading him to visit me; his absorption in his work, it seemed, had now grown almost total. He had promised her he would call on me at the end of the week; but Lady Mowberley clearly doubted whether he would keep to his word.

Fortunately, although he was exceedingly late, George did in the end arrive. I had almost given him up when he was finally shown into my rooms, complaining bitterly at being forced from his Bill; I made him strip, which helped to silence him. I could tell at once that Lady Mowberley was perfectly justified in her fears, for his appearance was indeed shocking. His face and body were thin and very pale; he had symptoms of fever although, bafflingly, a normal temperature as well. Blood tests revealed no abnormalities; certainly no anaemia. I experimented, adding a drop of my own blood to his slide; to my great relief, however, there was no phagocytic response – the appearance and behaviour of white cells instead quite normal. There was evidence of cuts, though, around the neck and wrists. Very faint, but disturbing to find them. There had clearly been considerable loss of blood.

I asked him about Lilah. At once, he grew defensive and almost surly. Most unlike George. It was as though, now I too had met her, he was jealous of me. I tried to determine the cause of the cuts. George was unable to offer any explanation other than the one that he had given me before – namely his carelessness with a shaving blade. And the lacerations to his wrist? No reply. I then asked him if the cuts had materialised during his visits to Lilah. He said not. I asked him about his bad dreams: had they been worst during the nights of these visits? Again a flat denial. Indeed, he claimed the opposite: he was most oppressed, he told me, when he had not seen Lilah at all. I can see no pattern or solution here.

Short-term treatment: transfusion of blood, Llewellyn and myself as donors, the operation completed satisfactorily. Immediate signs of improvement. I advised George to cut back on his work, but I suspect this advice will be ignored. Indeed, he barely listened to me, so impatient he was to leave; I did not try to hold him, but instead escorted him as far as Commercial Street.

On the way, a horrific incident occurred. Outside a tavern we passed a cluster of drunk, rough-looking men and their prostitutes. One of the women in particular caught my eye. Her face was violently painted, and it took me a second to recognise Mary Jane Kelly. Her eyes were gleaming and her mouth was twisted; even through her cosmetics, I could tell she was very pale. At first I assumed that it was the sight of me which was upsetting her, and I was just preparing to cross the street so as to spare her embarrassment when I suddenly realised that she had not even noticed me, but instead was staring at George. She glanced down at her wrist and I saw her whole face seem to melt into an expression of the utmost loathing and fear. She screamed violently and jabbed a finger at George. 'My blood, look at it, that's my blood on his face!' Her voice was that of a madwoman. She launched herself at George, knocking him down into the street. Remembering the fate of the poor dog she had attacked, I was on to her quickly. I pulled her away from George and, calling out for help, was able to drag her back to the surgery. George, meanwhile, was fortunately unhurt, with only a few minor bruises and scars. Needless to say, he was utterly baffled by the whole affair. 'Charming neighbourhood you've got here,' he kept muttering, 'charming neighbourhood.' He left in a hansom as soon as he could.

Since then, Mary Kelly has remained feverish. Sometimes she will throw herself against a far wall, apparently attempting to escape. Her desperation is the same as on the previous occasion when this mania occurred. During her brief moments of lucidity, I have attempted to ask her why she attacked George. But she can give no coherent explanation, beyond saying that she had imagined his face to be streaked with her blood; felt a terrible rage, imagining he had stolen it from her; then remembered nothing more. The orderlies have told me that she sometimes mutters of asylums, sobbing and wailing, and is clearly terrified of being taken to one. Let us hope it does not come to that.

Her mention of asylums, however, reminds me of what the police told me some months back, that there was a second prostitute who was drained of her blood and yet survived the attack. I would be interested to visit the asylum where she is held. I have looked up the address.

Bram Stoker's Journal (continued).

... The summer passed, however, and Eliot's interest in the case seemed to decline. Instead, he appeared increasingly absorbed in issues of medical research, and as a consequence I saw him even less than before. On the few occasions when we did meet, he would update me on the state of Mary Kelly's health, but otherwise he remained silent on our adventure of a few months before. I asked him once if he believed Lucy still to be in danger. He fixed me with his hawk-like stare. 'Not if I can help it,' he answered shortly, and then would say no more. I did not attempt to press him, for I could see he was determined to keep his suspicions to himself.

I was relieved, though, that Lucy should have such a guardian. I felt this not only as a man with feelings of personal friendship for her, but also in my role as theatre manager, for she was increasingly shining as one of our brightest stars. One day Mr Oscar Wilde expressed to me an interest in her abilities, and since I knew that he was planning to write a comedy very soon, I determined that I would effect an introduction between the two of them. For it appeared to me that I had a duty to raise the profile of such a promising young actress; accordingly, I began to plan a dinner party which might promote her cause. I invited several guests whom I judged might aid Lucy in her career; and then, since he was an associate of us both, I decided also to invite Dr Eliot.

I walked across to Whitechapel one bright July morning. I caught Eliot just in time, for as I rounded the corner of Hanbury Street I saw him approaching a cab. He seemed pleased to see me, and when I extended my invitation to him he accepted, though with the proviso that he was not obliged to be witty or bright. I assured him, however, that I had never met any man more clever than himself, and he appeared gratified by this compliment. He shook his head, however, and gestured towards the cab he had been preparing to board. 'You see there, Stoker, proof of my inadequacy. You remember Mary Jane Kelly?'

I assured him that, naturally, I did.

'Very good,' he continued. 'Then you may also recall that I recently discharged her. Her condition, however, has suddenly taken another turn for the worse. My treatment of her, I confess, has done her no good at all.'

'I am sorry to hear that,' I replied. 'But tell me, Eliot, what is the significance of the cab?'

'Why, merely that it will convey me to New Cross, where I hope to visit Lizzie Seward, the prostitute who survived an attack very similar to that inflicted upon Mary Kelly. The unfortunate woman has since been committed as insane.'

'May I accompany you?' I inquired.

'If you have the time,' he replied, 'then it would give me great pleasure to have you by my side once more. I should warn you, however,' he added, as we climbed into the cab, 'that the visit will not be a pleasant one.'

Eliot's foreboding was justified. We arrived at the institution, which to my eye seemed more like a jail than a hospital, and were shown at once into the office of Dr Renfield, the asylum's head. Eliot explained his interest in Lizzie Seward; Dr Renfield almost glowed with pride, and he described his patient's condition as though boasting of a prize exhibit in a zoo. It seemed that Lizzie Seward liked to tear animals to shreds; she would then drink their blood and rub it across her skin. 'I have even coined a phrase,' Dr Renfield said, 'to describe her condition.' He paused for effect, looking pleased with himself. 'Zoophagous – the consumption of living beasts. It sums her up very nicely, I think.' He rose to his feet and gestured with his arm. 'This way, please.'

We followed him down a long passageway and into the wards. The patient's condition was terrible. Locked in a tiny cell, caked with dry blood, surrounded by feathers and tiny bones, she stared at us with uncomprehending eyes. 'Watch this,' said Dr Renfield, giving us a wink. He turned to a cage, evidently stored there purposely, and removed a dove. He opened the door and released the bird into the cell. I observed that its wings had been clipped; it started to flutter vainly. Lizzie Seward had meanwhile shrunk back into a corner, and was watching it through narrowed eyes. Suddenly, she gave a hideous cry of pain and rage, and seized the dove. Twisting off its head, she proceeded to drink the blood, sucking at the flow desperately as though expecting to discover some magical property in it. She then ripped apart the bird's stomach, rubbing the blood and intestines across her face and hair rather as though she were soaping herself. Gradually, she sank down on to the floor of her cell. Prostrate amidst the feathers and gore, she began to weep.

Eliot's face, I saw, was pale with anger at the sight of this spectacle, but Dr Renfield seemed not to observe his guest's displeasure. 'And the fun is not over,' he whispered. 'Just watch now.'

As he said this the patient started to twist and buck, her whole body arching as though preparing to vomit up some noxious substance. But after much retching she could only scream, the sound as piercing as Mary Kelly's had been; she then launched herself against the far wall of her cell. She attempted to climb the stone, scrabbling with her bare nails until I saw blood start to flow from her fingertips. When Eliot protested to Dr Renfield he gave my companion a reproachful look, then shrugged and summoned two orderlies. They entered the cell, seized the patient and bound her into a leather harness. She was then strapped down to the plank which served her as a bed. The operation was conducted with quite unnecessary force. 'I am now absolutely resolved,' Eliot whispered in my ear, 'that Mary Kelly shall never enter such a place.'

He then asked Dr Renfield for his diagnosis. 'Zoophagous hysteria,' the Doctor replied, seemingly hurt that Eliot had forgotten his phrase. 'Incurable,' he added, clearly content that this should be the case. Eliot nodded; he seemed not to have any further questions to ask, and I imagined he would be disappointed by the fruits of his trip. Once outside the asylum, however, he seemed not disheartened at all; indeed, he appeared almost pleased with himself. He said nothing to me, however, and since the hour was now growing late I did not have time to bother him with questions. Hailing a cab to transport me to the Lyceum, I ordered him not to forget my invitation and to call on me, as ever, if he needed any help. He assured me that he would. I left him, frustrated by my companion's taciturnity, but roused as well at the thought that our adventure might not quite be finished yet . . .

Dr Eliot's Diary.

6 July. – A visit to New Cross, to observe Lizzie Seward. Met Stoker on the way, and he accompanied me. The head of the asylum worse than incompetent, and the conditions in which the patient is kept are a disgrace. The visit not entirely wasted, however – one suggestive line of inquiry opened up. I observed, during one of Seward's fits of madness, how she clawed at the wall as though attempting to break out. As we left the asylum I observed the layout of the building, and my conjecture was confirmed: the wall Seward had attacked faces to the north, towards Rotherhithe. Mary Kelly, I realise now, had thrown herself against a wall facing south-east – also towards Rotherhithe.

I determined to proceed there immediately, to see if I could not find more information concerning this seemingly mysterious coincidence. Stoker unable to accompany me: the Lyceum waiting. As we parted, he bade me good luck; he had evidently been shocked by what he saw of Lizzie Seward. Hope it does not affect his imagination too strongly. I continued alone to Rotherhithe.

I told the cabbie to drop me by Greenland Dock. Searching through the back streets, I located the pub mentioned by Mary Kelly in her account of the events that had led up to her assault. The bar crowded. My first inquiries met with hostile incomprehension, but I stood a few drinks and tongues began to loosen. It seems there are dark whisperings abroad in Rotherhithe. No one remembers the specific case of Mary Kelly, but the rumours of a beautiful woman stalking the docks for prey had been heard by almost everyone at the bar. One man told of a friend who had disappeared; others had heard stories of similar cases. But when I asked for a description of the mysterious woman, there was remarkable disagreement. Some spoke of a negress, glimpsed through the window of a curtained carriage; but others described a blonde, and their terms reminded me of the woman that I had seen following me. Unfailingly, though, with both women the same aura was insisted upon: a beauty which terrifies, appals, turns the blood to ice. I described Lilah; no one had seen a woman like her, nor were there even any rumours of such a woman being glimpsed. But Lilah's beauty too could be described as unnerving. Hard to know if this is just coincidence; hard to reach any conclusion at all. This business seems to lie beyond rational analysis.

I stayed in the pub for several hours. When I left, it was late afternoon; the side roads were dusty and deserted; the odd wagon rumbled past, and even a hansom, but nothing corresponding to a private carriage of the kind that Mary Kelly had described. It seems impossible that such a vehicle could stay hidden for long. And then, just as I was thinking this, I found myself by the turning to Coldlair Lane, and I remembered the difficulty I had suffered before when I had searched for a warehouse, an entire building, and failed to find that. I was suddenly struck by a feeling of panic, of a kind that I had not known since Kalikshutra, when I had been similarly confronted by inexplicable facts, when the structures of logic had seemed just as close to collapse; and I felt how dangerous were my efforts to resolve the case. I turned back to the High Street, and wondered what I should do next. As I deliberated, I stared at a shop-front across the road. A wagon went by laden with produce from the docks, and obscured my view. It passed, and once it was gone I saw a little girl standing by the shop. She was dressed neatly in coat and hat, and wore ribbons in her hair. She held a hoop. It was Suzette. She smiled at me, then turned and began to bowl the hoop down the street. She didn't glance round. I called out her name, but she didn't even pause and I began to run after her. Another wagon rumbled by. I lost sight of Suzette. The wagon passed, but still I couldn't see her. I scanned the High Street, up and down, but there wasn't a trace of her. I breathed in deeply.

Suddenly, from behind me, I heard the rolling of her hoop again. It was strangely amplified, and I realised with a shock that all other noise – the rumbling of the traffic, the sounds from the street – had fallen utterly away. I looked down a side alley. For the fraction of a second I could see Suzette, just a tiny figure running away from me, and then she was gone again. I followed her. At the turning of the street where she had disappeared I heard the rolling of the hoop, echoing as before down an empty lane, and then, pursuing it, I heard it suddenly clatter to the ground and fall silent. Round a further corner, I recognised the street which led to the warehouse door. Suzette was standing by it, waiting for me. As I approached her, she smiled shyly and reached out to take my hand; with her other, she rolled her hoop. I did not even think to hesitate; my will no longer seemed my own. Together, we passed in through the open door.

Waiting for us in the hall was the wretchedly deformed dwarf. He removed Suzette's coat and hat; she smiled up at me and clutched my hand again. 'This way,' she said, pointing towards the stairs. Their twisting of proportion was as startling as before; we were climbing only one of several double stairways, all spiralling in seeming defiance of gravity and reaching into heights that I knew could not be there. And yet they were; and I felt that same strange giddiness I had just suffered on the street, the sense that my frameworks of understanding could not deal with the mysteries being opened up to me. There was a difference, though: before, I had felt helpless; now, with my sense of what was possible dissolving before my eyes, I began to glimpse amongst the wreckage of my old assumptions new forms, new ideas, and felt not afraid but excited, even moved. 'Lilah has been waiting for you,' said Suzette, 'a very long time. She did not think you would stay away for so long.' We were standing on a balcony next to a wondrously crafted door, inlaid with Arabic designs of indigo and gold. Suzette reached up and opened it. 'You must tell her you are sorry,' she whispered. I passed through.

Beyond was the room I remembered from before, yet it was subtly changed. It took me a second to understand this; then I realised that along the side of the room, where before there had been curtains, now there was a wall of glass made from panes of different colours – blues, dark greens, nasturtium oranges and reds – so that the light, like the scent of perfumes in the air, was remarkably rich and deep, and seemed almost to possess the texture of water, stained perhaps by a setting sun. Two doors were open in this wall of glass, and I saw that beyond them stretched a conservatory. I heard the bubbling of water; passing through the doors, I saw two small fountains, spaced at equal distance along a pathway of marble, with trees and plants on either side and further pathways, running and disappearing into heavy green shadows. The air was as rich as before, but the perfumes now were of orchids and vegetation, sweeping tropical trees, flowers of an impossible brightness and strange, flesh-coloured plants which seemed to palpitate before my gaze, as though shuddering beneath the pollen and its suffocating kiss. I felt a touch, as soft as blossom, brushing my hand. I turned round.

'I am upset,' said Lilah, 'that you did not come sooner than this.'

'Yes,' I replied. 'Suzette told me I had to apologise.'

'Well, do so.'

I smiled. 'I am sorry.' Lilah took my arm; she met my smile. 'Here,' she said, gesturing towards a side-path. She brushed aside some lilies that obscured our way, and we walked beneath the warm, ripe shade of the trees. I glanced at her. She wore a sari and across her long, braided hair, fastened by jewels, hung a veil of the purest diaphanous silk. The effect should have been to cloak her; and yet in truth the sight of her, her touch, the scent on her clothes acted on me as the arboretum did, oppressing but also stimulating me, inducing a strange reverie, a sense of being close to new sensations and ideas. Whether it was truly her presence or the closeness of the air, I hesitate to say, but I began to experience thought differently, as though concepts and reasonings were nothing but dreams, my brain a hothouse in which strange things might flourish and grow. I longed for some relief from the vegetation; and hearing a fountain ahead of us, I suggested to Lilah that we pause there for a moment. Next to the fountain was a stone seat covered with cushions and rugs. Sitting down, I watched the flow of the water from the fountain's mouth. Lilah whispered something so softly that I couldn't catch what she said, and at once, from the shadows, the panther came slinking. Lilah smiled; she snapped her fingers; the panther leapt up beside her on to the seat and Lilah curled up next to it. I realised I was staring at her like an idiot, like some green young boy. I struggled to tear my eyes away from the sight of her bare arms against the panther's black fur, from the curve of her breasts beneath the sari's satin fold, from the fullness of her bright lips, from the fullness of her smile. I knew I had to escape it, this hothouse lust – this muggy, sapping, destructive desire, which I had always despised before and learned to ignore. I would not surrender to it now. With an effort, I looked down at the stone slabs of the pathway. I forced myself to think. I forced myself, in short, to be Jack Eliot once again.

And as I did so, so I returned to the mystery which had first brought me to Rotherhithe. I began to ask about the phantom woman supposed to haunt the docks, and although Lilah shrugged she did not seem surprised by the question. She could not help me, though; and so instead I told her about Mary Kelly and my work with her; then I asked about the strange attraction that both Kelly and the poor lunatic in New Cross seemed to feel towards the scene of their assaults. Could she explain this remarkable phenomenon? Lilah took my hand; she began to talk. There was no magic, she said; she had told me that before. But there were many ways to understand the secrets of nature; I had realised that, surely; why else had I come to Kalikshutra, and worked there for so long? Yet it was not just in Kalikshutra that these secrets could be found; there were many places haunted by the darkness of such mysteries; and London too was one of them.

'You mean Rotherhithe?' I asked. 'Now, here, for as long as you stay?'

Lilah smiled and retouched the edge of her veil, as though to cloak herself from my inquisitiveness; yet the gesture was a tantalising one and the effect, as she must have known it would be, was to concentrate in a single moment all her fascination and loveliness and power, to hint at the depths which I had barely skimmed, and appear to offer them up to me.

'For as long as I stay?' she murmured softly. She laughed, but I knew that I was right, that wherever she was, wherever she had been, there mystery would also be – that dark, unexplored dimension of the world which I could not explain, but knew now to exist and could no longer deny. For the truth will always gather followers; and Lilah, for those afflicted by what they could not understand, might indeed seem to represent a form of truth. I thought of the darkness that was rising in Rotherhithe, outside Lilah's door, and of all the creatures borne on its tide. The negress in the carriage. Polidori. Myself.

This last thought made me start. Lilah squeezed my hand, then she raised it to her lips. Her kiss almost froze me; I blinked, struggling to recapture my thoughts. I began to ask about Polidori. I explained my involvement with Lord Ruthven and I thought – or perhaps I imagined it – that at the mention of his name, Lilah's eyes appeared to gleam as though excited or disturbed. Certainly, I had never seen her respond with such evident interest to the mention of any other name; and I wondered what power Lord Ruthven might possess to unsettle such a woman even as Lilah. But though her eyes had betrayed her, she said not a word; and would only agree, when I pressed her further on the topic of Lord Ruthven, that he and Polidori were indeed afflicted by the same disease. What that disease was, I did not need to be told; but remembering my studies on Lord Ruthven's blood, and eager to pursue the implications they had suggested for haemotological research, I began to share with Lilah my theories and hopes.

Never has the pursuit of knowledge seemed more intoxicating to me. As we talked, I began to see – to understand – to feel unsuspected truths almost tangible in my grasp. How long did we sit there together? No time at all, it seemed, so oblivious to all but our conversation had I grown, yet when at length we finished and I returned to the streets outside, the moon was pale in the sky and the first hints of dawn were rising in the east. I had been with Lilah for ten hours; I hadn't eaten, I hadn't drunk, I had only talked, and in that time, it had seemed to me, I had spanned the world of medicine and travelled far, far beyond. If I could only repeat it all now, speak it into this phonograph, what a revolution in knowledge might I not pursue!

But I remember nothing. The inspiration is gone. All my insights and certainties, the whole edifice of understanding that Lilah and I had raised up – it is disappeared, melted away on the morning light like the phantom fabric of a castle of air. And yet it was more than that – more than a phantom: it was there last night, I know it, in my head. The truth may have faded; but the truth remains the truth. Is that what I am searching for now? Is that where this case is leading me to? Not away from, but back to scientific research? The stakes I am playing for seem to heighten with time.

Letter, Hon. Edward Westcote to Mrs Lucy Westcote.

Alvediston Manor,
Near Salisbury,
Wiltshire.

7 July.

My dearest L,

You are funny. Why would I blame you? I'm hardly the man to forbid you anything. If I were, I doubt you would have married me. Dammit, Lucy, you've always been strong-minded. That's the way I like you. I could never bear to carry on like the Pater, dishing out orders all the time. Hate orders, always have done. It's perfectly true, I didn't want you to visit my parents' house again; but that wasn't because I was afraid you might intrude or any of that rot, only because I feel there's something wrong there and I don't want you mixed up in it. And I was right, wasn't I? You shouldn't have gone. 'Some shadow of evil' – yes, I liked that. Nice phrase. Puts it pretty well.

But actually, Lucy, it seems the shadow may be lifting soon. I've had the most splendid news, you see. Got a letter last week, from India. Not from the Pater himself (he's off slaughtering the heathen somewhere on the frontier), but from some other chap I've never heard of, a subaltern of his. It appears that my sister may not be dead after all. She's been seen, apparently, up in that region where she disappeared. It's not absolutely certain but sounds pretty hopeful, according to this subaltern, and they've sent off a mission into the hills. Really, Lucy, have you ever heard more ripping news? I can't wait for you to meet Charlotte. I'm sure you'll turn out the most tremendous friends.

I've been in such a state of excitement over this letter that I'm a little behind on my business down here. I'll certainly aim to have everything over and done with in time for Mr Stoker's dinner party, though. And, yes, *of course* I remember Jack Eliot. We met in your dressing room. He was in India too, wasn't he, up in the hills? Maybe he knows the region where poor Charlotte disappeared. I'll be able to ask him at the very least.

Darling Lucy, I'll be back soon. I miss you more than I can put into words. But you know that.

All, all love, my dearest, to you and Art,

Your doting husband,

NED.

Dr Eliot's Diary.

16 *July.* – For just over a week, I have been working hard on my research, attempting to recapture the spark of understanding I had felt with Lilah, which at the time had seemed so genuine. But the toil has been fruitless. Lord Ruthven's leucocytes have remained unchanged, which should have acted as a spur to my theorising, but instead has served to paralyse my thoughts. I can see no way past the problem they represent. There is a sample beside me on my desk as I speak. Beneath the microscope the cells seem to mock me with their unceasing movement, while all around sheets of paper covered with scribblings mount up on my desk. They amount to nothing; I am lost in a maze which I cannot understand.

Yesterday, so dull and distracted did I feel that I went so far as to call on Lilah again – purely to see if she could lighten my spirits. There was no difficulty in finding her warehouse this time. I had not realised, until I was with her again, how much I had missed the stimulation she provides. We sat in the conservatory, Suzette with us, scribbling notes in a magazine: *A Study in Scarlet* again. I promised her I would read it. There was only limited opportunity for conversation of the kind that Lilah and I shared last week, for I could spare only a few hours away from the surgery. But Lilah is always intriguing company; we were together long enough for me to recapture the spark I had enjoyed before. But now it is faded again; and I feel nothing but distraction and bafflement.

Only the discharge of Mary Kelly this afternoon, after a satisfactory recovery, has served to lighten my mood. But even so, I am still unable to explain the cause of her relapse, nor am I confident that she is wholly cured. I have warned her on no account to return to Rotherhithe, nor to travel near it, even along the opposite bank of the Thames. For her own comfort of mind, I have agreed to take possession of a spare key to her room in Miller's Court. I have placed it prominently next to the clock in my rooms.

20 *July*. – No choice in the end but to take the afternoon off. I had been trying to concentrate on my research, but the inspiration was as absent as before; the longer I worked, the greater my sense of depression grew, and I was getting nowhere. I went for a long walk, to try to order my thoughts.

Passing through Covent Garden, I called on Stoker, but he was busy and so I continued my walk across Waterloo Bridge and back along the Thames. Without really having intended it, I found myself in Rotherhithe. I called on Lilah. To my surprise, the door was answered by Polidori. He did not seem pleased to see me.

'She's not in,' he snarled, and would have slammed the door in my face had I not blocked it with my foot. 'If you don't mind,' said Polidori, as rudely as before, 'I'm rather busy.' He turned his back on me and I saw that behind him, standing in the hall, was a man

I recognised from the opium den. His eyes were open but quite without sense, and his head lolled as though his neck had been broken. Instinctively, I stepped forward to see what assistance I could give him, but Polidori pushed me roughly aside and took the man by his arm. 'Nothing for you to worry about,' he told me, speaking close to my face so that I received the full blast of his breath and had to look away. From the corner of my eye, I saw Polidori grin and turn back to his companion. 'He can't handle his smoke. Had a bit too much of it, haven't you?' He slapped the man on his cheeks, but the addict made no reply. Polidori lifted his chin and breathed full on his face; but still the man stared as dully as before.

'He needs help,' I said.

'Not yours, though,' replied Polidori rudely. 'I thank you, Doctor, but I do have some medical training of my own.'

'Then at least let me help you.'

'Oh! So your knowledge of opium is the equal of mine? You understand the principles of addiction as well as me? You have devoted a lifetime to studying it, perhaps? No. I didn't think so. Very well, then, would you please' – and even his expression of politeness remained a mocking leer – '*fuck* off, Doctor, and not pester us?' He brushed past me and began to lead his patient across the hall, towards a door that I recognised from my first visit; it led to the room in which Stoker and I had discovered George.

'What will you do with him?' I called out.

Polidori paused in the doorway; he glanced back at me. 'Why, what do you think?' he asked. 'Dry him out!' He hissed with laughter, then slammed the door in my face and I heard a key turn in the lock.

'Why does he upset you so much?'

I looked round. From the balcony above the hall, Suzette was watching me. I shrugged.

Suzette held out a hand. 'Come and wait for Lilah with me.'

I sighed; then I walked across the hall and up the stairs. 'You *do* hate him, don't you?' asked Suzette, as she reached up to take my hand.

'I don't hate anyone,' I replied. 'That would be a waste of time.'

'Why?'

'Because it is always a waste of time to surrender to emotion.'

Suzette considered this. Her solemn face wore a frown. 'So what should you surrender to instead?'

'Your judgement.'

'Of what?'

'Of what you estimate someone's effect to be on their fellow men.'

'And if it's bad, you should hate them?'

'No. I said – never hate. Attempt to . . . counteract.'

'Counteract.' Suzette repeated the word, as though impressed by its length. 'And so you want to . . . "counteract" . . . Polly?'

I stared into her wide eyes. She was very young, but I was uncomfortable with the way the conversation was turning. I had the sense – extraordinary with a child – that she might almost be playing with me. 'I don't trust him,' I said at last, 'that is all.'

Suzette nodded solemnly. We had reached the main room by now. I sat on a divan and Suzette clambered up to join me. She continued to fix me with her unblinking gaze. 'You don't trust him because he gives people opium, do you?'

'Opium?' I frowned. 'You're too young to know about that.'

'But I live next door to Polly's shop. How could I not know about it?' She hadn't smiled, but I thought I could detect a glint of amusement in her eyes. 'Besides,' she added, fiddling with a ringlet in her hair, 'Lilah tells me that it's good to know things.' She looked up at me again. 'Do you think it's not?'

'It's not good to know about opium, no.'

'But you do.'

'Yes. Because I have to know about what makes people ill.'

'Have you taken it yourself, then?'

I frowned, but her expression remained as interested and solemn as before. 'No,' I said at length.

'Why not?'

'Because I prefer my brain to be clear and sharp. I do not want it clouded. The desire for opium becomes a craving, Suzette. Do you understand what a craving is?' She nodded. 'Very good,' I said. 'I have a craving, but it is for a *natural* excitement, for the stimulation of my reasoning powers. You understand that, don't you, Suzette? I have seen you playing chess – you like problems and puzzles, just like me.' Again she nodded slowly. 'Then promise,' I said, 'never, *never* take opium.' I tried to look as stern as I could. 'If you must be an addict of anything, then be an addict of the excitement that your own powers can give you – an addict of mental exaltation.'

'Like Sherlock Holmes.'

'Yes,' I said, not wishing to admit that I had failed to read the story yet. 'If you like.'

Suzette nodded. 'So in that case ...' she said, fiddling with her ringlet again.

'Yes?' I encouraged her.

'If you like to feel all sharp and alert ...'

'Yes?'

She looked up at me. 'Do you like to take cocaine?' she asked.

She must have observed my surprise. But still she didn't blink, and her face remained the picture of innocent inquiry it had been before. I looked away and thought that George had been right after all, she did need a nanny – at the very least. And just as I was considering that I would tell Lilah this, I heard footsteps approaching up the steps outside, and Suzette scrambled from the divan and ran across to the door. 'Lilah!' she cried, as the door opened. She reached up to hug Lilah, and Lilah swept her up in her arms. Behind them, I realised, still on the balcony, stood a man. He was in evening dress, dark-faced and bearded, with a turban round his head. It was the Rajah: I recognised him at once.

And then, a fraction of a second later, I remembered that this man was actually George. Such errors of the memory are always suggestive; on this occasion especially so for, staring into his face, I was struck as I had been before by the transformation in my friend's appearance. Quite simply, I could not recognise him; instead of the honest, jovial features of Sir George Mowberley, I was staring at a

267

man stamped with jealousy and lust. 'George,' I said, almost inquiringly. I held out my hand; George stared at it, and his lip seemed to quiver as though with hatred for me. Then he controlled himself and took my hand; as he shook it I suddenly shuddered, for I was struck – I couldn't say why – by a most extraordinary surge of dislike and fear. I remembered how both Lucy and Stoker had described their response to the Rajah; now I too, even while aware of his true identity, found myself affected in a similar way. George must have noted my revulsion, for he began to frown; to cover myself, I started to compliment him on the quality of his make-up and dress. I smiled as good-humouredly as I could manage. 'Quite unsettling.'

'Yes,' said Lilah, taking his arm, 'you look perfectly sinister,' She reached up to kiss him, long and lingeringly. George tried to hold her, but as he did so Lilah slipped away from his grasp. 'Not in front of the child,' she murmured.

'Damn the child.' George glared at Suzette, then muttered something else beneath his breath. Suzette suddenly began to laugh. George's frown deepened, and I saw how his hands were clenched into fists.

Lilah must have observed it too, for she took George's arm again and began to guide him away. 'Come on,' she said, 'we must wash that make-up from your face.' She led us into the conservatory. As I accompanied her, I observed how she too seemed changed, though nothing like as profoundly as George. She had painted her face, not thickly but strikingly; her hair had been deliberately set to seem unstyled; her jewellery I recognised as Kalikshutran gold. Her dress, even more daringly than before, was in the latest *d'ecollet'e* style. She seemed quite unlike the woman I had sat with on my previous visit. Again, I found the transformation unsettling to behold.

We stood by a fountain, while George bent down and wiped the make-up from his face. I observed, before it was washed away on the fountain's flow, how the paint stained the water in the manner of blood. Interesting, especially in view of what Lucy saw in Bond Street when George had been *applying* the make-up; hard to explain, since the finish on the face looks nothing like blood. I was relieved when George had completed his ablutions; as he sat down beside us, he seemed his old self again. No – almost his old self, I should say, for there remained in his eyes the gleam of suspicion, and his features seemed even more gaunt than before. He is still clearly weakening. I requested him to visit me within the next few days. He promised me that he would, once his Bill was passed; it seems the vote on the measures is due for next week. Whether George does come, of course, I can only wait and see.

I rose and excused myself shortly afterwards. The situation is potentially awkward. Evidently, if I am to see Lilah in the future, it must be when I don't have to share her with George. God knows what he has been imagining.

24 *July*. – An unpleasant incident, which I am almost embarrassed to record.

A couple of days ago, I had finally obtained a copy of *Beeton's Magazine*; that same evening, I spent an idle hour skimming through *A Study in Scarlet*. By an odd coincidence, it turned out to have been written by Arthur Conan Doyle. I haven't seen him since our university days. His hero, Sherlock Holmes, is an obvious caricature of Dr Bell, for their deductive methods are exactly the same. Evidently Doyle did gain something from Bell's lectures, after all.

The story itself was an amusing one, if implausible. I wondered how much of it Suzette had understood. The following evening, frustrated yet again by the progress of my research, and therefore at somewhat of a loose end, I thought I might visit Rotherhithe and attempt to find out. It was soon clear that Suzette had understood it perfectly well. For one so young, she is admirably sharp. We had a lengthy discussion on the art of deductive reasoning. In particular, Suzette was intrigued to know if there are situations where the method would not work. She returned to her old question: what happens if you are in a case, and you don't know the laws? I attempted to explain to her that in the field of human behaviour, with all its irrationality, there can be no certain laws; that detection depends on observation; that reason itself must always be applied.

'Applied to what?' Suzette asked.

'To the evidence,' I replied. 'If it seems mysterious, then a logical explanation must always be found for it.'

Suzette furrowed her brow. 'But what if a logical explanation does not exist?'

'It must do.'

'Always?'

I nodded. 'Always.'

'So if it didn't ...' – she glanced back down at her magazine – 'then Sherlock Holmes wouldn't be able to solve the case.'

'No, I suppose not.'

She nodded very slowly, then looked up again. As she stared at me, she narrowed her eyes. 'And nor would you, would you, then?'

At this point Lilah began to scold her lazily. 'You're such a provoking girl,' she said, taking her on her knee. 'What would Uncle George think? Little girls aren't meant to worry about difficult things.'

But I had to wonder. Once Suzette had been packed off to bed, I asked Lilah about her. It seems she is the only child of a beloved friend. 'A very old friend,' Lilah added with a distant smile.

'Has she always been this precocious?' I asked.

'Precocious?' Lilah nodded. 'Oh yes.'

'And her intelligence, her learning – you have been teaching her yourself?'

'Of course. Suzette is far too much trouble for a teacher, I'm afraid.' Lilah paused, as though catching some noise from the hallway below. She stretched out her fingers and smoothed back her hair. 'One thing, though,' she murmured; 'George's suggestion – perhaps he was right. Suzette could do with a nanny; she needs to be tamed.' She paused again. Now I too could hear footsteps, coming up the stairs. Lilah glanced at the door, then turned back to me. She smiled. 'I shall have to start looking for a suitable girl.'

George burst into the room – terribly haggard and pale. As he stared at us he seemed to tremble, and I was afraid he was about to collapse. I rose to go to his aid; as I crossed to him, he shouted something almost unintelligible, but clearly to the effect that I had betrayed his trust. I tried to calm him; I reached out to take his pulse, but as I did so, George raised his hand and, clenching it into a fist, suddenly struck me upwards on the chin. The blow caught me unawares. I staggered back and George stumbled after me; he raised his fist again and caught me a second blow, this time on the side of my head. Instinctively, I returned the punch; George was knocked down to the floor and I hurried abashed to his side, for he had seemed so weak that I was afraid I might have injured him. But still he refused my assistance; he struggled to rise, hissing accusations at me, and his eyes still burned with the most implacable hate.

Lilah, who had been watching as though faintly intrigued, now intervened, covering George's prostrate body and asking me to leave. I protested that George needed help. 'Maybe,' replied Lilah, 'but he won't accept it from you. Don't worry, I will treat him. Just go, Jack, go!' I stood hesitantly; then I turned and left. By the doorway, I glanced round again; Lilah was kissing George and embracing him, as she propped him up. I turned again and walked out through the door.

What a wretched, sordid business! I cannot believe how thoughtless I have been. I should have known that George would take things the wrong way, he is so overworked and ill. And now I have lost the chance to treat him. Earlier this evening I visited his house. I was informed by the butler that Sir George was not receiving guests that night.

Letter, Lady Mowberley to Dr John Eliot.

2, *Grosvenor Street.*
24 *July.*

Dear Dr Eliot,

I am afraid that I must request you not to call on my husband again. I do not know what quarrel you have had – George himself refuses to tell me, so I presume it to be serious – but whatever the cause, he is now quite implacable. I must repeat, therefore: do not call on him again.

It is with the utmost regret that I pen such an instruction – I have so few friends in this city. I must shortly travel to Whitby to settle some family business there; and thinking as I have been about my childhood home, I am all the more reluctant to forgo the companionship of a man such as yourself, a man who makes me feel not altogether alone in this great wilderness of London. I hope and trust that you will appreciate this. Indeed I confess it quite readily, Dr Eliot, that I am almost tempted to remain in Whitby once my business has been concluded, and never return. I am quite at my wits' end with George, so altered he seems. It is his illness, I am certain, which is responsible for this change in his character; either that, or the thought of the speech he must give when he concludes the business of his Bill next week. Perhaps once that is done and out of the way, he will become himself again. We must certainly hope so.

Once again, then, Dr Eliot, yours in profound regret,
ROSAMUND, LADY MOWBERLEY.

Dr Eliot's Diary.

25 *July.* – High melodrama from George, in the form of a letter sent by his wife. Should be grateful, I suppose, that he has not challenged me to a duel. Clearly delusional; he must be very sick. He will not let

me near him, though. There seems nothing I can do.

A hard day in the ward, for which I was grateful. Late afternoon, resumed my study of Lord Ruthven's blood sample. I am still floundering but equally reluctant to give up on the challenge yet. The leucocytes remain alive – that fact alone is a miracle. But no – the word 'miracle' will not do – and therein lies my problem. I am beyond the bounds of medical orthodoxy – I seem far beyond the bounds of science itself. In such a dimension, I am quite lost. And yet I am comforted by remembering an argument of Lilah's, that there are many paths to the mysteries of nature. Repeating that now, I sound like the worst breed of crank – but when I was with Lilah that night in her conservatory, I believed it to be true. No – more than that – I *saw* how it was true. That mood, that spirit of mental exaltation ... somehow, I have to recapture it. But still the problem: which path do I take?

28 July. – Still no breakthrough, and the leucocytes continue to tantalise me. It is perfectly clear now, I think, that the samples I possess cannot be studied in isolation: for the purposes of my research, I must have reference to the organism from which the blood cells came. And yet I have cut myself off from Lord Ruthven; I can expect no further illumination from him.

29 July. – It is useless. I can go no further. I have neither the resources, nor the experience, nor the wit to carry on.

30 July. – The weight of my failure is still heavy. I cannot bear to admit to it, yet it is clear, I think, that I must. I have been deluding myself for far too long.

Thank God for Stoker's dinner party tonight. Would not have relished an evening spent alone.

Bram Stoker's Journal (continued).

... I therefore looked forward to seeing Eliot with more than usual impatience, for I was hopeful, with the possible development of his investigation, that he might have been rendered more communicative. Indeed, I was informed that he had called on me one afternoon at the Lyceum, but I was engaged with Mr Irving at the time and hence unable to see him; I therefore resigned myself to waiting until the evening of my dinner party. I do not know what I expected or feared, but as I awaited the arrival of my guests, I increasingly found myself almost nervous, as though in expectation of what Eliot might have to reveal.

Although not the last, he was very late. I was relieved to see him, for I had almost persuaded myself that he would not arrive, but as he stepped into the light my initial relief was transformed into dismay. For the period of a month had wrought a terrible change in his appearance. The flesh seemed barely to cling to his bones; he had a haggard and haunted look in his eyes. 'Good Lord!' I exclaimed, staring at his gaunt features. 'What has become of you?'

Eliot frowned. 'My work,' he muttered, 'it has not been going well.'

'Work?'

'Yes, yes,' he said impatiently, 'a project of research, nothing that would possibly interest you. Now please, Stoker – are we to stand out here all evening, or will you introduce me to your guests?'

'Yes, of course,' I answered, somewhat abashed. I left him with Lucy and Oscar Wilde, trusting that his taciturnity would not survive the companionship of two such exuberant guests, yet nervous of his evident irritability. And indeed, when I rejoined them some minutes later it was to hear Wilde gushing on the subject of fashion, and Eliot suddenly asking him whether an interest in such a topic was not a waste of intelligence and time.

Wilde laughed at this; but Lucy, fortunately, was there to interpose. 'You must excuse him, Mr Wilde,' she said, taking Eliot's arm. 'Jack thinks nothing is of value unless it is dead, and lying on a slab.'

'A most commendable attitude,' replied Wilde. 'You are obviously acquainted with Lady Brackenbury. But not everyone is so displeasing to the soul and eye. What of those who are beautiful?'

'Why? What of them?'

'You have accused me of wasting my time, of not being serious. But is not the beauty of a young boy serious? Or indeed' – he glanced at Lucy – 'a girl?'

'Serious?' Eliot frowned. 'No. What lies beneath the surface, in the mind, or the flow of blood through the veins – that is serious. But not beauty – I have seen the flesh and bone which constitute it.'

'How charmingly gothic of you,' murmured Wilde. 'I should never look so far. I always judge by appearances. But in that, of course, I am merely a herald of the age – only the superficial is important now. It is that which makes the tying of a cravat so exquisitely serious, and beauty itself a form of genius and truth – higher, indeed, than either, as it needs no explanation. In that lies its reassurance – and, perhaps, its danger too.'

'Well,' Eliot said after a slight pause, 'it is lucky, then, that I am not a designer of cravats.'

Wilde laughed. 'And lucky I am not a surgeon,' he replied. 'You see, Doctor, you are perfectly correct. It is just that I prefer to preserve my ignorance. It is such a delicate flower – the one touch of reality, and it loses its bloom. I doubt my views would survive the sight of too much blood.'

Eliot smiled, but made no further answer, and the silence was filled by the dinner bell. 'We are a little late,' I apologised, 'We have been waiting for our final guest. He has just arrived, however, so if you are ready we can sit down to eat.' I then led the way into the dining room, and we all took our places. As we did so, our final guest joined us with a murmured apology for being late. I greeted Lord Ruthven warmly, then showed him to his place. Eliot, who was opposite him, appeared somewhat surprised, and indeed glanced at me almost reproachfully, I thought. I recalled that he could not have met Lord Ruthven since that first time in Lucy's dressing room, and doubtless was unaware of his

Lordship's interest in his cousin's career, and the oft-repeated marks of his concern and support. I could scarcely have failed to invite him to such a gathering; and yet Eliot continued to appear upset, and his reluctance to talk with Lord Ruthven was evident.

Instead he busied himself with Edward Westcote, which surprised me, for Westcote – while a personable fellow and a worthy husband to his wife, no doubt – had always struck me as an insipid conversationalist. Eliot, however, appeared quite animated with him; I made an effort to overhear what they were talking about, and caught Eliot discussing India. Specifically, he was discussing the myths of that area in which he had stayed, and some of its more intriguing superstitions. Lord Ruthven too had begun to listen, I observed, and soon the other guests were as well, pressing Eliot with queries of their own. Eliot himself appeared suddenly reluctant to continue; and when Lord Ruthven asked him to describe some myth of immortality current in the Himalayas, he simply shook his head and sat back in his chair.

Wilde, however, was clearly intrigued by the turn of the conversation. 'Immortality?' he inquired. 'You mean eternal youth? Why, what a charming idea. The ephemeral rendered perpetual. I can think of nothing more delightful.' He paused. 'But you do not agree, Dr Eliot?'

Eliot gave him a sharp glance. 'Perhaps,' he replied, 'it would make of beauty what you claim it to be – a serious matter.'

'But not delightful?' pressed Lord Ruthven, a faint smile on his lips.

For the first time Eliot met his eyes. 'That, my Lord,' he said at length, 'would depend upon the price one has to pay.'

'Price!' exclaimed Wilde. 'Really, Dr Eliot, it is most vulgar to talk like a stockbroker when you are not one at all.'

'No,' said Lord Ruthven, shaking his head, 'on this issue at least, he is surely correct. It is the definition of a pleasure, is it not, that it must exact a due? Champagne, cigarettes, a lover's promise – all perfectly delightful, but the pleasure they afford is momentary compared with the suffering we must then endure on their account.

Imagine – just imagine! – the due that would be levied on eternal youth.'

'What do you think it might be?' Lucy asked, staring at him with rapt concentration. The whole table, I saw, was similarly transfixed, gazing at the beauty of Lord Ruthven's pale face. Lit by the candle flame, it seemed touched by gold, a thing quite unearthly and not human at all.

'My Lord,' said Lucy again, prompting him, 'you were talking of the due on eternal youth.'

'Was I?' asked Lord Ruthven. He lit a thin cigarette, then shrugged faintly. 'It would have to be damnation, at the very least.'

'Oh, the *very* least,' agreed Wilde.

Lord Ruthven smiled, and blew out a wreath of blue smoke. He watched as it curled above the candle flames, then lowered his eyes to stare at Wilde across the table. 'You think the loss of your soul a cheap price to pay?'

'Yes, indeed,' replied Wilde. 'Certainly I would prefer it to exercise, or respectable living. After all, when set against good looks, what is morality? – only a word we use to ennoble our own petty prejudices. It is better to be good than ugly – but it is better by far, my Lord, to be beautiful than good.'

I saw how disturbed my dear wife was at the turn the conversation was taking. 'No!' I exclaimed with some violence. 'You are being too flippant, Oscar. To be damned, and yet still be alive, for ever … It would be … too awful. That would be not life, but a … a …' – the horror of the idea seemed suddenly to possess me – '*a living death.*'

Lord Ruthven smiled faintly at this last phrase, and breathed out another plume of thin smoke. He glanced across at Wilde, who was staring at him with parted lips and a gleam in his eye. 'How much would you be prepared to suffer, Mr Wilde?' he drawled.

'For eternal youth?'

Lord Ruthven inclined his head. 'Or indeed, for any youth.'

'Youth,' said Wilde, his expression suddenly solemn, 'is the one thing worth having. It is the wonder of wonders. The only true source of happiness.'

'You truly think so?' Lord Ruthven laughed.

'You disagree, my Lord? But that is because you yourself are still beautiful. You will age, though. The pulse of your life will dim and grow sluggish. You will become lined, and loathsome, and sallow-cheeked. The light will fade from your dulling eyes. And then, my Lord, you will suffer terribly, remembering the passions and the delights that you once believed were your own by right. Youth, my Lord, youth! There is absolutely nothing in the world but youth!'

Lord Ruthven stared into his wine. 'The beauty you speak of, Mr Wilde, is an illusion. A face that did not age would be nothing but a mask. Beneath its show of eternal youth, the spirit would be withering, a hideous mess of corruption and evil. Mr Stoker is right. Beauty can conceal, but it cannot redeem.'

Wilde stared at him, a slight frown on his brow. 'You surprise me,' he said. 'You would not be tempted yourself, then?'

Lord Ruthven stubbed out his cigarette. I observed how he glanced suddenly at Eliot, but otherwise he made no reply.

Oscar Wilde laughed. 'You are too honest for your own argument, my Lord. You are a hedonist, of course – with your beauty you could be nothing else – and hedonists always succumb to temptations. It is the only way to get rid of them, after all.'

Lord Ruthven leaned back in his chair. 'Yes,' he nodded slowly, 'you are probably correct.'

'Of course I am,' said Wilde. 'For in the end, what is suffering when weighed against beauty? For beauty, anything may be forgiven. You, my Lord, you might be guilty of the most horrific sins, you might be damned for all eternity, but your beauty would still obtain forgiveness for you – your beauty, and the love it would inspire.'

'*You* would forgive me, then?' The emphasis appeared strange to me and I noticed, as Lord Ruthven asked the question, how he glanced again at Eliot.

'I forgive you?' replied Wilde languidly. 'I would not need to. Why, I prefer a beauty that is dangerous. I *prefer* to feast with panthers, my Lord.'

'Say rather,' murmured Eliot, 'sup with the devil.' He rose suddenly to his feet. 'Stoker,' he announced, 'I am afraid I must depart.' Everyone stared at him in surprise – everyone except Lord Ruthven, who smiled faintly and lit a cigarette – but Eliot, I observed, still avoided his eye. Instead, he turned and thanked my wife for the dinner, then hurried from the room; I joined him in the hall. I had expected to find him overwrought, but he seemed on the contrary almost cheerful in his manner. I pressed him to explain his sudden departure, but he would not, only thanking me instead for what he termed a 'revelatory meal'.

'Revealing what?' I asked him; but again he shook his head.

'I will see you shortly,' he said, 'and when I do, I may have some answers for you. In the meantime, though, Stoker, I must wish you a good night.' And with that he was gone. I was left, if anything, even more perplexed than before.

Eliot had been right, though. Shortly I was indeed to be given answers; and answers more terrible than I had ever dared imagine . . .

Dr Eliot's Diary.

30 July. Late. – The breakthrough I had hoped for may now be very near. I met Lord Ruthven tonight – the last of Stoker's guests to arrive. I had not even suspected he would be present. I sat opposite him at table, but made every effort not to engage in conversation and instead talked with Edward Westcote for much of the meal. Lucy had spoken to me earlier about him, in a low urgent voice as we repaired to the dining room. There are rumours, it appears, that Westcote's sister is not dead, after all – reports from some subaltern have reached him, saying that an expedition had been sent into the hills. Lucy, not surprisingly, is very concerned that her husband will be disappointed; it seems that she half-expects some cruel hoax. I asked her why and she shrugged faintly. 'The letters he has received,' she replied, 'they don't seem quite right. Why, for instance, if his sister has truly been found, has Ned heard nothing from their father? He is out there in India too – yet he has not written at all, only ever this subaltern.'

'But who would have an interest in practising such a cruel hoax?'

'I don't know. But please, Jack – I am certain that Ned will ask you about Kalikshutra, for he knows now that you have had some experience of that place yourself. Deal with him gently. I cannot bear to think of his spirits being raised so high, only to be dashed again.'

Indeed not. And yet in many ways, I hope that his sister *is* truly dead, for if she is not then I dread to contemplate what state she may be in. As Lucy had asked me to do, I attempted to lower Westcote's sense of expectation; he bore it well, and I knew he did not entirely share my pessimism, for he continued to ask about Kalikshutra. Naturally, Lord Ruthven pricked up his ears at this, and I was reluctant to continue; but I knew I owed it to Westcote to tell him all I could. Inexorably, inevitably, I began to talk of the disease in the hills, and the fears and superstitions it had bred. This brought in Lord Ruthven; and soon all the other guests. A general conversation on the philosophy of death. Lord Ruthven's contribution unsettling. He spoke with his customary grace and wit, so that the horror of what I knew to be self-analysis seemed almost charmed away. Almost, but not quite; for the horror remained, concealed beneath the beauty which Lord Ruthven himself chose to describe as a mask, laid over agony and rottenness. Occasionally, just occasionally, I would see this mask slip; I would glimpse what lay beneath; I would have no choice but to recognise the agony. Shaken by this, and lacking the social art necessary to disguise it, I determined to leave. I needed time to be alone, to prepare myself. For I knew that Lord Ruthven would follow me.

I walked from Chelsea back along the Thames. Before Vauxhall Bridge, I heard the roll of a heavy carriage's wheels. As I glanced round, the carriage began to slow down, then stopped by the pavement where I stood. The door swung open, I clambered in; Lord Ruthven rapped on the door with his silver-headed cane.

'I am sorry,' he whispered, 'if you feel I intruded tonight.'

I listened to the carriage as it began to rumble forward again.

Lord Ruthven sighed. 'I was wondering, you see, if you might not reconsider your decision.' There was a silence; I assumed he was waiting for an answer from me. However he turned, pressing his cheeks against the glass of the window, and stared out at the moon-stained Thames. 'You saw it tonight, did you not?' he asked.

'Saw it?'

'When you fell silent. You understood. I know you did.'

'Diseased souls are not my field, I'm afraid.'

Lord Ruthven laughed softly. 'It is not my soul I am asking you to heal.'

'Then what?'

'My blood – you have told me so yourself, Doctor – the disease is in my blood. I am right, aren't I? There may be a physiological cause.' He had leaned forward, taken my hands; as he looked into my eyes, I recognised the glitter of desperation in his own. 'You must help me – for my own sake, and for all those whom I threaten.'

'And if I do not?'

Lord Ruthven shrugged. 'Nothing. You will be in no danger from me, Dr Eliot, if that is what you mean. I do not wish you to continue your work under duress. It is perfectly true that I kill, but only because I also have to drink. You have seen the cells; you understand why – I can no more help myself than your patients can help the effects of their diseases. But I am not a wanton murderer. At least ...' – he paused – 'that is, I mean, in the main ... in the main, I can select my victims ...' He swallowed; a shadow passed across his face; again I do not know how, but for a second his agony seemed naked before me. 'You *must* help,' he murmured. 'In the name of' – he smiled bitterly – 'humanity.'

For a long while I did not reply. 'I cannot,' I said at last. 'What you are asking me to find for you – the removal of the craving for blood from your cells – such a cure, as I have said, would mean immortality. *Immortality*, Lord Ruthven. That is beyond my or any man's power to find.'

'No,' answered Lord Ruthven very shortly. 'It must be possible.' He leaned across to me. 'Find it for me, Doctor. Do all that you can. Somewhere, somehow, you must find me hope. Me, and all my breed.' He squeezed my arm, and his fingers gouged deep. 'Do not turn me down, Doctor.'

The carriage had halted by a junction. I broke free from his grasp and rose to my feet. 'I will get out here,' I said. Lord Ruthven watched me as I opened the door and climbed out into the street; he did not try to hold me back. 'We could take you to Whitechapel if you wished,' he said.

'I need to walk. I have a lot to think about.'

Lord Ruthven arched an eyebrow. 'You do indeed.'

I looked up at him. 'I will do all that I can,' I said. 'But for now – please – I must be on my own.' And then I turned, and crossed the road, and walked into a tangle of streets where his carriage could not follow. As I went, I smiled to myself. I realised that I felt almost exultant. Perhaps my research was not doomed, was all that I could think; perhaps now, with Lord Ruthven as my patient again, I would attain the breakthrough I had been working towards so painfully and for so long. Immortality – that was too much even to contemplate – but there were other goals I might now perhaps reach. I would need Huree, of course. He was the expert on the vampire's world. And as I spoke this word to myself, 'vampire', I realised how reluctant I had been even to utter it before. No wonder my research had been a failure – I had never dared admit what its true object had been. I could have no such qualms now. I could not hold back as I had done before.

Circumstance seemed determined to bless this resolve. I reached home after half an hour's walk; as I climbed the stairs that led to my rooms, I saw that my door was ajar and a light flickering from inside. I approached the door carefully; the light, I could see now, was very weak. I entered my room. Propped up on my desk was a picture of Kali. It had been garlanded, and in front of it were candles and bowls of burning incense. Beneath one of the incense burners a book had been left. I picked it up, and read the title: *The Vampire Myths of India and Roumania: A Comparative Study*. Tucked inside the first page a note had been left. I removed it. *'Thought you never went out. Things must have changed. Will see you tomorrow and get all the news. Yours, Huree.'*

Surely, together, we cannot fail?

31 July. – Huree round this afternoon. He is still the master of disguise. Did not recognise him at first, since during the course of his European travels he has transformed himself into something almost Viennese: *pince-nez*, goatee beard, ghastly Alpine hat. His bulk betrayed him, though; he is even rounder than before. Offered to put him up but he refused, saying he was damned if he was going to live in a slum. Instead, he is staying in Bloomsbury with an old lawyer-friend of his from Calcutta. This lawyer has a servant who can cook Bengali food. Huree keen to catch up, after a month of nothing but Parisian *haute cuisine*. Afraid, having languished in such a gastronomic wilderness, that he has been reduced to skin and bone. I was able to reassure him he has not.

I then narrated the events of the past few months. Huree pretended to keep his calm, but I could tell it was a show; he is excited and disturbed. Not much discussion or analysis from him as yet, but that will come, I am sure. For now, our most pressing task is to identify the cause of George's illness; and, if it should prove to be what we both suspect, somehow to secure his safety. Not easy, in view of George's refusal to see me, but I suggest to Huree that he attend the debate in the House of Commons tomorrow. The vote is to be taken on George's Bill and George himself, as the Minister responsible, will be summing up for the Government. I have my own responsibilities, and will be unable to attend; but Huree at least should have the chance to study George. I will await his conclusions with considerable interest.

Only one hint that Huree is already developing theories on the case. As he left me, he paused and turned round. 'Polidori?' he asked. 'Our opium-peddling friend – you are sure his name is Polidori?'

'Yes. Why? Does he mean something to you?'

'Is he a doctor, perhaps?'

I stared at him in surprise. 'Yes. At least, according to Lord Ruthven, he was.'

Huree smiled. 'Ah! Lord Ruthven!'

'Huree, tell me, how did you know?'

He smiled again. 'I remember,' he said, 'in your investigations in the past, you preferred to keep your cards close to your chest. Well, now the boot is on the other foot. Don't worry, old man, it is just a little hunch of mine.'

I shrugged. 'As you wish.'

Huree nodded and continued on his way down the stairs, when he suddenly paused and turned again. 'You know, Jack,' he said, 'you have not attained the breakthrough in this case because you are not yet expecting the impossible. Your reason is no bloody use to you now. You must search for leads that should not logically be there. That is why you have been needing me. I can lead you where you wouldn't think to go. Just remember, Jack – anything is possible now.' He smiled, and bobbed his head. '*Anything.*'

Yes. He is right, of course. Just as Suzette was. The rules of this game are like nothing I have known. It is time I at last began to master them.

Hansard's Parliamentary Debates, Vol. CCCXXIX [August 1, 1888].

ORDERS OF THE DAY

IMPERIAL FRONTIERS
(INDIA) BILL.—[BILL 337.]
(Sir George Mowberley.)

CONSIDERATION.

Bill, as amended, *further considered.*

THE SECRETARY OF STATE FOR INDIA (Sir G. Mowberley) (Kensington) moved that in view of the overwhelming support for his Bill in both Houses, he would accept no more amendments. The frontier proposals were in the best interests of both the Indian peoples, and of the British Empire. The full and unconditional recognition of the independence of the kingdoms of Bhushan, Kathnagar and Kalikshutra, in particular, was in full accord with the principle of securing a lasting peace on the frontier of the Indian Empire. The attention of Honourable Members was drawn to the Imperial Defence Bill [Bill 346], and any further questions on military expenditure were requested to be referred to The Secretary of State for War (Mr. E. Stanhope). The Secretary of State for India concluded by thanking Hon. Gentlemen in all parts of the House for the assistance they had given to him in his endeavours to settle the great and complicated question which could now at last be considered as resolved.

Question put, and *agreed to.*

Bill read the third time, and *passed.*

Cutting from The Times, *2 August.*

ILLNESS OF SIR G. MOWBERLEY

The illness of Sir George Mowberley, Secretary of State for India, is reported. Shortly after the successful passage of the Imperial Frontiers (India) Bill through the House of Commons late last night, a measure on which Sir George himself had delivered the concluding speech, the Secretary of State was taken ill in the Lobby Hall. He was transported to his home in a state of unconsciousness.

His condition at present is reported to be stable.

Dr Eliot's Diary.

2 August. – In the papers, George was reported as having collapsed. Huree called on me early; he confirmed the news but added – what the papers had not mentioned – that George had also been taken ill while giving the speech itself, and had needed to rest for a minute before continuing. Obviously, at the distance he was sitting from George in the Visitors' Gallery, it was impossible for Huree to arrive at a firm diagnosis; he saw nothing, however, to contradict our initial hypothesis.

I wonder now though if our suspicions may not have been premature – at least with regard to George. Huree is still convinced; I am not so certain that the evidence will support the inferences we have been placing upon it. Certainly, when we called on Lady Mowberley this afternoon she seemed less afraid for George's health than she had been before. She is convinced that he is suffering from exhaustion, and nothing worse than that; indeed, was quite insistent on the point. She clearly feels he can be in little danger, for she is leaving for Whitby tomorrow on her family business and will be away from her husband for almost three days. Sadly, she could not permit me to inspect George myself, since it appears that his hostility towards me continues unabated, but when Huree mentioned the cuts to George's wrists and neck she was able to tell us that even these had disappeared. She hopes to persuade her husband to travel abroad, to the South of France, perhaps; in the meantime, while he continues so weak, she feels at liberty to meet with me again once she is returned from Whitby. She has promised to inform us of any further developments.

I will not take Huree to meet her again, though. He was very short and rude with her. Virtually accused her of lying about the state of George's health. He sometimes has a very unfortunate manner – cannot bear his theories to be disproved. I recognise the same trait in myself, of course.

6 August. – Huree absent for several days now. I still don't know what he is working on.

Took out my papers, and samples of blood. Reviewed my research so far. Must visit Lord Ruthven soon.

8 August. – Late night spent reviewing the case with Huree. We have agreed to suspend judgement on George's illness, for lack of evidence, but to continue our search for the murderer of Arthur Ruthven. If we assume that it is indeed a vampire for which we are searching, then the field becomes somewhat narrow. Huree is keen to meet Polidori. We shall travel to Rotherhithe tomorrow.

Letter, Mrs Lucy Westcote to Mr Bram Stoker.

12, *Myddleton Street,*
London.

9 August.

Dear Mr Stoker,

I am afraid I will be a terrible disappointment to you and Mr Irving, but you must warn Kitty to start rehearsing my lines, for I am ill and unable to act in tonight's performance. I am not quite certain what my malady is; I have been suffering from bad dreams, and woke this morning so weak that I was barely able to lift myself from bed. You will doubtless think I am being true to my background, and playing the society lady; but I assure you my faintness is entirely genuine, for I feel dizzy all the time, and have grown very pale, and in short am an abject picture of woe.

I know it is bad form to let you down like this. But I have been feeling ill now for almost a week, and I am sure that a day's rest will restore me to full health. I plan to be with you again in an evening or two.

Until then, Mr Stoker,
Your wretched friend,

LUCY.

Dr Eliot's Diary.

9 August. – A frustrating morning's work. I took a hansom to Coldlair Lane, but Polidori's shop was bolted up, without a sign of movement or light from inside, and a piece of paper with a scrawled message was attached to the door: 'Closed due to unforeseen circumstances. Normal business will resume on my return.' Huree took this sheet of paper with evident gratification, and slipped it into his coat pocket. I am not convinced of its value myself. I am aware of the uses that the science of graphology can sometimes have in the field of detection; but in Polidori's case I doubt that his handwriting will tell us much we do not already know. Of course, Huree may want it for some other purpose; he is still reluctant to discuss his ideas.

Searched for the entrance to the warehouse, but could not find it. Neither of us, I think, greatly surprised. Returned to Whitechapel. This afternoon, must continue to work through my research papers.

5 a.m. – Woke from a strange dream. Had fallen asleep while working at my desk. Most unusual. I had imagined I was in India again, on the summit of the temple in Kalikshutra. Flames were raging and corpses were scattered everywhere, but there was a deathly silence and I seemed to be the only living person there. I had to heal the dead, bring them back to life. There was a terrible urgency which I didn't understand, but seemed all the more real for that very reason. I couldn't do it, though. No matter how hard I worked, they wouldn't come alive. I knew there was some secret I was missing, hidden away from me. I began to dissect the bodies – with a scalpel at first, then with my bare hands. Lucy was there, and Huree, and everyone I knew; I ripped open their stomachs, probing their organs, then shredding them apart, desperate to find the cure that would bring the corpses back to life. I was starting to slither and slip in the mess I was creating. I tried to clean myself, even as I continued to dissect, but I was too stained with blood and I couldn't wash it away. I was wading now in blood. It was sucking me down . . . it submerged me. I couldn't breathe. I thought I was dead.

I opened my eyes. Lilah was standing before me. She was naked. Her lips were red and cruel; her eyes gleamed black below painted, drooping lids; her beauty was quite impossible and yet it was there, a beauty that seemed formed from man's most fantastic passions, his most exquisite dreams, from the very desires of the world, yet to be something more than any of these and therefore, for that very reason, touched with over-ripeness and corruption. And as I understood this, I felt myself wanting her all the more, and I stepped forward and she took me in her arms. I'm writing nonsense, of course; but I felt it – as I feel it even now, when I close my eyes. She kissed me. As she did so, my mind seemed to unfurl and expand, and all the secrets, all the mysteries which had been my torments before, seemed ready to be unveiled and given to me. I could feel myself waking. I struggled to stay asleep, for I wanted the fulfilment that I knew would then be mine, if I could only stay asleep, if I could only stay asleep. It was there, this fulfilment, a distant prick of light, but as I moved towards it I realised that it was also the point at which I would have to awake, and leave Lilah's arms and be myself again. I reached out to touch it; I opened my eyes. I was sitting at my desk, slumped in my chair. I was quite alone.

As I said, a very strange dream.

6 p.m. – Continue distracted. Don't know what the problem can be. Seems pointless to continue with my work in this present mood. Perhaps I should visit Lilah?

11 August. – I have been away for two nights. It seems impossible. I am a doctor; I have always been precise in my time-keeping; yet while I was with Lilah, I was evidently oblivious to the passing of the hours. Huree was waiting for me when I returned home from Rotherhithe to Hanbury Street; he is disturbed by Lilah, he says, and by the influence she appears to be gaining over me. I understand his concern; but I am not convinced it is justified. The seeming breakdown of time, for instance: that appears to me not as an indication of a malign influence, but a sign that I am on the right path, that I am passing beyond the frameworks of direct empirical observation to an understanding which may well prove remarkable in both its scope and implications. Huree may disagree, but I believe the progress I am making must justify any risk.

Certainly, I feel I have already glimpsed great possibilities, without any apparent threat of danger. Lilah seemed almost to be waiting for me when I arrived. She was in the arboretum, seated on a bench; Suzette was with her, tracing lines in a book, and when she heard my footsteps she looked up and showed me the open pages. There was a maze drawn on each one, the first of remarkable complexity and beautiful design, the second simple and clumsily drawn.

'Which do you prefer?' Suzette asked. I pointed to the first one. Suzette smiled. 'That was mine,' she said. 'I win, then. We've been having a competition, you see.'

'We?' I asked.

Suzette nodded. 'Me and ayah.'

'Ayah?'

Suzette pointed. I turned and looked. Standing in the shadows, holding a tray of sweetmeats and drinks, was a plump young Indian girl. She flinched as I stared at her, and bowed her head. I glanced at Lilah inquiringly.

'I took George's advice,' Lilah said, her eyes glittering. 'I found Suzette a nanny.'

'She's stupid,' said Suzette.

'That's all she needs to be,' Lilah replied. 'She only has to look after you. Woman's work,' she drawled, 'as I think George described it once.' She stretched out her arm and beckoned lazily. 'Sarmistha.' The girl lowered her tray and came scurrying across, as though terrified. Lilah ordered her to put Suzette to bed, and as Suzette opened her mouth to complain she silenced her with a glance. The ayah stretched out to take Suzette's hand; Suzette stared at her with a malevolence that was quite unlike a child's, so cold and passionless it seemed, then took the ayah's hand and allowed herself to be led down the path. As she went, the ayah glanced back over her shoulder. She raised her sari to cover her head, as though embarrassed to be seen by me; then she turned again and led Suzette out through the arboretum door.

I asked Lilah if she had seen George recently. She shrugged, and said that she had heard he was sick; but now that the Bill is passed she doesn't seem greatly to care. Reminded by my own fears for George, I began to discuss the state of my research, and specifically my agreement to work with Lord Ruthven again. Lilah was intrigued by this news; Lord Ruthven appears to fascinate her, though she claims never to have met him; doubtless she has heard stories from Polidori. Pressed her on this, but she was reticent; instead returned the discussion to the state of my research. Talked for ... well ... I am unable to say for how long. We left the arboretum, and climbed the stairs to the dome of glass where we could watch the stars. Conversation seemed expanded by the view. One avenue of thought particularly suggestive: what if there are instructions programmed into each individual cell – instructions that might be identified, and perhaps amended or rewritten? The search then would be for nothing less than the building blocks of life. Hopeless, perhaps; at least, that is how it strikes me as I sit here now. But talking with

Lilah, the prospect seemed full of hope; my ideas energetic; my brain alive.

One thing in particular I remember her arguing, and Suzette and Huree in their own ways have said it too: insight cannot belong purely to the conscious mind. Reason is insufficient in itself; there must be a surrender to what lies beyond, a point of liberation, a taking off into flight. With Lilah, I experience this; without her, I don't. When I am with her, watching her, listening to her thoughts, I seem conscious of profound distances waiting for me.

What is the cost, though? What do I need to understand before I can decide how far I should go?

12 *August.* – A visit to Lord Ruthven has been arranged: requested by Huree and required by myself. It is evident, I think, from my study of the remarkable case before me now, that Virchow's concept of cellular pathology is fundamentally correct, and that there is no morphologic element beyond the cell in which life is able to manifest itself. Clearly, then, I must focus my analysis of Lord Ruthven's disease upon the bone marrow, to see if the production of cells has been affected – and if it has been, then to identify how. I suspect a cancer mutating the white cell lineage, though its origin, let alone its cure, is impossible as yet to divine.

13 *August.* – A visit to Lord Ruthven this evening, with Huree in attendance. We did not bother to disguise Huree's identity; Lord Ruthven had read his work and did not protest when I introduced him. A warning, though, to keep the secrets revealed to us: this was not given in words; instead, a vision of ourselves with gashes to our throats and our tongues extruding from the open slits. The images in both our minds, we discovered later, appeared to have been identical, so if nothing else, a remarkable demonstration of tele- pathic power.

Lord Ruthven agreed at once to the operation I proposed. He waived my offer of anaesthetic; instead he laid himself upon a table, and within seconds his eyes began to glaze and he appeared to lose consciousness, though when I tried to close his eyelids I could not make them shut. Uncomfortable at first, operating on him, and when I had to cut through the muscle to the hip bone could not believe there was no expression of pain. But even once I had parted the tissue and begun to drill through the bone to the marrow, the patient remained perfectly motionless, and the operation proceeded without difficulty. Will continue work on the marrow sample over the next few days. Lord Ruthven, when he woke from what I can only describe as his self-induced hypnosis, appeared to feel no pain at all. He is eager for results, I can tell, though he did not press me, and ordered me not to rush my work. I hope his faith is justified. I do not feel confident. The problems in arriving at a cure for his condition seem at best intractable. I must hope for inspiration again.

Huree, by contrast, brimming over with self-confidence. His observation of Lord Ruthven this evening has clearly confirmed some theory of his. I asked him to tell me about it but Huree shook his head. He wants to be certain, he told me, and still has some further research to do. He then changed the topic immediately; began to ask if I ever read much poetry.

'No,' I replied. 'Why?'

Huree shrugged, and smiled and bobbed his head. 'A pity,' he said, and would add nothing more.

Poetry. Huree's mention of it cannot have been wholly random. But I fail, as yet, to see any link. I am afraid that my powers may be waning.

Letter, Professor Huree Jyoti Navalkar to Dr John Eliot.

British Library.
14 August.

Dear Jack,

I must humbly request your forgiveness, but I shall not be meeting with you today as we had previously arranged. I have a trip to make, you see, a tour that is of the utmost urgency, the length and breadth of your beautiful land. It will be a delightful opportunity to view the English countryside. I must go to the Cotswolds first, to Kelmscott Manor. Have you heard of it? The painter and poet Dante Gabriel Rossetti lived there; since he has long been one of my favourite artists, the chance to visit the scene of his final years is not one lightly to be thrown aside. Then I must proceed to Nottingham. I will return to London as soon as I can, i.e. jolly quickly.

I trust that your own work will go well. One request: please, Jack; while I am away, do not pay a visit to Rotherhithe. I am afraid of who – or what – may be there. We will talk of this further when I get back.

So long, old man,
Toodlepip!

HUREE.

Dr Eliot's Diary.

14 August. – The evidence of the marrow sample as I suspected; below the microscope's lens, the smear revealed to be generating an uncontrolled explosion of leucocytes. Compared these cells with the leucocytes extracted from Lord Ruthven's blood almost three months ago: they are identical. It is, to all intents and purposes, a vision of immortality.

We may then, very tentatively, begin to talk of a pathology of vampirism. The locus of any investigation must indeed be the bone marrow, and its infection by what would appear to be a cancerous process affecting the production of white blood cells. I am reminded of my discussions with Lilah, and our positing of a 'code' of instructions within every cell. Assuming this hypothesis to be correct, we might further explain the mortality of cells by reference to an instruction within the 'code' of each one – instructing it, as it were, to age; in the vampire's case, however, this 'code' would presumably have been mutated or destroyed. But how would the cancerous process have been initiated? Through oral contact, perhaps? Some enzyme in the saliva which would then act on the cells of the bone marrow? But how? I need to know more about the folklore; the various legends that Huree has collected from around the world must surely contain some reference to genuine case-histories, however distorted. But where is Huree when I need him? – gone on a tour of the countryside. He tells me not to visit Lilah; but to whom else can I turn when confronted by this need for primary evidence? If needs be, I will have to ignore his advice.

Because all the time, of course, the central challenge, the problem of problems remains smeared across my slide. I prick my finger; I add blood to the marrow sample; I watch my cells being attacked and absorbed. Here is the demonstration of vampirism, a need for alien haemoglobin which, when translated from the level of microbiology, becomes a murderous hunger for blood. How am I to counter this dependency? Succeed, and Lord Ruthven's immortality need no longer be counted a disease. Fail – and it is not only Lord Ruthven who will continue to pay. What should I do? What line of inquiry should I be following now?

I cannot wait for Huree indefinitely.

Letter, Mr Bram Stoker to Hon. Edward Westcote.

The Lyceum Theatre.

15 August.

Dear Edward,

I have asked the cabby to deliver this note to you, along with your wife, because I fear that Lucy will make light of what happened to her this evening. But it is my duty as the Manager of this theatre, as well as an admirer and, I hope, as a friend of Lucy's, to ask you, please, to tell her to remain in her bed. She collapsed this evening in the middle of the second act, and was carried from the stage unconscious. She recovered some twenty minutes later and assured me that it was only a temporary dizziness; I am certain, however, that her condition is something more threatening, and so it is that I have sent her home. I am aware that you have been at your parents' Wiltshire residence for the past few days; Lucy may therefore not have told you that she missed two performances as a result of illness earlier in the week, and that ever since her return she has seemed faint and pale. For her own good, she must accept the fact that she is sick – whatever the illness may prove to be.

Might I suggest that you consult Jack Eliot? He appears to be an excellent doctor, and Lucy would accept instructions from him she might otherwise reject. If there is any way that I could help, then I am, of course, always willing to oblige.

Yours sincerely,

BRAM STOKER.

Dr Eliot's Diary.

19 August. – Again, the sensation of transcending pure reason; and again, as though it were a necessary corollary of this experience, the curious distortion of time. I was certain I had been in Rotherhithe for no more than twenty-four hours; but according to my calendar, and the intemperate note left by Llewellyn on my desk, I have been absent from Hanbury Street for almost three days now. I must go and make my apologies; but first, let me talk into this phonogram and see if I cannot make some sense of my memories before they start to dim and grow uncertain. Such urgency would not usually be required; my powers of recall are generally more than capable; but on my memories of Rotherhithe, I have found, my mind has a tendency to play strange tricks. What I consider my greatest gift as both detective and doctor — my unloading of the burden of trying to remember unnecessary facts – in Rotherhithe seems exactly reversed. I recall the ephemera; but the most important details and insights fade away.

I wanted to speak to Polidori. In the continuing absence of Huree, I needed corroboration on details of my research; to whom else could I turn but Polidori, who had been a doctor himself before the sickness claimed him? His shop, when I arrived in Coldlair Lane, was still dark and boarded up, but the door was open, and climbing the stairs I smelt the familiar poison of the opium fumes. No one attempted to seize me as I walked through the addicts' den; it was as though they recognised me now as one of their own, and I was relieved when I had left them behind and crossed the bridge into the warehouse beyond. I passed through the hallway, and as I did so realised – as I had not before – that the statues of the women in the far alcoves all wore Lilah's face. It must have been a trick in the expressions, for the variety of periods and races on display was immense; and yet, studying them now, there could be no doubt – I recognised Lilah in every one.

There was a sudden cry. I turned from the alcoves, regretting the lack of time to peruse the statues further, and began to hurry down the corridor that led from the hall. As I ran, I heard a second scream. It was a girl's; very high-pitched but short, as though someone had cut it off, and it had come from the door I was heading towards. I lengthened my stride; I paused by the door; I could hear music coming from inside, a quartet for strings. I opened the door and stared around me in sudden surprise. I was in the nursery again: pink walls, dolls stacked in the corner, a rocking-horse with ribbons in its mane. The musicians, dressed as before in their frock-coats and wigs, continued to play their piece, quite oblivious to my sudden entrance. Suzette, however, did glance round. She was sitting on a sofa in a neat party frock, swinging her legs to and fro and playing with the ringlets in her hair. She smiled at me, but I did not reply in kind. For standing in front of me with a cane in his hand was Polidori, and kneeling in front of him with her bare back exposed was Suzette's nanny, Sarmistha. She was shuddering; across her shoulders stretched a single red weal. A line of blood began to trick down her back.

Polidori glanced round at me. He grinned.

'What are you doing?' I asked.

Polidori grinned again. He bent down and dabbed at the girl's blood with a fingertip. He held it to the light, then licked it with his tongue. 'Research,' he said. He hissed with laughter, kicking the girl's legs apart, then kneeling down between them. He reached up with his hand beneath the bunched folds of the ayah's skirt.

'Let her go,' I said.

Polidori ignored me; I saw him move his arm to and fro. He glanced up at Suzette. 'Yes,' he leered, 'female. No doubt at all. How *does* she do it?'

I took him by the neck, pulled him away and flung him to the floor. Polidori looked up at me, surprised; then slowly he began to grin again. 'Sir *fucking* Galahad,' he whispered. He picked himself up and stared into my eyes; he raised his cane, then turned back to the girl. 'She's just some slut, some dirty foreign bitch.'

'She pulled my hair,' said Suzette, 'when she was dressing it.'

Polidori turned back to me. 'Did you hear that?' he asked. 'The girl can't even attend properly to her young mistress here. You would think that even the most stupid girl might manage that. But not this little *whore*. I think she deserves' – he swung round and raised the cane again – 'punishment.'

Before he had brought it down, I caught him on the jaw. Polidori staggered and fell into the lap of one of the musicians, who still continued to play – conscious of nothing, it seemed, but the instrument in his hands. Slowly, Polidori picked himself up. He rubbed disbelievingly at his jaw, then stared at me. 'What have you done?' he whispered. 'What have you done?' He seemed to tense; and then before I had even seen him move I could feel him at my throat, his nails ripping at my neck, and I fell with a crash into the sofa and heard Suzette scream as my head knocked her knees. Then Polidori was on top of me; he was shaking, I realised, his eyes rolling wildly, and the stench of his breath was moist with spit. 'I'll kill you,' he whispered, 'I'll slice open your fucking heart.' I struggled desperately as I felt his fingers on my chest, pinching into the flesh, and then I heard Suzette as she screamed again.

'Polidori!' She stamped her foot. 'No!'

Polidori glanced up at her.

'She won't allow it. You know she won't. Stop it at once!'

'I don't care what she wants.'

Suzette did not reply; but she continued to stare at him, and slowly Polidori lowered his head, and I felt his grip on my chest start to weaken. I sat up; and Polidori slipped off me and rose to his feet. He shuddered and clasped himself, and then he stood utterly still. 'Don't tell her,' he whispered.

Suzette tossed back her curls. For a few seconds more she continued to stare down her nose at Polidori; then she turned to me. 'Well, come on,' she said, turning towards the far door.

'No,' I replied. I glanced at Polidori. 'I need to ask him some questions. That's what I came here for.'

'Oh, don't be so silly!' exclaimed Suzette impatiently, stamping her foot again. 'He won't answer any questions from you. Will you, Polly?'

Polidori licked his lips; then he grinned and slowly shook his head.

'I told you,' said Suzette. 'You see how he is. It won't do. You must come with me instead.' She reached out and opened the far door. As she prepared to walk through, she paused and glanced down at Sarmistha who was still prostrate on the floor. The girl looked up; Suzette widened her eyes and nodded; then she passed on through the door. Sarmistha rose uncertainly to her feet, clutching the torn shreds of her sari to her naked body, and I saw to my shock how thin she had become. As she readjusted the folds of her garment about her I caught a glimpse of her breasts, and saw how they were tattooed with tiny red dots like puncture marks; but I did not have a chance to inspect them further, for the girl covered both her body and her head, and scurried past me. I followed her out through the door. Ahead of us were the double staircases I remembered from before, spiralling away to impossible heights, rising up through empty space. Suzette was running, her tiny feet echoing through the silent distances that stretched in every direction from the stairs; looking behind me, I saw that even the door had gone and I was standing on one of the steps – suspended, it seemed, in naked air, with nothing else to see, and only darkness all around.

I began to climb the spiral, following Suzette and Sarmistha. They were both running, and I began to run as well. But no matter how fast I went, I could never catch them up; they were always ahead of me, their footsteps fading into the darkness. I stopped. I traced the configuration of the two stairways, and realised – what at first had been impossible to tell – that I was on a different stairway from Suzette and Sarmistha. I looked up for them. They were gone. Instead there was a balcony, and at its end a door. It had a fresco painted on it, in a primitive style that I didn't recognise, depicting a goddess with her head amongst the stars, and mortals licking at the toes of her feet. I passed through the door. I entered a beautiful room. The air was perfumed; radiance glittered from jewels and soft flames; the bed wore hangings of the deepest red.

As in my dream, Lilah was naked. Her face was painted, her nipples and labia touched with gold. She extended her arms; I crossed the room and joined her on the bed. The touch of her skin enhanced a curious sensation I had experienced since entering the room: the apparent fusion of an erotic response with an urgent intellectual curiosity, so that the two extremes of emotion and reason appeared blended into one. I had no cause now to restrain my mood of sexual arousal, for far from threatening my capacity to think with due clarity, it seemed on the contrary to stimulate it. Again, I remembered my dream: the promise of some revelation, some point of ultimate comprehension; this was waiting for me again now, not on the margin between sleep and consciousness but on the crest of sexual climax, and so I pursued it, and passed through it, and continued to pursue the climaxes beyond. What did I see in them? Everything. Simply ... everything. So expanded had my cognitive faculties become that I comprehended intellectual problems in the same way as I felt the sexual bliss – infinitely – without limits at all.

How can I explain this experience? I cannot. For now it is passed and I remember ... I remember nothing. Or at least – I remember the pleasure of understanding, but not how or what I had understood. This is not a rare frustration; I have always recognised it in the sexual act: a summit is no sooner reached than it disappears. But now I find that the most intense intellectual experience of my life has faded in the same way; that my thoughts were no better than cheap synaptic thrills. How could this have occurred? Perhaps I am suffering from some hallucination; perhaps my memories are nothing but delusions. I do not think so, though – the experience was too vivid and strong ... it was real. No. I must confront the truth. There is a far more likely alternative.

For it is clear, I think, that if my intellectual and erotic exaltations were indeed blended, then both were dependent upon Lilah's presence by my side. When did she leave me? I don't remember. I don't even remember falling asleep. But I must have done, for I woke up suddenly and found I was alone, lying naked on the floor of an empty room. My clothes were in a bundle next to me. Above my head there was a painting of Lilah; it was illumined by a single candle; the rest of the room was a soft, crimson dark. It had been dark before, of course, when Stoker and I discovered George lying on the floor just as I was now, beneath the image of Lilah and her silent smile. I rose at once and dressed, then hurried from the room. Outside Sarmistha was waiting, her head bowed, holding my coat. I took it from her; she turned and began to run. I called out after her – asking if she needed attention or help – and she paused, turning to glance at me, her large eyes tear-stained, and then before I could approach her she was running again and had disappeared. My last memory, then, of my time spent in that place, was of a young girl's misery and her helplessness. The spell of the warehouse seemed suddenly dissolved. And yet how wrong I was.

I left the hallway and began to walk down the streets. The further I went, the more the details of what had happened began to fade from my mind, the more painful I found it to continue home, *the more desperately I needed to turn and go back.* The longing was almost a physical pain; like the pain I have read in the case-histories of withdrawal from opiates. Perhaps that is what I have become, an addict, like those wretches in Polidori's den, or more specifically, I suppose, like George himself – an addict to Lilah's company. I wanted it more than anything. I still do now. More than anything I have ever known in my life.

Should I fight it? I remember the poor Indian girl – the glimpse of the cruelty which exists in Lilah's world, which I had suspected before but never seen until then. It has always been a maxim of mine that our subconscious is a dangerous and threatening place, for we cannot control the desires that it may choose to breed; and what else is it that Lilah has offered to me, if not the desires of my unconscious mind? I am afraid to surrender to these again; afraid to lose my self-control; afraid – yes, I admit it – to see what these desires might lead me to. I will not visit Lilah again. I will stay true to myself. I will remain who I am.

I will not visit Lilah again.

11 p.m. – Have apologised to Llewellyn and sent him to bed. Poor fellow, he looks exhausted. No crises while I was away, though, except that Edward Westcote has called on me; it seems that Lucy has collapsed on stage from exhaustion and been confined to her bed. I would call on her now, but it is very late; not the best way to cure exhaustion, waking the patient at 11 o'clock.

Will call on her tomorrow, then.

Telegram, Professor Huree Jyoti Navalkar to Dr John Eliot.

20 August.

Fear Lucy Westcote in terrible danger. Guard her. Urgent. Repeat – urgent.

HUREE.

Dr Eliot's Diary.

21 *August.* – A terrible couple of days, with the prospect of many more still to come. Early yesterday morning a telegram from Huree arrived, warning me of a danger to Lucy. Startled, in view of her husband's news that she had been confined to bed, so abandoned my morning's work to Llewellyn and left for Myddleton Street at once. Westcote relieved to see me. 'I'm sure it's nothing,' he kept muttering, 'just overwork', but I could tell he was disturbed. Asked to see the patient. 'Quiet,' said Westcote. 'She's asleep.' Crept upstairs, where Lucy lay in bed. Needed only a glance; arrived at my diagnosis at once.

Lucy looking deathly pale. But worse: across her neck tiny scars, identical to those I had seen on George. I asked Westcote when they had begun to appear. The beginning of the month, he replied; almost three weeks before. And when had Lucy first begun to complain of feeling faint? Westcote swallowed and glanced at his wife. 'Three weeks ago.'

He was desperate to know what I thought. I didn't answer him at first. Instead, I crossed to the window and tried to open it. The catch was locked. I glanced at Westcote. 'These have only recently been closed,' I said. 'Look, I can see the pattern of dust.'

'Yes,' Westcote agreed, 'we closed them last week.'

'Why? The heat has been terrible recently.'

'Lucy insisted.'

'Bad dreams?' I asked.

He looked startled. 'How did you know?'

'What was it? An intruder? Some strange threat?'

Westcote nodded slowly.

'Tell me.'

He blushed. 'I don't know,' he said at last. 'It was ... yes – just some strange threat.'

I frowned; he was clearly embarrassed by something. I studied his face, then shrugged and turned back to the window lock. I inspected carefully. Then I beckoned to Westcote. 'Look,' I said. 'The paint is chipped around the edge of the lock. Someone has been forcing it.'

Westcote stared at me, appalled. 'You mean ... no ... It's impossible ...' His voice trailed away. He took out a key and unlocked the window, opened it and stared outside. 'But there is a sheer drop,' he said. 'How could anyone have reached this ledge?'

I glanced across at Lucy. 'Edward,' I asked him, ' these past three weeks – have you been in the room with her? At night, I mean?'

He flushed again.

'Please,' I said impatiently, 'the situation is too pressing for coyness. Have you been sleeping with her?'

Westcote shook his head. 'For much of the time I have been in Wiltshire, preparing my parents' home for Charlotte's – that is, my sister's – arrival back from India.'

'You have definite news?' I asked, surprised.

'Yes. She is on a steamer from Bombay even now.'

'Then I am very happy for you.'

He smiled faintly, and nodded. 'As you can imagine, there is a great deal of preparation to be done. Indeed I only returned to London a few days ago, to discover a letter from Mr Stoker waiting here, telling me that Lucy had been taken ill. Lucy herself hadn't written to me at all. She continues to claim there is nothing much wrong. But she is clearly very ill, is she not?' He stared at his wife; she stirred and moaned, but did not wake, even when she began to gather the sheets about her as though warding off some threat. Edward Westcote turned back to me. 'She has been like that since my return. I lay beside her on my first night back, but I could not sleep; her dreams were so bad, and when she woke she told me I had made her nightmares worse ...' He paused, and blushed again, then stared down at the floor.

'Nightmares,' I said softly. 'What nightmares?'

Westcote looked up at me. 'A woman,' he muttered. 'A woman comes to her.'

'Yes? And what does she do?'

He stared about him uneasily. 'I can't tell you,' he said at last.

'Why not?'

He blushed again. 'I just can't,' he said.

'Why? Does she dream that the woman feeds on her?'

'No. Perhaps. No, not all the time. No. I'm really not sure.'

'Is there sexual contact? Is that what you mean?'

'Doctor!' Westcote stared at me in agony. 'Please!'

I met his stare. Then I took his hand and clasped it firmly. 'Edward,' I whispered. 'I understand how upsetting this must be. But please, you must tell me – it is of the utmost importance – has Lucy told you what this woman is like?'

Westcote turned from me to stand by his wife. He gazed down into Lucy's face; for almost a minute he stared at her; he reached out to take her hand. 'She was veiled,' he said at last. 'Lucy has never been able to see her face. Why?' He glanced up at me, as though suddenly struck by the implications of my question. 'Do you think that this woman might be more than just a dream?'

I glanced at the window again, and the drop to the street below. I shrugged. 'I have a friend. He is away at the moment, but when he returns he should be able to answer that question much more authoritatively than I can. But in the meantime' – I crossed to the bed, and stood by Lucy's side – 'I will see what I can do for her medically.' I took her pulse; it was very faint. 'She has clearly lost a good deal of blood.'

'But . . .' Westcote stared at his wife in disbelief. 'She hasn't gone anywhere. I don't understand. There hasn't been any blood on the sheets.'

I pointed to Lucy's neck. 'And these scars?' I asked. 'What about them?'

Westcote frowned, then he shrugged helplessly. 'I don't know,' he replied.

'Well,' I said, trying to sound as confident as I could, 'let us wait and see what my tests have to show.' I took a sample of Lucy's blood and then, just to be certain, of Westcote's as well. I left him with strict instructions not to move from the side of Lucy's bed; then I returned to Whitechapel as fast as I could. Closeted myself in the laboratory. Lucy's blood, thank God, revealed no serious abnormalities: certainly no mutation of the leucocytes. The red cell count was lower than I cared to see, but fortunately an analysis of Westcote's blood revealed a compatibility of sanguigens. My own sanguigen, however, incompatible. Not unduly worried, though: Westcote a strong-looking man.

Preparing for the transfusion, I was reminded of George. In view of the evident similarities between the two cases, and bearing in mind George's affection for his ward, I thought it might be worthwhile to call on him again, to see if he wouldn't relent and talk with me; a comparison of his condition with Lucy's, I thought, might prove mutually instructive. When I arrived at the Mowberleys', however, it was to be told that George had recently gone away to the South of France, for the purpose of recovering his health. Lady Mowberley, who informed me of this departure, assured me that his condition was already much improved: a promising development, since it suggests that a transplant from the scene of the attacks can indeed result in recovery. At present, however, Lucy is far too weak to travel; we must do all we can to restore her strength. Lady Mowberley very concerned to hear of her condition; offered to help in any way she could. In particular, volunteered to look after Lucy's child should there be any threat of infection in the house; I assured her there was not. On second thoughts, though, perhaps that is not strictly correct. I may mention her offer to Edward Westcote tonight.

On my arrival back at Myddleton Street I found Bram Stoker in attendance on Lucy, evidently much distressed by the state of her health. In confidence, he told me that her appearance had deteriorated badly since the week before, when he had sent her home from the Lyceum. Like Lady Mowberley, he has volunteered to help in any way he can; he has time at his disposal just now, it seems, since the Lyceum's season has recently come to an end. Was able to employ him at once, helping with the transfusion of Westcote's blood. The operation a modified success: Westcote left very weak, but some colour restored to Lucy's cheeks and her pulse is now more regular. However, it is an indication of the seriousness of her condition that although her husband was bled almost to the point of danger, Lucy's own strength has only partially been restored. At least she now seems stabilised; there has been no deterioration since the transfusion yesterday, and she has even been able to sit up and talk. She has added nothing, by the way, to what Westcote had already told me: the woman in her dreams, she confirmed, is always veiled, though there is perhaps something, she thinks, which is familiar about her manner. Have asked Lucy to consider this further. Perhaps she will observe more during the next visitation.

Nothing last night, however. Westcote and myself took it in turns to sit on guard; Stoker is staying tonight. I will grab a few hours' sleep; and then return to relieve him and take my own place on watch.

22 *August*. – Huree still not here. I don't understand where he can be. If he knows that Lucy is in danger, then surely he also knows that he should be by her side. I don't have the experience to handle this affair on my own.

Lucy herself still in a stable condition. An interesting event last night, though, around 3 a.m., shortly after my arrival to replace Stoker on guard. I heard a curious scratching at the window; I rose to see if I could make anything out, but my path was blocked by Lucy who had likewise risen and crossed the room. Her eyes were open, but when I spoke to her she was oblivious to my call; she brushed past me and began to open the window, and I heard the scratching at the pane again. But when I crossed to stop her she suddenly flinched, like a patient wakened from a mesmeric trance, and stared at me in a puzzled way. 'Jack?' she whispered. 'What are you doing here?' Then she fainted into my arms. I returned her to her bed. She began to dream, moaning again and clutching at her throat; then her dreams deepened and her convulsions died away.

Nothing else of any interest to record. No further scratchings at the window pane.

23 *August*. – The bounds of logic and probability have already been

so strained by the events of the past few months that, really, I should have ceased to be surprised by anything. Nor am I, in fact. No – I am *not* surprised – although it reassures me, I think, to believe that I am. After all, the web of connections was an elementary one; I would normally have recognised and traced it myself. But I had not yet wholly accepted Huree's favourite dictum, that the impossible is always a possibility. Once that is granted, then in a peculiar way the laws of logic can reassert themselves. Perhaps there is hope for my methods, after all.

For Huree himself, despite the startling nature of his premises, has undoubtedly displayed a flair for deductive investigation. He arrived early this afternoon and went up to see Lucy immediately. He knelt by her bedside, staring at her in silence for a good while, then glanced up at me suddenly. 'Kirghiz Silver,' he said. 'Not available in London, I suppose?'

'Everything is available in London,' I replied. 'But probably not from the costermonger.'

'Garlic, then,' said Huree. 'It will have to do. Its effect is much weaker, but perhaps it will serve to keep him at bay.'

'Him?' I asked in a tone of surprise, for I had told Huree of Lucy's dreams. But he smiled at me and tapped at his nose, then lumbered to his feet.

'Come,' he said, 'I have something most interesting to show to you.' Together we went downstairs; Huree told Westcote of the need for fresh garlic, and when Westcote looked at me, startled, I inclined my head. Huree and I then proceeded out to Farringdon Road, where we hailed a cab. 'Bethnal Green,' said Huree to the driver. 'The National Portrait Gallery.'

This was not a destination I had been expecting, but I knew better than to inquire. Huree smiled at me, or rather he smirked; as the cab began to jolt away, he drew out some papers from under his coat and handed me one: it was the message that Polidori had left on the door of his shop. Huree then handed me a second sheet of paper, a letter this time; I saw at once that the handwriting was identical.

'Where did you obtain this from?' I asked.

Huree smirked again. 'Kelmscott Manor,' he replied.

'Where Rossetti lived?'

Huree nodded.

'What was it doing there?'

Huree's smirk began to stretch beyond the tops of his ears. 'It was among Rossetti's papers. I wasn't surprised; I had expected it would be. Jolly simple, really. He was Rossetti's uncle, you see.'

'Who was? Not Polidori?'

Huree bobbed his head and turned out to stare at the passing street. 'Dr John William Polidori,' he murmured. 'Died, supposedly, by his own hand – 1821. Physician, student of somnambulism, occasional writer of unreadable tales . . .'

'Yes,' I said, suddenly remembering. 'Stoker mentioned him. I never thought . . .'

'Did Stoker tell you *what* he wrote, though?' inquired Huree, his eyebrows darting up and down as he spoke.

I shook my head.

'His most famous tale, Jack, was called "The Vampyre". Can you guess the vampire's name?' He paused, in his showman's way. 'No? Then let me help you with that one too. He was an English aristocrat. An English *Lord*, to be strictly precise.'

'Surely not Ruthven?'

Huree beamed.

I sat back in my seat. 'Extraordinary,' I murmured. 'And Huree, I must congratulate you – your zeal and intelligence have evidently been put to their customary good use. How did you find this story out?'

'Child's play!' exclaimed Huree, snapping his fingers with relish. 'You forget, Jack, that the vampire has long been a quarry of mine. It would have been pretty poor if I had been ignorant of Polidori's work. You only had to mention his name, and I remembered his reference to a vampire named Lord Ruthven. It came to me at once' – he snapped his fingers again – 'like that! But it was only the beginning. Wait and see. My journey round England has been most profitable. I have been finding out who Lord Ruthven really is.'

I frowned. 'What do you mean, who he really is?'

Huree smiled, then rapped on the side of the cab. 'Let us go and look,' he said as the cab slowed to a halt. He paid the cabby, then trotted towards the Gallery entrance-way. 'Oh yes,' he giggled. 'Let us go and jolly well look!'

I followed him up stairways and through canvas-laden rooms. At last, by an imposing doorway, he halted and turned. 'You will kick yourself, Jack. You will be jolly cross that you ever missed this.'

'Why?'

'Mr Stoker told you about Polidori. But did he tell you whose physician Polidori had been?'

'Yes,' I replied. 'Lord Byron's . . .' And then the syllable froze on my tongue as I spoke it. Lord Ruthven. Lord Ruthven! That was why Huree had wanted to see him! That was why he had asked me, when we left Lord Ruthven's home, if I read poetry! I must have stood there quite numbed, for I never even felt Huree take me by the arm. He led me into the Gallery and across to a painting on the wall. I stared up at it. Lord Byron, dressed in the scarlet and gold of some eastern uniform. Only it was not his face I saw smiling at me from beneath a fringed turban, but another man's, a man I had met, a man whom I knew, not as Byron, but as Ruthven. 'Good Lord,' I murmured. I turned to Huree. 'It seems impossible, but . . .' I stared back up at the painting again.

'But it is not,' whispered Huree, completing my sentence for me.

I nodded slowly. 'So who else might be out there, do you think, drinking people's blood? Beethoven? Shakespeare? Abraham Lincoln?'

Huree smiled and shook his head. 'I believe not. The circumstances connected with Lord Byron, you see, are most particular.' We began to leave the Gallery, and as we did so, Huree explained the course of his research in Nottinghamshire graveyards, and lawyers' firms, and assorted public records offices. He had traced the first mention of Lord Ruthven back to 1824 – the year of Byron's death in Greece; he had demonstrated that Lord Ruthven had been the major beneficiary of the dead poet's wealth; he had searched for a Ruthven family tree, anything which might disprove that the Lords Ruthven and Byron were one and the same. But he had searched in vain. There was no Lord Ruthven: the title was nothing but an alias.

'But Lucy?' I asked. 'Arthur? Where are they from?'

Huree's expression darkened; he lifted a hand. 'This is where it grows serious, Jack. You remember the telegram I sent?'

'Naturally.'

'Yes, jolly good, of course you do.' Huree paused. We were out in the sunshine by now; he lifted his face to the rays, as though invoking the daylight for assistance, then looked round for a bench and sat down on it with a sigh. I joined him. Huree was taking out his papers again. He laid them on his lap; he stared at them in silence for a while; then he dabbed at his brow and looked up at me again. 'Lucy's family line, like the references to Lord Ruthven himself, go back only as far as 1824. Logical conclusion? – the Ruthvens are descended from Lord Byron himself.'

I frowned. 'Logical?'

Huree raised his hand again. 'There's more.'

'Indeed?'

'It is not very cheerful, Jack.'

'Tell me.'

Huree nodded. He reached for a sheaf of papers and handed them across. 'These are copies of death certificates. Each Ruthven, once he or she has had a child, has then died within a year. The moment the bloodline has been perpetuated – pouf!' – he snapped his fingers – 'the parent at once becomes expendable. It is an absolutely infallible rule, you see, Jack. Cast iron! And even that is not the worst: their deaths, when you know what to look for, all seem to result from a catastrophic loss of blood. Your friend Arthur is only the most recent example of this.'

'But Arthur never had a child.'

'No. But Lucy did.'

I shook my head in disbelief, and stared up at the sky. 'It seems impossible,' I muttered, 'impossible. And yet you truly believe this,

Huree, that Lord Ruthven has been feeding on his own blood-line, draining them dry?'

'I am convinced of it. What other theory can fit all the facts?'

'But is there any tradition,' I asked, 'of the vampire feeding on his blood-line like this?'

Huree shrugged. 'There are many traditions. Vampires are not like some bloody microbe, Jack; you cannot just study them, and say what is true and what is not.'

'But we *can* study Lord Ruthven. I have his blood under my microscope even as we speak.'

'Yes,' said Huree impatiently, 'what of it?'

'It seems strange that he should employ me and then drink from under my very nose.'

'Not at all,' said Huree. 'Use your damn brain, Jack. That is precisely what explains his desperation. He is a slave of his passions.'

'But it is over a year since Lucy had her child. Why should he start to feed on her *now*?'

Huree shrugged. 'Perhaps you should look at it the other way. Perhaps he has come to you because he has felt his hunger growing worse, and he knows that he cannot withstand it any more.'

'Then it is a race, you think? Either I cure him or he drains Lucy dry?'

Huree nodded. 'That is one way of approaching the matter.'

'And a fairly desperate one, I'm afraid. I do not feel encouraged by the progress of my research. There must be something more we can do.'

'Kirghiz Silver,' said Huree. 'Infallible.'

'Yes, but if we can't find that, what other course should we take? Do we confront Lord Ruthven?'

'He is dangerous.'

'Thank you, Huree, I had deduced that for myself. Yes, he is dangerous – but is he indestructible? There must be some way we can stop him, even destroy him if needs be.'

'I will need time to work on this.'

'Unfortunately, you may not have much of that.'

'No.' Huree sniffed contemplatively. 'But at least now we know who our adversary is. And that has to be a start.' He rose to his feet. 'Don't you agree, Jack? That has to be a start!'

Yes. A start. But perhaps not on the course that Huree believes us to be on. His discoveries have certainly been an excellent piece of work; his knowledge of vampirism is unexcelled, and his conclusions on the blood-line must surely be correct. But I am still not entirely convinced that we do know who our adversary is; we may be missing something here. Even taking into account all Huree's revelations, Lord Ruthven is not the only suspect we have; the proof against him is damning, but not *conclusive*. I need to sit down and think about this. There are other factors to take into account.

1 a.m. – Stayed up late, working on the bone-marrow cells. No breakthrough. The more I consider my dealings with Lord Ruthven, the less likely I find it that he is preying on Lucy, although I do not doubt that she is in terrible danger from him; for I remember, the first time I met him, how he smelled Lucy's clothes, having clearly detected the trace of her blood. Doubtless, also, it was he who killed Arthur Ruthven; it was shortly after Arthur's death, after all, that Lord Ruthven came to me with his request that I work to cure him of his thirst; psychologically, then, such a theory rings true. But with Lucy, by contrast, the psychology is all wrong: she is my patient; for Lord Ruthven to be feeding on her while also employing me would be a virtual act of treachery. I do not believe, odd though it may seem, that he would behave in such a way. Am aware, of course, that this is hardly a logical assumption to make.

As it happens, though, there is a second problem with the theory of Lord Ruthven's guilt. Why does Lucy imagine her intruder to be a woman? Huree has attempted to brush over this question. But it is surely possible that our adversary is Haidée. We know almost nothing about her. What is her relationship with Lord Ruthven? Even more importantly – what is her relationship with Lucy? Does she too have common blood with the Ruthvens? Until we have the answers to these questions, we must consider Haidée a suspect as well.

And there is a yet further possibility: we may not be searching for a Ruthven at all. There are other predators abroad in London at the moment. Female predators. My thoughts – as they have so often seemed to do recently – start to turn again towards Rotherhithe.

24 August. – A day in the laboratory, working on the leucocytes and bone-marrow cells. As yet, no real developments. I begin to think wistfully of the insights I have experienced in Rotherhithe. I wonder if the risk is worth taking. Difficult to decide.

As it happens, Lilah has been on my mind for another reason. This morning, during the surgery, Mary Kelly was one of the out-patients. Her health good; no hint of any relapse; her vital signs stable. Only one thing troubling her, she reported: she had begun to have nightmares, vivid, so that they would seem very real at the time. She would dream that she was in her bed in Miller's Court, and hear a woman's voice calling out to her. Going to a window, she would see the negress standing in the street below. Despite her fear, she would feel a desperate longing to obey the woman's call. She would leave her room, then follow the negress through the empty streets; she would realise they were walking through Rotherhithe. The negress would start to kiss and fondle her lasciviously, and then, as she had done before, slice her wrist above a golden bowl. The blood would start to flow in a great stream, until Mary Kelly would imagine she was drowning beneath a sea of red. She would struggle to wake, would imagine that she did so. She would find herself in a dark room, with a picture of a beautiful lady on the wall lit by a single candle. She would feel a curious longing to lie there for ever, to surrender herself to the lure of the dark. But she would remember my warnings of the danger that lurked for her in Rotherhithe. Again, she would struggle to wake. This time she would be successful and find she was standing in some unfamiliar street, sometimes more than a mile from her room. If true, and I have no reason to doubt her – indeed, just the opposite – then she is reporting a most remarkable display of somnambulism.

I have two reasons for feeling particularly concerned. The first is that on a couple of occasions Mary Kelly has reported dreaming not of a negress, but of a European woman with long blonde hair. Disturbing, because although her description exactly matches the woman I have seen, I have never told Kelly of these experiences and there is therefore no possibility of her having known of them.

The second reason: again, a description of something I recognise. The room, with the picture of the lady and the single candle. I have seen it. I know it. I have lain there myself.

It is a room in a warehouse in Rotherhithe.

25 August. – Early morning, an urgent summons to Myddleton Street. Westcote kneeling by his wife's side; Stoker, ashen-faced, standing behind him. Lucy herself as ghastly-looking as before the transfusion; the bones of her face standing out prominently, her complexion chalky and drained of all colour. Conducted immediate emergency transfusion; as before, Westcote left very weak, and Lucy's pallor only moderately improved. As I conducted the operation I saw how a pane of the window had been shattered, and asked to be told how the attack had occurred.

It had come while Stoker was on guard; he had been on duty by Lucy's bed for the second half of the night. At around 4 a.m. he had felt a desperate urge to sleep. He had begun to pace around, but still he couldn't keep himself awake, and before he knew it he was dreaming confused snatches of nightmare: some terrible threat, trying to break in; being frozen in ice, struggling to break free; a human form on Lucy's chest. I pressed him to describe this form. It had been a woman, eyes gleaming beneath her veil; as she drank from Lucy, she had been embracing her victim and fondling her.

'Fondling her?' I asked.

Stoker swallowed and glanced at Westcote. Even beneath his beard, his blush was evident. 'Fondling her *lewdly*,' he whispered at length.

I nodded. 'And you are certain – quite *certain* – that it was a woman beneath this veil?'

Stoker nodded. 'Absolutely.'

Poor fellow, he was bowed by guilt. I assured him that he had no cause to blame himself; he could have no understanding of what we were up against. Stoker nodded; he said that Huree had hinted as much. I asked where Huree was, for I had been surprised not to see him, but it seemed that he had already arrived, and then hurried off almost at once in a state of great excitement and urgency. 'The medallion,' said Westcote, 'the coin that was found in Arthur Ruthven's hand – the Professor observed it hanging round Lucy's neck, and asked to borrow it. I hope Lucy will not object. The Professor insisted it was very significant.' Interesting. I wonder what fresh trail Huree might be following now.

Returned to Whitechapel. An orderly's sanguigen proved compatible with Lucy's; hurried back with him to Myddleton Street. During the transfusion, Lucy restless and half-awake; once the operation had been concluded, she began to clutch at her throat – not at her wounds, I realised, but at where her medallion had hung. She woke suddenly, demanded to know where it had gone; I explained, but she continued angry and upset. Then she began to ask where her baby was in a low, desperate scream, thrashing about in her bed from side to side. I told her that Arthur had been sent away to a place of greater safety. She demanded to know where; I told her. At the mention of Lady Mowberley's name, Lucy sighed and smiled contentedly. 'I am glad,' she whispered; and then her eyes closed and she returned back to sleep. Much calmer now; her complexion likewise restored to full colour. The second transfusion an evident success.

Prompted by my exchange with Lucy to call on Lady Mowberley. Concerned to warn her of the events of the previous night; Huree had been convinced that Arthur was in no danger and Lady Mowberley, although warned of the possible threat, had rejected our offer of protection. She was at home when I called; although obviously concerned for Lucy's health, she listened to my account with the utmost calmness and once again refused my suggestion of guards. Did so quite categorically.

I asked her, remembering the visitation in her own room all those months before, whether she had ever seen the same intruder again.

She stared at me, a faint smile on her lips. 'My husband's mistress, you mean?'

I bowed my head. 'Yes, Lady Mowberley – your husband's mistress.' I paused. 'Have you seen her recently, perhaps?'

She frowned and suddenly shuddered, rose from her seat and crossed to the window, clutching at herself as though feeling the cold. She stared out in silence at the street below. 'Yes,' she said suddenly, 'I have seen her.'

'When?' I asked.

She turned to face me. 'Last night,' she answered. 'I hadn't been able to sleep. I was standing here, just as I am now. I saw her pass in the street below.'

Very calmly, not wanting to alarm her, I crossed to where she stood. 'Lady Mowberley,' I asked; 'do you remember, perhaps, what time this would have been?'

'Indeed, yes,' she replied. She turned to look out at the street again. 'I remember it very precisely. There was a clock beside me, and I glanced at it. It was twenty minutes before four o'clock.'

26 August. – I had to go. For upwards of an hour after completing my diary entry last night, I sat curled in my armchair, marshalling the fragments of evidence. It was clear to me then, as it is clear to me now, that the locus of our investigation must be Rotherhithe. But still there are details which elude my grasp. It is very frustrating, as though I am being denied the final fragment of a puzzle which otherwise would be perfectly simple to understand. Indeed, if anything, the situation appeared clearer last night. All the evidence then seemed to point towards Lilah; it still does, I suppose, but I am somehow less certain of that now. Must talk with Huree. He has left me an intriguing letter on my desk, if a little florid. For all his evident over-excitement, it seems he is clearer to understanding who Lilah might be. Will visit him shortly. First, though, must record what I can of last night.

I was met at the door by Sarmistha, the Indian servant girl. She was even thinner than before; her dress hanging loose about her and her expression one of the most abject terror. I tried to question her, but she would not speak to me, covering her face instead and hurrying up the stairs. She led me to the conservatory where Lilah and Suzette were playing chess. They both looked up as I strode towards them. Lilah glanced at Suzette, and I saw how she smiled.

I stood before her, in silence, for what seemed like an eternity. Perhaps it was. I wondered what to say. Suzette watched me solemnly; Lilah, by contrast, continued to smile. I swallowed and felt suddenly ridiculous; then angry with them both, ragingly angry. 'What are you?' I asked. I shook; then clenched my fists; I could not surrender to my emotions now. 'Are you vampires?' I asked, as calmly as I could. 'Or something worse? Tell me. What is your purpose in London? What is your purpose with me and my friends?'

Lilah glanced up at Sarmistha, then back at Suzette. 'I think he is very close now, my dear.' She moved a chess piece. 'Check,' she said.

Suzette continued to study me as solemnly as before. 'Why, Dr Eliot?' she asked at length. 'What is it that Lilah is meant to have done?'

I took a step forward. I was fighting to control my anger and fear. 'Lucy Westcote is dying,' I said. 'Some – creature – some monster – is draining her of her blood.'

Not a flicker of surprise crossed Suzette's face. 'And so?' she asked.

'A woman has been observed drinking from Lucy's throat.'

'What of it?'

'You know what.'

Now Suzette did smile. She glanced at Lilah, then down at the board. 'How sad,' she whispered, as though to herself. 'I still don't think he is close enough.' She moved a piece and took Lilah's king. 'Disappointing.' She stared up at Lilah. 'I think I have won the game again.'

Lilah looked down at the board; she laughed, then swept away the pieces with her hand. She rose to her feet, adjusting her dress as she did so with a movement of such grace, of such simple elegance, that all my desire and need for her returned, focused it seemed in that single simple gesture, so that I was enslaved again and knew I could not fight her, that I would follow her anywhere she cared to lead. She took my arm; 'Come with me,' she murmured. 'Come with me for always.' I felt, what I had never understood before meeting her, how terrible and fathomless a woman's beauty can be, how dangerous, and how utterly incomparable. I knew, if she would have me, I would indeed never leave. I clung to her arm as though to hold her for all time.

'I am not the one,' she whispered, 'who has been drinking from your friend. I have no need of anyone's blood. You do believe me, don't you, Jack?' She kissed me. I imagined I was dissolving on her lips. 'You do believe me?'

And of course, I did. I pressed myself closer against her and felt the softness of her breast against my side, smelled the perfume on her skin. We were still walking. Ahead of us stretched a long, dark passageway. There were animals around us, birds above our heads. I remembered it from before, when Suzette had left us, running across the stones, leaving Lilah and myself alone for the first time. And now we were still alone, but it was we who were walking down the passageway. We came to a door. Lilah opened it. Beyond, the crimson-hung bed was waiting for us ...

I woke again, naked and alone as before. The room was still dark; the candle still burned beneath the picture on the wall. I dressed, then left the room; Sarmistha was waiting with my coat in her hands. She handed it to me and fled, and though I pursued her she was lost in the dark. I returned and left the warehouse. Outside, I found that a whole day had passed. But I was safe. Unharmed. What danger, though. If Huree is even half-right – what danger!

And yet ... her words are in my ears, in the whorls of my brain. 'It was not I who has been drinking from your friend. I have no need of anyone's blood. You do believe me, don't you, Jack?' Yes. And I still do. Why? Can there be any reason other than my infatuation? Any reason at all? I need to think. I need to clear my head.

I will visit Huree now. He evidently has much to reveal to me. Will take his letter and peruse it in the cab. Cannot dismiss it out of hand.

Letter, Professor Huree Jyoti Navalkar to Dr John Eliot.

26 August.

Jack–

Where the bloody hell are you? Not with that bloody woman, I hope. Because if you are, you're a damned bloody fool. Oh please, dear God, you have not gone there, and if you have, you will come back safe and continue unharmed. If you read this, come to me at once. By night – my room in Bloomsbury. By day – the Reading Room of the British Library, Seat N4. I have been reading much. There is a good deal I have to reveal to you.

Because, Jack – I know who she is! I know who – or rather what – we are fighting against. It reduces me, I confess, to a state of near despair. I have become a nervous timid creature who shakes all the time. What hope do we have? We creatures of clay – of mortal flesh and blood! But I am losing my thread. Please – I must remain philosophical. We die; we are born again; we flow towards God. Let us be brave, then, and great-souled. But I am sorry – I am losing my thread again. Let me start at the beginning – the coin I found hanging from Lucy's neck.

You never told me it was from Kirkeion. I suppose it did not seem important to you – an unknown Greek town, vanished for ever from the history books – why should it have done? But to me, Jack, Kirkeion is not unknown at all – dear me, no. It is not in the history books you should have been looking, but in the legends of the Greeks, in the hermetic records of the ancient mystic rites. Search amongst the forbidden texts, smuggled from the library of Alexandria – there you will find mention of Kirkeion.

It was a town of the dead, Jack, where men lived as the slaves of the Goddess, lost for ever to the flow of mortal life, in agony because they knew this themselves, yet on the rack of remembered pleasure too, for they had seen the face of the Goddess as they fell and so, for all the horror of their fate, could not regret the things they had become. What these things were, you may guess when I tell you the Goddess's name. She was spoken of in the epics, in the *Odyssey*, and yet Homer did not know the whole truth, for he was drawing on rumours for his portrait of the sorceress, Circe the terrible, transformer of men. You will remember your Classics, I am sure, and the island that Odysseus visited, filled with strange animals, his own men amongst them, reduced to rutting swine. Please, Jack – do not think me mad. Do not go all damned sceptical on me again. You think it fantastic that a place such as Kirkeion should have truly existed? Well, don't! Damn it, Jack, don't! Apply your damned laws of observation if you wish. Do as you have always done – extrapolate from the evidence you have studied yourself. There are animals in Rotherhithe, are there not, and humans twisted into strange, distorted shapes? There is Lucy's coin, with the name '*KIRKEION*' stamped around its edge. And above all, Jack – *above all* – there is Lilah . . . Circe . . . call her what you will.

For she has had many names. She was known in China and Africa; in the voodoo rites of the jungle glade; on the blood-smoked pyramids of Mexico; in her honour, the queens of Canaan and Phoenicia would prostitute themselves; for her, the walls of Troy were toppled into ash. As Amestris, she watched the only breasts on earth more beautiful than her own cut from her rival's living flesh; as Yielâ, she was known to Jericho and Ur, the first cities in the world, and yet already she was older than them, as old as man himself. Her cheeks are the colour of the blossom of pomegranates; her lips as red as blood; her eyes as deep and timeless as space. Lilah, you call her. Do you not hear the echo, as you pronounce the syllables, of the most terrible and ancient name of all? לילית it is written in the Hebrew – Lilith. In Jewish myth, she was the first wife of Adam before Eve was made, expelled from Eden for her terrible crimes, and preying on humanity in revenge ever since. Why, in some traditions, Jack, she was the wife of God Himself.

Lilith, Jack, *Lilith* – eternal harlot, bather in blood, queen of the demons and the succubi. Avoid her. I know you must think I am raving – and yet just pause, and remember what you have experienced and seen for yourself. She is all the legends I have described above, and something more – a principal of darkness, active in the world, beautiful, seductive, terrible. I fear for you, Jack. I fear for us all. Come to me as soon as you humanly can.

May our assorted gods be with us, and all those we love, as my own thoughts, dear Jack, are with you now.

HUREE.

Letter, Dr John Eliot, to Professor Huree Jyoti Navalkar.

Surgeon's Court.

11 p.m.

Dear Huree,

I was convinced, if not that you were raving, that you were a little drunk at the very least. Lilah as Circe, transformer of men? I was going to call on you, to sober you up. However, yet again I must apologise. Coming to visit you, I put on my coat again. I slipped your letter into an inner pocket. As I did so, I felt a second slip of paper against my fingertips, only a scrap really, but not one I could remember having put there. I took it out. I read it; and as you will understand when you have done so yourself, I realised I could not come and call on you tonight. I have a more pressing visit to make.

The implications of this letter are evident; not just for the theory you have outlined in your own letter, but for the whole course of the investigation. I see now how culpably blind I have been. Dear God, Huree, pray we are not too late.

I will write to you again as soon as possible – tonight, I hope. Before anything else, I must corroborate what George says and rescue him if I can.

The handwriting, by the way, is undoubtedly his.

Get Stoker.

JACK.

Attached to the above letter.

Jack – it's me – for God's sake – the girl – the one who met you at the door, who hands you your coat – it's me. How? I don't know. I was taken – Polidori came – and then ... no. Horrible, Jack – horrible. But it was over at last. Opened my eyes. Brown skin – I lifted my hand – God, Jack – *breasts* – there on my chest. I screamed – screamed and screamed. Couldn't believe it – how could I have done? – kept waiting, wake from the nightmare, be myself again. But no change. Weeks have gone, and I'm still here, and I'm still – a girl – me, George Mowberley, Minister for India – *some bloody wog girl.* Lilah's joke, I suppose. Not funny, though – terrifying, Jack – God, I'm always so bloody terrified. Afraid my brain is going too, you see – can't think straight – can only work – scrubbing, serving, tending Suzette – otherwise, the terror comes back – unbearable. Tried to escape once; almost paralysed, the terror grew so great. Forced myself, though – stole a boat – got across the Thames to the docks. You remember, Jack? You followed me there one night. Where the gentlemen go – cheap whores – fuck them. All there again that night – the gentlemen – looking for their whores. One of them got me – couldn't escape – God, Jack – no – *no.* Save me, Jack. You have no idea. Lilah wants to send me back. Fucked for coppers. The filth – inside you – violated – the pain of it – damp. Better though, perhaps, than Suzette. Calling me now. Weight on my stomach, forces me on to the floor – her teeth, Jack – sharp – tiny razors – a child, Jack, God, *a child* – sucking on my breasts – no milk, though – blood – draining my blood – her sucking lips – my blood.

She's coming now. Terror again. Help me – *please.* My God. My God. *Help me!*

Letter, Dr John Eliot to Professor Huree Jyoti Navalkar.

2 a.m.

Dear Huree,

Excuse illegibility – am writing this in the back of a cab. I am safe – other news though, I am afraid, grim. Arrived in Rotherhithe – found streets to warehouse without difficulty. They were dark and empty – as I followed them, however, could hear the faintest sound of skipping feet, a young girl's, ahead of me beyond each turning. Occasionally, on the wall, a shadow, nothing more. Arrived at the warehouse doorway. Tried to enter, but the door was locked; hammered, shouted – no response. Then saw bundle, discarded in the gutter.

It was a woman's body. I turned it over. Recognised Sarmistha at once – George, I should say – George. George was dead. No fluids – drained dry. Tongue withered, a tiny stump in the back of the throat; hair thin and white; body a sack of rattling bones. Tried to lift the corpse. Felt it start to crumble, the arms turning into powder in my hands. Stared at the face. It was no longer Sarmistha's – for a brief second it was George's again – I recognised my friend. Then gone. Nothing but dust. A mound of ash and rags on the side of the street.

Tried to scrape up the dust – useless. Rose to my feet. Turned and walked, then began to run. A child's voice, singing some rhyme over and over, ahead of me. Again, though, no sign of the singer – no sign of Suzette. Terrified. Worse than Kalikshutra. Reached the main street at last. Hailed the cab. Shall never go back.

Are you with Stoker at the moment? The cab will have dropped me at the end of Grosvenor Street; the driver has instructions to take you there now. I shall be in the doorway of the Shepherd's Arms, directly opposite the Mowberleys' house. Come fast. We are drawing into Grosvenor Street as I write this.

You still have your revolver, I trust?

JACK.

Bram Stoker's Journal (continued).

... Not a fortnight after the dinner party I had held in her honour, Lucy fell sick; and in circumstances so remarkable that I at once began to harbour the darkest fears as to the nature of her malady. Her symptoms seemed to parallel all too closely an illness studied by Eliot in India, which he had first mentioned to me during our pursuit of Sir George, and which he had never thereafter discussed without expressions of the utmost horror. Delirium, catalepsy, severe loss of blood: all these marks of woe, first observed by Eliot in the Himalayas, he now found reproduced in poor Lucy, and I could tell from the urgency of his manner that he feared the worst. Yet still he would not draw me into his confidence: instead, he preferred to stay closeted with Professor Jyoti, an acquaintance from his Indian days and an expert, it seemed, on Lucy's mysterious disease. These two men appeared to be preparing themselves for some great adventure; and remembering how it was I who had previously been Eliot's confidant, I cannot deny that I felt a little undervalued. I was deputed to guard Lucy in her illness – a task I willingly fulfilled! – but I could sense that she was menaced by some yet greater threat. It was this danger I longed to tackle and, indeed, for which I started to prepare myself; for I could not believe in the final reckoning that my assistance would not after all be required.

The summons finally came one hot August night. Professor Jyoti arrived alone to call me from my bed; despite my demands for an explanation, however, he continued as inscrutable as before, and would repeat only that Lucy was in the utmost danger. I dressed hurriedly, frustrated but intrigued; then, having kissed my dear wife farewell, I climbed with the Professor into the back of his cab and accompanied him back to his rooms in Bloomsbury. Once arrived there I began to press him again; but still he would speak only of some dark and terrible danger, before asking me if my assistance could be counted upon no matter how great the horror. Naturally, I replied that it could; but I also pointed out with some force that I would be better prepared if I knew what the horror might be. The Professor stared at me, his pudgy face frozen suddenly into an expression of the utmost seriousness. 'We are hunting a woman,' he said. He then asked if I remembered a dream I had reported, in which a veiled form had appeared to lap at Lucy's blood.

'We are hunting a dream?' I exclaimed in disbelief.

The Professor smiled wryly. 'It is something more than just a dream, I am afraid. You are a man of the theatre, Mr Stoker. Remember *Hamlet*. "There are more things in Heaven and Earth" – etcetera, etcetera.' He chuckled suddenly. 'Not everything in fiction is fictional. Prepare for the worst, Mr Stoker. Prepare, if you like, for the impossible.'

These were scarcely encouraging sentiments; yet I felt a surge of excitement at confronting the stuff of an adventure tale again. I asked the Professor about Eliot, whether he would be accompanying us; but at that very moment there was a knocking on the door, and the Professor rose at once and hurried me outside. There was a cab waiting for us; the Professor greeted the sight of it with relief, although he had evidently been expecting it, for he did not bother to give the cabby instructions beyond shouting at him, as before, to drive with the utmost speed. He began to read a letter, which I supposed the cabby must have delivered to him; he frowned; once he had finished it, he screwed it up and flung it away. He leaned forward again, and again urged more speed. Our journey, however, was not very long; we were soon passing through the streets and squares of Mayfair, and just by the entrance into Grosvenor Hill the Professor instructed the driver to turn aside and halt. We climbed out, and the Professor led me through the shadows towards the doorway of an inn. 'You inquired after Dr Eliot,' he said. He smiled and gestured with his hand. 'Here he is, Mr Stoker, waiting for you.'

Eliot was pleased to see me, I was gratified to observe. But his face seemed even thinner than before, and something in his wasted expression told me that his nerves were at their highest pitch. He turned to the Professor. 'You did not tell Westcote anything?' he asked.

The Professor shook his head. 'There was no need. He is watching over Lucy tonight. He will be of more use there, I think – especially if our quarry knows we are on her track.'

'Which she may well do, I'm afraid,' said Eliot. He turned and glanced up at a house on the opposite side of the road. 'You see how her windows are dark. I have been unable to catch a hint of movement from them.' He turned again, and glanced at a bulge in the Professor's jacket. 'You have brought your revolver, I see. You have one for Stoker as well?'

The Professor nodded and handed the weapon over to me. 'Keep the revolver hidden, Stoker,' Eliot whispered. 'We do not wish to be mistaken for burglars.' Then he walked up the front steps and rang on the bell.

There was no answer. Eliot rang the bell again, hard, pulling on it for upwards of thirty seconds. At length he paused and we heard footsteps approaching us from the hallway inside. The door was unbolted and opened; a man peered out at us, a sleepy frown on his face. 'Dr Eliot!' he exclaimed, with a sudden start. 'What on earth is your business at this hour?'

'Your mistress,' Eliot asked, 'is she in?'

The butler – for such he clearly was – frowned again and shook his head. 'I am afraid not, sir. She left this evening, to join Sir George in the South of France.'

'And the child ...' Eliot paused and swallowed. 'Mrs Westcote's child – Arthur – did Lady Mowberley take him as well?'

The butler looked puzzled. 'Yes, sir. It was all agreed with Mrs Westcote. Did she not tell you?'

Eliot struggled to control his expression, but his disappointment and anguish were evident. For a second his shoulders slumped, as he stood bowed in thought. 'The cab,' he said suddenly; he turned back to the butler. 'You ordered it, I assume?'

The butler nodded.

'Can you give me the address of the company?'

The butler hesitated; then he nodded again. 'A moment, please.' We waited on the doorstep, Eliot stretching his thin, nervous fingers

327

one by one and then glancing at his watch. At length the butler returned and gave us a card. Eliot seized it with a quick dart of his hand, and without a further word hurried down the street. The Professor and I followed him. As we went, I struggled to marshal the implications of all I had just heard. 'We are pursuing *Lady Mowberley?*' I finally asked, not bothering to conceal my disbelief.

Eliot glanced at me. 'Her husband was found murdered this evening,' he said. 'He had been abducted from his house, a crime which was then concealed from me for almost a month by Lady Mowberley. His disappearance, if not his subsequent death, could only have been committed with the full connivance of his wife. Do not worry, Stoker. The case against her is watertight.'

'But why should she have taken Lucy's child?'

'That,' said Eliot impatiently, 'is what we are trying to find out.'

'And where would they have gone?'

Again, Eliot glanced at me impatiently. 'Why do you think we have come to the cab stables?' he asked. He turned his head, and I saw that we had arrived at the address given on the butler's card; Eliot began to pull on the bell, and after a second lengthy wait we again heard footsteps coming downstairs. The door was opened to us, most grudgingly, and we were met by a volley of proletarian abuse. Eliot prevailed upon the doorman's better nature, however, by insisting on the importance of the case in hand; and indeed, his mood of urgency was evident. A ledger was taken down, studied; the record of the evening's business was found. 'Here,' said our man, 'ten o'clock. A cab was called to Grosvenor Street. Number Two.'

'And its destination?' asked Eliot impatiently.

The man drew his finger across the page. 'King's Cross Railway Station,' he said, looking up.

'Of course,' said Eliot, seemingly unsurprised. 'Thank you.' He passed across a guinea. 'You may very well have just saved a young child's life.' He turned to the Professor and myself. 'Come, gentlemen,' he said. 'We still have a long night ahead of us.'

I did not understand his confidence, for it seemed to me that we were no nearer knowing where Lady Mowberley might be. 'If she travelled from King's Cross,' I said, as we walked towards Oxford Street, 'then she might be anywhere in the North.'

Eliot shook his head. 'If she has taken a train at all, then it will be to Whitby.'

'How can you be so certain?'

'Because Whitby is where the skeletons in her cupboard lie hidden.'

'Skeletons?' I exclaimed.

'Lady Mowberley, Stoker, is neither who nor what she seems. You will perhaps remember the theory I expressed to you, consequent on our pursuit of Sir George, that someone had been attempting to influence him for political ends?'

I nodded. Eliot had indeed mentioned this theory to me some weeks before, and his reasoning had struck me as perfectly exact.

'Good,' said Eliot. 'Then it is clear also, I think, that the subterfuge practised by Lady Mowberley – or rather the woman who calls herself Lady Mowberley – is part of this same conspiracy. You will not have been aware of this, but Rosamund was engaged to George Mowberley whilst still a child. They were then separated for several years. George would scarcely have recognised his fiancée at the time when they married.'

'But in fact,' I exclaimed, 'it was not the fiancée at all whom he married, but the woman we are now chasing who had taken her place! Is that what you suspect?'

'Exactly so,' nodded Eliot. 'You are on excellent form tonight, Stoker. I congratulate you on your perspicacity.'

'You believe, then,' said the Professor slowly, 'that she has fled to Whitby to cover her tracks? There is evidence there which may prove what she has done?'

'It would seem probable,' Eliot replied. 'She visited there quite recently, less than four weeks ago. However . . .'

'We must hurry to King's Cross at once!' I insisted, interrupting him, for it seemed to me that we had no time to lose. 'We must book our tickets for the very next train!'

'Yes,' said Eliot. 'That should certainly be done. *However* – as I was going to say – I do not think that all three of us should depart on the chase. The false Lady Mowberley is evidently a woman of the most remarkable intelligence and malignity. Her talent for deception is an extraordinary one.' And as he said this it seemed to me that he spoke of his adversary almost with admiration, rather as a duellist might compliment his foe. But then Eliot's frown deepened, and his face grew dark once again. 'Who knows what web she may have spun around poor Lucy?' he muttered. 'She has fooled us once – she may do so again. Our journey to Whitby may prove nothing but the wildest of goose-chases. I would be reluctant to abandon Lucy to one man's care alone.'

'But Westcote has his own friends,' I protested, 'who will help him to watch over his wife. There is no reason why Lucy should be in any greater danger just because we are temporarily absent.'

The Professor nodded. 'I am inclined to agree with Mr Stoker. The false Lady Mowberley, as you have said yourself, Jack, is a woman of quite diabolical powers. It will require all our combined skills and bravery, if we are to track her down and confront her successfully. We have all of us, in our different ways, been involved in this case from the start. I do not believe it would be wise to separate now.'

Eliot bowed his head. He looked unhappy. 'If you are convinced of that,' he said.

The Professor nodded his head. 'The forces we are engaged against are not lightly to be approached. We will call on Westcote now and explain the situation to him. But we must hurry. Every minute that passes loses us the advantage.'

By now we had reached Piccadilly Circus, and even in the early hours of the morning that mighty hub of the metropolis was crowded with vehicles. We hired the first hansom we came across and ordered it to drive to Myddleton Street, where we found Westcote still sitting up by the side of his wife. Eliot warned him on no account to leave Lucy unattended, and in our absence to allow no one into the house except those whom he knew, and could absolutely trust. Eliot repeated this warning over and over again, in the grimmest of tones: no one! No one at all! Then at last he turned to

Lucy and kissed her lightly on the cheek. We all of us, I think, felt upset to part from the fair object of our concerns; yet I for one was grateful for our brief visit to her sick-bed, for I knew that the image of her would now be constantly before my eyes, reminding me in the most vivid manner possible of how pressing and desperate our mission was. In such a mood, I thought as we left for King's Cross, might a knight of old have departed Camelot.

We reached the station at shortly after five a.m. We had to wait almost an hour for the first train north but during that time we were able to ascertain that a woman answering to Lady Mowberley's description had indeed been observed the evening before, boarding the last train for York. She had been seen, furthermore, with a baby in her arms, and both the guards who remembered her commented on the peculiarity – that a woman of her evident rank did not have a nursemaid for the child. I could see that this news disturbed Eliot, and when our own train finally departed he sat slumped for much of the journey in thought. 'It seems too obvious,' he muttered, 'actually to be carrying the child in her arms. She must be very confident. Either that – or else ...' His voice trailed away and he slumped once again into pensive silence.

Fortunately, our train made excellent speed, and we arrived in good time to catch our scheduled connection. Despite Eliot's evident forebodings I felt a good deal more cheery by now; and certainly, sitting on the Whitby train gazing out at the August sunshine, and surrounded by the cheery babble of holidaymakers bound, like us, for the Yorkshire coast, the fears of the previous night appeared quite banished from my mind, and I was confident our foe would soon be run to earth. I thought of all the hints which my companions had given me, that she was somehow more than human; how utterly ridiculous these appeared to me now! Not even our arrival at Whitby itself, which had been cast by my imaginings as a place of menace and fear, could dim this mood of optimism; for it was in reality a most lovely spot, built around a deep harbour, and rising so steeply on the eastern side that the houses of the old town seemed piled up one over the other, like the pictures we see of Nuremburg. Only the ruins of the Abbey, lowering over the town on the eastern cliff, immense and romantic, suggested that Whitby might indeed correspond to the place of my imaginings; but in the evening sunlight, even the Abbey seemed more picturesque than anything else.

A few inquiries soon established where George's fiancée, Rosamund Harcourt, had lived. We drove a couple of miles along the coast to where Harcourt Hall stood, an imposing pile almost on the edge of the cliffs. Having alighted by the entrance to the driveway, we advanced through gardens grown wild and tangled with as much circumspection as the fading light would allow. No one intruded on us, however, and by the time we had arrived at the house itself I was starting to doubt whether anyone lived there at all, for many of the windows had been boarded up and the general impression was one of emptiness, so that I began to fear our journey there had indeed been a fool's errand. But then Eliot pointed to the gravel of the forecourt, and I saw the marks of a single line of footsteps; so it was evident that someone at least was around. 'A woman,' said Eliot, crouching by the indentations in the gravel, 'judging by the smallness of the feet – but who?' He glanced at me; I patted the bulge of the revolver in my coat. He nodded, then climbed the steps and hammered on the door.

An answer was a long time coming; but it came at last. An old woman, evidently an ancient servant of the Harcourts, finally opened the door; and at the sight of her lined and withered face, I watched Eliot's own expression visibly lighten. She proved to be the house-keeper, appointed to maintain the house until such time as the Mowberleys should choose to return; she had been a servant to the family for over fifty years, and clearly mourned the house's empti-ness and state of disrepair. She was taciturn at first, as I believe is often the Yorkshire way; but once Eliot had hinted that her mistress might be in danger, she opened up remarkably and proved eager to assist us in any way she could. At first, however, this seemed likely to be not very much. No, she told us, she had not seen Lady Mowberley for more than two years – not since before her wedding, indeed. No, she had observed no strangers in the neighbourhood. No, there had been no mysterious or unexplained sicknesses. 'Not since Her Ladyship herself were ill,' the old woman added, 'before her marriage to Sir George.'

'Ill?' Eliot inquired.

'Pale, like – thin – awful weak. Queer, she grew. Like she were numb in the head. That's when she arranged her wedding, you see, even though her own mother were only just dead. Carried on, she did, wouldn't hear no. Two months later it were done. Married!' The housekeeper shook her head. 'Sad affair, it were, sad and strange.'

'Strange?' asked Eliot, clearly intrigued. 'In what way? Apart from its hurried nature, that is?'

The old woman shook her head. 'It were that private, it were wrong, all wrong.'

'How do you mean, private?'

'Just her and Sir George, and Sir George's best man. Arthur, I think he were called. Gentleman from London, anyhow.'

'No relatives?'

'No, none to be had. Her Ladyship were the last – the last of the Harcourts. The only one left.'

'And so there was just her and the two others in attendance at the church? You are absolutely sure of that? There was no one else at all?'

'As I said, only the three.'

Eliot's frown deepened. 'And afterwards? Did you see your mistress then?'

Again the housekeeper shook her head. 'No, she went right off. Her and her husband. I told you. We never saw them at all.'

'So – let me be perfectly clear about this – Sir George and Lady Mowberley left on their honeymoon straight away? Is that correct? And before that, for her own wedding, your mistress had had no relatives about her, no friends – *no one she knew at all?*'

'Aye, but it were her own will. She were like that, solitary, since she went ill with the sickness in her head. Wouldn't have nowt to do with us servants – brought in new ones of her own. I weren't allowed near her on her wedding day at all, even though I'd been with her since she were a little babe. None of us were.'

Eliot glanced at the Professor. He nodded in reply, as though confirming some private suspicion of which they had both spoken before. Eliot turned back to the old woman. 'You have been most helpful,' he said, 'but please – one thing more. On the night before the wedding, did any other strange event occur? Anything you remember? Anything at all?'

The housekeeper thought; then she shook her head. 'No. Nowt – save for the general queerness of Her Ladyship's mood.' Then she paused, struck by a sudden remembrance. 'There were the disturbance by Mrs Harcourt's tomb . . .'

'Mrs Harcourt?' Eliot interrupted. 'That would have been Lady Mowberley's mother, of course?'

The old woman nodded. 'Aye. Someone had forced open the entrance to her crypt. But that weren't here; that were back in Whitby, in St Mary's Church.'

Eliot had suddenly tensed, quite rigidly, and his nostrils had dilated as though literally with the scent of the chase. 'Just let me repeat this,' he said slowly. 'On the night before Lady Mowberley's wedding, there was an incident involving the Harcourt crypt? What? – someone trying to break into the coffin, perhaps?'

'Aye.' The housekeeper nodded. 'Perhaps. Though why they'd want to do that, I couldn't say.'

Eliot nodded as though in triumph. 'Thank you,' he whispered. 'Thank you very much.' He pressed the old woman's hands; then he turned and without a further word began to hurry down the drive.

The cab was waiting for us; Eliot ordered the driver to return us to Whitby, then sat in silence with his lips compressed and his eyebrows drawn, his eyes expressive of a puzzle solved. I myself, of course, remained as mystified as I had been before; but I remembered Eliot's dislike of being questioned and judged it best to wait until he should speak of his own free will. When he entered a shop, however, and ordered a pick, a shovel and a heavy hammer, my curiosity could no longer be restrained.

'Tell me your thoughts, Eliot,' I demanded once we had left the store. 'You are now certain, I presume, that Sir George did not marry his real fiancée?'

'Of course,' replied Eliot. 'The solution is apparent, I would have thought.'

'But you are forgetting,' said the Professor, 'that Mr Stoker is not fully conversant with the background of the case.'

'Background?' I inquired. 'What in particular?'

'In particular?' The Professor smiled, then stroked the bulge of his stomach as he thought. 'Mind control, for instance.' His smile faded. 'There is a way – I have seen it myself, so I know it to be true – for the mortal brain to be seduced and utterly enslaved. The victim becomes nothing but another person's tool. Such a fate may have been – no, surely was – Rosamund Harcourt's.'

'Her "queerness", you mean?'

'Exactly so,' said Eliot. 'The wedding, the hiring of new servants, the demand for privacy – all would have been done at another's behest, for her thoughts by then would not have been her own. And in following such commands, Miss Harcourt would have been preparing her death. Death, I say' – he frowned – 'or something even worse.'

'Worse?'

Eliot glanced up at the eastern cliff where the Abbey stood framed against a bank of darkening cloud. 'That is what we have to find out,' he muttered. He shivered suddenly and concealed his shovel beneath the folds of his coat. He glanced up at the sky again. It was almost green; the air was heavy with a sultry heat and that prevailing intensity which, on the approach of thunder, affects persons of a sensitive nature. 'There will be a storm tonight,' he said. 'That can only help us.' He glanced at his watch; it was now just past nine. 'Come,' he said, 'we should have something to eat. What we must do tonight should not be attempted on an empty stomach.'

What he meant, I already suspected – the shovel and pick had not been bought on a whim – but I had no wish as yet to have these dark thoughts confirmed. I ate as heartily as circumstances would allow;

and it was not long off midnight before we finally left the inn. The heat, if anything, seemed even worse now than it had done at nine o'clock; and the closeness of the air was most oppressive. I was grateful to be walking along the harbour's edge, for Eliot was leading us along the foot of the eastern cliff towards the headland on which the Abbey stood. Then suddenly, I heard a rumble of thunder; gazing out to sea, I saw a mass of fog in a ghostly white wall, rolling in through the harbour mouth. There was another roll of thunder; and without any further warning the tempest had broken. With a rapidity which seemed incredible, the whole aspect of nature at once became convulsed: the waves rose in growing fury, breaking over the piers and the harbour front; the wind roared as though in competition with the thunder; the sky overhead seemed trembling under the shock of the footsteps of the storm. For a second, the fog lifted and broke; gazing out at the sea again, I saw boiling mountains of water and foam, rising in an immeasurable grandeur and cast a brilliant silver by the lightning overhead; and then the view was swallowed by the fog and we too, on the harbour's edge, were swallowed as well, so that I could barely see the faces of my companions through the dankness of the mists.

Eliot took my arm. 'This way!' he yelled in my ear, pointing towards the old town above us. We began to climb through the gale-buffeted streets and then up a curve of steps, hundreds of them, leading from the town up the side of the cliff. As we neared the summit, there was a break in the sea-fog once again; looking ahead of me, I could just make out the form of the Abbey, but the view was obscured by a second church rising from the cliff-edge, and surrounded by a graveyard full of tombs and crooked stones. 'St Mary's!' yelled Eliot in my ear; he began to cross the graveyard, bending with the wind to avoid being swept from the cliff, and weaving through the stones. I followed him; and I soon realised that our destination was the largest tomb I could make out, a squat crypt of rectangular stone on the very edge of the headland, looking out across the sea. As Eliot neared it, he paused and stared about him, evidently checking to ensure we were alone; but the storm, as he had prophesied it would be, was our ally that night, for we were in its very teeth and there was no one else abroad to dare its rage.

As I reached the crypt there came another rush of sea-fog, greater than any hitherto – a mass of dank mist closing in on me as though with the clammy hands of death, so that I could see nothing and only hear, for the roar of the tempest, the crash of the thunder and the booming of the mighty billows came through the dank oblivion even louder than before. I felt my way along the side of the crypt until I came to its corner; then I felt along the succeeding edge. I saw a shape ahead of me; it put out its arms and I recognised Eliot. I peered into his face, and saw how it was frozen and terribly pinched.

'Get out your revolver!' he screamed in my ear.

I must have frowned, for he reached into my pocket and took it from me; he looked around as he returned it, then he gestured with his arm. I too looked down; I was staring at the side of the crypt; I now saw for the first time how the entrance way had been smashed into pieces, so that an oblong of darkness was waiting, jagged like bared teeth, grinning at us.

Above the shrieking of the wind, I heard a sudden giggle. 'Who goes first?' asked the Professor from behind my shoulder; he giggled again. I glanced round at him and smiled grimly; then I crawled in through the gap.

The darkness, after that of the storm, seemed unbearably still. I reached in my pocket for a box of matches, struck a flame, then cupped it in my hands, at the same time struggling to keep hold of my gun. But when I looked around, I could see no trace of anyone else in the crypt; there were tombs in a melancholy line along the edge of the wall, but none of them seemed disturbed, nor could I make out any hint of foul play. Eliot and the Professor had both joined me by now; they too stared around the crypt, and I could see the disappointment on Eliot's face mingled with relief. Then suddenly he started. 'What's that?' he asked. He stepped forward, then knelt down by one of the tombs. There was an envelope, I saw now, propped against its side. With feverish haste Eliot picked it up; he ripped it open; he removed a single sheet of paper, read it, then closed his eyes.

'I had dreaded this,' he said in a distant voice.

'Why, what in God's name is it?' I asked.

He turned round slowly. Never had I seen etched upon a human face a look of such ghastly agony. 'See the date,' he said, pointing. 'The fourth of August.' His shoulders slumped. 'That was when she came here. I remember her at the time telling me she had to visit Whitby on business. And now we know what that business was.'

'But the guards,' I protested, 'the guards at King's Cross. They saw her on the train last night! Her and Lucy's child.'

At the mention of Arthur, Eliot seemed to flinch. 'She – they – may have embarked on the York-bound train,' he said slowly, 'but they never arrived in York. No,' he went on, scanning the note once again, 'our quarry would have been off at the first stop and back to London – leaving us to head on and find nothing but this long-prepared taunt. See how confident she was that we would swallow her bait.' He brandished the note despairingly. 'Why, she has even signed it!'

'Let me see,' I said. Eliot shrugged and turned away as he handed me the note. '*A good try, Jack,*' I read out loud, '*but not quite good enough. You are too late. Rosamund, Lady Mowberley, née C.W.*' I looked up. 'What does C.W. mean?'

Eliot glanced round at me. 'Why, it can only be the true initials of the woman we have been pursuing. She has no need to hide her identity now. Our pursuit was in vain.'

'Not altogether,' said the Professor, who had been silent until now. He reached for the pick.

'What do you mean?' I cried, seeing that he intended to force open the tomb.

The Professor glanced up at me. 'There is still some good we can do in this place.'

'It is Mrs Harcourt's tomb?' Eliot asked.

The Professor strained with the pick; then he gestured at a name on the coffin lead and nodded. 'Here,' said Eliot, 'let me help. Stoker, please. You are stronger than any of us.'

'I will not be a party to this desecration.'

The Professor looked up at me. 'Mr Stoker, it is not desecration we are about but an act of the profoundest mercy. Help us, and I will explain everything. But I could not tell you before – you would not have believed me – not until you had seen the full horror for yourself.' He handed me the pick. 'Please, Mr Stoker. Trust me. Please.'

I hesitated, then took the pick; with all the strength I had, I began to lever up the tomb's stone lid. The weight was prodigious; but at last I felt it start to give, and, with a groan of effort, shifted it across. A stench of rottenness and death rose up from the blackness I had exposed; I bent down to inspect it closer; and as I did so the match that Eliot had been cupping in his hand flickered and went out. I heard him scrabbling with the match-box as he hurried to light a second one; and then I froze, for there was suddenly a second sound in that crypt – a clicking – and it was rising from the tomb I had just opened up. We none of us made a sound; there was another click, amplified by the silence; and then a spurt, as Eliot lit the match.

Cupping it in his hands again, he held it over the open tomb. I stared; and as I did so my heart grew cold as ice. There was a skeleton there, not yet wholly decomposed, lying amongst the mouldy rags of her shroud, her eyeless sockets staring up at us blindly. But the corpse of Mrs Harcourt – for such I judged it to be – was not alone, for there was a second body lying alongside hers – not a skeleton, but withered and incalculably lined, and her eyes were open and gleaming bright. She was alive! The creature – I say creature, for she bore no resemblance to the girl she must once have been – the creature was alive! Her mouth, as she stared at us, was open wide, her teeth as sharp as an animal's fangs, and when she closed them, I recognised the clicking we had heard before, and knew instinctively that she was hungry for blood. How I knew, I am still not absolutely certain: the cruelty in her eyes, perhaps, or the dryness of her skin which wrapped her bones like centuries-old parchment – but whatever the reason, I knew – yes, I knew – with horror and the utmost certainty – what it was we had found ... what nature of thing.

339

I turned to the Professor. 'It is Rosamund Harcourt?' I asked.
He nodded.

'She is a . . .?' I could not pronounce the word.

'Vampire?' The syllables echoed from the cold stone walls. The
Professor repeated the word; then he nodded to himself. 'Yes. Two
years she must have lain here, since that night before her wedding.
You remember, Mr Stoker, what the Harcourts' old housekeeper
said about the disturbance at the crypt? That must have been when
Rosamund was brought here, her place to be taken by the fiend we
still pursue. A cruel fate,' he whispered, 'doubly cruel. Incarcerated
with the body of her mother, dreaming of blood, withering slowly
into the creature you see before you now. Too weak to rise up, too
weak even to stir.' Again there was the clicking from the vampire's
hungry jaws. The Professor gazed at her almost with tenderness as
he reached for the pick. 'This is not death we give her – she has that
already – but release. Release again into the flow of life.' He placed
the point of the tool over the creature's heart. His hands never
trembled, nor even quivered. He raised the pick; then he swung it
down with all his might.

The Thing in the coffin began to twitch, and a hideous blood-
curdling screech came from the lipless mouth. The body shook and
twisted in wild contortions; the white teeth champed together till the
gums were torn, and the mouth was smeared with an oozing black
foam. The Professor raised the pick and swung it down again; a thin
spume of black slime rose from the wound and trickled over the
creature's withered flesh. The Professor reached for the spade; his
face was set as he raised it, then brought it down hard so that the
creature's neck bone was snapped and its head quite severed by the
single blow. The body bucked and writhed; then at last it lay still. The
terrible Thing was dead at last. Our grisly business in that place of
death was done.

But not in the broader world. I need not describe our urgency as
we left the churchyard and hurried through the town. Cruel was our
wait at the station; not until seven were we bound at last for York,
and once arrived there we had a further hour's wait for the London

train. Eliot used the time advantageously to wire a telegram to Westcote; but no reply was sent back to us, although Eliot had expressly asked for one, and so our dread of the mysterious C.W. and our fears for Lucy and her missing child grew ever more profound. I remembered Eliot's doubts, his reluctance to leave for Whitby; and as I did so I felt an especial guilt, for it was I who had persuaded him to accompany us. For I could see now all too clearly what he had most feared, how C.W.'s flight had been nothing but a ruse designed to draw us away from London, so that our hellish adversary – returned long ahead of us to the capital – might practise God knew what terrible designs. I doubted we would see little Arthur Ruthven again, for C.W. would now have had a day to dispose of him, and cover her tracks; any leads we might find would now be long cold. And as for Lucy – dearest Lucy! – I dreaded to think what might be threatening her . . .

The journey back to London appeared to last for ever. We dozed fitfully, and when we could not manage to sleep the Professor would tell me of the nature of our adversary, the vampire, that terrible creature of superstition and myth, risen to haunt us from the mists of time, stalking even through London, even through our scientific, sceptical age, our matter-of-fact nineteenth century. I still found it almost impossible to believe; and yet I could not doubt the reality of what I had seen that previous night. 'For it is certain,' the Professor said, 'that the vampire has been known everywhere that men have ever been. Why should he not still be abroad? What makes you think our own age so privileged?' Eliot listened, and nodded; but he said nothing himself. He was brooding, I knew, on what he counted as his mistake; the taunt of C.W. had seared deep into his heart.

We pulled into King's Cross at last, just before five o'clock. Within a quarter of an hour we were knocking on the door in Myddleton Street. Westcote himself answered it; his face was nervous and drawn. 'Your telegram,' he said, 'I returned here too late to answer it. Is everything all right?'

'That is what you can tell us,' replied Eliot. 'Lucy . . .'

'Is well. She is being tended by my sister even now.'

341

'Your sister?' exclaimed Eliot.

'Yes.' For the first time in a long while, I saw Westcote smile. 'That is where I was this morning when your telegram arrived – meeting my sister at Waterloo. She arrived in England last night, and in London at nine today. Dear girl, she has been with Lucy almost all afternoon. They are already as fond of each other as if they had been friends for years. My sister has herself been through terrible suffering, of course. But just like Lucy, Charlotte was always strong.'

'Charlotte.' Eliot suddenly staggered.

'My dear fellow,' said Westcote, 'are you feeling all right?'

Eliot stared at him, and his expression was a ghastly one. 'Your sister,' he said softly, '*Charlotte* – she wrote you a letter, no doubt, a note telling you she would be arriving at Waterloo?'

'Yes,' said Westcote, looking puzzled now. He felt in his pocket and drew out an envelope. Eliot snatched it from his hand. A single glance at the handwriting satisfied him. 'C.W.,' he whispered; then he turned and sped from the room. The Professor had understood too; he followed Eliot up the stairs at once. It took me a second, though; and then I too understood. 'C.W.!' I exclaimed. '*Charlotte Westcote!*'

'What is it?' Westcote asked desperately. 'What on earth is going on?'

I took him by the arm and we ran as fast as we could up the stairs. By the entrance to Lucy's bedroom, I saw Eliot checking his revolver; then he slid open the door and passed inside. One by one, we all followed him.

For what seemed an eternity, we stood frozen by the scene we saw displayed for us there. Words cannot describe the horror of it, nor the sense of disgust that rose up in my breast. Lying on the bed was the naked figure of Lucy; she was moaning softly, and writhing on her sheets. Her breasts were smeared with blood; her belly and hips as well. Bending over her, her knees between Lucy's thighs, was a young woman; her lips were pressed close to one of Lucy's breasts while with her free hand, she ... no ... I blush even to remember it. Had I not seen the vileness of her practices with my own eyes, I would have deemed them impossible, nor shall I pollute this narrative by describing them now. For several seconds, as we all stood there, this woman continued as we had discovered her – pressing herself close against Lucy's naked flesh and drinking from her bloodied bosom; then, with a slow deliberateness which seemed almost mocking, she raised her head and turned to look at us. There was a gloating voluptuousness about her expression which was both thrilling and repulsive, and as she arched back her neck she licked her lips with an almost sensual delight. She paused; then she smiled, and I saw the trace of Lucy's blood on her sharp white teeth.

'Hello, Jack,' she said. She swept back her hair, then rose to her feet. 'How was Whitby? Not too boring, I hope?'

'My God!' exclaimed Westcote, finding his tongue at last. 'Charlotte! What is this?'

She smiled again, and glanced down mockingly at Lucy as she continued to writhe on the bed. 'I congratulate you on your wife, Ned. I could never understand what you saw in her, the rude little trollop, but now I've had her I can almost understand. Who knows? I might even keep her for myself.'

Westcote suddenly screamed something, an unintelligible cry of horror and rage. He wrestled the gun from Eliot's hands and, aiming it at his sister, fired at once. The bullet hit her in the shoulder; as the blood flew up from the wound, I imagined that she laughed; and then she was fading before our very eyes, turning into a vapour which rose up on the blood and spilled out through the window, vanishing into the night so that nothing of her was left behind. The Professor hurried across to the window, while Eliot and Westcote ran to Lucy's side. She touched her breast, then raised her gore-stained fingers to her eyes; at the sight she gave a scream so wild and so despairing that it seems to me now that it will ring in my ears till my dying day. Westcote tried to hold her; but she would not allow it, writhing instead as though terrified of him, gazing out at the window and moaning all the time. Her face was ghastly, with a pallor which was accentuated by the blood which smeared her lips, and cheeks, and chin; all across her body more blood was smeared, or trickled from her wounds in a ruby flow.

'Did I shoot her dead?' screamed Westcote, still struggling to hold down his wife. 'For God's sake, Professor, is my sister dead?'

The Professor locked the window; then he slowly shook his head.

'I will hunt her down!' Westcote cried. 'My God, I shall see her pay for this if it is the last thing I do.'

Again the Professor said nothing; but he glanced at Eliot, and I saw the perturbation and horror in his eyes. I wondered if he knew how the vampire might be killed. I wondered if he thought we had any hope at all.

Later that evening, once Lucy had been tended to and sedated, we met for a conference in the drawing room. Eliot described to Westcote our pursuit of the woman we had known as Lady Mowberley; then, in response to the poor man's disbelieving questions, the Professor explained the nature of vampirism and its prevalence in a land of which I had already heard much, the kingdom of Kalikshutra where his sister had been lost. 'Lost in every way,' muttered Westcote. 'Lost in hell.' He glanced at the Professor. 'Is there any hope for her, do you think?'

The Professor reached for Westcote's hand. The gesture spoke louder than any words.

'The letters, then,' asked Westcote, 'the ones I received from my father's subaltern – fakes, you think? All of them – fakes?'

The Professor nodded, still wordlessly.

Westcote buried his head in his hands. 'So there was never any need for her to have been found in India – for she had been in England all the while. What an idiot I have been!' he cried. 'What a dupe! But how could I have known?' He lifted his head and stared round at us imploringly. 'How could I ever have guessed it? – that my sister was ... that she had become ...'

'A vampire?' It was Eliot who had spoken. 'Yes, that is the word you must use. It is difficult, I know, even to utter it, still less to contemplate the full horror of its meaning. You must, though. For they thrive on their victims' scepticism, as I know to my own cost all too well.'

Poor Westcote ran his fingers through his hair. 'But why? What has been her purpose? Why this adoption of the role of Lady Mowberley?'

'She has been acting as another's agent, I believe.'

'Another's?'

Eliot nodded. 'The solution is regrettably self-evident. Your sister was lost in Kalikshutra, where she was presumed to be dead; but in fact, as we now know, she had come to England to serve the purpose of those who had made her what she was – a vampire – a creature of their will. And it was as such a creature, no doubt, that she travelled to Whitby, where she destroyed and took the place of Sir George's bride-to-be.'

'But why such interest in Sir George?' asked Westcote in disbelief. 'Why go to these remarkable lengths?'

'Because Sir George, at the time, had just entered the India Office, with responsibility for the Indian frontier – on which, as you will remember, Kalikshutra lies. Do not forget also the peculiar circumstances of Sir George's engagement: he had not seen his wife-to-be for almost seven years and it was this, I am certain, which sealed both their dooms, for it ensured that an imposter would be able to pass unrecognised. Clearly, your sister had been seized and bent to the will of someone who had needed just such an imposter, as part of her scheme to protect Kalikshutra from possible annexation. She had wanted an agent in the Minister's very bed.'

'She?' exclaimed Westcote. 'But who is this "she"?'

Eliot made no reply; instead, he rose and stared out into the darkness of the street.

'Answer me, Eliot! Who is this person? Damn it!' he exclaimed in sudden fury. 'This "she" may have Arthur, my child!'

Eliot turned to face him again. 'No,' he said slowly.

'What do you mean, no?'

'Lady Mowberley ... Charlotte ... it is she who has your child.

Forget this other person. She is beyond our reach. It is your sister we must hunt down.'

'But how can you be so certain that she is the one who has Arthur?'

'Because Charlotte has an interest in your son which is hers alone.'

'What do you mean?'

Eliot approached Westcote; he touched him on his shoulder. 'When Lucy married you,' he continued gently, 'she presented Charlotte with an unexpected problem. Clearly, your sister could not allow herself to be seen by you – that would have exposed her identity utterly. Hence the refusal even to meet with you once. But Lucy's marriage also presented her with a source of unexpected pleasure. You will recall, perhaps, how eager she grew to see Lucy once your child had been born?'

'Yes. Encouraged by you, as I seem to remember.'

Eliot bowed his head in a gesture of regret, but Westcote seemed scarcely to observe this. His face appeared numbed by a rising sense of fear. 'Go on,' he whispered at length.

Eliot swallowed. 'The vampire is drawn to shared blood.'

'Shared?'

'The blood of a relative,' interposed the Professor. 'It gives them, as Jack has put it, an especial pleasure.'

'You mean Arthur?' Westcote stared at him in horrified disbelief. 'My son? Charlotte has been attracted by her own nephew's blood?'

The Professor shifted and sighed. 'I am afraid so, yes.'

Westcote's face crumpled. 'Then by now, she will have . . .'

'Killed him?' The Professor shook his head. 'It is, of course, possible. However, from my study of these creatures I think it unlikely. It appears to be the custom to leave children until they are of an age to breed.'

'To breed?'

'The blood-line,' said the Professor softly. 'It must be – perpetuated – you see. If anyone is in danger from her . . .'

'Yes?'

346

'Then I'm afraid that it is you.'

Westcote nodded slowly. 'Yes, of course, of course.' Suddenly his face seemed positively to beam with relief. 'Then there is hope, you think? My son may still be alive? You think that is possible?'

'I am sure there is still hope.'

'How are we to find him?'

Eliot sighed. 'It may be difficult. While we were away on our wild goose-chase to Yorkshire, your sister would have had all the time she needed to conceal your son. Judging by the skill with which she has orchestrated the rest of her plot, her hideaway will have been carefully prepared.'

'But what can we do? We can't just wait here, doing nothing at all.'

'For now,' replied the Professor, 'difficult though it will be, we have no other choice. And in the meantime, of course, there is always your wife to protect.'

'Yes,' said Westcote, 'yes, of course.' And again his spirits seemed to revive. 'She, at least, we *know* is still alive.'

'Exactly so!' exclaimed the Professor, clapping together his hands. 'And let us do all we can to ensure she stays that way. After all – we are not defeated yet!' And as he proclaimed this, I could almost imagine he believed it to be true; as we sat there, we four, drawing up our plans, with all the Professor's knowledge of the Undead at our service, and Eliot's keen brain, and Westcote's courage, I could truly believe that the game was not yet lost. The Professor spoke encouragingly of a plant by the name of Kirghiz Silver, an infallible cure it seemed against the vampire's threat; he would travel the next day to Kew, and search for it in the hothouses of the Gardens there. Eliot, meanwhile, would tend to Lucy; Westcote would guard her; and I – I would stand guard over both of them. And so it was.

That night, Westcote and I stayed on watch in Lucy's room. The poor girl was still sound asleep – the effect, no doubt, of the sedatives – but although she would stir occasionally and mutter in her dreams, I could still – looking upon her dear, sweet face – remember the Lucy of a month before, and pray that she would soon be restored to us all.

My hopes, so badly damaged by recent events, began to stir and flutter feebly again.

And then at four o'clock, shortly before we were due to be relieved, I heard the rumbling of a carriage from the street below. It halted directly outside Westcote's door; several minutes passed, and still it did not continue on its way. Feeling perturbed by now, I crossed to the window and stared down at the street. The carriage was directly below me; a cloaked figure was leaning out from it, smelling the air – or more properly, I guessed, the scent of someone's blood. He or she – I could not make out the sex of the figure – glanced up at me for the fraction of a second; I had the general impression of a remarkable pallor, and then the figure had withdrawn and the carriage was on its way. Even now, I am still not certain who it was I saw that night. At the time, of course, I assumed it to be Charlotte Westcote; but a conversation I overheard some hours later, while the Professor and Eliot were together on watch, alerted me to the likelihood of it being the mysterious "she".

'I must visit her,' Eliot kept saying, 'you know that. It is the only way we will ever have a resolution. I *must* visit her.'

The Professor disagreed. 'It is too dangerous. She is deadly.' I strained to catch more, but at this point they lowered their voices, and what else they talked about I couldn't tell. Of one thing, however, I was certain; the woman they were discussing was not Charlotte Westcote.

Despite my feelings of unease, however, I slept soundly from then on, for the last two days had been tiring ones, and when I woke again it was almost midday. I rose and, as I was climbing the stairs to Lucy's bedroom, met the Professor coming down. The moment I saw his face, I knew his tidings were bad; I asked what news there was and he, without a word, turned and led me back up to Lucy's room. Eliot was bending over his patient; he looked tired and distressed, and when he rose to greet me I at once understood why. For I could see now that Lucy had been bound to her bed: she was writhing uncontrollably and hissing almost like a snake, while her face was a parody of the one I knew so well – cruel, voluptuous and adamantine. I stood over her; and when she saw me her eyes blazed with unholy light, and the face became wreathed with a wanton smile. 'Free me, Bram,' she whispered. 'You have always wanted me, haven't you? So fresh and soft – so unlike your wife.' She laughed. 'My arms are hungry for you, Bram. Free me and we can rest together. Free me, Bram, free me!'

There was something so diabolically sweet in her tones, like the tingling of glass when struck by a knife, that it was all I could do to look away from her. 'My God,' I asked Eliot, 'what is happening to her?'

He compressed his lips. 'The disease,' he said, perfectly calmly, 'appears to be spreading through her veins.'

'Is there nothing you can do?' I asked.

Eliot shrugged. 'I have taken a blood sample. I will try to run tests on it. However ...' – he paused – 'I must be honest with you ... I am not hopeful.'

The Professor grunted. 'There may still be cures beyond the reach of science.' He turned and wandered back across to the door. 'I shall be leaving now as well. I have a cab below, to take me to Kew. We will see what effect the Kirghiz Silver has.' He bowed to us both in the Hindoo fashion; then he trotted down the stairs. Eliot followed him. I was left alone with – Lucy, I was going to write ... but let me say rather – the Thing which wore Lucy's name and form, for of her former sweet nature there was nothing left at all. The girl I had known was gone; sitting there with her that day, I felt like a mourner at her wake.

And now, with a dread heart, I approach the climax of this tale. I was joined that afternoon by Westcote. He had clearly been forewarned of Lucy's condition, for he concealed his evident agony and sat with her patiently, despite the combination of blandishments and abuse with which she sought to persuade him to set her free. I realised how grievously I had underestimated him; for the man I sat with that afternoon was a husband worthy of Lucy's love. The hours passed and Westcote's fortitude was tested to the limits; yet he never once wavered in his duty to his wife.

At around six there was a knocking on the door; Westcote left the room and stood listening on the balcony; it was a letter which must have been delivered, for I heard the maid coming up the stairs to where he stood, and when he returned to Lucy's room he had an envelope tucked into his jacket pocket. He did not mention its contents to me, however, and so I did not choose to press him; I assumed its business was private. He sat down again by Lucy's side; he held her hand but she wrenched it free. He tried to hold her; she spat in his face. The pain in his expression was terrible to witness. He rose, with her laughter ringing in his ears, and moved to the window, where he repeatedly clenched and unclenched his fists.

'I cannot bear this,' he said as I crossed to join him.

'The others will be back soon,' I replied, trying to comfort him.

'Yes,' said Westcote desperately, staring at his wife, 'but when? They have been away for hours.' He gestured at Lucy. 'Look at her, Stoker. She is growing worse. Eliot should be here. I have half a mind to go and fetch him myself.'

'We should wait,' I repeated.

Westcote shook his head. 'We can't,' he said simply. He stared into my eyes. 'Stoker – please. Go to Eliot. Tell him it is urgent.'

'I don't want to leave you.'

'Damn it,' said Westcote, 'it is my wife, not myself, we should be worrying about now. Just look at her!' He pointed at Lucy again. 'Damn it, she needs Eliot as soon as she can. Now, Stoker, *now!*'

I saw, in short, that he would not be appeased until he had had his way. It was with a heavy heart, though, that I left for Whitechapel, urging my driver to go as fast as he could. Eliot, when I found him, was still hard at work, crouched over slides and tubes, but once I had explained the situation to him he rose and came back with me immediately. He told me as we went that he still did not hold out much hope; his research, it seemed, was not proceeding well. For my own part, my regret at having left Westcote alone with his wife was intensifying all the time, so that neither of us was feeling greatly at ease.

Unfortunately, since my drive across to Whitechapel, the traffic had grown considerably worse, and it took us longer than it should have done to return to Westcote's house. By now, such was the nature of the presentiments affecting us that we were almost desperate. We ran up to the door; and when the maid answered our hammerings I at once began to ask her if all was well in the house. She seemed puzzled. Of course all was well, she replied. Her master and mistress were both still upstairs; why, they had even had a visitor.

At once, I froze. Who had the visitor been, I inquired. Her master's sister, the servant replied. Miss Westcote had brought Arthur with her, she added, as we sprinted up the stairs. She had heard Miss Westcote leave perhaps twenty minutes ago.

I scarcely registered that final comment; yet once I had entered Lucy's room and seen how her bed was empty, with all the restraints snapped and tossed on to the floor, I understood at last what the maid had said. 'She has taken Lucy!' I exclaimed, before the horror of it struck me dumb, and I slumped on to the bed in a numbed state of grief.

'Here,' said Eliot, from behind the open door.

'What is it?' I asked, scarcely lifting my head.

Eliot shut the door and I saw there was a chair against the wall. Westcote was slumped in it, for all the world as though taking an afternoon nap. Carefully, Eliot lifted his chin. I saw to my shock, but scarcely my surprise, that he was quite dead; his skin had been bleached to an unnatural paleness, and the bones beneath the flesh seemed brittle and thin. There were dreadful gashes to his stomach and throat, but again the wounds seemed perfectly dry. Eliot continued to inspect him.

'Drained,' he said at last. 'There is scarcely a drop of blood left in him. But it is puzzling . . .'

'Why?' I asked, as his voice trailed away. 'Surely it is his sister's doing?'

'Oh, evidently,' Eliot replied, 'but that is not what is puzzling me. No, what is strange is that he appears to have put up no fight. It is almost as though he sat here and welcomed it . . .' He continued to frown; and then suddenly I saw his haggard face light up. He leaned forward and took something from Westcote's pocket. 'You mentioned a letter that came for him.' He held up an envelope. 'Was it this one?'

I inspected it shortly, then nodded. 'It may have been.'

'And it was after receiving this letter that Westcote demanded you go away?'

Again I nodded.

Eliot removed the letter from the envelope. 'Let us see what was in it, then,' he murmured, almost to himself. He scanned the letter. 'I recognise the handwriting, at least. Lady Mowberley's – or Charlotte Westcote's, I should say. Now then. To the letter itself.' He began to read. '*Dear Ned – It is no good, you know. You will never defeat me. Ask Jack Eliot – he will tell you as much, for he knows it in his heart. But I have a bargain to propose. I must have Westcote blood, you see – if not yours, then another Westcote's will do. I think you understand me. A life for a life, Ned – yours for your son's. What do you say? I know you have one of your friends with you now. Send him away. When I see him go, I will accept that as a signal that you have agreed to my proposal and I will join you promptly. I am so sorry, Ned. But as you may have realised, I am no longer myself. Such is – or was, at any rate – life. Your loving sister, C.*'

Eliot paused, then folded the letter away. He stared down at Westcote again; he closed his eyes.

'So Westcote agreed then, you think?' I asked. 'He sat here and allowed her to drink his life away?'

'Evidently,' replied Eliot.

I was struck again by the horror of what we were confronting. I gazed about the room, making certain – after what I had heard Eliot read – that Arthur had indeed been taken, and was not there after all. But there was no sign of him. 'She betrayed him,' I said bitterly. 'He gave her his life, and still she betrayed him.'

Eliot too had been studying the room. 'I am not so certain,' he replied.

'What do you mean?' I asked.

'There is a mystery here.' He gestured at the door. 'Observe the hand prints on the very base.'

I had not noticed them before. But now that I looked, I saw that Eliot was perfectly correct and that there were indeed hand-prints, very tiny, marked in blood.

'Only a young child could have left these,' said Eliot, 'which corroborates the maid's evidence: Arthur was indeed here. That should not be surprising, of course – Westcote would hardly have surrendered his life so willingly if Charlotte had not brought Arthur with her. But the evidence surely suggests that these prints were left here once Charlotte had gone. When else would the child have got the blood on his hands? Not during the attack itself – that is highly improbable. No, no, it must have been when he was left here alone with his father's corpse. Doubtless he clung to his father, seeking comfort; and when none was forthcoming he attempted to scratch his way out through the door. Yes,' said Eliot, staring at the handprints again, 'it is all quite clear.'

'But in that case . . .' I said slowly.

'Yes?' Eliot asked.

I looked about the room again. 'Where *is* the child?'

Eliot gestured at the windows. For the first time I saw that they were open, and had obviously been forced for a pane of glass had been smashed from the outside on to the floor.

'So you think . . .' – I swallowed – 'what . . .? – someone came in through there?'

He nodded shortly.

'But . . . Charlotte – when she took Lucy – they left through the front door. The servant girl heard them.'

'Then doubtless,' said Eliot, 'we are dealing with someone other than her.'

'Another vampire, you mean?'

He shrugged faintly. It was as good as a nod.

'Who?' I asked.

'That,' said Eliot, 'is the mystery.'

And so it remains. That Eliot had his own suspicions, I was certain at the time; and subsequent events have confirmed as much. For he was eager all that afternoon to pursue the leads which he believed would still resolve the case; once the Professor had returned from Kew and seen for himself the catastrophe, Eliot began to speak to him in the same terms I had overheard the night before, talking of the 'she' who had to be confronted – not Charlotte but another, even deadlier. The Professor, however, refused to countenance the attempt, not until they were better prepared; brave man though he is, he insisted that the woman was too dangerous as yet; he demanded that Eliot delay his attempt. Reluctantly, Eliot appeared to agree; and so we left it on the evening of that terrible day. Before we parted, however, the Professor gave us all a bulb of Kirghiz Silver, which he promised would preserve us from the vampire's thirst. It was certainly a remarkable looking plant, and reassuringly out-landish. I have worn it about me ever since.

Whether Eliot did, however, we may never know. For despite his promise to delay his investigation, that very same evening he disappeared. Neither the Professor nor myself have caught a glimpse of him since. He left no message in his study, not even a scrap of paper; instead, he has vanished as utterly as Lucy or her child. I wonder whether we shall ever see any of them again. The Professor and myself have continued our search, but we have very few clues and those we did have now seem to be gone. For the Professor revealed to me – what I had not at first guessed – that the woman mentioned by Eliot and himself had lived in Rotherhithe, in that very same warehouse from which we had rescued Sir George. Of course, as soon as it was evident that Eliot had disappeared, we sped there at once; but there was now no trace of the warehouse at all – it was utterly gone. Even Polidori's shop had been boarded up, and although we forced our way inside, we found no evidence there which might have helped us with our search.

What else we can do, I find it hard now to know. We have contacted the police, of course, but a case such as this is beyond their ability to solve; they are in any case preoccupied at the moment with the Whitechapel murders, and the demands of the public that their perpetrator be found. In effect, we remain as we were before: alone. The Professor is content that this should be so; he knows that the reality of the vampire is all too easily scorned.

But for all his expertise, we remain no nearer a solution to the case: Eliot, Lucy, her child, all are gone, and the vampires too are dispersed God knows where. Somewhere in the foul shadows they must be lurking – not only Charlotte but also the mysterious, unnameable 'she' – and I hope there may yet be a breakthrough in our investigation; but I have my doubts. I wish I did not have to finish my narrative in such a despairing frame of mind, but since it has been my determination to invent nothing throughout, I conclude, as I started, by telling the truth. I lay down my pen now in the hope that one day I have cause to pick it up again. Pray God, when that occurs, I may have something happier to write.

Letter, Professor Huree Jyoti Navalkar to Mr Bram Stoker.

16, Bloomsbury Square.

20 September 1888.

Dear Mr Stoker,

I must thank you most gratefully for the loan of your narrative. I believe it to be accurate in all the essentials. If you wish to pursue vampirology further, perhaps I could recommend a book of my own, *The Vampire Myths of India and Roumania: A Comparative Study.* Although I say it myself, it is excellent. However, beware! – although the nature of the vampire is unchanging, different cultural understandings of this nature can be exceedingly varied. As a Britisher, you will be more familiar with the Roumanian as opposed to the Indian breed. May I suggest in particular the chapters on Transylvania? Jolly interesting.

I have also been remembering our conversation, where you discussed with me your intention of adapting your narrative into a novel or a play. It was very kind of you, I must say, to consider me as a model for the hero of such a work. Please, though, Mr Stoker, I must insist that you abandon that particular idea; if you can make of me the hero of a romance, then I am a Dutchman. Invent, Mr Stoker – always invent. Otherwise, no one will believe you at all.

I will, of course, inform you at once if I hear any news. My hopes for our dear friend, though, are fading by the day.

Guard yourself, Mr Stoker,

Your colleague,

HUREE JYOTI NAVALKAR.

Reminiscence composed by Detective Inspector 'Steve' White, relating to the events of 30 September 1888.

For five nights we had been watching a certain alley just behind the Whitechapel Road. It could only be entered from where we had two men posted in hiding, and persons entering the alley were under observation by the two men. It was a bitter cold night when I arrived at the scene to take the report of the two men in hiding. I was turning away when I saw a man coming out of the alley. He was walking quickly but noiselessly. I stood aside to let the man pass, and as he came under the wall lamp I got a good look at him.

He was about five feet ten inches in height, and was dressed rather shabbily, though it was obvious that the material of his clothes was good. His face was long and thin, nostrils rather delicate, and his hair was jet-black. His complexion was inclined to be sallow, as though he had been for some time in the tropics. The most striking thing about him, however, was the extraordinary brilliance of his eyes. They looked like two very luminous glow-worms coming through the darkness. The man was slightly bent at the shoulders, though he was obviously quite young – about thirty-three, at the

356

most – and gave one the idea of having been a student or professional man. His hands were snow-white, and the fingers long and tapering.

As the man passed me at the lamp I had an uneasy feeling that there was something more than usually sinister about him, and I was strongly moved to find some pretext for detaining him; but the more I thought it over, the more was I forced to the conclusion that it was not in keeping with British police methods that I should do so. My only excuse for interfering with the passage of this man would have been his association with the man we were looking for, and I had no real grounds for connecting him with the murder. It is true I had a sort of intuition that the man was not quite right. Still, if one acted on intuition in the police force, there would be more frequent outcries about interference with the liberty of subject, and at that time the police were criticised enough to make it undesirable to take risks.

The man stumbled a few feet away from me, and I made that an excuse for engaging him in conversation. He turned sharply at the sound of my voice and scowled at me in surly fashion, but he said 'Good-night' and agreed with me that it was cold.

His voice was a surprise to me. It was soft and musical, with just a tinge of melancholy in it, and it was the voice of a man of culture – a voice altogether out of keeping with the squalid surroundings of the East End.

As he turned away, one of the police officers came out of the house he had been in, and walked a few paces into the darkness of the alley. 'Hello! what is this?' he cried, and then he called in startled tones to me to come along.

In the East End we are used to shocking sights, but the sight I saw made the blood in my veins turn to ice. At the end of the cul-de-sac, huddled against the wall, there was the body of a woman, and a pool of blood was streaming along the gutter from her body. It was clearly another of those terrible murders. I remembered the man I had seen, and I started after him as fast as I could run, but he was lost to sight in the dark labyrinth of the East End mean streets.

357

Telegram, Professor Huree Jyoti Navalkar to Mr Bram Stoker.

8 November.

Join me at once, 'Jack Straw's Castle', Highgate Hill. Urgent. Extraordinary developments. Will tell all when I see you.

HUREE

PART THREE

Letter, Professor Huree Jyoti Navalkar to Mr Bram Stoker.

Mahadevi,
Clive Street,
Calcutta.

31 October 1897

My dear Stoker,

It was good to hear from you after so many years. My thanks for the copy of *Dracula*, which I read last night. It is nonsense, of course – but entertaining nonsense. I predict that it will survive. The market for such stuff seems as enduring as your vampire Count himself.

It is because of this intuition – that *Dracula* will still be read in fifty, maybe even a hundred years – that I am sending you the enclosed bundle of manuscripts, and a book just published, *With Rifles in the Raj*. Read together, I trust they will provide an adequate record of those terrible events of almost a decade ago. It had always been my intention to preserve the papers, so that they might serve as a warning to those menaced by a similar threat; yet the very existence of much a record must inevitably endanger those who keep it, and I have been much troubled by the need to advertise what must at the same time be kept secret.

The publication of your novel, however, presents us with a possible solution: for while *Dracula* is clearly tinged throughout with melodrama and fantasy, yet for all that it is not so distant from the truth. It is my hope that those we aim to reach – those poor unfortunates menaced by the Living Dead – will recognise in your novel an echo of the dangers which they are facing themselves, and will consult your papers to discover what you know. Therefore – do this: deposit the enclosed collection of manuscripts with your lawyers; keep the collection's existence concealed; but leave instructions that those who claim to be menaced by creatures such as your Count, and seem truthful, are to be shown the papers. Such an arrangement is hardly perfect, I know; but I can think of no alternative. It is vital that the papers themselves should survive.

I have thought it best to leave their ordering to you. Quite apart from your novelist's eye, you experienced some of the events described and should be familiar with the narrative. An episode which will surprise you, however, is detailed in a letter I received a couple of years ago. It provides a solution to many of the mysteries which puzzled us at the time and remained unanswered, even after that terrible night on Highgate Hill – as well as some other mysteries besides. I have placed the letter directly beneath this.

Good luck, Stoker. May the blessing of your god be with you.

Your old comrade in arms,

HUREE JYOTI NAVALKAR

Letter, Dr John Eliot to Professor Huree Jyoti Navalkar.

August 1895.

Huree,

Are you surprised, I wonder, to have this letter in your hand? It has been a long time since we were last together that night on Highgate Hill – I suppose you might have forgotten me. But I doubt it, somehow; just as I doubt you are surprised to be reading this, for I did promise you all those years ago that one day I would tell you everything. I like to think that I am a man of my word.

It was the box which persuaded me to go to Rotherhithe. I had not intended to confront her; not intended to flout your advice. You were right, of course, Huree: I should never have gone; it was folly, not courage, which took me there. And yet ... I repeat – there was the box as well, which I could never have ignored.

It was waiting for me that night of Westcote's death, waiting on my desk. It was made of rough wood and painted red; there were Chinese letters down one of the sides; clearly it had once been used for the transport of opium, but not now, I knew – not now. With trembling hands, I removed the lid. Inside, the box was empty save for a piece of stiff card. I inspected it. I had observed the handwriting at once, of course, purple like that on the card sent to George; a cursory inspection proved the ink to be water and blood. The script, also as before, was clearly feminine; this time, however, there had been no attempt to disguise the hand, for it was of a quite remarkable elegance and not clumsy at all. Indeed, in the beauty of its style it seemed almost to belong to a different age. Its message was one you may recognise. *'How often have I said to you that when you have eliminated the impossible, whatever remains,* however improbable, *must be the truth?'* Literature records this as a saying of Sherlock Holmes; but it was in truth a maxim of Dr Joseph Bell, the teacher of both Conan Doyle and myself, and one which I had often mentioned to Suzette. She, in turn, had answered me by phrasing my own growing fear: 'But what if the impossible *is* the truth?'

As I held that card, alone in my room, I knew for certain she had written it. I saw quite clearly – suddenly understood – the web of evil which had been woven around me, all those long past months, by the darkness lurking like the spider in its heart – spinning, endlessly spinning, sensitive to every thrashing movement I had made, binding and drawing me in all the time. And now, I knew, that darkness was very close. The crisis had arrived. How could I escape it? There was no escape. I could only face it and play the game to its end.

I left that night. I took a gun with me, and the bulb of Kirghiz Silver worn in a pouch concealed beneath my shirt. I had expected to discover Lilah's warehouse straight away, but although I searched I could not find the streets which led to its door. Frustrated, I returned to the High Street and thence to Coldlair Lane. Polidori's shop, as before, was boarded up. I knocked on the door; there was no reply. I tried to force it, but the lock was too strong. I took a couple of steps back into the street and stared up at the top-floor window, but there was no light that I could make out, not even the flicker of an opium pipe, and just as on our previous visit it seemed as though the place had been utterly abandoned. Disappointed thus a second time, I turned and began to walk from the shop; then – on an instinct, I suppose – I glanced round again and, as I did so, for a second saw a face. It was pressed against a window pane, staring wildly from the top floor down into the street, and although it was gone as soon as I had glimpsed it I had recognised it immediately. The face at the window had been Mary Jane Kelly's.

I realised I would have to break through the front of the shop. Fortunately the street was deserted, and my efforts at pulling down the boards were not observed. Once I had smashed the window and passed inside, I hurried upstairs, braced for anything, but when I pulled aside the curtain it was to find that the room was empty after all, wholly denuded of people and furniture, with nothing to suggest they had ever been there. Only when I inspected the window pane did I discover evidence that I had not indeed been hallucinating, for fingerprints in blood had been left smeared upon the glass, and when I studied the floor carefully I found further traces of blood in a line of tiny dots. These ran towards the door in the far wall – beyond which, you will remember, was the bridge across the water to the warehouse door. Naturally I tried to force my way through, but the door had been secured too well and this time, unfortunately, there seemed no other way of breaking through.

To my intense frustration, therefore, I found I had little choice but to leave the room and go back into the street, as distant from my goal as I had been before. I began to wander down the High Street. A mist was rolling in from the Thames. At first, such was my self-absorption, I was scarcely conscious of it, until I suddenly realised that it had blotted out not only the lights, but also the noise from the taverns and pubs, the rattle of vehicles, the footsteps of other men on the road. I stared about me but I could see nothing, hear nothing: I seemed utterly alone. I called out; my voice was swallowed by a bank of brown fog. I stopped, and after a few minutes there came a gap in the mist, but as I stared along the street I realised that I was still alone, for although the lamps were flickering the street was quite deserted and the windows of the houses and taverns were dark. I called out again; still there was no reply. Then the mists began to thicken again and I felt their dankness sucking on my skin.

Suddenly, I felt a touch on my shoulder. I spun round. There was a man behind me, but his face was hidden beneath a muffler and cap. 'Looking for something?' he asked. Beneath the folds of his scarf, he seemed to wink at me. 'Looking for some fun?'

'Fun?'

'Fun!' The man began to laugh. He pointed back up the street. I stared, but could see nothing. The man was still laughing like an idiot. I reached for his scarf, I pulled it away. His eyes were quite dead, his skin like a corpse's; I remembered how the riverman had shot him on the Thames. 'Fun!' he kept repeating, over and over, and pointing with a bleached finger back up the street.

From the muffled depths of the fog, I heard the rolling of a carriage's wheels. Slowly, I began to walk towards the noise. The fog seemed to be dizzying my brain, much as I remembered the opium had done when I had gone with Stoker into Polidori's den. I peered back through the wreaths of brown haze. The dead thing was still watching me, laughing all the more. Then shadows of spokes began to wheel through the mist, and I turned again. There was a whinnying and a clattering of hooves, and I heard the carriage rumble to a halt. I could see it now, a blot of darkness waiting for me in the shadows beyond the street lights' yellow gleam. I walked past the horses and stood by the carriage's side. The silence, like the mist, was thick all around me; the very horses seemed frozen by it. Then suddenly there was a click from the carriage door, and I saw it hang ajar. I felt desire in a hot flush reach into my bones.

'Come to me.' The whisper seemed to arise from nowhere and seep through my every emotion, my every thought.

'Lilah,' I answered. 'Lilah.' I reached for the door; I opened it . . . I stepped inside.

I knew her at once. She was just as I had always glimpsed her: Lilah, and yet not Lilah: skin as pale as the gleam of ice, lips as red as a venomous flower, eyes cold, bright with lust and malignant pride. I reached out in wonder to stroke the coils of blonde hair that framed her deadly, perfect face, more beautiful than it was possible for a woman's to be, fairer than heaven, crueller than hell, lovely beyond terror and human belief. 'Lilah,' I whispered again. It was not a question but a shudder, rather, of comprehension and need. She smiled; her bright lips parted and I saw the gleam of teeth behind the flaming red. She stroked my neck; her touch was a wonderful, impossible thing.

'Come to me.' The words were like caresses, scorching my mind. 'Come to me.'

I gasped. I turned, seeking her mouth, but her finger was on my chin and I felt her lips touch my throat, and then my skin seemed to be melting – absorbed into the moisture and warmth of her kiss, oozing and running in a stream across my chest, a sticky, fleshy brew that was mingling with her own. I reached to touch the flow; and as I did so my fingers brushed the bulb in its pouch.

I heard a snarling, stinging hiss, like a cat leaping back from a singeing flame; and then I was alone again. I looked about me. I was lying on a dark corner of pavement, my head against a wall. I heard the sound of distant laughter, the chink of bottles from noisy pubs; wheels were rumbling across cobblestones; footsteps hurrying. The air was quite clear; the mist was gone; of the carriage and the woman, there was no sign at all. Slowly I rose to my feet; I rubbed my eyes. I began to walk down the High Street again.

The turning which led to the warehouse was where I had expected to find it. As I entered the unlit street, the noises behind me faded again; soon there was no sound at all but that of my own feet, taking me towards the warehouse door. It was open. I passed through it.

Inside, Suzette was waiting for me. She raised her arm, and pointed. 'Very close now,' she whispered.

'I know,' I replied. I walked across the hall, I opened the door. Inside the single candle was burning as before, beneath the picture of Lilah where it hung on the wall. I stared at it without looking to either the left or the right; then I shut the door behind me. As I did so I heard a splash: liquid hitting liquid. Slowly I turned. I stared into the darkness . . . and found that I could see.

A body was hanging from a hook, skewered through the feet. It was quite naked, and very white. I recognised the corpse from its face: one of the addicts from the opium den. A droplet of blood was welling out from the nostrils; it stretched; it fell. Then another: blood on blood. There was a bath, filled with blood. The bath was made from jewel-emblazoned gold, but the blood was even richer – even more lovely than the finest gold. It shimmered; if I stared long enough, I knew, I might see beauties undreamed of by the human mind. There was another splash. How wonderfully it was received, and stilled, and absorbed. All the world might be so absorbed ... all the universe ... stilled into blood. I took a step forward. The blood and gold seemed to merge, then pulse and ripple like waves of purest sound. I wanted to be a part of it, I wanted its mystery. Another splash – I looked up at the addict's frozen, drained face: his eyeballs were bulging like skinless grapes. I shuddered suddenly, and reached for the bulb in its pouch around my neck.

I heard laughter, so mocking and terrible that I had to put my hands to my ears. 'You clutch and paw at your talisman,' I heard; 'but still you come.'

She stirred in her bath. Her blonde locks were quite unstained; her ice-white arms still gleamed through the red. She washed her breasts with a lazy sweep of her arm; then lolled back again with a languorous sigh. 'Yes,' she murmured, 'still you come.' She inclined her head and fixed me with her stare. 'How amusing you are.' She smiled. 'So desperate for what I have. So afraid of what you might become. I am really very grateful. It is rare for a mortal to entertain me, you should know.'

She smiled again, then stretched and laid her head against the gold. With a caress of her hand, she wiped her pale cheeks with blood. When she removed her fingers, not a streak or stain was left: it was as though her flesh were a sponge, I realised, drinking up the blood, gorging on the fluids of another person's life. With a contented sigh she lowered her head, smoothed out the tresses of her blonde hair through the blood. 'More,' she murmured, 'more, this one is almost drained.' She waved vaguely with her hand. 'Hurry, Polidori, I want a flood of it.'

He must have been standing in the shadows, for I had not observed him previously. Now, as he stepped forward, he fixed me with a twisted leer of acknowledgement and contempt; then he turned and tugged on a golden chain. The corpse began to sway and come swinging down. From the corner of my eye I watched Polidori lay the body on the floor, then start to ease the hook out from the ankle bones – but I could not concentrate on the sight. How could I have done? For she was washing herself again, soaping her breasts and cheeks with the blood; and as she did so her skin seemed to radiate and pulse. It was changing, growing darker; her blonde hair too was shimmering into black.

'Bring her,' she ordered. The voice was still Lilah's, but her appearance was now that of an African girl – as terrible, as lovely as she had been before. I remembered Mary Kelly's description of the negress who had taken her and bled her wrists – a beauty so great that it chilled the very heart. I lowered my eyes before her gaze; and as I did so I heard the negress start to laugh. 'Bring her!' she cried; I imagined her laughter rising up within my mind.

'No,' I muttered, 'please, no.' Still she laughed. It seemed as though the noise were flaying me. Louder and louder it grew; and as it did so I heard the chinking of the hook as it swung on its chain. I turned. Polidori had a naked woman in his hands. He gripped her hair, forced her to her knees; with his other hand he reached for the hook. As he did so, his grip on the woman's hair yanked back her head. Her face was a mask of terror and pain and I scarcely recognised Mary Kelly. 'No!' I cried. I took a step forwards; I reached for my gun. 'No!'

For a second there was silence. The negress stared down the barrel of my gun; then suddenly she burst out laughing again. 'Let her go!' I said desperately. I turned the gun on Polidori. 'For God's sake, let her go!'

The negress tried to speak, but her words were lost on her laughter which broke like a wave, drowning everything she said.

'I will fire,' I said.

She only laughed the more.

Very coolly, I aimed the revolver. 'Let her go,' I repeated. Then I fired, once, twice. The bullets tore into her chest; for a second she looked surprised as she stared down at the wounds; then her eyes gleamed with delight.

'Wonderful,' she exclaimed, 'quite wonderful!' She paused, her laughter dying away. 'It's starting to bore me, though,' she said suddenly. She turned to Polidori. 'You may kill her now.'

Polidori reached for a knife. As he did so, I felt within my shirt and removed the Kirghiz Silver. At once there was a hissing intake of breath. I looked across the room at Polidori; he had lowered his eyes. He had begun to shake, I could see. I held out the bulb; he shuddered even more. Slowly I advanced on him, holding out the Kirghiz Silver in my palm, and as I stepped towards him so he shrank back and his hands fell by his sides. I reached out to take Mary Kelly's arm. She was still shivering in dumb amazement; only when I pulled her did she rise and follow me. I reached for her clothes, I handed them to her; with a sudden desperate comprehension, she slipped on her dress.

'Run,' I whispered in her ear, 'and keep hold of this.' I pressed the Kirghiz Silver into her palm. She stared down at it, still seeming utterly petrified. 'Do you understand?' I asked. 'Keep hold of it.' Mary Kelly looked up at me, her fingers closed around the bulb; then she nodded, and turned, and I heard her start to run. Her footsteps echoed away across the hall; there was the slamming of a door. I breathed in deeply. So she was gone; she had managed to reach the street.

'How wonderfully noble of you!'

The words were so mocking, they seemed like ice down my back. I looked about me. We were quite alone again, as we had been in the carriage in the street. The air of the room now was suffocating: ripe red, heavy with pollen and scent. Despite myself, I breathed it in. There were lilies and white roses, dotted with blood; in golden tripods perfumes burned: ambergris, champak and frankincense.

'But was I supposed to be impressed?' Lilah asked. 'Was I

supposed to be inspired? Was I supposed to send you forth with my blessings on your head, moved by your offer of sacrifice?' She paused, smiling up at me lazily. 'Or did you offer it as I take it – as an amusing joke? Certainly, it makes the fate I have in mind for you even more entertaining. Yes – even more droll!'

She laughed, glancing at her nails, her bright lips pursed. 'I have delayed this far too long, I think,' she murmured. One last time she stretched in her bath; then she stirred, and the whole room seemed to fall away as she began to rise – remorselessly, impossibly high, like Venus born from the foam of the sea. Blood, in a mantle of glistening scales, winked on her naked limbs, then shimmered and disappeared, so that she had the look of a serpent sloughing off its skin, chysalid and glittering in the low burning light. She wore only her jewellery, her bracelets and rings, while in her ears and round her neck gleamed the Kalikshutra gold; on her forehead was the mark of the eternal eye; set amidst her hair was the goddess Kali's crown.

'A Socialist,' she whispered, gazing at me, 'a labourer for the good of his fellow men.' She clapped her hands. 'How delightfully progressive!' She reached out and took me, and clasped me to her breast. 'I shall certainly keep you, and add you to my collection.' She smiled. 'Yes, for ever, I think.' She kissed me. Her words seemed to echo down the coils of my ears, ripple in waves through the whorls of my brain. It disoriented me. I could feel myself falling – down, down, into the waiting blood. I clung to Lilah. I was still in her arms. I looked about me. We were no longer in the room but running down steps – an infinity of steps, all different colours, curling in double spirals through space. I had climbed such staircases in the warehouse before; but never had I seen so many, mutating before my very gaze, a web of shifting colours, patterns and shapes. Dimly, I felt afraid of them – as though what I were seeing was mutating *me*. I had to escape. I had to break free from Lilah, from her twisting, softening limbs. But I was wedded to them; I could not even stir. For the blood she had absorbed was now sucking on me. I remembered how my neck had felt before, in the carriage, when it had seemed to melt and blend with the touch of her lips. But now my whole body was oozing away into a sticky quagmire of humid flesh, and I could gradually feel myself absorbed and then enclosed, sealed utterly within a womb of secretions that were fishy, salt and dank, distorting the distant pulse of my life, so that hearing it my existence seemed scarcely mine at all. Nor indeed was it – no – my blood was being pumped by another creature's heart. I was Lilah's thing now: jelly, placenta, albumen. A teeming mass of algae and buzzing cells ... a soup of tiny dots. And then, even they were gone. There was only red, beating with the pulse of Lilah's blood. Soon that too was silent. There was nothing at all. Nothing but darkness. Oblivion.

For how long I was lost, I do not know.

An eternity.

A second.

Both, perhaps.

The moment came, though, when I opened my eyes.

'She is waiting for you,' said Suzette.

'Waiting?'

'By the boat.'

She was smiling, I saw as she bent down and kissed me on my forehead. I stared at her and frowned. She seemed changed. How can I describe it, Huree? She was still Suzette, still the same little girl with party frock and plaited hair – but equally she was something quite different as well. I saw a face I had never glimpsed before: a woman's, of perhaps twenty-five to thirty years of age, stately, beautiful, brilliant. Distinguishing her, I would lose Suzette; and then Suzette would return and the other face depart. There are designs, ocular tricks – perhaps you have seen them – where a rabbit is also the head of a duck, or a goblet the profiles of two lovers preparing to kiss; both images are present, but the mind is unable to glimpse them simultaneously. So it was with Suzette, only in a way much more infinite and extraordinary; so it was with everything I saw. For standing by me, with fresh clothes in his hands, was the twisted dwarf; so ugly he was that I had barely been able to endure his presence before, yet when I looked at him now I could see how long-limbed he was, and beautiful; indeed the handsomest man I had ever seen. When I crossed the hall, and watched the panther sleeping curled up on the steps, it was not just an animal I saw; a woman was there too, dark and lovely and arrogant, her form and the panther's at once different and utterly the same. All the animals, all the creatures and beings in that place – I looked at them, and saw how they were all souls transformed, and I felt, to my surprise, not horror but exultation; not disgust but delight.

I turned to Suzette. 'And me?' I asked. 'Show me. What have *I* become?'

Suzette – or rather, the woman who was also Suzette – smiled faintly. 'Here,' she said. We were in the conservatory. She led me across to one of the ponds. The water was as still and pure as glass. I stared into it, then I shut my eyes. Opening them, I looked again. 'I don't understand,' I murmured. 'What has happened?' For my face, in the water, seemed exactly the same.

Suzette took my arm. She began to lead me on.

'Has there been no change at all, then?' I asked.

Suzette did not reply. Instead, she paused by a wall of iron and glass; she took out a key and unlocked the door.

'Tell me,' I said. 'What have I become?'

Suzette gestured at the darkness that lay beyond the door. 'Hurry,' she whispered. 'Lilah will be waiting for you. She has a game to play, then you will understand.' She turned and ran; I was left alone. So I did as she had ordered, and stepped out beyond the glass.

I was in the open again, in the London night. There was a staircase of winding metal ahead of me which clung down the side of a grimy harbour wall. I could hear the lapping of water from below; at the foot of the steps was a tiny boat, and I began to climb down towards it. At the oars was the creature who had rowed it before. Although I stared at him, I could not see what other form he might once have worn. 'Jack!' cried Lilah. She was waiting for me in the prow of the boat. She smiled. 'My very own philanthropist.' Her smile deepened. 'Hurry, Jack, hurry.' I joined her and she folded me in her arms. She gave the order to pull away; the oars began to chop and we glided out from between the narrow walls. Beyond was the mighty expanse of the Thames.

We joined the river's flow. As the creature pulled at his oars, Lilah nestled my head on her lap and began gently to stroke my hair. I stared up at the sky. It was a dull and ominous shade of red. For some reason the very sight of it cast a pall across my spirits; my mood of exaltation began to fade, and in its place I felt a gnawing sense of unease. I stirred; I couldn't bear not to see the stars, blotted out by the glow of the city, as though London were seeping across the sky. I remembered the vision Lilah had shown me – of the city as a creature flayed of its skin, with the Thames as its artery, thick with living blood. I shifted again, stared out up-river; but the waters did not seem like life-blood now. I trailed my fingers through them, and they felt as they looked, greasy with ordure, and putrefaction, and death. Beyond their flow I could see the lights of the City winking mockingly at me; bright, they looked, exceedingly bright – but again, I wasn't fooled. For death was there too, bred from the dung of gold and human greed; death was in everything, everywhere I looked, in the seething darkness of that monstrous, brooding town. I remembered a visit I had made once to a patient's house, when I had brushed against a wall and knocked out a lump of crumbling brick; I had looked at what lay beneath it, and seen a solid block of swarming, creeping things. I shuddered at the memory; then stared at the river bank ahead of us again. If I were to knock against it, tumble the buildings like plaster to the ground, I would see the very same thing I had seen in that house: vermin, blind and crawling, feeding on dung.

There was a jolt; I woke from my thoughts. We had reached the quays on the northern bank. I heard drunken, reechy laughter; saw twisted silhouettes beneath shrill jets of flame. I shuddered. The very thought of stepping on to such a place filled me with disgust. I wrapped myself in my long black cloak as Lilah smiled and helped me from the boat. As her own cloak parted, I saw for the first time that she was wearing an evening gown. I too had been garbed in formal attire: top hat on my head, tails beneath my cloak. I wondered where we could be going that night. I asked, but Lilah just pressed a finger to my lips. 'You are going to entertain me,' she whispered very softly in my ear. Then she turned back to the boat and took a black Gladstone bag from the oarsman's outstretched hands.

'What is it?' I asked, as she passed it on to me.

'Why, your medical bag,' she replied.

'Medical bag?'

'You are a doctor, aren't you?' She laughed; then led me, before I could ask more, across the filth-littered quay. A carriage was waiting for us. We both climbed in; the wheels began to turn, slicing through mud. As we jolted, I heard the pulping of rotten vegetables and fruit. I looked out through the window – again, the shudder of physical disgust. The buildings like a fungus, risen from the dirt. People everywhere I looked – greasy, stinking, predatory; quivering sacks of intestine and fat. How was it I had never realised this before – how ugly the poor were, how loathsome, the way they dared to live and breed? We passed a tavern. I heard the smacking of lips and the splash and swirl of liquids down throats, the belching of gas, the animal laughter and slobber of chat. One of the men turned and stared at me. I wanted to vomit. His hair, Huree – his hair was damp with grease; his skin slimy; there was nothing in him, not the faintest spark, nothing at all that seemed worthy of life. I leaned back against my seat.

'For God's sake,' I gasped, 'we must get out of here.'

Lilah stroked my brow.

'Tell me,' I insisted, 'where are we going?'

She smiled. 'Why, to Whitechapel, Jack. They are so wretched there. Don't you remember? They need your help, your philanthropy.'

'No.' I shook again. Noise, noise all the time, crowding in on me from the streets outside. The stench and the darkness seeping from the crowds. I could feel my anger on thin, insect legs, crawling across my every emotion and thought. It couldn't be borne. I had to escape it, it had to be crushed. I leaned out from the window. 'Here!' I cried. 'For God's sake, stop!' The carriage began to slow. I slumped against the door; it opened and I staggered outside. I was standing on the pavement of Whitechapel Street. I breathed in desperately. Surely the air would cool me? But the beat of life was everywhere – copulating, breeding, defecating life. As remorseless as time, it sounded; as remorseless as the monstrous crawling of my anger, inching forward on its thousand insect legs, prickling the sponge of my livid brain. Each step now was like a needle's stab. Deeper and deeper; deeper they would spear. The horror was within my skull, piercing behind my eyes. Not just in the street but in my very thoughts – their faces, their laughter, the scent of their blood. It would drive me mad. No one could survive such pain. And still my anger crawled, and spread, and stabbed.

I sought darkness. Leading from the main road was a narrow, unlit street. I hurried down it. For a moment, there was almost a silence in my thoughts. I breathed in deeply and leaned against the brick of a warehouse wall. How long would I have to stay there, I wondered? The thought of leaving the silence and darkness was unbearable. Lilah – she must have seen where I had gone. She would come, and drive me back, and take me away from this sewer with its bubbling, foetid life. Otherwise ... No, no. I closed my eyes. I ran a hand through my hair. To my faint surprise, I realised that my other hand was still clutching the medical bag.

Suddenly I heard footsteps. I looked up. At the far end of the street was a solitary lamp. Two figures were standing beneath it, a woman and a man. The woman bent over and raised up her skirts; the man took her with an urgent, quickening grind. I could hear his breathing, very amplified; I could smell the humid stench from his genitals. He had soon finished. He dropped the woman down on to the pavement; then I watched him leave and heard his footsteps fade away. The woman still lay where she had fallen in the dirt; she hadn't even bothered to smooth back her skirts. She stank: my nostrils were assailed by the odour of rotting fish, of underclothes sticky with semen and sweat. At length, she did stagger to her feet. I knew her: Polly Nichols – I had treated her once for venereal disease. She began to sway towards me. Her tattered dress was covered in filth; I imagined it would cling like a second skin: she would have to peel it off if she were ever to be naked, and clean again. The thought made me nauseous. For her own skin would be greasy, pitted with sores and bleeding spots: that would have to be peeled away as well. She was big-boned. There was a lot of skin . . . a lot to be cleaned.

I stepped out in front of her, and she shrank back, evidently startled; then she recognised my face, and flashed a toothless grin.

'Dr Eliot,' she cackled. 'Ain't you looking smart?'

'Good evening, Polly,' I said.

Her breath stank of gin. It would be swilling about inside her now, in her stomach, her bladder, her liver, her blood. Rotten – every putrid, stinking organ, every putrid, stinking cell. The legs of the insect on my brain were now like claws.

'You have a disease,' I said. I smiled. 'Let me cure it.' I reached into my bag. She never had a chance to protest. The knife sliced through the windpipe, and the blood came pumping out in a crimson, glorious stream. I knew at once, ripping her throat from ear to ear, that I had done the right thing. As her life ebbed away, my own came flooding back. The wash of blood was so sweet and good. My anger was dead: I could feel the insect shrivelling, its legs becoming straw; I laughed as it dropped off from my brain. I looked down at Polly. Her severed gullet was oozing and flapping. I cut the throat again, back to the spine . . .

I stared up to see Lilah. 'Jack,' she murmured, kissing me, 'my darling Jack. What a wonder I have made of you.' I laughed. I was drunk on her kisses, and the life that I had shed. I returned to the corpse and continued to slash. Lilah held me tighter; I melted on her touch. I cannot describe what she gave to me; words cannot approach it. But I did not need words. I merely opened, and accepted it.

A long time it persisted. The glee was still with me as we stood in the dark afterwards, watching the constables puffing on their whistles, the scurrying of the doctors, the nervous, eager crowds. How I laughed when someone fetched Llewellyn, my very own assistant, to certify the cause of death. If only he had known! And there I was behind him, with Lilah, unobserved!

We breakfasted that morning at Simpson's, raw oysters and blood-red wine. Back in Rotherhithe, the pleasure was a glow which stayed with me for days – days, I say, translating it into the equivalent that you would understand, for to me, with Lilah, there was no such thing as time. There was only feeling, and so I judged by what I felt – the slave of all I had sought to repress. Dimly I knew this, for beneath the fog my reason and my old self still endured. As the contours became clearer, so my horror began to grow; the more I understood what it was that I had done. Soon I knew nothing but abject self-disgust; it crushed me, paralysed me; I could scarcely bear to stir. And yet I was at last myself again; and knowing that, I could finally act.

I knew I had to escape. I left, not across the river but towards London Bridge. No one sought to bring me back. I was not deceived, of course. I doubted that Lilah would let me slip her clutches for long. But in the meantime, there were those whom I could try to alert. 'Whitechapel,' I ordered my driver as we crossed London Bridge. 'Hanbury Street.' I had to warn Llewellyn; I had to tell him, before my reason was extinguished again, of what had been done to my brain, of the monster I had become. But my reason was already fading, the further I journeyed from Rotherhithe; the insect's legs were starting to crawl through my mind a second time. I clenched my fists, I shut my eyes; I fought to clear my thoughts of the stabbing pain. But remorselessly it grew; and with it, my desperation for the cure.

At last we reached the turning into Hanbury Street. The driver would take me no further; he was a decent man, he told me, and it was very late at night. I nodded, scarcely understanding him; I thrust all the money I had into his palm, then staggered like a drunken man into the dark. The pain now was searing; but I knew there was only a short way to go. I would do it. I glanced at a woman leaning against a street lamp. It was fortunate, I thought, that I was so close now to the surgery; otherwise I would never have passed her by. I stopped, I stared at her. How ugly she was. She smiled at me. Like the other one, she stank of unwashed crevices and sweat. The thought of her body, its life, made me shake. I wanted to shriek, the pain was so intense. One step at a time. One step at a time. I would do it. I was walking, after all. I was moving down the street. It wasn't very far.

'How much?' I asked.

The woman grinned at me; she gave me a figure. I nodded. 'Over here,' I said, pointing towards the dark. 'Where we can't be seen.'

The woman frowned. I realised I was shuddering, and struggled to control myself. She must have misinterpreted my eagerness, however, for she smiled again and then took my arm. So she really imagined that I wanted her! Wanted to explore her stinking, oozing slit! The very idea redoubled my disgust. The pleasure of killing her was almost greater than before. I hacked her throat to shreds; ripped the stomach, then pulled it apart. The intestines were still fresh to the touch; with what relish I scattered them over the ground! – tissue on dirt – dust to dust! I sliced free her uterus. How delightful it was, to see it flopping and sliding like a landed fish! There was no chance of life being grown within it now. I slashed at it a few times, just to make sure. Putrid and turned into dung, though, I thought suddenly, it might blossom with flowers. I pictured them in my mind's eye: white, and sweet-smelling, and delicate – a pretty bloom to spring from such a source! I would take the uterus, present it as a gift. Lilah was at the end of the street. She received my offering with laughter and a kiss.

We returned to Rotherhithe. The pleasure persisted as it had done before. No other mental function could counter the delight; memories of the world beyond the warehouse walls were blotted out by it, and details of my life there now seemed hopelessly remote. I only truly understood this after meeting with Lady Mowberley again – Lady Mowberley, I say, for I could barely recall her true identity at first, nor even how I had known her or ever seen her face. It appeared before me one evening, though, as I was staring into the flames of an incense burner, tracing patterns of blood in the fire; suddenly I could see her before me, this barely-remembered woman, risen it seemed from a world of my dreams.

'Jack,' she whispered. 'Jack.' She smoothed her hand across my brow. 'Do you not know me?' she asked.

I frowned. She seemed a phantom, unreal. But slowly I did indeed begin to remember her, and how desperately I had once searched for her, and at the memory of that I had to laugh. Was it really true that I had fought her in the cause of preserving human life? Of *preserving* it?

She assured me that it was true; then she joined in my laughter. 'I apologise,' she said, 'but as you find now for yourself, there are certain needs we have no choice but to obey. Do not blame me, Jack, and do not blame yourself. We are Lilah's toys. I fought it once too, on the mountain peaks of Kalikshutra, so long ago now, it seems, so long ago, when I first felt her teeth and lips against my skin, and her thoughts inside my brain – my Lilah – my beloved, bewitching queen . . .' She paused; and reaching out for me, stroked my cheek gently with her nails. 'Yet now,' she murmured, 'if I had the choice – I would not return to being mortal again. I have learned too much – felt too much. Why – I have toys of my own. You remember Lucy?' She smiled. 'I am sure she would want to send you her regards.' She paused; but I did not understand; for my brain felt too dizzy to recall Lucy's name. My companion frowned; then smiled, as though she had understood. 'I am sorry, Jack,' she whispered, 'that I deceived you for so long – and yet I – you – *we* cannot help ourselves.' She kissed me on the lips. 'We cannot be but what we are made.'

'You deceived me,' I echoed suddenly, in puzzlement.

She frowned. 'Why, do you not remember?' she asked.

I glanced past her at the flames of the incense burner. Faintly a memory stirred, of another fire in another room. 'You came to me,' I murmured. 'We sat in chairs beside my hearth. Is that not so?'

Lady Mowberley, or Charlotte Westcote as I could now remember she was called, smiled at this. 'We wondered how long it would take you,' she replied, 'to suspect the client who had hired you on the case.'

'*We* wondered?'

'It was not I who devised the game.'

379

'Game?' I stared at her wildly. 'It was a *game?*'

Charlotte inclined her head.

'Whose?'

'Surely you can deduce that?' she asked. 'No?' She laughed, then turned and gestured. 'Why, La Señora Susanna Celestina del Tolosa.'

I looked and saw Suzette – not the little girl, but the woman I had glimpsed before: graceful, haunting, beautiful. 'No,' I whispered, shaking my head. 'No ... I don't understand ...'

Suzette smiled. 'But you will, Doctor – you will.' She crossed the room towards me. 'You are scarcely yourself at the moment, after all. But when your pleasure fades – then you will remember, and for a brief while be Jack Eliot again.' She took my hands, stroked them. 'You should be proud; you entertained Lilah and myself a great deal.'

'Entertained?' I struggled to remember through the fog. A story somewhere? In a magazine? Something she had talked of and persuaded me to read? I began to ask her, but Suzette rose again and with a gesture cut me off.

'Over the centuries,' she told me, 'I have composed many enchantments – many games. You gave me the chance, though, to practise something new. We were certain, you see, that you would eventually discover the trouble George was in. Your old friendship with him – your powers of observation – your experiences in Kalikshutra ... yes; it was inevitable that the case would attract you in the end.' She glanced at Charlotte, then smiled and took her arm. 'When Miss Westcote learned of you from George, we were initially disturbed by the reports of your background and your powers. We had spun a tight mesh around Mowberley, you see; and yet you, it now appeared, might untangle it again. I wondered whether to dispose of you – and then, I happened to chance on *Beeton's Magazine*. Surely you remember it, Doctor? Sherlock Holmes? The first consulting detective in the world?'

I nodded. Yes – I could recall it all quite clearly now.

'I recognised in it,' continued Suzette, 'the inspiration for a wholly novel type of game – suitable to this new age of reason, this scientific century, before whose sceptical gaze all superstition must die. Lilah was quite entranced by the idea. We set you on the case; we observed your progress; we followed each turn you took through our maze. You did very well – it was a privilege to watch – but you failed, of course, in the end, to understand.' She smiled, and turned away. 'As I had always known that you would.'

'Why?'

'I have already said. You are a child of your century, of your rational age.'

I stared at her blankly.

'It was the single most intriguing aspect of the game: to test your arrogance, and see it fail.' She handed me something. 'Do you remember this?' she asked. It was the card I had found in the opium box.

I nodded. Yes, I did remember it. I read it out aloud: '*How often have I said to you that when you have eliminated the impossible, whatever remains,* however improbable, *must be the truth?*' I shook my head, then laughed wildly as I tore up the card. 'Yes,' I agreed, 'you were right – what arrogance.' I laughed again. 'How could I have been so blind before?' I asked. 'How could I not even have suspected the truth – what possibility might be ... or pleasure ... or experience? But now, thank God' – I raised my hands, and looked around me – '*thank God, I do.*' I laughed again, hysterically. Thank God, indeed! I had never known such a happiness, I had never felt so boundless – so blissful – so *free*. What limits could there be on *anything*?

I started to remember, though, very soon afterwards – just as I had done after the first murder. Like a painting cleansed of its accretions and dirt, my guilt was reappearing again, dim at first, then with ever greater clarity; and as it did so, the palace around me was slowly transformed back to a gaol. I knew better now, of course, than to attempt to escape it; and so I remained with the other captive beasts adorning the menagerie, an amusing trophy set amongst the rest. I was privileged, I realised, looking around me, to have been permitted to retain my human form; I could have been a monster, a spider, a snake. As Suzette explained to me, Lilah took inordinate pleasure in choosing the form to which her victims were reduced. 'Always something apt,' she smiled. 'A punishment crafted to fit the crime.'

'Crime?'

'Yes ... of boring her. For she will always be bored in the end by human love – though she also loves and feeds on it. The dwarf, for instance – a French vicomte from some two centuries ago, exceedingly handsome but dangerously vain. The panther – an Ashanti girl, arrogant and cruel, who sought to stab Lilah in a jealous fit. Sir George' – she smiled – 'well ... you saw him for yourself.'

'But you killed him; you bled him to ash.'

Suzette turned away. 'I am a vampire,' she said at last. 'I must have blood.'

'*Must?*'

She glanced back at me coldly. 'You should understand the need to kill.'

'Should I, though? Is that what I am – a vampire, like you?'

Suzette frowned, then shook her head slowly. 'Perhaps not,' she murmured. 'I had assumed you were. But Lilah can make her victims into anything. Perhaps you are a killer and nothing more. For if Lilah had transformed you into a vampire, then believe me – you would recognise your own taste for blood.'

'I like to shed it,' I replied, 'sometimes.'

'But not to drink it?'

'No.'

She shrugged. 'Well, then – you are not a vampire.'

'But you?' I pressed her. 'Was that what Lilah made of you?'

She turned back to me, and there was not a trace now of the child in her woman's face. Terrible it was, radiant with intelligence and loveliness. 'When Lilah met and seduced me,' she said at last, 'I was a vampire already.'

'When?'

'A long time ago.'

A trace of my old wonder stirred, my forgotten disbelief that such things could be. I swallowed. 'How long?' I asked.

'In the courts of the Moorish kings of Spain,' she replied. 'A thousand years ago – eleven hundred, perhaps ...' She turned away from me again. 'It is so hard to remember now.'

'And Lilah – that is where she met you? In one of those kingdoms in Spain?'

Suzette nodded shortly. As she gazed into the distance of the night, she stroked back her hair – her elegantly braided woman's hair. 'I lived,' she murmured at length, 'when I first met her, amongst the fountains and courtyards of Andalucia, where learning and all the arts of civilization flourished as they had rarely done before. My mother was a Jew, my father a Christian; I lived amongst the Arabs of the Caliphate. The different cultures were mine to sample, for I belonged to each one and none of them; and with this displacement came its birthright – mockery of them all. Knowledge was my passion – and amusement the perpetual condition of my mind. Lilah I loved, for she seemed to share these qualities of mine, yet infinitely amplified so as always to challenge and fascinate me. We left Spain. Across the whole world we roamed for two – three – however many centuries. Always, though, we would return to her favourite shrine, her kingdom amongst the Himalayan peaks, which is her one true home, and which, as you have witnessed for yourself, she will always defend. Others she has abandoned, to empires, cities, the various encroachments of man ... but never Kalikshutra. She – and I with her – have lived there far too long.'

'Yes,' I exclaimed, remembering suddenly, 'I saw you, a statue, in the jungle shrine. You were standing by her throne.' And then I frowned, staring at her, seeing not the girl but the woman still. 'When the statue was made, though ...' My voice trailed away. 'You must have already been transformed by then ...'

'Yes,' she said, her smile both self-mocking and sad. 'It happened in the end, of course. I came to bore Lilah.' Suzette paused. 'Just as she bored me. I told her that I intended to leave. Her demands for amusements, for perpetual entertainments – they had started to fatigue me, to wear me down. I was tired of games; I wanted something more.' She smiled again and turned away. 'I told her, as I left, that she was like a little child.'

There was a long silence. At length she glanced round. 'So you see,' she murmured, gesturing wide with her arms, 'she came after me. I did not escape her after all.'

'You are a prisoner here too, then?'

Suzette didn't answer.

'You could leave if you wanted to, surely?' I pressed. I swallowed. 'Surely . . . I mean, your powers . . . you couldn't be stopped?'

Suzette turned from me and gazed out at the stars. We had been climbing the staircase towards the dome of glass; now we passed through it and beyond, into the night outside. 'Look at me,' she whispered, and I stared. Once again she was a little girl. I sought to find the woman beneath the plaits, the ribbons, the pretty party dress. But she was gone. I suddenly remembered the creature from the boat; his former self had been absent as well, when I had looked at him out on the river and searched for his past in his present face. I swallowed. Sweat was starting to form on my brow.

I stared at the crimson glow of London spread out before me. I could feel the prickle of anger again, borne on the breeze. The marks of my own change were returning to me. 'I must get inside,' I muttered. As I turned, I staggered; Suzette smiled and took my arm. We passed back through the door. As we did so, the prickling ebbed and died away. When I looked at Suzette, she was a woman once again.

'So there can never be escape.' I pressed my forehead against the glass. 'Never.'

'You can leave,' replied Suzette. 'But what she has made you here – no – you can never escape that.'

'And that is true for all of us, then? In this . . .' I paused, and stared about me. 'In this . . . place – this prison.'

'Prison?' Suzette laughed. 'You think this is a prison?'

'Why? What do you think it is?'

Suzette shrugged. 'What you were promised. What, in the end, you grew so desperate to find: a sanctuary from the laws of probability, where human science would no longer apply. Hasn't that been your goal all this time? And now you have it – you exist in it.' She paused, gazing at the dome of light above our heads, the blaze of stars. 'Wherever she lives,' she murmured softly, 'wherever in the world, she recreates this dimension for herself. The finite is all around us – but here, where we live, is infinity.'

'Yes.' I followed her gaze, then shivered. 'But burrowed out from the warehouse walls.'

'That disturbs you?'

'Of course.'

'Why?'

'It reminds me too much . . .' – I paused to consider – 'of the hole in which the antlion traps its prey.'

She raised an eyebrow. 'Antlion, Doctor?'

'Yes – its larval form, to be strictly accurate.' I smiled ironically. 'You will recall the funnel it digs, into which inquisitive ants are then lured. The larva feeds on them, drains them of their fluids, tosses their shrunken skins aside. What is waiting here if not just such a trap? The jaws are open – the ants blunder in.' I paused. 'Ants like the wretches in the opium den.'

Suzette stared at me, then shrugged. 'I do not share your outrage. It is hard to feel concern for the fate of ants.'

'So I am right? The opium den does serve as the rim of the trap?'

There was a lengthy pause. 'Yes,' said Suzette at last. 'Clearly.'

'And Polidori?' I asked.

She narrowed her eyes. 'What do you mean, Polidori?'

'He is its guardian. Is he not a part of Lilah's collection, then? Not one of her trophies?'

'Polidori? No.' Suzette stared at me coldly, then laughed. 'She would never choose him as her lover.'

'That is a prerequisite?'

Suzette inclined her head.

'So is that why Charlotte Westcote is here?'

'Charlotte Westcote does not live here; she was merely a tool.'

'So...'

'She has never been with Lilah – no. We needed a wife for Sir George, that was all. English, of course. So we took the Westcotes on the mountain road. The mother was too ugly – we fed on her. But Charlotte Westcote made a pretty vampire. She was clever too, just what we required, and with a remarkable and immediate aptitude for vice.'

Evidently,' I agreed. I paused. 'And Polidori? What is he doing in this menagerie? Was he made a vampire by Lilah too?'

'No, Doctor. As you know very well.'

'Then by whom?'

'You know.'

'Lord Byron?'

Suzette inclined her head.

'And so that is what Polidori is doing here now? Pursuing a vendetta against Lord Byron and the whole Ruthven clan?'

Suzette shrugged faintly. 'His Lordship, I gather, still has scruples about killing those who share his own blood. Polidori likes to send his descendants to him — just to remind Lord Byron of what a monster he is. Arthur Ruthven was one of those descendants. So you will recognise – in response to your original question – that Polly and Lilah had a certain *congruence* of aims.'

'But Arthur Ruthven is long dead now. Lucy, his sister, though, is still alive.' I swallowed. 'Tell me, Suzette – do Polidori and Lilah still share their congruence of aims?'

'Doctor.' Suzette smiled and raised her hand. 'I have answered quite enough, I think, for now. The game is finished.' She turned, and this time did not wait for me. 'You have lost, Doctor,' she called out as she left me alone. 'Be content with that.' She laughed. 'Be a sportsman, if you must.' And then she was gone. Slowly, I too descended the stairs, considering all I had gleaned from her. As I did so I felt, with a sudden thrill of recognition, how my mind seemed almost my own again – restored almost to its former sharpness and resolve. Yes, I had lost the game. It was too late for me. But it wasn't myself I was playing for now.

Polidori, it was clear, held the key. My conversation with Suzette had confirmed a suspicion I had pondered on before, that the world of Lilah's palace was indeed like a burrowed hole dug within the fabric of the warehouse brick – and that the entrance to it lay through Polidori's shop. That was how the addicts had been drawn in, after all; that was how Stoker and myself had come through; that was where reality seemed to blend with the unreality beyond. For elsewhere – the entrance from the High Street, for instance, or the moorings on the Thames – the border between the two states seemed more like a wall than a meeting place, guarded by Lilah's unsleeping consciousness, through which no one could penetrate except on her desire. Penetrate – and, of course, withdraw as well. But through Polidori's shop, perhaps ... Polidori's shop ... What opened into infinity, after all, would surely lead from it too – and might Lilah not then be oblivious to the escape if I left through that exit, yes, *through Polidori's shop?* The data, it was true, was scarcely conclusive; the reasoning barely supported by facts; but I had no other options, no choice but to try. After all – could the penalty for failing be worse than to endure as I was?

Naturally, if I was to make my attempt through Polidori's shop, then I would have to cultivate the man himself. His attic, I found, had begun to fill once again like a well-stocked larder, as I told him myself. I could see now, as I had not done before, how some of the addicts had already been bled – but it was less their pallor which betrayed them, rather their reaction to me. For my presence would fill them with terror, even rage; sometimes they would cower before me, at other times spring at my throat – just as Mary Kelly, I remembered, had once leapt at a dog, or Lizzie Seward, in her cell, had ripped the head from a dove. These violent reactions had always puzzled me before; but now, recalling the beasts of the menagerie and how they had been formed, I wondered if the women had not somehow sensed the transfusion of their blood and sought to reclaim it, during their bouts of insanity, from any beast that might happen to fall into their hands – just as the addicts now sought to reclaim their lost blood from me. Certainly, whatever the explanation, the effect of my presence in the attic was undeniable; and to Polidori, as the addicts' keeper, it afforded endless delight. He would often be reduced into a frenzy of his own, so violent was his laughter, and since I was always careful to share in the joke he began to encourage me, for his own amusement, to visit him more. He never liked me – he never liked anyone – but his hostility grew slowly less evident. Once, I went so far as to try to reach the shop on the floor below; Polidori froze immediately and ordered me back; yet by turning with a show of the utmost unconcern, I was able to preserve his good humour with me. For I was satisfied at that stage merely to see my suspicions confirmed; the issue was not yet ready to be forced. First of all, Polidori had to be won.

But I was confident, if I were lucky, that I could tempt him in the end. For there was something else I had deduced from my talk with Suzette: that Polidori didn't know where Lucy Ruthven could be found. That he did indeed want her, a few discreet questions were sufficient to establish; for just as he had sent Lucy's brother to Lord Byron and his death, so also, I discovered, had Polidori been promised Lucy herself. But for now, I theorized, she was Charlotte Westcote's; certainly it was Charlotte who had taken Lucy from her room, and since I had now established that she was not with us in Rotherhithe, I had a reasonable idea as to where she might be hiding instead – with poor Lucy, presumably, beside her as her prize. Had she not told poor Westcote as much, after all, when we had discovered her on that dreadful afternoon – that she would keep his wife as her concubine? All this, during my rambling conversations with Polidori, I was able to intimate in passing references, and whispers, and hints. I was careful never to incriminate myself, never to propose a naked bargain to him; and likewise, Polidori never offered one to me. But the seed, I hoped, was planted; and so I paused and waited, to see if it would grow.

And yet in truth, even if I had wished to force the crisis and make the one attempt I would have to escape, I found I had little choice anyway but to delay. For my mental powers – which for a brief, precious moment had seemed my own again – had now begun to cause me fresh concern; not from any dulling of my responses but rather from the opposite, the constant process of their heightening. How can I describe the effect? At first, as you might imagine, it had been a rather pleasant one, welcome even, for it had seemed to arise from my recovered powers of reasoning, and to promise yet further resources of insight. But I was wrong. The insights arose, certainly; but only to fall and be at once swept away. It was as though my brain were like a heart which was pumping too fast; just as an exhausted man must gasp for oxygen, so my mind was starting to crave endless stimulation for itself, merely to satisfy its racing demand, which was pulsing, speeding, growing all the time.

You will remember, Huree, that the desire for mental exaltation had always been a feature of my character; yet now I was becoming its absolute slave, for the more I sought to banish the threat of boredom from my brain, the more my thirst for fresh excitements would grow. I could no longer concentrate on the details of my escape from Rotherhithe; no longer plan or evaluate; my efforts would shrivel and crumble instead. Puzzles, cryptograms, games of chess: I tried them all, exhausted them, threw them aside. I gave up trying to think or sit down; the fire-storm of boredom would engulf me at once. Instead I came to wander ceaselessly through the mirror-like hallways, the twisting flights of stairs, searching in vain for some escape from my mind – so burning now, so vivid and bright, demanding fuel to feed its hunger, its desires. Sometimes I would see Lilah, the barest glimpse, and my craving, for that second, would be satisfied; then she would be gone and the pain would return. If I could only find her, she would extinguish the flames. If I could only find her ... But I was trapped in emptiness, on the endless flights, and I was alone. I would mount the stairs, but when I reached their summit I was back at their foot. Was there anything other in the world than these loops of steps and time? Hopelessly I climbed them, endlessly. The coals burned hotter and hotter in my brain. Every thought, every feeling would burst into flames. There was nothing the heat did not incinerate.

'Here,' said Suzette.

I looked down at her. She had on her prettiest dress and wore pink ribbons in her plaited hair.

'Here,' she said again. 'Seven-per-cent.'

I took the needle. For a second, I gazed at it; then I rolled back my shirt-cuff and pinched at my vein.

'Deep,' whispered Suzette.

'Deep,' I replied.

I thrust the point in; I plunged the piston home. For a moment all seemed clarified. As the drug purged my veins, I breathed a long, contented sigh of relief. Suzette laughed, I smiled at her. And then I screamed, for the effect of the cocaine was fading away; the flames were returning, the relief was gone. I gripped the syringe in my shaking hand. 'No,' I shuddered, 'no!' I touched the needle with my finger tip; I pricked a jewel of blood; then I stabbed the point into my arm again. This time there was no effect at all. Again I plunged; again and again, until my arm was punctured with a pattern of dots. I licked at the blood, I smeared it on my lips, but it gave me no pleasure. I looked up. 'Help me,' I asked. 'Please help me, Lilah, please.'

She paused in her embraces. Her lips, like mine, were touched with red, as she bowed her head again, licking and sucking on Suzette's naked breasts. Together, girl and woman, they laughed in my face as they twisted and writhed, their limbs entwined, their bodies clinched tight. I took a step forward. My brain was a furnace of burning sands. Lilah paused; broke away from her kisses; turned to look at me again. Her eyes were aglitter; her lips bright and moist.

'Poor Jack,' she murmured. She smiled. 'Ripping Jack.' I clasped my ears. Her laughter was rising on the flames in my brain. I couldn't block it out. I needed her. Only her touch would extinguish the heat. I tried to move, but my limbs were stone and I could only watch. How greedily they kissed. I clenched my eyes shut. But like their laughter, their lovemaking filled up my thoughts. The pain was such that it couldn't be borne. I screamed. The noise streamed like blood, then was burned up in the flames. It would surely end now . . . the heat was melting the sponge of my brain. It would surely end . . . it would surely have to end.

'Here,' said Lilah. The silence was suddenly heavy and calm. We were standing beneath her portrait. There was no other light in the room but the single candle, flickering as before. Lilah was holding a golden dish which held a liquid that was dark like communion wine.

'Wash your face.'

I did so. At the touch of the blood I knew what to do; where to go.

'See,' said Lilah as she held the dish up to my face. The reflection was my own and yet not altogether my own. My skin was very pale, my eyes very bright; it seemed the face of an avenging angel of death.

'Go,' said Lilah. She kissed me. 'Find your peace.'

And so I turned and crossed the river, to where the slums were rankest and darkest with life. I welcomed my anger now, for the purpose it gave, and the promise it offered that the fire-storm would fade; one glimpse of blood, and my head was cooled; one glimpse of blood and the inferno was tamed. As I ripped the whore, the agony of dullness seemed to ebb with her life and the arid pain slipped away, purged by the flow from the gashes to her throat. The rush of sudden joy surprised me; I rose from the body and stumbled through the streets – each sensation, each thought, each emotion precious now. I stared at the filthy streets, and felt gratitude, towards the rubbish, the excrement, the faces in the gaslight, that I could see them and not suffer pain as my response, but rather the opposite, a sense of wonder and relief. Like blood through cramped limbs, I felt my disgust returning, flowing through my thoughts. I stood amongst the sewage, and on long, ecstatic breaths gulped in the scent; I touched it with my finger and tasted it. As I did so, a whore brushed past me. Her clothes were greasy and damp. I watched her as she continued down the street. She was lard-breasted, loose-hipped, reeking of flesh. I felt the prickle again, on the margin of my thoughts. Suppose I were to kill again? Just suppose! But no sooner had the thought come to me than I sought to bury it. I had already killed once; I couldn't murder a second time tonight. Once was enough. Surely? Yes, surely. It was time that I left.

The desire still flickered as I hurried from the slums, but I fought it down, though my mouth was very dry. The City was ahead of me; as I reached Aldgate I heaved a sigh of relief, for I had now crossed from the East End and left Whitechapel behind. I lowered my pace. Idly I wandered up Mitre Street. All seemed silent and still. Suddenly, from a passageway just ahead of me, I saw the beam of a torch; I shrank back into the shadows as a policeman turned out, then walked past me down the street. Once he was gone, I approached the passageway; I could make out a church beyond it, a small square, some ugly warehouse fronts – nothing of interest. I shrugged, and turned and prepared to walk on. Then suddenly, as I did so, I heard a woman start to sing.

She was clearly very drunk. Even at that distance, I could smell the gin. With a shiver of delight, I turned again and walked down into the square. The woman was leaning against a wall. She glanced up at me. Her face was blotchy and red. She smiled, muttered something, then collapsed at my feet. I opened my bag; I tried to tell myself that even though I now held my knife in my hand, I would not use it – I could not justify it, not twice in one night. But even as I pretended this, a rush of excitement was lightening my veins, and indeed, as soon as I had gashed her, the pleasure was like nothing I had ever known. 'Oh, yes,' I moaned, 'yes!' as I slit across her cheek from her ear to her nose. The surgery was soon completed. Before departing, I was careful once again to amputate the uterus. I slipped in into my pocket. Then I rose, and left the reeking mess, and hurried from the square. As I turned into an alley behind the Whitechapel Road, I stumbled and almost fell into a policeman's arms. He stared at me strangely; then he shook his head and bade me good night. How I laughed. For as I walked away from him, I could hear the first cries of horror rising from the square. The policeman turned and sprinted after me; but by then it was too late. I had already melted into the vile air of the slums; faded like a mist. But it wasn't over yet. There would always be more. I was Jack the Ripper. I would always be back.

I would always be back. The joy of the prostitutes' deaths began to fade; but this one thought, mutating from an affirmation of triumph into a cry of despair, still remained with me. For it was the case, I realised, that the rhythms of my transformed state had been written into my very cells: murder, euphoria, disgust, then pain; and in the end, inexorably – murder once again. How long would it persist, this cycle of horror? A thousand years, Suzette had said, a thousand years and more she had been drinking human blood. As I woke from the pleasure of my double killing, the dread of this eternity seemed more terrible than the worst agony I had yet experienced, and I was determined – in the brief moment of lucidity that I knew would be granted to me – to attempt my escape. If I could only reach you, Huree, I thought, we might rescue Lucy from Charlotte Westcote's arms; and perhaps – just perhaps – I might be rescued from myself. Was that ever possible, do you think? Would you have known what to do? I was never to ask you, of course. But you were the object of all my hopes, Huree, as I plotted my flight. And in that place, hope was much more precious than life.

Nor did it seem altogether baseless. For I was even given the time when I would have to make my attempt. The scale of Polidori's hatred of Lord Byron had become increasingly evident; once having acknowledged it to me he could never stop referring to it, scratching at it like some festering sore, and he would sit muttering and cursing to himself, sometimes shouting abuse, or just staring for hours into the brazier coals. He would speak of Lucy; his eyes would light with pleasure at the thought of sending her to Byron, and her death. My own role in the fulfilment of this ambition was still never spoken of openly; but Polidori told me one evening that Lilah would be bathing the following night.

'Bathing?' I asked.

Polidori grinned and gestured at the bodies on the floor. 'Very – seductive – she finds it, bathing,' he whispered. 'Quite loses herself in the pleasure. Nothing distracts her from it – nothing at all.'

I nodded slowly. 'I see.'

'Good.' He leered at me; then stirred and, feeling in his pocket, drew something out. It was an opium pipe which he handed to me, together with a small velvet bag. 'We're both doctors,' he hissed. 'We know the reason why opium's prescribed. Cuts out the pain, doesn't it? Even the most terrible pain.' He giggled to himself, then rose to his feet. As he did so, he stumbled over the body of a prostrate addict. He swore violently; he seemed ready to strike the man, but then paused and turned back to me, giggling again. 'Never mind,' he whispered. 'I'll be even with him soon.' He winked, then bared his teeth. 'Don't forget. *Tomorrow night.*'

And so it was. The following night. I made my attempt at eight. The anger settled on me the moment I had left. I struggled to keep an image of Lucy in my mind, to contemplate how best we could rescue her, but such chivalrous musings did little to abate my pain. I came straight to you, but if I barely spoke then it was because I needed all my efforts, all my strength, not to succumb to the anger and eviscerate you. A reasonable excuse for silence, I think you will agree. Did you ever suspect? No. How could you have done? But perhaps you will remember, Huree, that when I did talk it was only ever through gritted teeth? I was afraid otherwise, you see, that I might have bitten out your throat. I had no weapon on me, after all. That was why we needed Stoker. I couldn't have trusted myself with a gun – still less with a stake, or anything sharp. Worse and worse, the desire to kill grew. I fought it for as long as I humanly could. Not until we had been in Highgate for some time, sitting in that inn, the Jack Straw's Castle, did I finally take out Polidori's bag and smoke the opium. The effect, for a while, was all I could have hoped. Stoker arrived not long after I had taken the drug; that was how I was able to talk – there was a numbness in my brain. You remember, Huree? Me telling you about the Westcotes' house? The power of the evil I had experienced there? For that brief spell of time, you see, I had been able to remember and concentrate; for almost half-an-hour, perhaps, as we crossed the cemetery and approached the house, the prickling in my head remained anaesthetised.

But inside, in that bedroom, where Charlotte slept ... So sleek-skinned they looked, didn't you think, in each other's arms, so rosy and gorged? We were lucky, you see, Huree, in one sénse, that they had only recently fed; otherwise, even with the Kirghiz Silver, we would never have surprised them. But the scent of their kill was heavy in the air; you could not smell it, but it paralysed me, and I felt – very faint but digging deeper all the time – the scratching of insects' claws in my brain. I stood there frozen, trying to banish it; but mementoes of killing were all around me in that room. Dry blood. Scraps of flesh amongst the tufts of the rugs. A single finger dropped by the bed. When you stabbed Charlotte through the heart and she awoke with that frothing, terrible shriek, I knew that I too would have to kill soon. The puncturing of her heart, and then the severing of her head – the soft swish as you cut the throat, the hacking of the neck, the final crack as the vertebrae snapped: these were delights I should never have observed. That she was dead at last, melted into a soup of intestines and blood – the cause of my own and so many others' misfortunes – this meant nothing to me; no, it was only the scent of Charlotte's death I could understand. Just as the guts spilled thick across the floor, so the touch of their perfume spilled deep into my brain – and I was damned.

You remember, Huree? – I could do nothing. I stood by the doorway. I was shaking so hard. Lucy had risen from her lover's bed – a dumb, frightened animal, cornered in a trap. You shouted at me not to let her go. But when she darted, Huree ... when she darted ... What else could I have done? Her eyes were so staring, so fleshy and ripe. I would have picked them out. I would have fed on the tissue from the optical nerve, as though sucking the meat from the claw of a crab. And if I had held her, Huree – then right before your eyes, right in that room, I would have ripped her hard with my naked hands, I would have ripped her apart. So I let her go. For a second our eyes met, hers uncomprehending; and then she slipped past me and disappeared. I heard your cry of protest; I turned to face you, and Charlotte's grinning head, dripping gore on to the rumpled sheets. My hatred and anger hollowed me out. How I wanted to kill you! The insect's claws were chittering now. An effort – and I turned.

I stumbled away, back down the stairs and out through the hall. It had begun to rain. My anger wasn't cooled. I searched for Lucy; I couldn't see her. There were the marks of carriage wheels though, left in the gravel, very recent and leading away from the house. I ran after them wildly, frantically. The rain was falling more heavily now. I had soon lost the marks of the carriage wheels.

I stood on Highgate Hill, breathing in the air. London. Below me. A stench of excrement and blood. I ran towards it for miles, through the night. I never stopped. Not until the stench was unbearable and my revulsion as ripe and vivid to match. Tonight, I thought to myself, I would enjoy the pleasures of hate. Previously, the other times, I had hurried and gorged much too fast; tonight, I wanted more time for my work. But there seemed to be policemen on every other street. What if I were disturbed? It would be unbearable: my climax interrupted, my pleasure curtailed. No – for tonight, I decided, I would have privacy. Someone's room. But whose? I looked about me and realised, for the first time, that I was almost in Whitechapel again. I continued to hurry through the narrowest, blankest streets. I met almost no one. I smiled. So the whores were too frightened of my knife to come out? It certainly seemed so; and indeed the terror was almost palpable, as sharp and cold as the autumn winds. I shivered as I realised that my clothes were wet through. All the more reason, then, I thought, to find a room – nice and snug, with a fire in the grate. No more cold pavements for me. I wrapped my cape about me. I bowed my head. Then I stepped out from the shadows into Hanbury Street.

No one saw me slip into my rooms. I was glad to find they had been left undisturbed; dust was thick everywhere. I crossed to my desk. My work, again, had been left quite undisturbed. There was still even a slide beneath the microscope. I peered through the lens: Lord Byron's leucocytes. They were as active as before, moving ceaselessly across the face of the slide. The sight of them, the flickering cells, sharpened my desire to take a life. I considered my options. I wondered about Llewellyn, whether he was on duty in the ward below. If he was, it might be difficult removing a patient from under his nose. I frowned. There had to be some way. My desire was not to be frustrated now. I bit at my knuckle in an effort to steady my hand. As I did so, I shut my eyes; then opened them again. I found myself staring at the mantlepiece. Next to the clock I could make out a key. Slowly, I smiled as I remembered whose it was. I crossed to the mantlepiece. I picked up the key. I slipped it into my pocket; then from my desk took a surgical blade. Silently, I descended the stairs and returned into the street.

It was not far to Miller's Court. I passed through a narrow arch and entered the yard. Mary Kelly's room was number thirteen. I paused by the door. I swallowed, then knocked.

There was no answer.

I knocked again.

A silence. Then a faint creaking from the bed. 'Go away.'

'Mary.'

'Who is it?'

'Jack.'

'Jack?'

I smiled. There had been unmistakable fear in her voice. I composed myself. 'Doctor Eliot.'

'Doctor?' Genuine surprise. 'I thought you were gone.'

'I need to talk to you.'

'My door's locked.'

'I've got the key.' I turned it, I pushed at the door. It swung open. I walked inside.

Mary was sitting on the bed. 'What is it, then?' she asked. I smiled at her ... and then suddenly, she knew. She saw it in my face, just as she had seen it in George's that time in Hanbury Street, when she had attacked him and tried to claw it from his cheeks – Lilah's mark, the mark of death. She rose, hatred and terror disfiguring her. 'No,' she whispered. 'No, please, not you.'

'Be quiet, Mary,' I told her.

For a second she stood frozen, then she tried to run for the door. I seized her arm, I twisted it back. 'Oh, murder!' she cried. Then her voice slipped away. Gently, it slipped and spilled across the floor in a soft, steady drip. She melted into my arms. I raised her and crossed to the bed. Tenderly I laid her out. How cold she was! I glanced around the room. By the fireplace I saw a bundle of clothes; I smiled, and placed them in the grate. They were soon burning merrily. The shadows flickered with orange and red. I stared at Mary again. Dyed by the flames, her naked skin gleamed. We would both be warm now. How content I was, as I settled down to work.

Damp and fragrant, Mary tempted me to hurry; but I was not as green in my pleasures now as I had been before: the greatest delights would always ride on patience. I caressed Mary gently with the edge of my blade: I severed her head from her neck until it hung from the skin; I sliced up her stomach and removed her organs; I placed her hand in the wound, so that she could feel it for herself. No life there now; I was purging it utterly, rendering her clean. I sobbed with joy. When I had finished, not a trace of her disease would remain. I stabbed her breasts. If she had lived, a child might have suckled on those. No milk rose up with the blood, but still I shuddered. The disease might have been spread: a child might have been born. Not now, though. To make certain, I stabbed the breasts again; then I severed them both with a delicate care. I stood back. Mary's face in the flickering light seemed to smile her approval at me. The flesh would soon peel from it, I thought, and the bones rub through; then she would smile for eternity. I kissed her; imagined I was kissing the teeth of her skull. I felt a sudden fury that she should still wear the face she had worn whilst alive. She deserved better; I had won her better. With a hacking of my knife, I removed her nose. Now she had a dead thing's nostrils. I began to hum, carefully peeling the skin off from her brow. The flesh beneath was sticky; I would have to shred that away too. But there was no hurry. Why, I might stay with Mary's body for days. I raised my head and glanced at the door. I should lock it. I got up from the bedside and fumbled for the key. I crossed to the door. As I did so I frowned; I hadn't remembered leaving it ajar. I froze. I couldn't hear a sound, not above the crackling of the clothes in the fire. I shrugged. I pushed against the door. Then I frowned again. The door wouldn't shut.

Gingerly, I pulled it back and peered out through the gap. A glittering stare met my own. 'Have you finished with her now?' Lord Byron asked.

At once I tried to slam the door in his face. But he held out his arm in the gap; I felt a great strength pushing against me and I was flung to the floor. Lord Byron stood in the doorway. He stared around the room. His lips narrowed; once – just once, but I saw it for myself – his nostrils flared in an expression of disgust. He stood aside and leaned against the wall. 'In the name of the saints,' he muttered. 'What is it about you medical men?'

I stared at him, then back to Mary where she lay on her bed. The red shadows flickered across her body, scarcely recognisable now as a thing that had lived – just a trunk of ordure, black with drying blood. 'She is mine,' I said. I inched back, still staring at my adversary. My hand, as I leaned against the bed, brushed against something moist. I looked down: her liver, glistening in the light of the flames. I picked it up; I kissed it, then placed it between her feet. 'You won't have her!' I screamed suddenly. I scooped up the cuttings of skin, and clutched them in my arms. Like a baby, I rocked them. I began to laugh.

'For God's sake,' exclaimed Lord Byron. I looked up at him. I saw horror stamped upon his handsome face. And he a vampire! I laughed even more. I laughed till I choked.

Before I was even aware that he had moved, Lord Byron seized my wrists. I stared into his contemptuous, tungsten eyes. I spat in his face. 'At least I don't spill blood to drink it,' I sneered. 'I have a higher purpose.'

'And what would that be?' asked Lord Byron, his voice suddenly low with rage. 'Why this slaughter-house, Eliot?' He shuddered, and flung me against the corpse on the bed. 'You were a good man. A compassionate man. What has happened to you?' He frowned. His nose twitched as he breathed in my scent. 'So I was right,' he whispered softly. 'You are not one of us. You are not a vampire at all. But what are you then? What have you become?'

'Why?' I stared again into Lord Byron's eyes. 'What business is it of yours?'

His eyes, so harsh and glittering before, seemed almost to shimmer now. He reached to stroke my cheek. 'I have need of you,' he said at last.

'Need of me?' I laughed wildly as I stared around at my butcher's work. 'You want to talk about your damned blood cells *now*?'

'Why not?' His voice was so cold, it froze my laughter dead. 'What better time could there be?' He frowned; he picked up the folds of Mary's dead skin and held them to the light. A muscle twitched in his cheek, and he dropped the shreddings down on to the table. 'With the proofs of your transformation so fresh about you...' Suddenly, he had seized me by the hair. It was me he studied now, me he held to the light. 'I knew,' he said slowly, 'when you vanished, that you must have fallen.' He glanced down at my knife. 'Jack the Ripper. The Whitechapel phantom. The bloodthirsty butcher with the surgeon's skills. Who else could it have been? So I started looking out for you, Doctor. I put a watch on Rotherhithe. Tonight we saw you leave. I knew you would lead me to Lucy. And I was perfectly right. You led me straight there.'

'You have her now?'

'In the carriage.'

I laughed again. 'Then Polidori will be pleased.'

'He wanted me to have her?'

'That was why he let me escape.'

Lord Byron frowned. 'But it wasn't Polidori ...'

'Who made me what I am?' Again, I could barely gasp through my laughter. I shook my head. Lord Byron, to my surprise, was smiling as well. He seemed almost relieved by my words.

He waited until my laughter had run its course. 'Of course it was not Polidori,' he murmured at length. 'He could only have made you a vampire like himself – not the creature that you are.' He paused. 'So do you hate her?'

'Lilah?'

He nodded.

I stroked Mary's skinless brow. I shook my head. 'Why should I?' I asked. 'When she has given me this ...'

Lord Byron's expression did not change. But his stare was icy again and, once trapped by it, I could not escape. 'I had hoped, actually,' he said, still standing over me, 'to find you at your kill. That was why I left you alone tonight, you see. I had wanted to surprise you with the mark of your slaughter still on your lips, your victim in your arms, so that your self-disgust would make you utterly mine. The vampire may have no choice but to drink – but that does not mean he cannot regret what he is. Some of his former self will always endure. That is the greatest torture of all: to understand what it is that he must do. You, though ...' He frowned. He held my cheeks. Deeper and deeper his stare seemed to burn. 'You have no sense of guilt. Not the faintest vestige of horror or shame. So my hope is confirmed – you are not a vampire at all. But *what* are you, Doctor? The time has come – we need to find out.'

I turned away from him, back to Mary, kissed her blackened lips. 'I don't understand,' I murmured. 'Why should it concern you what I have become?'

Suddenly I felt his thoughts inside my skull. What was he doing? 'No,' I muttered, 'no.' I clung to Mary's trunk. I felt Lord Byron's fingers on my head. He pushed my face into the skinless flesh.

'See what you have done,' he hissed. Again I felt him stabbing through my mind. I shuddered. I could feel my exultation burning up, it was all gone. White, blinding white; irradiating white; and then nothing but Lord Byron's voice deep inside my brain. 'There must always be death,' he whispered, 'so long as there are butchers – generals – creatures like myself ... But this? Look at it, Doctor. What has happened to you?' He dragged back my head. 'Look at it!'

I did. And suddenly, I understood. Hellfire, and before me her skin peeled off – Hell. I had done this. The horror was my own. 'No!' But still I had to look. I stared at Mary Kelly's eviscerated corpse and suddenly, in the shambles I had created, in the mess of blood and intestines and flesh, I saw my own oozing form, lying in Lilah's arms, melting slowly across the warehouse floor.

'Yes,' Lord Byron whispered from deep within my thoughts. 'That is very good. And now show me all. What happened to you, Doctor? What happened next?'

I closed my eyes, but there was no escape. Even shut, my eyes could see. I looked about me. I was floating through a sea of transparent blood. Cells the size of my head were splitting and mutating before my gaze, while again – as they had done before when I had melted into Lilah's flesh – steps in strange helixes were coiling from me, twisting into patterns and forms yet stranger still. They were thickening all the time, and I began to struggle against them, for I could feel them against my limbs like strands of algae, sucking and soft, and as I brushed against them, so I was absorbed into their touch, and was no longer myself. I struggled, but I was fading fast away, for there was nothing now but these double spirals above me, below me, all around, and I screamed, for my consciousness no longer seemed my own, and then, as before, there was nothing but dark.

'Very good,' said Lord Byron.

I felt rain on my brow, I opened my eyes. I was lying in the yard. 'You saw it?' I asked.

He smiled. 'The transformation?' he replied. 'The breakdown of your cells?' He nodded. 'Yes.'

'Transformation – but into what?'

'We must wait and see.'

'What do you expect?'

Lord Byron glanced down at me. 'Around Lilah,' he asked, 'the creatures like you – do they age and die?'

I shook my head. 'Never,' I whispered. I swallowed. 'Never!'

'And yet,' he continued, 'as you said yourself, they do not need to drink blood. I am right, am I not?'

Slowly I rose to my feet. 'You believe my blood is what we have been searching for? A ... what? – an immortal's?'

Lord Byron shrugged. 'We know that it is.'

'But ... what I am ... the monster I've become ...'

'Is irrelevant. You do not require another human's blood to rejuvenate yourself. That is what matters – that is the opportunity, the hope we have. To study your cells. To find an answer at last.'

'But I am Lilah's. I cannot escape her.'

Lord Byron met my stare. His lips curled into the faintest smile, then he turned on me and began to walk through the mud.

'Where are you going?' I asked him.

'To Rotherhithe, of course. To make you truly mine.' He paused, waiting for me, but still I couldn't move. I was suddenly aware of the flickering of flames and I stared back through the door.

'They mustn't find her,' I mumbled, 'no, not like that.' I turned, but Lord Byron seized hold of my arm.

'Leave her,' he said. 'You require a sentimental parting, after what you have done?'

'Please.'

Lord Byron laughed bitterly and shook his head. 'If you want to serve her, then come with me now.'

Still I gazed at the door. Inside, the carcass, disembowelled, defaced ... Not Mary, not Mary any more. He was perfectly right, there was nothing I could do. 'The key,' I muttered, feeling in my pocket. 'At least ...' I pulled it out. 'She mustn't be disturbed. Not found like that.' My hand was shaking, but I locked the door. I stood for a second, then felt another pull on my arm. I was led from Miller's Court. We began to walk along the cobbles of Dorset Street. We trod through a puddle of sewage. With the stench of the effluent, it came to me again, what it was that I had done, the horror ... just – the horror ... I gasped for some air. I breathed the sewage into my lungs. But though I vomited, vomited for minutes, I could not empty myself – not of that room. Soon I was retching up nothing but air. The butchery remained. I sank to my knees. I rested the palms of my hands in the filth. I felt it bubble and ooze across my skin. I was grateful. I used it to wash away the blood and scraps of flesh.

I looked up. 'What will you do?' I asked.

'Destroy her,' he replied.

'And if you cannot?'

Lord Byron sighed. He wrapped his cloak about him to ward off the rain. 'If I do not destroy her,' he said at last, 'then she will destroy me. Now, come.' He gestured with his cane. 'I need to tackle this business before dawn.'

He began to walk again. On the far side of Brushfield Street I saw two carriages parked by the market place. Lord Byron led me across to them. He rapped on the side of the first; the curtain parted and the door swung ajar. Lord Byron opened it. 'How is she?' he asked.

'Dead,' replied a woman's voice. I peered inside the carriage and recognised one of the vampires from Fairfax Street. She was shaking her head. 'Stupid and slow, as the dead always are.'

'Not Lucy?' I murmured involuntarily. 'Not dead?'

The vampire smiled. 'See for yourself.'

I took a further step forward. I could see a woman now, crouched like a beast on the floor. She looked up at me; her eyes were blank, her skin leprous and damp with rot. 'Lucy?' I asked, disbelievingly. I glanced back at Lord Byron. 'But...' – I swallowed – 'she isn't dead.'

'Is she not?' Lord Byron sighed. I realised he had taken up a bundle in his arms; he cradled it, then held it out towards Lucy. At once her expression grew cunning and alert; her eyes seemed lit by an animal greed; her lips grew plumper and began to dribble and smack. Suddenly, she started forward, and would have leaped through the door had Lord Byron not slammed it shut with his cane. His own face, I saw, seemed troubled and almost as hungry as hers. 'Here,' he muttered, 'take it.' He handed the bundle across to a second vampire, who had been standing in attendance by the carriage's side. Lord Byron shuddered. 'For God's sake,' he whispered, 'don't let it near me again.'

'What was it?' I asked.

'Arthur,' replied Lord Byron, 'Lucy's child.'

'It was you who took him?'

'Naturally. His father was dead at the time. His mother...' – he gestured at the carriage door – 'well, you saw her for yourself.' He shrugged faintly. 'I am Arthur's only relative now. I would have preferred to leave him to his mother's charge for a few years, but as it is – do not worry – I will ensure that he is brought up safely enough. It is in my interest, after all, to see him one day propagate an heir. I am sure your Professor will have told you that.'

'But Lucy?' I asked. 'What has she become? A vampire? – no – her mind seemed gone...'

'Rotted,' said Lord Byron curtly, 'as her flesh will also rot away. Her mistress, Charlotte Westcote, is not wholly destroyed, for no mortal can destroy a vampire of her strength; but your Professor has grievously harmed her, and while she is injured Lucy will continue to decay. For she is nothing outside her creator's existence; nothing but her slave, her harlot, her toy. And this is the second reason, Doctor, why you must come with me now. For you have seen such creatures in India. You have seen how rapidly the sickness can spread. Imagine it, the plague of the dead infecting a city of eight million souls! I may be a vampire and a peer of the realm – but in my own way, I am also a democrat. I do not wish to see London become a wasteland of serfs. It is Charlotte who has begun to spread the sickness; but it was Lilah who infected Charlotte first of all. We must strike at her: Lilah – Lilith herself – the evil's very heart. Strike her down.' He glanced at me. 'And see, while we do it, if we cannot rescue you.'

'Now?'

'If you are ready.'

I nodded.

'Good.' He turned and ushered me through his carriage door. For the length of the journey I sat in silence, the horror of what I had left in Miller's Court paralysing my capacity for observation and thought. But as we at last entered Rotherhithe, my determination to extract a revenge from the being who had made me what I was, and my dread of her strength, alike served to reawaken my mental powers. And yet as I considered the struggle ahead of us, and the terrible evil we would have to confront, so also I found it harder to contemplate the prospect of success – for a hope that is destroyed is worse than no hope at all.

'Is it not possible,' I asked Lord Byron suddenly, 'that we are entering a trap? That it was not Lucy whom Polidori was fishing for when he let me escape, but you? It was you he has been promised, you whom Lilah will teach him to destroy?'

Lord Byron shrugged. 'I would almost welcome that.'

'Would you, though? Lilah's destruction is not always death.'

'Indeed?'

I held out my hands. 'See what she has made of me.'

He shrugged faintly again, and turned away.

'Beware, my Lord.'

He stared back at once, his eyes very cold. 'Beware?'

'Lilah is a being of terrible powers.'

He smiled, then glanced out through the window, for the carriage was rolling to a halt. He turned back to me. 'And so am I,' he whispered. 'So am I.' He squeezed my arm, then opened the carriage door and climbed out into the street. I joined him. We were standing in Coldlair Lane. Before us, dark-windowed, was Polidori's shop.

The door was open. We passed through it. The attic upstairs was empty. I frowned. So Lilah had indeed been bathing. An image of her, unbidden, arose in my mind: her limbs damp and porous, heavy like a sponge with blood, waiting to enfold me in their placental embrace. Lord Byron raised an eyebrow; he must have scanned my thoughts, for I felt his presence in my mind; but though I had no doubt he understood what he saw, his pale face remained otherwise motionless. He led the way across the wooden bridge and then, with a pause to check the revolver he had hidden beneath his cloak, on through the warehouse door.

From inside, I heard him laugh. I followed him, then stood frozen in amazement by what I saw. A colossal domed hall stretched away before my gaze. Torches rose from the rim of the dome, soaring to form a great pyramid of fire. Around the wall were massive pillars, and stairways winding in rows up the side; in the very centre of the hall, beneath the point of the pyramid of torches, stood a tiny Muslim shrine of the kind I remembered from my days in Lahore.

Lord Byron pointed to it. 'In there. That is where she will be.'

'You recognise this place?' I asked.

Lord Byron nodded. 'The vampire who created me,' he murmured, 'haunted a pleasure-dome very much like this.' He began to walk across the hall, his footsteps echoing through that colossal empty space. I followed him. We paused at last by the doorway to the shrine. Lord Byron gestured upwards, at a face carved out from the stone above the arch. 'Is that Lilah?' he asked me. I stared at it, then nodded. Lord Byron smiled. 'Lilith is come,' he murmured to himself. 'Lilith the blood-drinker is come.' Then he swept back his cloak. 'Polidori!' he shouted. 'Polidori, come out!'

There was silence. Lord Byron laughed. 'You wanted me here, didn't you? Well, here I am.' He walked in through the door. I saw him turn and aim his revolver at a shadowy, cringing form. As I followed him into the shrine, I recognised Polidori. He was kneeling on the floor. On his face, however, was his customary leer.

'So pleasant to meet you again,' he whispered, '*Milord*.' He spat out the title as though it were the worst insult he could give, then he giggled. 'My lord and creator. My noble lord. Always such an honour.' His face began to twitch; he wiped at his sweat as it trickled from his brow. 'Been waiting for you,' he shouted suddenly. 'Knew you would come.'

'And Lilith – she is waiting too?'

'But, of course, *Milord*.' Polidori gestured at a blackness stretching down into the earth; then turned his head and gave me a wink. 'Bathing,' he grinned. 'Just like I said.'

'Well,' murmured Lord Byron, 'then I am sure we shall get along splendidly. Even the prettiest woman looks better for a bath. And Lilith – by all accounts – is not unpretty at all.' He removed his cloak and tossed it to Polidori. 'Keep hold of that while I visit your mistress. Guard it well, and you may earn yourself a tip.' He turned to me. 'Come, Doctor. Let us visit our Enchantress of the Bath.' He began to descend. With a glance at Polidori, I followed him. Dark, very dark, the steps stretched ahead of us, but Lord Byron seemed to know his way, and so I was careful to follow the course of his footsteps, as we went deeper and deeper, into the earth. At last, ahead of me, I saw a faint red glow, and Lord Byron turned and waited for me. 'We are almost there,' he whispered once I had joined him. 'Take this.' He handed me a knife. He turned, then paused and took my arm again. 'Remember Miller's Court,' he whispered. I nodded. We continued to descend. And all the time, the glow of the fire grew ever more bright.

At length, ahead of us, I made out a doorway of stone. Lord Byron passed through it without a second's pause but I froze, for I knew that beyond it Lilah was waiting, Lilith herself, whose terrible powers I had seen for myself, extraordinary, impossible, infinite. Suddenly I was certain we would fail. Lord Byron too, no doubt, had remarkable powers; but he could not hope to rival Lilah – not destroy her as he planned, for she was older and greater and more cruel than he. In the red shadows flicking on the stone, I saw only the flames of Miller's Court; and in my mind's eye the face of Mary Kelly, skinless, noseless; shredded by my knife. I sank down, crushed by the horror of the memory; and then I forced myself to walk on through the door. My last, best chance – I could not squander it. And one comfort, at least, I had; whatever destruction was wrought upon us, it could not make worse the Hell I had now.

Lilah was standing against a wall of fire. She seemed barely silhouetted, for her own body was glistening red; and seemed to rise and change with the flames behind her back. The floor of the chamber was still awash; by Lilah's feet was what seemed to be an altar, streaked and sticky with viscera. So she had finished her bath, I thought. I gazed on her naked form. It would be sodden, I knew, with blood; and yet how perfect she seemed – how blindingly and terribly beautiful. She smiled at me. Her face too; the depths of her eyes. All my loathing of her shrivelled and was dead. I would stay hers – now, and for all time. Whatever the cost I could never leave.

And Lord Byron, I wondered numbly, what did he feel? Lilah was gazing at him. I could not see his expression as he stared at her.

'I have waited,' said Lilah eventually, 'a long time to meet you.'

Lord Byron inclined his head. 'How exceedingly flattering.'

'Oh, it is,' Lilah smiled and smoothed back her hair. 'More than you know. I am not accustomed to take much interest in your breed.'

'My breed?' Lord Byron laughed. 'But you yourself are a creature of blood.'

'How different though, my Lord! As you well know. Is that not why you are here after all?' She gestured at me contemptuously. 'To fight for him and his rich prize of cells, to unlock their secret and find yourself your cure? Yes, you see, I know your deepest hopes. But they are worthless, my Lord. They cannot help you change. They cannot help you become like me, however great you may be, the greatest of your kind – still you are nothing, compared with me.' She flickered and rose before us, growing with the flames. 'Do you see, my Lord? I change – and I am the same. I am the first and the last; the high and the low; all things . . . and none.' Again she stood before us in the form she had worn before. 'You see, my Lord. I am not like you at all.'

'Indeed you are not.' His voice was very cold.

Lilah stared at him for a long while. Then she turned, and the flames behind her died away, and I saw, instead of the close, subterranean dark, the burning of stars in an unpolluted sky. I looked about me: the mountains were purple with the coming dawn; the jungle rich in vivid shadow; Kalikshutra, as lovely as I remembered it from my last day there.

'Jack.'

I turned round. Lilah was beside me, seated on a throne. She pointed, and smiled mockingly. 'So brave, weren't you?'

I looked. I was standing, I realised, on the topmost point of the temple's dome. Below us, the barricade I had erected from the shattered statues was blazing furiously; the army of the dead was beyond it; and behind it, sheltering from the attack, were you, Huree; the soldiers; and yes – next to Moorfield – me as well. I had a torch of burning wood in my hand. I was waving it and jabbing it in the faces of the dead. They surged forward suddenly; I remembered the moment: it was when our flank was turned, and I had smelled our fate on our assailants' breath.

Lilah laughed, and rose to her feet. 'Should I save you?' she asked.

'Save me?' I frowned. 'But I *was* saved.'

'No.'

'I am here now.'

'Yes – for the moment.' Lilah smiled and inclined her head. 'You. Me.' She glanced round. 'The noble lord.' She sat down again, slowly, into her throne. 'But we need not be at all.'

Lord Byron shook his head. 'What is this?' he asked.

Lilah gestured with her hand to me. 'If he is killed on the barricades now, he will never meet me – he will never meet you. The whole fabric of the plot will be torn, and unravel into nothing. Our standing here need never occur.'

'No.' I ran my hand through my hair. 'I don't understand . . .'

'But of course not!' Lilah clapped her hands with delight. 'And you never will! But I understand; it is perfectly simple. And I would do it if I chose, Jack, just because I can. However' – she smiled at me – 'I choose not to this time. You have had your chance and wasted it. I do not intend to pass up what happens as a result of this decision. I wish to meet Lord Byron – and yes, Jack, even you.' She clapped her hands again. 'And now, my Lord, see how the corpses drop. Yes! Down they go, withering away. Dust to dust – their natural state.' Her eyes gleamed with pleasure. 'And see our bold defenders – saved at the last!'

I watched as Moorfield stepped round the barricade. As he did so, the flames began to rise; I saw them grow black with the bodies of the dead and leap higher and higher, up towards the stars. I searched for Moorfield; I searched for myself; but no one living seemed left on the dome. I remembered what I had felt at the time, and which you reported, Huree, and Moorfield too: a sense of being wholly alone in that place, and then suddenly, the six women, the vampires, seen in the fire. I looked now, from where I was standing with Lilah, and saw them again. They turned; they stared up; they prostrated themselves. And suddenly I remembered another thing I had glimpsed when I had seemed alone on that place: a throne, surmounting the very pinnacle of the dome; a shadowy form seated on the throne; and by its side, two other shadows, similarly dark, and I recalled, what I had forgotten until that moment, how one of those shadows had worn my face.

Lord Byron frowned; he had read my thoughts; he had sensed my shock and my bafflement. 'But how can this be true?' he asked. 'That the figure you saw . . . now proves to be yourself?'

I stared at him; I made no reply.

'It cannot be true.'

'But it can.' Lilah smiled. 'Oh, it can, my Lord. And you thought ...' She laughed; she stretched languorously, and closed her eyes. 'You truly thought you could challenge me?' She shook her head. 'When I am more than nature, more than time – and certainly more than your world of spirits, my Lord: I am control and the uncontrollable; union and the dissolution; I am truth – and also iniquity.' She laughed again. 'So enjoyable it is – being so much all at once.' She opened her eyes. 'You cannot fight me,' she whispered as she reached for his hand. 'But you have seen now, I hope, what I might give you instead.'

'I have indeed.'

Lilah ignored the coldness in his voice. Instead, she gestured with a sweep of her hand. The temple was suddenly still and empty, its pinnacle touched by the first rays of dawn. The stonework seemed impossibly steep; it appeared to grow from the mountain-side, and tower high into the oxygen-less air, yet I experienced no discomfort, only the pleasure I had felt in Lilah's bed, when the knowledge of the whole world had seemed opened up and revealed to me. The mountains stretched away before us: the plains, the rivers, the jungles, the seas. I looked to the east. The sky was rosy now, and fresh with the promise of regeneration, of hope. My soul seemed flooded by a blaze of light.

'And yet,' said Lord Byron very softly, 'I have also seen what was done in Miller's Court.'

'What, squeamish, my Lord?' asked Lilah. 'A blood-drinker like yourself?'

'All this beauty, all this wonder and hope ...' – he swept with his arm – 'the earth, the air, the stars – can it only be bought with the skinning of a whore?'

Lilah's eyes narrowed. 'And if that were true?'

Lord Byron shrugged. 'Then I would not be interested.'

'And yet you kill.'

'Yes. But you know why: because I have no choice. It is not a great comfort, I admit, but it is better than killing without reason at all.'

Lilah laughed. 'And the Doctor, here – if he were like you – killing only in order to survive: would that make him happier, do you think?'

Again Lord Byron shrugged. 'You would have to ask him that yourself.'

Lilah glanced at me as I tried to think. Suddenly the dawn, the mountains, the sky seemed shrunk to a room lit with darkness and fire. 'No.' I said. 'No. Anything but this.' Mary's corpse, her hand in her stomach, ripped and skinned, lay stretched before my gaze. 'No,' I said again, burying my face in my hands.

'You would rather kill, then, to slake a thirst than for pure amusement's sake?'

Slowly, I uncovered my eyes. Mary's face was gone; instead it was Lilah who was watching me. We were in the vault again, deep underground, beside the wall of fire. 'I would rather not kill at all,' I replied.

'No, no,' she laughed, 'you are forgetting, that what the Gods give, they cannot take away. And yet' – she stroked my cheek and smiled – 'for all that, I am compassionate.'

'Compassionate?' Lord Byron's smile was dark with bitterness. 'You are the damnedest politician I have ever met.'

'Unfair, my Lord. Politicians promise what they cannot give.'

'Yes, of course, my apologies – you are perfectly correct – you have already shown us tonight what you can give. No.' He shook his head. 'No, I will not have you. Even as I am, the slave of my thirst, I am freer than I would be as the slave of your gift.'

'But if that gift were freedom from your thirst?'

'I will not be beholden to you.' He smiled suddenly and glanced back at me. 'But I will fight you for it,' he whispered softly.

Lilah stared at him. A shadow of sudden anger crossed her brow. 'And that is your final decision?' she asked.

'You heard me. Cant – cunt – whatever it is you are hawking – I will have none of it.'

Lilah smiled thinly. 'How regrettably obdurate of you,' she

whispered. 'How regrettably *base*.' She turned, and clasped herself, and gazed into the fire. 'Well,' she said at length, 'it is no great loss. You will still be mine. Yes' – she smoothed back her hair and turned round again – 'you should make an entertaining addition to my menagerie. Your friend, Doctor Polidori, has offered me several suggestions as to what you might become – all quite amusing. I will give you to him, I think. Yes. As a reward for his honest and devoted months of service. Would that not be fitting, my *Lord*?'

She spat out the word as Polidori had done. Lord Byron surveyed her with a look of faint amusement; he turned to me. 'A tigress robbed of young,' he murmured, 'a lioness – or any interesting beast of prey – are similes at hand for the distress – of ladies who cannot have their own way.'

'Very pretty,' smiled Lilah. She reached out to stroke Lord Byron's cheek. 'But have you ever' – she kissed him – 'met a lady quite like me?' Their lips met again, then she broke away. 'I doubt it, my Lord. Even so praised a Don Juan as yourself. I doubt it very much.'

Again she kissed him; she held him in her arms; and I saw blood, thickened to a fleshy slime, oozing from her body and sucking on his. From behind me I heard a sudden intake of breath. I looked round. Polidori was crouching in the doorway, his eyes gleaming, his teeth parted in a greedy smile. Lord Byron staggered. Polidori leaned forward even further, and bit on his knuckles so hard that they began to bleed; and as he did so, Lord Byron smelled the air and looked round, and saw where Polidori was watching him. Lord Byron laughed; but his face was very cold, and stamped not with fear but with pride and contempt. He raised his arms; blood streaked with jelly ran in strings from Lilah's skin, but they snapped, and fell, and Lord Byron's arms broke free. He combed her hair away from her neck; she struggled to twist back from him, but his grip tightened as, with a sudden moan, he bit. Lilah shuddered; she too moaned; locked, they staggered and fell, body against body, limb against limb.

Still, Lord Byron drank; and still the bog of Lilah's blood and mucus sucked; and still they rolled across the sticky floor. The wall of fire enveloped them, flickering and twisting gold about their forms, as they continued in their embrace, nothing but dark shadows now, so tightly locked they seemed like one, and yet they were moving still, and then one was breaking free, and though I drew closer to the flames, and tried to peer through, I could not make out who it was, body arced backwards, arms upraised, and then falling, so that the two forms were joined once again. Suddenly, so ghastly that I could barely endure it, a shriek filled the vault, rising on a note of horror and disgust that seemed to dim the flames, for as I stared at it, the fire was dying away, and fading into the dark. Again a piercing shriek of revulsion, mingled now with disbelief; and this second time I knew I was hearing Lilah's voice. I stepped forward; where the fire had been there were now only stones, and the light was very faint, but I could see, ahead of me, Lilah's body stretched out. Lord Byron was lying on her. Slowly, he rose to his feet. I looked down; I held my hand to my mouth. Lilah was marked with Mary Kelly's wounds.

Lord Byron stepped back. 'Get aside,' he ordered numbly. But I continued to stare. Still beautiful she was, as lovely as before, despite the mutilations to her body and face. No blood though. No blood from the stomach, or the thighs, or the throat. 'Get aside,' repeated Lord Byron. I saw he was holding his revolver in his hand. He waved it at me and I took a single step back. He fired; then again; and again and again. He dropped the gun; he looked around the room; then he knelt by the corpse and beckoned to me.

'Do you still have your knife?' he asked.

I removed it from my cloak.

Again he glanced round the room, making certain Polidori was gone. He closed his eyes, then turned back to me and clasped my hand, gripping it tightly round the handle of the knife. He did not speak to me, but I understood at once what it was I had to do. I swallowed my disgust. I cut out the brains and the living heart. I finished the job, and slumped back. As I did so, I heard the crunching of glass.

I looked about me in surprise. The vault was gone; we were

kneeling on a warehouse floor, amidst shattered bottles, and bricks, and clumps of weeds. I stared up: through the roof I could see the early-morning sky; through a paneless window the gleam of the Thames. I looked for Lord Byron. He was limping slowly across the rubbish-strewn floor. By a pile of boxes, he paused and, brushing a couple aside, uncovered Polidori as he crouched amongst the weeds. Lord Byron held out his hand; Polidori flinched, then scrabbled through the boxes and passed up a cloak. Lord Byron draped it over his arm, then felt in his pocket and tossed Polidori a coin. He continued towards the bridge, and I joined him there. Together, we crossed into Polidori's shop, and down into Coldlair Lane where the carriage was waiting for us. 'Mayfair,' ordered Lord Byron. I climbed in, then sat back dumbly as the wheels began to turn.

I gazed out at the streets: at the workmen drinking their breakfast gin, the early-morning traders, the bedraggled whores. I saw the newsboys, with their placards and their gleeful cries: 'MURDER – HORRIBLE MURDER – MURDER IN THE EAST END.' I shuddered, of course, as the image of Mary Kelly rose before me; but though I knew the horror of what I had done would never leave me, yet I felt no prickling, no anger in my brain. Again I looked out at the streets. They were teeming now, for we were drawing nearer to London Bridge, and the crowds were a ceaseless, thickening flow; yet still I felt nothing. Or rather – I felt what I had always felt in the past, before Lilah, before my mind was changed; but of hatred, of revulsion, of disgust . . . not a trace. I was no longer the monster she had made me. I was myself again. I turned to Lord Byron. I smiled. 'She is dead.'

He glanced at me. 'Do you think so?'

'Why? Do you not?'

He smiled faintly, then gazed out through the window. His silence disturbed me. 'No,' he said at last. 'No, she isn't dead.'

'But . . .' The words froze on my tongue, as I stared out again at the filth and the crowds. Still no prickling. 'But you saw her . . . What I did . . . What I feel now in my head . . .'

'And what do you feel?' he asked.

'Nothing.'

'Nothing at all?'

'Well ... no. I feel – as I did before but almost – stronger – reborn.' I breathed in deeply. 'The very air – it's as though I am tasting it for the first time.' I met Lord Byron's stare. 'I am myself again. Only somehow, even more so than before.' I paused. 'No, I'm not making sense.'

'But you are, Doctor. Perfect sense.' He smiled. His expression, though, was mocking and almost sad.

I stared at him. 'I don't understand.'

'What?'

'How you can think that she isn't dead? Surely it is over. And soon we shall have our prize. Immortality, my Lord – freedom for ever from your hunger for blood.' I held up my wrist and nicked it gently. I dyed my nail with a touch of red, and held it up to the morning light. 'Look at them, my Lord. My precious cells.'

For a long time he did not reply. Then he frowned. 'When I held her,' he murmured, 'I would have felt it. I would have known ...'

'But you defeated her ...'

'Really?'

'You saw ... What we did ...'

'Yes.' He shrugged faintly. 'But I was stronger than she had ever thought.'

'So you agree? She might indeed be dead?'

He sighed. 'Yes, perhaps.' He shrugged again. 'But we shall know for certain soon, anyhow. If Lilith is dead – then Charlotte Westcote is dead. If Charlotte Westcote is dead – then Lucy is dead. But if Lucy is alive ...' He glanced out through the window. 'We shall be in Mayfair very soon.' He hunched himself up in the folds of his cloak. 'Let us wait until then.'

And so wait I did, in silence, until our carriage had stopped in a quiet Mayfair street, before the steps which rose to Lord Byron's door. I climbed out and walked up with him; as the door was opened, I saw a shadow pass across my companion's pale face and then, almost simultaneously, a gleam of pleasure and desire in his eyes.

His nostrils widened; and as I watched him smell the air, so too, just faintly, I caught a scent myself. It was rich, and golden, and like nothing I knew; as we walked through the hall it grew progressively stronger, until, by the time we had arrived in the dining room, I was conscious of almost nothing but the pleasure it was giving me. Lord Byron too seemed similarly entranced; I asked him what the perfume was, but though he smiled at me faintly he didn't reply. I wondered if it were not some drug we were breathing in, which had the power thus to affect the olfactory nerves; and I knew, with a surprised shock of utter certainty, that whatever it might be I had to have more. You will know, Huree, that I was never a man of intemperate tastes; I was surprised, now that Lilah's curse had been purged from my brain, that I should desire anything quite so strongly; I wondered if, perhaps, I was still not quite myself. I would recover soon, no doubt. And yet in the short term my enslavement to the drug seemed, if anything, to be growing; and my desire to taste it felt almost like a pain.

Lord Byron breathed in deeply; he leaned against the wall. 'Where is she?' he asked.

Only a single candle lit the room. I stared into the shadows, expecting not to make anything out; but to my surprise I found I could see perfectly well. A couple of vampires were lounging over a bottle of wine. They both smiled at me, and I saw their eyes gleam.

'Where is she?' Lord Byron asked again.

One of the vampires drained her glass. 'Below,' she replied.

'With Haidée?'

'But of course.'

'And has she . . .?

'Haidée?'

Lord Byron nodded.

'No.'

'Doctor . . .' Lord Byron reached for my arm. 'You had better . . .' He stared into my eyes, then he shook his head. 'This way,' he murmured. He led me through the dining room and on through the hall. We began to descend a flight of spiral steps. The scent was almost unbearable now; the further we went, the more desperate I grew. By a large oaken doorway, Lord Byron paused and smiled at me and pressed my arm. Then he opened the door and passed inside. I followed him. The scent, in a wash of gold, flooded my brain.

Dimly, I could make out the room we were in. The floor and walls were stone; but the fittings were wonderfully beautiful: glittering ornaments, many-coloured rugs, rich woods, bright flowers, paintings, rare books. These meant nothing to me, however; nothing at all; I wanted only one thing . . . I wanted the drug. I stared about the room, searching for it. I breathed in deeply; then saw two women seated on a bed, the one rocking the other's curled body in her arms. Lord Byron had already crossed to them. The woman cradling the other looked up; she seemed remarkably lined and old, and I knew her at once: Haidée, whom I had met one evening at table with Lord Byron, and who had asked me to help cure her disease. But it was not her I was smelling. No. It was the other one, the girl in her lap, I was smelling her *blood*. That was what the perfume had been; that had been the drug – human, mortal, living *blood*. I remembered Lilah's question. 'If Dr Eliot were like you,' she had asked Lord Byron, 'killing only in order to survive: would that make him happier, do you think?' And at once I knew, Huree. I knew what I was.

I watched as Lord Byron took Lucy by the hand. Her eyes were glazed, but otherwise she seemed the very picture of health: fresh-skinned, rosy-cheeked – vital . . . fresh. For several minutes Lord Byron spoke with Haidée; and all the time my hunger was growing worse, and I was almost tempted to seize Lucy myself. But at length Lord Byron shook his head, and turned away; Haidée screamed after him, but he made no reply and, walking past me, led Lucy through the door.

'I can never resist temptation,' he said.

'No', I replied.

He motioned me to shut the wooden door. I did so. Lord Byron nodded, his smile now a terrible and chilling one. He led Lucy on up a further spiral of steps; then he seized her by the arms; he thrust her against the wall. He was shaking violently, but as he unbuttoned Lucy's dress his expression seemed almost tender, and his eyes were half-closed as' though reluctant to watch. Suddenly he bowed his head; for a second he froze. 'I am not like Haidée,' he muttered. Again he paused. 'And even she – one day – even she will give in.'

'Haidée?' I asked.

Lord Byron glanced round at me. 'It is not just my blood' – he stroked Lucy's neck – 'which flows in these veins.' He shuddered; he seemed ready to bite; then he paused and turned to stare at me again. 'Almost eighty years,' he whispered. 'Haidée has endured, growing older, and drier, and more withered by the hour.' He laughed softly, despairingly. 'How long, Doctor? How long will you wait, now you have realised what you are?'

With his nail he punctured through the skin of Lucy's neck. The blood began to pump from the jugular. Lucy moaned softly, as she slumped into his arms, and I closed my eyes as I smelled the flowing blood. Lord Byron was on his knees; and I knew I was weak, that I couldn't fight the scent. He glanced up at me. 'Hungry?' he asked.

I tried, and failed, to reply.

'I shouldn't really waste this blood on you,' he said, 'but I feel guilty. You wouldn't be here if it hadn't been for me.' He reached up for my hand, and pulled on it. 'Come, Doctor. Join me. Have your first taste.'

A minute more I resisted. Then I staggered; I fell to my knees, I gazed at the blood. Lord Byron laughed and gave me her wrist. 'There,' he murmured. 'Bite deep. It's always best that way.'

I stroked the veins.

I glanced at Lucy's face.

I bit, as Lord Byron had advised, very deep . . .

Like a couple of dogs, we fed on our prey.

'I am compassionate' – so Lilah had claimed. Yet even now, the game was not quite over; there was one last joke to be played. It was waiting for me in my study in Hanbury Street. I had returned there to pack, just the barest essentials I would need, for I could not stay in London; the whole world was now my exile. Indeed, I almost missed Lilah's parting gift, for I had not at first planned to take my microscope. My work, my dreams, seemed like dust to me now.

Yet at the last moment, I found I could not abandon either – not altogether. I crossed back to my desk. As I approached the microscope, I saw the slide of blood beneath the lens. I frowned. I remembered it quite clearly, for I had looked at it before leaving for Miller's Court: Lord Byron's leucocytes – a film of white cells. I bent down. I peered at the slide with my naked eye. The sample was now red. Thick, vivid, haemoglobin-rich red. I adjusted my microscope's lens. I stared through the glass. I inspected the slide.

The leucocytes were still alive as they had always been; but now the red cells were active as well. Somehow the slide had been doctored; somehow, the structure of the blood had been changed. For there was no phagocytic activity; no absorption of the red cells by the white; instead both seemed utterly stable. I remembered, from my researches into the structure of vampire blood, how Lord Byron's white cells had broken down and fed on alien haemoglobin; I rushed downstairs, to the astonishment of Llewellyn and the attendants who had clearly given up on me for good; I took a sample of blood from a patient; back upstairs, I added it to the blood on the slide. Still there was no activity. I waited, speaking to Llewellyn, lying in response to his questions as best as I could manage, and all the time wondering, wondering what I had. At length I inspected the sample again. Still nothing; no phagocytosis; no reaction at all. The alien blood had not been consumed. Nothing had changed, Huree – *nothing had changed.*

Nor has it ever done. I have the sample before me now. I am never parted from it. Sometimes, when my depression grows too great, I will inspect it again, just to check that it is truly unaltered – truly unchanging – a true immortal's blood. Lilah's, in other words – for it could have come from no one else's veins. It was what Lord Byron fought her for, after all – fruitlessly, as it now proves, since his blood remains a vampire's, and I still do not know how its structure can be changed. For the sample of Lilah's own blood resists my every effort to fathom its secrets; it has offered me no illumination, no breakthrough, no cure. Instead, it offers me only one thing I did not have before – the certainty that immortal cells can indeed exist. It is, after all, Lilah's final parting gift; her most refined and delicious torture: the torture of hope.

I have not told Lord Byron, since I know that Lilah intended me to. One day, perhaps, when I am nearer the source of her joke; but not until then. For, on him, the torture would be infinitely worse.

Help me, Huree – help me, please. Use what I have told you to warn those you can. And meanwhile, I am waiting.

As I have waited these past seven years.

As I will always wait . . .

For ever, it seems.

For now, and all time.

JACK.

AUTHOR'S NOTE

Detective Inspector 'Steve' White's report on pages 356–7 is taken from Donald Rumbelow's *The Complete Jack the Ripper* (W.H. Allen 1975). My thanks also to Dr Ric Caesar and Captain Damien Bush for our many late-night discussions on a possible pathology of vampirism.